A MARKED MAN

Ada Cambridge was born in Norfolk, England in 1844, the eldest daughter of Thomasine Emerson and Henry Cambridge. In 1870 she married George Cross, a clergyman, and accompanied him to Australia where she contributed regularly to journals and periodicals and established herself as one of Australia's literary pioneers with her three volumes of poetry, two autobiographical works and twenty-one novels. She died in Australia in 1926.

Debra Adelaide was born and now lives and works in Sydney. She has B.A. and M.A. degrees in English Literature and is interested in Australian women writers, particularly those authors 'lost', neglected or forgotten. She is co-editing, with Dale Spender, a collection of essays on these writers, and is working on *Australian Women Writers: A Compendium*, forthcoming from Pandora Press.

PANDORA

AUSTRALIAN WOMEN WRITERS:
THE LITERARY HERITAGE

AUSTRALIAN WOMEN WRITERS
The Literary Heritage

General Editor: Dale Spender
Consultant: Elizabeth Webby

Pandora is reprinting a selection of nineteenth- and early twentieth-century novels written by Australian women. To accompany these finds from Australia's literary heritage there will be three brand-new, non-fiction works, surveying Australian women writers past and present, including a handy bibliographical guide to fill in the background to the novels and their authors.

The first four novels in the series are:

A Marked Man: Some Episodes in His Life (1891) by Ada Cambridge
Introduced by Debra Adelaide

The Bond of Wedlock (1887) by Rosa Praed
Introduced by Lynne Spender

Lady Bridget in the Never-Never Land (1915)
Introduced by Pam Gilbert

The Incredible Journey (1923) by Catherine Martin
Introduced by Margaret Allen

And forthcoming in Autumn 1987:

Uncle Piper of Piper's Hill (1889) by Tasma

Outlaw and Lawmaker (1893) by Rosa Praed

An Australian Girl (1894) by Catherine Martin

Three companion books to this exciting new series will be published in 1987 and 1988:

Australian Women Writers: The First Two Hundred Years
by Dale Spender

A lively and provocative overview history of the literary scene and the position of women writers in Australia which shows that any image of the country as a cultural desert was not based on the achievement of Barbara Baynton, Ada Cambridge, Dymphna Cusack, Eleanor Dark, Katherine Susannah Pritchard, Christina Stead and the many other women who have enjoyed tremendous international success.

Australian Women Writers: The Contemporary Scene
by Pam Gilbert

There are a number of outstanding contemporary women writers about whom relatively little is known. This book fills that gap with a comprehensive discussion of the work of Jean Bedford, Blanche d'Alpuget, Helen Garner, Beverley Farmer, Elizabeth Jolley, Olga Masters, Fay Zwicky, Patricia Wrightson and Jessica Anderson.

Australian Women Writers: A Bibliographical Guide
by Debra Adelaide

Covering over 200 Australian women writers, this invaluable sourcebook outlines their lives and works and puts rare manuscript collections throughout Australia on the literary map for the first time. A comprehensive guide to the articles and books written about these women is also included.

A MARKED MAN

Some Episodes in His Life

ADA CAMBRIDGE

Introduced by Debra Adelaide

London

First published in 1891 by
William Heinemann
this edition published in 1987 by Pandora Press
(Routledge & Kegan Paul Ltd)
11 New Fetter Lane, London EC4P 4EE

Published in Australia by
Routledge & Kegan Paul
c/o Methuen Law Book Co.,
44 Waterloo Road, North Ryde, NSW 2113

Published in the USA by
Routledge & Kegan Paul Inc.
in association with Methuen Inc.
29 West 35th St., New York NY 10001

Set in Linotron Erhardt
by Input Typesetting Ltd
and printed in the British Isles
by The Guernsey Press Co Ltd
Guernsey, Channel Islands

Introduction © Debra Adelaide 1987

British Library Cataloguing in Publication Data

Cambridge, Ada
A marked man: some episodes in his life.
—(Australian women writers. The literary heritage)
I. Title   II. Series
823[F]   PR9619.2.C34

ISBN 0-86358-131-5

CONTENTS

	Introduction	vii
	A Note On The Text	xv
I	Dunstanborough	1
II	A Rebel In The Camp	6
III	How Dicky Kept Out Of Mischief	15
IV	The Creeping Tide Crept Up Along The Sand	21
V	At The Coastguard Station	29
VI	A Faithful Watchdog	37
VII	New Lights	43
VIII	A Mistaken Policy	50
IX	Defiance	59
X	Danger	66
XI	Caught	75
XII	The End Of The Wedding Day	83
XIII	Dicky Plays The Man	88
XIV	The Son Proposes: The Father Disposes	96
XV	Dicky Stands To His Word Of Honour	102
XVI	His Last Wild Oats	108
XVII	The Irrevocable Deed	115
XVIII	Swift Repentance	122
XIX	A Last Chance	128
XX	Goodbye	137
XXI	Five-And-Twenty Years After	141
XXII	In The Next Generation	149
XXIII	Moonlight Confidences	155
XXIV	The Camp Of Refuge	162
XXV	Noel Rutledge	169
XXVI	Sue Shows Her Defective Education	175
XXVII	An Old Story	182

XXVIII	A Sequel To The Story	189
XXIX	Love and Duty	196
XXX	Sue Takes A Message	204
XXXI	How The Message Was Answered	209
XXXII	The Skeleton Is Locked Up	216
XXXIII	Three Months Later	223
XXXIV	A Camp Meeting	229
XXXV	Her Father's Daughter	236
XXXVI	The Court Of Final Appeal	242
XXXVII	How Lord Boyton Overdid It	250
XXXVIII	The Broken Bonds	259
XXXIX	Nature Unadorned	264
XL	His Misfortune, Not His Fault	271
XLI	The New Departure	276
XLII	'We'	282
XLIII	The Goal	289
XLIV	The Prodigal's Return	295
XLV	'Evening Coloured With The Dying Sun'	302
XLVI	'Like A Basking Hound'	310
XLVII	Two Years Afterwards	316
XLVIII	'While Darkness Is Quick Hastening'	323
XLIX	The Wages Of Love	329
L	The Wild Beast's Lair	335
LI	The Bo'sun Hauls Down The Lantern	341

INTRODUCTION

In considering the case of Ada Cambridge and her works one is struck, as a feminist, by the wearisome truth of a certain familiar pattern: like countless women writers before or since, Ada Cambridge's substantial contribution to her country's literature has been overlooked. No better proof of this could be found beyond the present edition of *A Marked Man*, for this is the first in nearly one hundred years.

When *A Marked Man* appeared in 1890 Ada Cambridge was the author of several novels, two volumes of poetry and a number of religious publications, and had already gained respect in the literary world. But this, her fourth published novel and the first that brought financial success, earned her much wider recognition at home and abroad and announced beyond doubt that here was no ordinary, genteel, lady writer inspired by mere religious devotion or the desire for amusement. The reviews of this novel were many and outstanding, ranging from the opinion that *A Marked Man* was one of the best-written stories of a 'mesalliance' to be found in modern fiction, to favourable comparisons with the works of George Eliot and William Makepeace Thackeray. It was forecast that Cambridge's name would be in the very front rank of modern writers. The subsequent lapse of Ada Cambridge and her works into relative obscurity is that old story of the suppression of women's literature assisted, no doubt, by the usual disdain of colonial writers both within and without their own country.

Undeniably, Ada Cambridge stood out in her own day. As early as 1896, when she still had more than ten books ahead of her, the literary historian Desmond Byrne upheld her readers' faith in her by devoting a chapter to her in his book *Australian Writers*. (He also included a chapter each on Rosa Praed and Tasma, thus making three out of his seven authors women: not a bad proportion for a man writing in 1896 and no small indication of the growing feminine influence on the Australian literary scene of the late nineteenth century.) Such a vote of confidence in Cambridge's work ought to have held weight, but except for a few obligatory references in accounts of Australian literature here and there, Ada Cambridge has, until recent years, been largely ignored, unread, buried in libraries, and out of print.

None of this is due to her ability as a writer which at the time was outstanding and continues to be so today, for if she had never written anything other than *A Marked Man*, her contribution to Australian literature would still have been considerable. Her own characteristic reticence and modesty concerning her talents, to be found in *Thirty Years In Australia* (1903), ought to be taken with the proverbial grain of salt. With the appearance of her first serialised novel *Up The Country* (1875) her mark on the contemporary literary scene was substantial enough to gain her access to the intellectually cultivated class she cherished, and yet in her autobiography she ascribes this success to nothing more remarkable than the fact of being pretty much the only author around at the time:

> My friend 'Rolf Boldrewood' had not yet received the worldwide recognition that he now enjoys; he was a 'Sydneysider', and supposed to belong to his own colony. Poor 'Tasma' had scarcely begun her brief literary career; Mary Gaunt, and others now on the roll, were mostly in their nurseries or unborn. So that I had the advantage of a stage very much to myself, which of course accounted largely for the attention I received.

In fact, Ada Cambridge was an extremely good writer whose work is characterised by conflicting impulses both to write within the bounds of convention – social, religious, literary – and to attack them. For the wife of an Anglican minister and a devoutly religious woman in her own right, she advances some surprisingly original and forthright views. And yet her novels frequently resolve with an inevitable bowing to the voice of convention as if in apology for the radical views tendered. But *A Marked Man* differs in this respect: it is a novel of integrity, artistically as well as thematically, in which epic scope, the deep and moving penetration of human emotion, and the credibility of character convince us that Ada Cambridge was possessed of remarkable literary talents.

The hero, Richard Delavel (who makes an appearance in *Fidelis*, 1895), makes a momentous error by thinking he can transcend the class barriers of his native England. The son of a wealthy and noble family, he determines to marry the daughter of a farmer, Annie Morrison. A combination of good-heartedness, youthful discontent, impetuousness and rebellion against the wishes of his family, who have earmarked him for the church, conspires to make him fall in love. With marriage comes the inevitable severance from his family and, on the very night of the wedding, there is the revelation of Annie's petty, grasping and exceedingly snobbish nature. Richard is foolish, but not hypocritical, and is determined to accept the consequences of his action: he resists Annie's entreaties to abase himself before his father and beg his forgiveness in the hopes of financial reinstatement, and decides instead to emigrate to Australia and make some sort of a living for himself. But this he does without Annie, who refuses even to consider the prospect of living in such an uncivilised place, and who will not countenance the idea of a husband stooping to the level of work 'in trade'.

Some twenty-five years later the novel introduces us to the Delavel household in Sydney. Richard has built a large and successful shipping business, and after the first five years had prospered sufficiently to be able to send for his wife; now they live in tasteful splendour in their Darling Point mansion with their only child, twenty-year-old Susan. Marriage relations are polite but deathly cold, and there is a good deal of tension relating to Sue, who is dutifully fond of her mother but, thanks to his supervision of her education, very much her father's daughter. With the appearance of the mysterious Constance Bethune, the story gathers interesting dimensions. Constance belongs to Richard's first years in Sydney. She befriended him, cared for him, nursed him through a serious illness, and finally fell deeply in love with him (as he did with her). She disappeared upon the arrival of Annie, never to be heard of again until Sue makes her acquaintance. Over the years Richard has suffered enormously from the conflicting demands of his love for Constance and his marital duty. Meanwhile a contrast to the thoughtless mismatch of Richard and Annie is found in the growing love between Sue and Noel Rutledge, an ex-clergyman. Unlike Richard, Noel yielded to the combined pressures of family influence and youthful inexperience and became a clergyman against his inner doubts. But the same 'fine intellectual rectitude' which led him to resign his hypocritical position is now being devoted to his courtship of Sue. Given his integrity and hard-won devotion to absolute honesty, and Sue's spirited independence and strongminded scorn for the values that have ruined her parents' marriage, then clearly Richard's reluctance to let them marry is based on ill-founded fears. True, their fortunes may not be matched, but their hearts, their intellects, their priorities are. And as for the consideration of class, Ada Cambridge suggests it is here in Australia that this hindrance to the happiness of marriage can be transcended.

Noel Rutledge is penniless, untitled, unconnected, a theological radical and renegade clergyman to boot. He can only proffer a distantly related bishop to satisfy Annie's demands for his credentials, and seems to have little chance of obtaining the mother's permission to marry Sue. But Annie Delavel's plans for her daughter face collapse, just as her cherished standards are on the verge of demolition. The young and genial Lord Boyton – naturally Annie's favoured matrimonial choice – whose courtship of Sue is conducted with remarkable good humour considering he no more wants to marry her than she does him, is also, ironically, partly responsible for Annie Delavel's death.

After Annie's demise Richard devotes himself to the retrieval of his beloved Constance, the tragic event being, as he unashamedly declares to his servant on the night of Annie's funeral, merely the release for which he has endured twenty-five years of misery. The rest of the novel is largely concerned with the search for Constance, their marriage and their remaining years together as seen from Sue's point of view, and it is a moving tale of a great love recovered after many wasted years. Particularly in this latter stage of the novel, Cambridge's fine control over the dramatic and intense subject matter is displayed. What could easily be cloying in the devotion existing between Richard and Constance is in fact sad and pathetic as we witness the desperation with which Richard is so vainly trying to make up for all those lost years. When, with the death of Constance, their three short years of bliss are over, and Richard retreats to his beloved beachside camp to die apparently of pneumonia but in fact from his unbearable loss, we know that Ada Cambridge has achieved something enduring in her portrayal of the anguish in human life.

One of *A Marked Man's* strengths is that it successfully resolves the conflicting impulses of radicalism and conventionalism which in many of the author's other works remain problematic. In *The Eternal Feminine* (1907) for instance, Cambridge makes hearty feminist gestures then unaccountably dives for cover in a reactionary ending, as if such things as her portrayal of Esther, medical student and sometime champion of the rights of women (until retracting her position by the end of the novel), is altogether too much of a challenge to the status quo.

Such contradictory political attitudes are certainly not uncommon – in any age or country – but in Ada Cambridge's fiction we find a hostility towards organised reform counterbalanced by a sincere desire for social change. This is particularly apparent in her novels which contain a good deal of satire, some of her characterisations are superbly comic, but which are undeniably quite conventional romances. Desmond Byrne noted that Ada Cambridge did not 'hate enough' in order to be an effective satirist. (If he could have read her autobiography which was not written until several years after his account of her work, he might have discovered something of her passionate anger.) But if it is possible that Ada Cambridge is unwilling to develop her flashes of irony and satire into fully articulated criticisms, if it is likely that radicalism is being deliberately compromised in the interests of retaining credibility with a reading public, then no doubt it is just as likely that even in her most problematic novels we are reading understated or disguised radicalism in texts posing as innocuous little romances. However, in *A Marked Man* Ada Cambridge's terms are made perfectly clear. Unlike some of her other, later works, this novel does not conclude with some reactionary backtracking, nor does it trivialise its subject.

In *A Marked Man*, Ada Cambridge's characters seem to be in a world upon the verge of great change; the novel looks forward to a time freed from the shackles of Victorian convention. This is certainly implicit in the characterisation of Sue who is a fresh and lively contrast to that legion of romantic heroines upon the verge of nothing more radical or exciting than matrimony. For while she does marry, this is not the ultimate object of the novel and, moreover, hers is a marriage liberated from the choking social and religious constraints found in the prejudices of her mother. Rejecting the attachment to wealth and social status held by her mother (to which, it must be remembered, Annie Delavel's claims are quite spurious anyway), Sue determines to marry for a whole set of reasons which her mother's generation disdains. And it is Sue who has optimistic (if naive) visions for the future:

'I'll tell you what I think of that money question,' she said. 'It is what my father thinks too – only he is preoccupied, his energies have been drained, and he has to consider others. We believe that the time is coming when people will be ashamed to be rich – I mean rich for merely their own purposes. It will be vulgar, it will be selfish, it will be mean; people will look down on the rich person instead of up, as they do now. And wealth will go out of fashion amongst well-bred people, and all that gross kind of luxury; and life will be more simple and sincere, more intelligent and refined; and the poor man will cease from the land then, without any bloody revolutions – if only he will be patient in the meanwhile. You are laughing at me and thinking me a visionary,' she exclaimed, laughing a little herself as she met his sympathetic eyes. (Chapter XXV)

Although this passage is tinged with irony, I think we can see, beyond Sue's somewhat impractical ideals, the author's genuine desire for social change, and it is unfortunate that this is hampered by her usual inability to discover just how a reversal of values might conceivably take place. This speech is made to Noel who in this chapter is attempting to summon up both courage and pedigree to qualify as a suitable son-in-law to Annie Delavel. Sue's rejection of a redundant value-system is matched in his rejection of orthodox religion. And this, we remind ourselves, is from the hand of a respectable wife of a minister of the Church of England.

Though undeniably a social thinker, Ada Cambridge would quite possibly be surprised to see her fiction discussed in the above manner; and indeed such an account should not be misleading. For apart from anything else, *A Marked Man* is a great romance in which, while we discover her most thoughtful and convincing social criticisms, we also find a strength and appeal in its themes of betrayal, exile and bitter estrangement – themes worthy of and handled in a manner that would have done credit to Henry Handel Richardson, to whose work this novel has been favourably compared.

A Marked Man also offers one of the strongest and most convincing female characters to be found in Cambridge's work: Sue's normal, healthy and unconventional good looks (her skin is brown rather than white), her rejection of petty-minded values and her intellectual capacity convince us that in her Ada Cambridge has discovered something enduring and compelling and particularly Australian about young womanhood. As much as Richard Delavel is the 'marked man' of the novel, his daughter stands out from the stereotyping of fictional heroines.

But this raises some interesting implications. Sue has been carefully moulded by Richard after his own image and, until the reappearance of Constance, is the mate and companion denied him in his marital choice. The author clearly wants us to sympathise with Richard's plight in his unhappy mesalliance and to side with him and Sue against Annie Delavel. And yet it is hard to agree that in this she has been entirely fair. What, after all, was Annie's great crime? Merely to be the unwitting recipient of Richard's blindly idealistic infatuation? Not to be the woman he, on a very brief acquaintance, has convinced himself she is? Of course, for such a mistake he suffers for the next twenty-five years, but that does not make Annie's fate any fairer. Annie Delavel is the victim of male idealisation but when, inevitably, her clay feet emerge, it is she who is found at fault. One gets the distinct feeling that while Ada Cambridge sympathises with women, she is also willing to concur in the masculine view of them. But then one also gets the distinct feeling that she is only telling the truth about the way women are treated by men. In thus giving with one hand and taking away with the other, Ada Cambridge is only making the compromises found among many woman writers.

Furthermore, the cause of Ada Cambridge's apparent compromises might be found in the reasons she advances for writing in the first place: to make money, to buy 'pretty things' for her children, and generally to boost the family's slender income. That this is not strictly true we know from such things as the fact of her having written and published well before her marriage, and her delight in being part of an emerging artistic scene and in having the friendship of other authors such as Rolf Boldrewood. Yet there is evidence to suggest (apart from the notoriously minimal stipend of the Anglican clergyman) that it was with more of an eye to immediate and financial, rather than long-term, success that prompted Ada Cambridge to take up her pen again, and that haste, coupled with the dictates of public taste, were some of the conditions under which she was obliged to write.

Considered as a whole, her novels are fascinating, provocative and very readable. They can also be frustrating, unsatisfying and depressing. Either way (and especially in view of the success she once enjoyed) they are not to be dismissed lightly. Whether or not all her novels are as accomplished as *A Marked Man*, they are the result of great skill and care, and all express to some extent a desire for balance and harmony in life and a belief in the worth of individual human endeavour.

Balance, whether of personality, ideals, or the conditions under which people must live, is the goal of her novels. In *A Marked Man* the tragic extremes of Richard Delavel's two marriages, the one bitterly frigid, the other desperately idyllic, are counterbalanced by the more sane and prosaic marriage of his daughter. The novel's ending relinquishes the exhilarating but destructive dimensions of human life and, in accepting instead this realism in human relations, is only consistent with the principles of optimism, faith and balance which were characteristic of Ada Cambridge's own life.

Debra Adelaide
Sydney, August 1985

A NOTE ON THE TEXT

———————————•———————————

A Marked Man was first published in book form in London in 1890 (Heinemann, 3 volumes). Originally, however, it was serialised in the Melbourne paper the *Age*, between 1888 and 1889, under the title 'A Black Sheep'.

Due to an early erroneous citation handed down through a number of otherwise authoritative sources, 'A Black Sheep' was until very recently always assumed to have been serialised in the *Australasian* in 1890. Thanks to the research of Elizabeth Morrison in Melbourne, this mistake has now at last been corrected.

The first one-volume edition, which seems to have been the one most readily available in Australia, was published by Heinemann in 1891. It is this edition which, for various reasons, has been used as copy-text for the current reprinting. Another edition, the 'Popular Edition', also published by Heinemann, appeared in 1894.

DA
April 1986

CHAPTER I

·

Dunstanborough

On the east coast of England there is a village which I will call
Dunstanborough, though it is not thus named in the *Directory*. On the
east coast it lies, its shallow beach washed by the waves of the German
Ocean; and yet, such is the conformation of that coast, that you can
see the sun setting straight before your eyes – shining upon the red
and white face of the chalk cliffs, and the white column of the lighthouse above, and the great rectangular boulders, draped with seaweed,
below – when you stand in the summer evenings looking seawards
from the shore. The sea which ebbs and flows there with such a long
sweep of tide is not altogether open sea, though very nearly; it is the
mouth of a broad and shallow inlet, across which you can see the
faint line of the opposite shore – that shore wherefrom no sea-setting
sun is visible – when the day is very bright or you happen to have a
good telescope. And, years ago, that strip of westward shore on the
eastward coast, sea-beach and village and park and farms, over all of
which one man held manorial rights – *cum wrecca et cum omnibus
pertinentibus suis et portum cum applicatione navium, cum soctra et sactra,
et Tot et Theam Infangtheof, et cum omnibus libertatibus et liberis consuetudi-
nibus, in bosco et plano, in pratis et in pascuis, in aquis et molendinis, in
vivariis et piscariis, infra et extra Burgum et in omnibus locis et in omnibus
rebus* – as the old dog Latin of the eleventh century charter so liberally
defined them – was a peaceful, pretty, rural place, unknown to fame
or fashion.

> A sleepy land where, under the same wheel,
> The same old rut would deepen year by year.

There were old families at the farms, whose tenancy of their lands
was hereditary, and, in a way, historical; and the humbler folk lived

in their ancient cottages, amongst the hollyhocks and cabbage roses of their plenteous gardens, from generation to generation. It was the ideal English village. The lower classes knew their place and kept it, dropping the loyal curtsey to their lord and lady and the young sirs and misses, not only in the street but in the church – out of which none would have ventured to budge when divine service was over until the Delavel pew was empty; and the great people looked well after the health and welfare, moral and physical, of their vassals – examining the children in needlework and the catechism at the national school, comforting the sick and aged with port wine and flannel petticoats, and distributing the best advice to young and old for their guidance in the small difficulties of their unimportant lives.

It was but a little village of one long, straggling street, half-a-dozen farms, and intersecting lanes bordered with high hedgerows and briar-tangled ditches – a place of no consequence whatever in itself. Its sole title to importance was its immemorial association with the Delavel family, with the old Hall which had housed the family's head for so many centuries, and with the old church where so much of the family's mortal dust reposed – where floors and walls and dusky windows were covered with the records of its great alliances and its famous deeds.

This latter edifice was an example of Early Decorated, much quoted by archaeological experts, and, like many other English rural churches, would have held the entire parish two or three times over. In it the effigies of dead and gone Delavels, male and female, knelt under arched recesses and pinnacled canopies, with rows of little Delavels in graduated sizes behind them; or lay prone on their altar tombs in helmet and wimple, with toes turned up and palms pressed together – a congregation to whom the church seemed to belong far more than it did to its living worshippers. The rectory was a stately and spacious house, fronting the church on the opposite side of the road, only its fluted chimneys showing over the trees and shrubs that curtained it from vulgar eyes. A cadet of the family, the Rev Maxwell Delavel-Pole, was the rector; a young man to whom the benefice had been assigned when he was a baby in the cradle, and for whom it had been kept and nursed by decrepid curates during his ecclesiastical minority. He had happened to take kindly to the profession chosen for him, and at the time of which I am speaking was doing the work of the new broom at Dunstanborough, whither he had come fresh from Oxford and his school-books only a year or two before, with commendable zeal and conscientiousness. He had matins every morning, winter and summer, and full services on saints' days; the congregation consisting for the most part of the inferior members of his own establishment, the parish clerk, and the old people of the almshouses – the latter sighing and groaning over their devotions in the deadly chill of the dank church when it rained and snowed, and their rheumatics were bad, but aware that they could only stay away at the risk of losing all the rewards of good conduct – their tea and tobacco, their coals and blankets, their soup and wine, the little comforts of their poor dependent lives. The farmers and well-to-do village folk, though most anxious to oblige, felt that life was not long enough for weekday churchgoing, and were in a position to indulge somewhat in the courage of their opinions.

Between the church and the rectory, on the side farthest from the village, the road continued a road for a hundred yards or so, wide, with grassy margins and overshadowing elm trees, and then it ended in a gateway – two prodigious square stone pillars, on which heraldic monsters of more than heroic size sat on their discoloured haunches, lifting weatherworn noses to the sky. These guarded two wrought-iron gates of a later period, with smaller gates on either side of them. Just within stood a venerable lodge covered with ivy to the chimney tops. This was one of the entrances to Dunstanborough Park and the Hall – the one used by the Delavel household and the village in their intercourse with each other. There was a private gate in the churchyard, but this was very private indeed, for the family only (when they chose to walk to church, as they mostly did), and not for servants, or tradesmen, or common folk of any sort. Within the green enclosure of the park, which was large enough for a considerable herd of deer to live in, with all the luxuries of shade and quiet to which those aristocratic creatures are accustomed, stood the ancient house which was the pride of the Delavels and the archaeological societies – a solid, wide-spreading, majestic, quadrangular building, with an unwholesome duckweedy moat all round it, and outside that a belt of gardens, not very well kept, but quaint and picturesque, with a good many yew trees about them, and tall hedges clipped into shapes of birds and beasts. The walls were of all ages, and some of them of a thickness suggesting the monumental stability of the Egyptian Pyramids. These portions were pierced with apparently unfathomable narrow slits, or had square stone-mullioned windows, in which sombre old stained glass or bottle-green discs and diamonds in leaden lattices scantily revealed the light and shut out the air; but later portions of the house displayed rows of tall Queen Anne sashes, and even a French casement here and there, set in a flat, dark surface of closely-trimmed ivy. Every kind of architectural irregularity was to be seen around the courtyard – once the scene of jousts and tournaments, afterwards paved with stone, but now grassed and gravelled like a college quadrangle – examples of many periods, from the unrestorable ruin of an almost prehistoric time to the French-windowed wall aforesaid, which only a learned person could describe in the proper terms; and this courtyard was entered by a vast gateway, like a railway tunnel, over the arched roof of which were vaulted chambers of stone, reached by spiral staircases, the grey outer walls being encrusted with crumbling shields chiselled with the numerous quarterings of the Delavel house – the carved work worn away by time and weather, so that it was a matter of guess-work which was which.

Within doors the house was a museum of treasures to the artist and antiquary. It was a fortunate thing that for several generations the Delavels had been hampered for money; for thus, though they had indulged themselves in new fashions from time to time, they had done so moderately, and had never made that clean sweep of old ones which might have taken place more than once had they been able to afford it. So there were still oak panels black with age, and chimney-pieces carved from floor to ceiling, and roofs upheld by open beams or ribbed with stone like a cathedral crypt. There were still tapestries and leather hangings, whereon stories sacred and pagan had been figured once and had faded away, and fine old Jacobean presses and settles that went out of favour with the Stuart kings. There were Louis Quatorze boule work and William of Orange marquetry, florid, pot-bellied, spindlelegged; and delicate Chippendale from the hand of the original Thomas, claw-footed, with slender, shining curves, and fine, flat carvings, wrought in that beautiful Spanish mahogany which is so rarely used in modern cabinetmaking. Some of them you see at this day in the loan exhibitions, with crowds of would-be possessors gloating on their antique charms. But in those earlier days of which I am writing they were sequestered and undervalued treasures, mouldering in unused rooms in different parts of the house – rooms beautiful and stately enough in their way, but also unappreciated, and, to say the truth, so comfortless and inconvenient as to be unfit for the requirements of nineteenth century life. The domestics had quarters in the old parts of the house, and the servants' hall was a glorious

Gothic chamber with an arched stone roof fit for a royal chapel. There were also some ghostly bedrooms, kept in habitable order with frequent fires and a great abundance of candles, where guests were put on the rare occasions of their entertainment, and where they invariably had bad dreams. But the family, in its ordinary life, confined itself to the wing with the sash windows, and there lived very much like other people, sitting on chintz-covered sofas, and enjoying the little comforts of that inartistic day.

The reigning Delavel was a tall, thin, high-nosed, stately man of sixty, the embodiment of all the feudal traditions of his race – a 'remnant', like his village, of a condition of things that had gone by without his knowing it. Lady Susan, his wife, was undignifiedly stout, a soft, simple, smiling woman, quite unlike her spouse; for which reason, possibly, it was that their three sons and two daughters were exceptionally strong young shoots of the family tree, which had put forth but feebly of late generations. Roger, the heir of the house, and the seventeenth Delavel of Dunstanborough in direct line, was a handsome young man of twenty-five, a cadet in the diplomatic service. The second son, Keppel, a year younger, was a lieutenant in the Guards. And the youngest son, Richard, was a fine lad of twenty, still keeping terms at Oxford. The daughters, Barbara and Katherine, were children of sixteen and twelve, in the hands of a governess.

These seven individuals comprised the family – the great family which within a certain radius was honoured and worshipped in a manner that Hapsburgs and Hohenzollerns might have envied. And the black sheep of the flock was Richard, the youngest son.

CHAPTER II

———•———

A Rebel In The Camp

Dicky, as he was called in those days, came home from Oxford to spend his long vacation at Dunstanborough. He had been very anxious to spend it elsewhere (with a college chum who had made arrangements for his inclusion in a mountaineering party), but there were three, if not four, good reasons for refusing him his wish. In the first place, he had failed for his degree, and was in disgrace, and did not deserve to enjoy himself; and secondly, his brothers, Roger and Keppel, were making their pleasures in the world so costly that economy was necessary in the case of one who could be compelled to save; and thirdly, Mr Delavel considered that his youngest son was too unsteady to be trusted with independence, and could only be kept safe and out of mischief under his father's eye. The fourth reason had reference to certain supposed good influences that might be brought to bear upon him if he stayed at home.

At this time the boy was overflowing with young life and vigour and ideas. He was a tall, slim, eager-looking lad, graceful and agile as a deer, and with the mettle of a young blood-horse, full of generous impulses and without a particle of meanness in him; and to call him unsteady was to express the purely conventional view of his character. The term was a label affixed to him by his high and mighty father, and therefore generally accepted as properly describing him, because of a certain startling and subversive tendency to think and choose for himself which he had developed with his growth to manhood, and which an otherwise irresistible paternal authority had been unable to put down. Being the youngest son, he was naturally destined for the Church (though the family living had been pledged to other uses before he was born, there were others as good to be had for the asking), and he had assumed from a child that such was his inevitable career; but on a recent return from Oxford, and quite suddenly, without giving any valid reason for it, he had calmly announced that he had changed his mind – as if the family politics had ever taken his mind into account – and deliberately refused to prepare for orders on conscientious grounds, to the intense wrath and indignation of his father, who called him an impudent young puppy to set up for opinions of his own at his age, and asked him how the devil he proposed to support himself.

Mr Delavel was sure that somebody had instigated his son to this unheard-of rebellion. And of course somebody had. The prototypical black sheep, but for whom our hero might possibly have been a lawn-sleeved bishop at this day, was a fiery-souled and frail-bodied young deacon – a curate-missionary to the Oxford slums – with a transcendental conscience and the zeal and courage of an early martyr, who, when the time for taking full orders arrived, which was during a period of close and affectionate intercourse with Dicky, came to the conclusion, after a hard struggle, that it would be wrong for him to become a priest. It does not sound a large matter to us, but in those old days, when Colenso was the infamous person of the time, it meant a great deal. The rebel made no parade of his rebelliousness; he did not seek to justify himself in public statements, like another person (then an innocent baby cutting its milk-teeth) who, many years later, was associated with Dicky under almost identical circumstances; yet he became a 'marked' man, at a disadvantage with the world. His honest scruples were ascribed to what a Yankee would call 'pure cussedness', to the promptings of a wicked heart, to demoniacal possession; like his more illustrious episcopal fellow-culprit, he was about thirty years before his time, and had to pay the fine that society imposes in all such cases. He was shunned as an 'infected' person, a sort of moral leper – practically excommunicated from the congregation of the elect.

Under these circumstances, Dicky, if he had been any one *but* Dicky – 'marked' himself with the seal of a distinct individuality – would have dropped the discreditable acquaintance. Instead of that, he cherished it more and more as it became less and less socially desirable, and naturally became more and more like-minded with the friend beside whom he stood and fought, and for whose cause he suffered. It was a brief if pregnant episode.

Simultaneously with the laying down of his clerical frock, the young deacon laid down his life, at enmity with the Church but at perfect peace with himself, having, it was popularly believed, done an immense amount of mischief and wickedness in his few years – having, at any rage, inoculated Richard Delavel with his high-minded eccentricity, whether for harm or good. The boy saw his friend laid in the grave – over which no clergyman could be found to read the words of hope, which were considered to have no applicability in this case, and straightway went home, with a new sternness in his young face, to tell his father that he had changed his mind with regard to his future profession. When asked why he so suddenly objected to enter the Church, he merely said that his conscience was against it, the absurd reason that drove his parent to frenzy. For was not the head of the house the hereditary keeper of the conscience of the family? And what business had a gentleman and a Delavel to have any ideas that were not those of his class? And what business had a boy barely out of his 'teens with ideas at all?

Mr Delavel refused to listen to him for a moment, and continued to believe that the natural order of things would proceed without serious interruption. Nevertheless, as time wore on and the stiffnecked boy showed no sign of yielding, the father began to realise that strong measures might be necessary. As the result of an interview that took place in this particular month of July, he resorted to the orthodox device for compelling a son to do his duty. He said to Lady Susan that the fellow should not have another penny until he 'came to his senses'.

Lady Susan was a soft-hearted mother, who always took her children's part. She thought Dicky entirely in the wrong, and yet she could not bear to see him thwarted. And she said she didn't see why he shouldn't go into the army, if he preferred it – the army, of course, being the only alternative present to her mind – especially as he had so fine a figure for a uniform.

Mr Delavel begged to inform her that it was as much as he could do to keep one son in the army. She must know as well as he did that to make allowances and pay debts for two would be out of the question.

'Dicky is not given to running into debt', the mother remarked. 'Both Roger and Keppel, when they were at Christchurch, had three times as many debts as he.'

The father gave him no credit for this convenient virtue, but went on to say that Roger and Keppel, whatever their faults, were true Delavels, and that he sometimes thought Richard must have been changed in the cradle. 'I suppose he takes after your people,' said the old man calmly; 'he certainly does not take after his own family.'

'Is not my family his own too?' inquired Lady Susan pathetically.

Her husband evaded that question. In marrying the daughter of an earl whose grandfather had been a money-lender, he had married much beneath him – in fact, Lady Susan's family was no family at all in his sense; and, though it was a constant wonder and irritation to him that she would not see it, he was too polite to wound her with explanations. But emphatically he did not allow her to be more than the wild stem on which the fine flower of his race was grafted.

Dicky, then, came home to Dunstanborough, to spend the long vacation where he would be out of mischief. There were great rejoicings at the Hall over his return – though he did come without his degree – particularly amongst the female members of the establishment; and for a day or two he stayed about he house and made himself a delightful companion. He chatted to his mother and escorted her about the garden, and put pillows at her back and footstools under her feet. He had his tea in the schoolroom, and conducted himself in various ways that were subversive of the usual discipline in that department, nevertheless charming the heart of the governess, who at forty-five was still susceptible to the fascinations of his sex. He teased his sisters, as women of all ages delight to be teased by the men they love, and he 'carried on' with the housekeeper, a venerable and obese person who had nursed him when a baby in long clothes, in such a manner that she declared with suffocating giggles that she would have to tell his ma if he didn't behave himself. The Hall was quite a cheerful place for the first few days after the black sheep's return.

Then a dreamy taciturnity came over him. Life at Dunstanborough did not yield him that spiritual sustenance which his large and growing appetite required. It was petty and monotonous, and he felt lonely, nursing great thoughts of his own with no one to confide them to, and building air castles which, in the present standstill stage of his career, he saw no chance of realising. So he left his family to their normal dulness and wandered away to remote coverts of the park; and there he lay amongst the bracken fern on the flat of his back, his long legs thrown one over the other, and his hands clasped under his head, and gazed into the branches above him for hours together.

On the fifth day he thought he would go and see his cousin Maxwell, by way of a change. Max was his brother Roger's friend rather than his, but they had all been boys together, and he thought it would be interesting to see how the young parson, as a full-blown rector and householder, was shaking down. On former occasions Mr Delavel-Pole's mother had been at the head of affairs – an aunt towards whom Dicky entertained the most undutiful sentiments; and that young man had given the rectory a wide berth and kept himself in careful ignorance of all that went on there. Now he heard that Max was his own master in his own house, and he thought he would go and ask him how he liked it. It was early in the morning when this impulse seized him. He was taking an aimless stroll before breakfast in the direction of the village, and chanced to hear the church bell ring for eight o'clock prayers.

'Matins,' said Dicky to himself. 'They're going on still. Well, it's rough on those poor old things to make them trudge to church at this time of day. He forgets they are not so young as he is.'

Then he made up his mind to go and speak to the old things, and ask them how their rheumatics and asthmas were getting on, and thought he might as well have breakfast with Max when he was there.

He strolled towards the hedge that divided two sides of the church-yard from the park, passed through the private gate, and stepped lightly round the church to the south door, by which all save the great family went in and out; and here he sat down on one of the two stone benches built into the side walls of the porch, and waited till the service was over. He could hear the rector monotoning the prayers with breathless rapidity in a low voice, and he knew he should not have to wait long.

In a few minutes the congregation came out. It numbered seven souls all told, of whom five were aged pensioners from the almshouses, hobbling along in various stages of decrepitude, who all curtseyed to the ground at the unexpected apparition of the young gentleman from the Hall, and seemed overwhelmed by the affability of his behaviour. The sixth was the parson's under-housemaid – the only one of the rectory servants who could be spared from his or her domestic duties. The seventh was a very pretty young girl.

Dicky Delavel was chatting to Sally Finch – old Sally, who had had seventy years' hard experience of life, yet looked up with cringing humility to the boy who had had almost none – when the seventh member of the congregation came out into the summer sunshine from the dusk of the church. The rector in his cassock was walking by her side, speaking to her as if he knew her very well, while she moved along with a fluttering gesture, her modest eyes cast down. Mr Delavel-Pole was in no hurry, though he had not had his breakfast. Nor was she. Not until he noticed the old people grouping on the footpath and caught sight of his cousin, did he shake hands with her, but then he dismissed her with little ceremony. 'Come to me at five o'clock,' he said; 'then we can talk it over. How do, Dicky? You are out early.'

'How do, Max?' said Dicky. His eyes were following the vanishing figure of number seven with an evident recognition of its unfamiliar charms, and he spoke a little abruptly. Indeed, the greeting was not overpoweringly warm on either side. 'Is it one of the privileges of a parson to have young ladies come to see you at five o'clock? Very pleasant sort of parish work that, I should think.'

'My dear fellow,' said Mr Delavel-Pole, with a little smile of disdain, 'there are no young ladies in Dunstanborough.' And his voice and manner implied his opinion that this was a very vulgar style of pleasantry.

'No? I didn't know that Dunstanborough was so bad as that,' rejoined Dicky. 'This is a visitor, then?'

'This? Who? Oh, you mean Annie Morrison. Didn't you know her? She has shot up a good deal lately. She helps me with the Sunday-school. She is a good little thing, but you would hardly mistake her for a lady, I think, if you looked at her closely.'

'I did look at her closely,' said Dicky. 'If she isn't a lady, she's an uncommon good imitation of one.'

'A very good imitation,' said Mr Delavel-Pole indifferently. 'That is boarding-school. She has taken the veneer very well; it looks quite natural at a little distance. You are coming in to breakfast, Dicky? Oh yes, you must come in – you haven't been to see me for an age.'

They had paused in the middle of the road, with their faces turned in the direction of the lane which was swallowing up the girl's figure – a trim and pretty figure neatly clad in blue cotton. The rector made a movement to enter his gate, and Dicky, mumbling thanks for the invitation, followed with rather an absent air. 'So that is Annie Morrison,' he said presently, as he rubbed his boots on the rectory door-mat. 'She wore a holland pinafore the last time I saw her.'

They entered the rich gloom of the house, and a man-servant came up softly, took off his master's cassock, and glided away with it. Then the two young men passed from the hall to the breakfast-room – a charming apartment, lighted by a deep-seated mullioned window that 'gave' upon a sweet green lawn, and solidly furnished with oak and leather, Turkey carpet, and dark wool curtains spangled with the cross and *fleur de lis* – where stood the rector's breakfast table, appointed like a lord's. Scarcely had they entered when the footman appeared with his silver dishes, and the young host sat down to entertain his hungry guest.

'How's poor old Woodford?' asked Dicky, when he had taken the first edge from his appetite with a couple of devilled kidneys that melted in his mouth. Woodford was the man who had turned out of Dunstanborough to let Delavel-Pole come in, now perpetual curate of the adjoining parish – a poor, lean, shabby old man, who had an invalid wife, eight children, and an income of £200 a year.

'I have not the least idea,' said the rector. 'I have not seen him for months.'

'Seems hard lines for him, eh?'

'What could he expect?' rejoined Delavel-Pole indifferently. 'His father was a miller, and he ought to have been a miller too. Bennet,' to the footman, with a severe face, 'go and ask the cook what she means by sending me in burnt toast.'

Dicky stayed with his cousin most of the forenoon. He was taken over the house to look at various improvements which had been made since he was there before; and he lingered long about the stables, looking at Max's new horse, and giving his opinion upon broughams and dogcarts. Then they went into the study, where, while he finished his morning pipe, they had a chat about Oxford and other interesting subjects. The rector talked much of his parish – the state in which Woodford had left it, and the uphill struggle on which he himself had embarked – and made serious inquiries concerning Dicky's views and prospects.

'I can't believe,' said Mr Delavel-Pole, who held a commission from his uncle to reason with this perverse and head-strong boy, 'that you are the sort of fellow to put your hand to the plough and then look back.'

Dicky's bright and friendly face clouded immediately. 'I am not aware that I am,' he said stiffly.

'What do you call it, then?' pursued the other. 'You have known all along what you were intended for.'

'I am not responsible for other people's intentions.'

'You never made any objections till now. Why did you not?'

'Because I never properly thought of it till now.' There was a little pause, and he added, looking up, 'Is there anything more you wish to know?'

The rector walked uneasily about the room. 'If it is that you fancy you are not fit for it,' he said, 'I honour you for the feeling. But that should not be a hindrance – that's a matter in your own hands. *I* did not feel fit for it once.'

'I should think you didn't,' replied Dicky, with a chuckle.

'But,' proceeded Mr Delavel-Pole, flushing a little, 'as time went on I saw that it was my vocation – I saw that I was called to it. Everything pointed that way, as it does in your case. And I obeyed the call, and I have never regretted it.'

'I don't want to judge others,' said the boy rather doggedly, as he knocked the ashes from his pipe. 'No doubt you felt it was all right. You and I are different.'

'I felt it was all right – yes. When the finger of Providence points out your path for you so clearly as that – when duty to God means duty to your parents as well – it seems to me there is not much room for doubt as to the right and wrong of it, Dicky.'

Dicky looked up at his cousin's thin, solemn, high-nosed face – the regular Delavel face, unsoftened by any touch of the genial spirit that irradiated his own – and said 'Ah!' in a meditative tone. The effect of this vague ejaculation was to raise a restive temper in the rector's breast.

'What do you mean by that?' he demanded sharply.

'Oh, nothing – nothing,' said Dicky, with an irritating chuckle; 'I was only thinking of the finger of Providence – that's all.'

'Are you going to deny that there is a Providence?'

'Not at all. But I do say it is a queer thing, when you come to think of it. I wonder how it strikes old Woodford?' His keen sense of amusement at his own train of thought, and at the spectacle of his companion's disgust and irritation, overmastered him, and he laughed aloud. 'I think you'd better not try to come the parson over me, old boy,' said he, rising, as he perceived that it was time to take his leave. 'It answers well enough, no doubt, with pretty young farmers' daughters, but I can't believe in you as they do. I'm very sorry, but I can't. Some men might influence me, perhaps, but not you, Max – not you. You'd better give it up for a bad job at once.'

'I have given it up long ago,' said Delavel-Pole haughtily.

'No, you haven't, for you are trying it on now. And look here – just you drop it' – his face changing into a nearer likeness to Max's own. 'I have got my own conscience, which is as good as yours – or my father's either. And I have made up my mind that I will *not* enter the

Church to please either of you – not if the finger of Providence points to a bishopric and ten thousand a year. I'm not over particular, but I draw the line at – well, at that sort of thing. I just warn you, you know.'

'You're a true Delavel for temper,' said Max, when rage would let him speak.

'You're another,' retorted Dicky.

And presently they parted, loving each other about as much as they had always done, since the days when they fought and kicked in their aristocratic nurseries as irreconcilable little boys.

CHAPTER III

●

How Dicky Kept Out Of Mischief

When lunch was over Dicky took an early opportunity to escape from his parents – who, pleased with his visit to that good young man, their nephew, seemed anxious to find out if it had had any effect – and disappeared, no one knowing whither. The warm morning had cooled; a film of coppery grey cloud was spreading like a veil over the clear sky; and a wind, that had risen in short little puffs, was beginning to moan bleakly in the tree tops. But these signs of coming rain and storm, which kept the girls and their governess in the house, did not keep him. With his terrier frisking at his heels, he strode at a rapid pace through unfrequented paths of the garden to the woods, where now the branches were dark and thick overhead, and the brushwood underfoot a lovely tangle of wild vines in flower, taking no notice of the delicate life that teemed around him. The crash and swish of his long-legged stride, in that midsummer solitude, when even the birds were silent, suggested the amateur poacher overtaken by untimely daylight.

He left the woods for the highroad at a point where it skirted the seashore, and gave off a lane that led to the Morrisons' farm. From the top of the park wall, which he reached by climbing an adjacent tree, he could see the farmhouse about a mile inland – or, rather, the stacks and garden foliage that marked its site; and, having dropped himself over, he took that road and lane, and shortly arrived at that house. He considered with himself that it would be a kind thing to go and have a chat with the old people. He had not seen old Morrison for ages – had, in fact, neglected him shamefully. And he was curious to see little Annie again; to shake hands with her and ask her how she did, and to apologise for not recognising her at the church door. He was afraid she might think him above noticing 'the likes of her', as doubtless many Delavels would be; and if there was a thing he abhorred more than another, it was to be suspected of class snobbery of that sort.

The farmhouse was a long, low building, with a honey-suckled porch, a steep, thatched roof, broken by an irregular line of dormer windows, and an air of old-fashioned neatness pervading it and its surroundings that was pleasant to see. The garden was fragrant with lavender and sweet peas and cabbage roses, and full of the sleepy hum of bees; the hay was in cocks in its surrounding meadow, and the cornfields beyond yellowing for the harvest. An old sheepdog, dozing on the doorstep, lifted his head and pricked his ears and growled a guttural growl under his breath at the approach of the intruders; and Billy the terrier responded in characteristic manner as he crept up at his master's heels.

Hearing the noise, Mrs Morrison – a comely, broad-faced dame, who waddled heavily as she walked – came out from the 'keeping room', as they called it, into the porch; where she stood aghast at Rover's presumption and her own remissness in having delayed to put on her afternoon gown and cap.

'Lord save us, Master Richard,' she piously ejaculated, 'you don't mean to say that's you, sir!' And she drove the old dog from the mat with contumelious kicks and threats, and besought her illustrious visitor to step in, backing into a corner to allow him room to cross the tiny entry and walk into the sitting-room before her. Following him, she hurried to open the door of the parlour within (it was superfluously termed the 'spare parlour' in those parts – a painful apartment, perfumed with beeswax and turpentine, and wonderfully adorned with bead and wool work and white antimacassars), but he would not notice the invitation. He had no sense of dignity, as a Delavel should have had, and preferred to plant himself in the Windsor chair from which she had risen to admit him. This was just opposite another chair in which the farmer, her husband, sat tightly wedged – his spotted handkerchief over his head, his empty church-warden beside him, his gaitered legs as far apart as possible, his hands folded placidly over his stomach – sleeping the sleep of the just after his noonday dinner.

The old man, being unceremoniously shaken and shouted at, roused himself with difficulty, and in his turn stared with astonishment at his visitor.

'What, Master Richard, sir, is it *you*?' he exclaimed; and when Dicky had again asserted his identity, Mr Morrison, collecting his faculties, supposed the squire had made his son the bearer of some message about 'them gates'.

'No,' said Dicky airily; 'I just happened to be taking a walk this way, and I thought I'd drop in and see how you all were. How are you, Morrison? Keeping pretty well?'

'Thank ye kindly, sir,' his gratified host responded; 'I'm as well as I can expect to be at my time o' life; and how's yourself?'

An interesting dialogue ensued, under cover of which Mrs Morrison escaped to attire herself smartly and get out her cake and wine. Dicky heard the whole history of 'them gates', of the state of the crops, of the danger threatening the hay, which 'might ha' been all got in in a couple o' days if it had held fine'. And so on and so on.

But there was no sign of Annie. In pauses of the conversation, and even when there were no pauses, Dicky listened with ears alert for the faintest sound of her step and rustle of her gown. Since he had entered the house without seeing her, he thought of her as upstairs in her chamber in the roof, braiding up her hair and putting on her best frock, perhaps, in honour of his visit. But time went on, and she did not come down, and the old people did not seem to expect her. Mrs Morrison returned, bringing in fruit and cakes and the best decanters; and when she required assistance in her hospitable ministrations she called one Eliza to her aid. At last Dicky's impatience got the better of a resolve he had made not to betray his sudden interest in the farmer's daughter. He felt that he *must* find out whether or not he had any chance of seeing her. So 'How are the young people?' he asked abruptly, in the middle of a long description of the surpassing merits of a new pony.

The father declared that the young people were fine and hearty, and that John, his son, was going to be married to Rhody Appleton, at the Coastguards.

'Indeed,' Dicky ejaculated, feigning an interest in what was evidently considered an event of importance.

'What, didn't my lady tell you? She was very kind to Rhody. She went to see her to wish her joy, and said she'd give her her teaspoons when she was married.'

'She goes to the Hall to sew sometimes,' added Mrs Morrison, as she poured half-a-pint of yellow cream over a huge plate of raspberries, 'and a beautiful needlewoman she is – I must say that for her.' The potential mother-in-law gave a little sigh, as of regret that she could say no more.

'They're to be married next month,' said the old man, who appeared more satisfied with the prospect, 'and they're going to live with us. There's room enough for us all, and Rhody'll brighten the house up. She's a smart gal, is Rhody, and as busy as a bee. You see we don't want to lose John, sir; and anyhow, the place will be his own afore long, in the course of nature, as one may say.'

'Just so,' responded Dicky, who, if he had properly heard what was said to him, would have told the farmer that he trusted it would be many a long day before John would step into his father's shoes. 'And how is Annie?'

Mrs Morrison replied that Annie was nicely. 'She's half a head over me now – looks down on her poor mother, I tell her. I never saw a girl grow as she's done the last couple o' years.'

'I think I caught sight of her this morning,' mumbled Dicky, his mouth full of raspberries and cream; 'at least Max – my cousin Delavel-Pole – said it was she. I didn't know her a bit. I thought it was a visitor at church.'

'Oh, was it at church?' inquired the mother, a shade anxiously. 'Yes, she goes to them early services whenever I can spare her. I don't mind in the summer, but I tell her she'll have to stop it when the winter comes. It's a long way, and I won't have her out in the dark mornings in the rain and slush, a-shivering in that cold church, with her clothes wet, and an empty stomach. I can't allow it, sir, and so I told Mr Delavel-Pole plump and plain. "Growing girls," I says, "are ticklish in their constitutions; and she's the only one we've got, and we don't want her to die o' consumption, nor yet rheumatic fever." He says she won't take no harm when she's doing her duty, but that's as may be. I don't hold with some folks' notions of duty, and Mr Delavel-Pole don't understand growing girls.'

'Delavel-Pole's an ass,' said Dicky, with irrepressible irritation, as he set down his empty plate. 'Don't you pay any regard to what *he* says.'

He spoke, of course, without remembering to whom he was speaking, and a moment of silent embarrassment ensued.

Then the old farmer began to chuckle and shake with an enjoyment that plainly betokened sympathy. He did not presume to think his rector an ass, of course, but he had the average male parishioner's instinctive grudge against the 'clerical sex' – it existed even in those remote days – and was delighted to share it with another, and such another. 'Oh, come now, young master, draw it mild,' he cackled, affecting to protest. 'Parson mustn't be spoke of like that, you know – Squire's nevy and all.'

'Of course not,' said Dicky. 'I was wrong to speak so. What I meant was that – that there were many things of which Mrs Morrison must be a better judge than he. For instance, she knows what's best for her own daughter. Of course Mr Delavel-Pole must be listened to – in his place.'

The farmer continued to regard his visitor with tears of laughter in his old eyes. For many a long day would he remember this delicious joke and repeat it to his cronies whenever the rector's name was mentioned – ' "Delavel-Pole's an ass," says he, just as cool as if 'twas that there dawg he was a-talkin' on. "Don't you pay no regard to what *he* says," says he. "You keep 'm in his place," says he.' And so on. But Mrs Morrison was honestly scandalised by Master Richard's plain-speaking and her husband's want of manners. She dutifully abstained from laughing.

'I'm sure I don't know whatever Annie would say – Annie thinks such a lot of Mr Delavel-Pole,' she said presently; and by that innocent remark she restored a decorous gravity at once. The farmer ceased to gurgle in his throat and wipe tears of mirth on his spotted handkerchief; a hint of constitutional moroseness obscured his jolly grin, and Dicky's face, like a mirror, reflected the change.

'The women's all like that,' remarked the old man, 'if the parson's young and good-looking and takes notice on 'em. 'Spose they think a man isn't flesh and blood when he puts a long-tailed coat on. And seems to me the parson knows how soft they are, and makes his account of it. That is, some of them do' (the farmer said 'du') – not Mr Delavel-Pole in particular, you understand, sir.'

'Oh, I understand,' said Dicky viciously; 'and I quite agree with you.' And then he told himself that it would be very improper to pursue that subject, and pulled himself up. 'Where is Annie?' he asked, point-blank.

Then Mrs Morrison told him that Annie had gone out for a walk. 'She said she was going to the beach to look for sea anemones while the tide was out. But I wish she was safe back,' said the mother, gazing anxiously out of the window. 'I told her to mind the weather, but she don't mind anything when she's after them things for her aquarium, and it's going to pour directly.'

Dicky rose, looked at his watch, and said he was awfully sorry, but he would have to be running home. His people did not know where he was – it was later than he had supposed – it would be as well to escape the coming shower, if possible. He refused cake and wine, on the ground that he had filled himself with raspberries, but his hostess was so crestfallen when he proposed to leave without taking any substantial refreshment that he asked her for a glass of beer – which she brought him foaming in a pewter tankard, and cool from the cellar, with great pride. He took it off at a draught, without drawing breath, and wiping his young moustache as he set down the mug, told her, with the air of giving a very weighty opinion, that there was no beer in Oxford to beat *that*. And then she was satisfied.

'Good-bye, Morrison,' he said to the old farmer. 'I shall come and see you again soon.'

'You're very good, sir,' replied Morrison, wondering. 'I take it very kind of you, Master Richard.'

'Good-bye, Mrs Morrison. Next time you must show me the aquarium, and your beehives, and . . . and the other things. Remember me to John. Tell him I wish him good luck and that I'll come to the wedding if Miss Appleton asks me.'

'Perhaps my lady wouldn't like her to take such a liberty,' said the farmer's wife, perplexed and pleased, and thinking that certainly Master Richard was the flower of the flock.

'What a dear young gentleman!' she ejaculated, as she stood in the porch to watch his departure. 'No pride about *him*. How nice he did speak of our John! And how he did enjoy his beer!'

'He always took notice o' John,' said the farmer.

It is, perhaps, needless to say that Dicky did not go straight home. No desire to allay his mother's possible anxiety as to his whereabouts, or kind wish to relieve the tedium of the schoolroom for his sisters, prompted his hurried leave-taking. He plunged down the lane up which he had come, and followed the cliff road in the direction of the village until he came to a place that allowed him, at the risk of his neck, to descend to the beach below. He would not yet abandon his mission of apology to Annie, after all the trouble he had taken, and he might, he thought, come across her somewhere in this locality before it was the time for her appointment with Max. In his secret heart he was more bent on forestalling and circumventing his cousin than anxious to see her for his own pleasure.

CHAPTER IV

•

The Creeping Tide Crept Up Along The Sand

The beach at Dunstanborough was spacious and level and firm –
everything that a beach should be, but so seldom is – and provided a
variety of opportunities for adventurous infancy and youth. When the
tide went out it went a very long way out, and left a miscellaneous
and interesting assortment of the treasures of the deep behind it. At
high-water mark there was a drift of foam and seaweed always thickly
studded with them, and at low-water they lay strewn in lavish abundance over the wide sweep of wet and wrinkled sands. Close in shore
the dark boulders, which were once the bases of rocks long since
worn away, and now so curiously resembled the crowded table tombs
of an old churchyard (say Haworth, in Yorkshire, for instance), though
covered to the very wall of the red cliff at one point, when the tide
was at the full, were left by the ebb naked but for their veiling of what
looked like fine green hair, and intersected by the loveliest little clear
pools that never went dry, each one of which was an aquarium more
rich and varied in its furnishings than any glass tank that I ever saw.
And even better than these pools for the curiosity hunter were the
mussel beds – two or three irregularly shaped dark blue patches on
the shining sands; but these lay so far out that they were seldom
visited. Here was the place for finding sea anemones in perfection –
flowering in the little runnels and basins between the spiky chunks of
the shellfish, in every shade of delicate translucent colour, lilac, and
rose, and orange, and silver grey – the full hearts expanded in clus-
tering tentacles that waved in the transparent water. But those who
went hunting to the mussel beds had need to keep a careful watch
for the returning tide, which had a way of stealing a march upon the
unwary, and surrounding them completely before they noticed its
approach. Not far from high-water mark there was a wide channel

that was always filled first and emptied (but never quite emptied) last. It was here that the bathing machines stopped when the tide was high; when it was going out they were taken further on, over shallow levels, into the gradually deepening mid-sea, or rather mid-estuary, water – often a long drive beyond call of the beach proper, where still the bathers might be left high and dry in a few minutes. The channel might be likened to a tightened bow-string, and the tide came up in the shape of the drawn bow; so that while a great plain of sand and the distant mussel beds remained uncovered, two strong currents were rushing swiftly round the arc behind, and into the line of the channel before them, isolating them from the mainland, and converting them into an island doomed in a very short space of time to be sunk deep beneath the sea. Accidents used to happen frequently from inattention to this peculiarity of the Dunstanborough coast, even to those who were perfectly familiar with it; and when Dicky Delavel reached the shore after his visit to the Morrisons' farm, one of those accidents was imminent.

By this time the sky was so dark, and the general aspect of things so cheerless, that the score or so of visitors who had spent the morning on the sands were no longer to be seen there; they had taken refuge in their lodgings up in the village from the threatening storm. The boy had walked a mile or two, swinging along as if life and death depended on his rate of speed, and had not seen a living soul. Even the coastguardsman, who should have been parading the top of the cliff with his telescope, was invisible.

'I have missed her,' thought Dicky; 'she has gone home by the road.' And he glanced up at the heavy sky and prepared to follow her example.

Suddenly he stopped. He had caught sight of a figure moving over the distant mussel beds – moving slowly in a stooping posture from place to place – and he could just see that it was a woman's. At the same moment he saw that the enemy was creeping upon her, and that she was too much absorbed in her occupation to notice it. Could *that* be Annie Morrison? Surely not. Annie was Dunstanborough born, and knew the ways of the sea as well as he did; she would never let herself be entrapped by the tide. Still, though it were only an ignorant visitor, in whom he could not be expected to feel the slightest interest, she had to be rescued, and he only was there to do it. Already it was too late for her to escape unaided. As he stripped off his coat the two currents came running up as fast as a fleet horse could gallop, and met together in the channel at his feet, where they began to rise and flow backward over the as yet large island of naked sand. Usually a boat was lying away on that island, with its anchor thrown out – perhaps on purpose for emergencies like the present; but boats were few at Dunstanborough, and this was now otherwise engaged. Moment by moment the gulf between him and that lone little figure grew wider and deeper, and in a few minutes he knew that sands and mussel beds would disappear beneath the waves. There was no time for hesitation. He kicked off his boots, flung coat and waistcoat above reach of the tide, looked up and down in a vain search for help, and then, accompanied by the faithful Billy, splashed through the tumbling waters of the channel, which washed his knees, and, reaching the dry sand, ran at his utmost speed towards the mussel beds, where the woman now stood upright and evidently aware of her predicament.

'Come along!' he roared, wildly waving his arms. 'Throw away your basket and run – *run*, I tell you!' And then, as she obeyed him and came speeding over the sands like a lapwing, he saw that it was really Annie Morrison after all.

There was no time for greetings, however. A flash of elation lit up his handsome face for a moment, and then it became strained and anxious as before. He snatched her hand, and dragged her back across the sands as fast as her legs could carry her; and as they ran the tide ran to meet them, followed them and surrounded them, so that when they came to the brink of the channel it was no longer a channel, and the dry land on which they stood was no bigger than a good-sized tennis lawn.

Now he stood still, breathless, and looked at her, still holding her hand in his, to which she clung in abject fright and helplessness. She was not a heroine in her behaviour at this moment, but she certainly was uncommonly pretty.

'Look here,' he said, trying to encourage her, 'walk as far as you can, and when it gets too deep don't be frightened – I can swim and take you with me. It won't be far. Do what I tell you and we shall get through all right. Hold my hand tight – I will take care of you.'

They entered the water together – or, rather, the water ran round them and drew them in – and, thanks to the even smoothness of that sandy floor, they were able to struggle along on foot until the tide reached up to Annie's shoulder. Then the girl lost her head and began to sway and flounder about and to shriek and cling to her companion in a way that made him clench his teeth and turn a little pale.

'We shall both be swamped,' he exclaimed, holding himself as still as he could for a moment while he tried to steady her. 'Do try and be brave – only for one second. Let me get a free stroke without pulling me down, and then put your hand on me somewhere – catch hold of my shoulder – my shirt sleeve – anything – and let yourself float; that's all you have to do. Otherwise we shall be drowned to a dead certainty.'

But she was beside herself with terror, and heard not a word. Desperate, he shook her off for a moment to take his plunge; and she screamed, and her head went down and her feet went up, and she clutched at him wildly – fortunately without getting hold of him; then she was dragged heavily to the surface by his hand under her arm, and his teeth in her frock; and thus, straining and struggling, and with such difficulty as taxed his strength and energy to the utmost, he managed to pull her through, by which time she was nearly insensible and lying a dead weight in his arms.

He made for the nearest point where he could get a foothold again, and this was under a jutting crag of cliff and amongst the fallen rocks – a rough landing place, where they were a good deal buffeted by breakers and bruised against the submerged boulders, but where they were past all danger of drowning. Up a steep slope of debris from the wave-worn cliff he scrambled, puffing and panting, and weighed down with his burden in her soaked garments; and he placed her in a niche in the red wall, where she would be sheltered from the now cutting wind and could draw breath again in peace. Here she leaned against him, with her eyes shut, and sobbed and moaned herself out of her stupefaction. In point of fact, she made an ignominious exhibition of herself. But this was not the way her conduct affected Dicky. Had she been like his sister Katherine, who had once thought it great fun to be precipitated into deep water with her best clothes on, he would not have found her half so interesting. Dear little timid, feminine creature! He had been nearly drowned through her cowardice, but he did not mind that now, as he sat beside her, trying to revive and comfort her. She made *him* feel so delightfully masculine and superior.

By-and-by she regained some sort of self-possession, lifted herself away from him, modestly drew her dripping clothes about her, and generally resumed her normal attitude, which, towards her 'betters', was entirely what the catechism inculcated, boarding-school notwithstanding. For the first time they looked at each other with leisure to understand their temporary relations and what had happened to them.

Dicky, with his wet shirt clinging to his strong young limbs and body, and his hair plastered to his head, was yet a handsome fellow for women's eyes to gaze upon. He had the fine-cut features peculiar to the Delavel family, with bright, straightforward eyes and a square and resolute jaw that were all his own, and with his cheek flushed and his chest heaving, filled with the triumph of his successful exploit, he was a lad that any mother would have been proud of, and that any girl must have admired. Annie was a deplorable little object, with her drenched petticoats clinging to the steels of her crinoline, her brown hair in rats' tails round her face, her battered hat hanging by its sodden ribbons to her neck; still she, too, had her surviving attractions – limpid brown eyes and soft pink lips and a bloom on her fair and healthy skin that terror and sea water could not quite wash out. She was the first to speak, and did so with much agitation.

'Sir, you will catch your death of cold! Oh, what will Mr Delavel and my lady say to me? Sir, do sit here, where you can be out of the wind.'

'Pooh,' he laughed. 'As if a wetting could hurt a strong fellow like me! It is you who will catch your death of cold, I am afraid. I wish I had my coat here to put over you. Sit a moment to recover yourself, and then we'd better get home as fast as we can. See, here is the storm. I thought it was not far off.'

The strong wind brought up the slanting rain, and it beat on their faces like a shower of bullets. Annie put down her head, and Dicky planted himself in front of her and spread himself as much as possible. It lightened and thundered, it hissed and howled; the grey plain of the sea was blurred, and the horizon was swallowed up in mist. The boy's whole body was exposed to the storm in order to protect his companion, who, however, could not well be wetter than she was; and the stinging of the violent rain upon his flesh and the trickle of cold streams inside his film of shirt were delightful sensations. Little did he think when he set forth in search of Annie Morrison that he was to be rewarded with such success as this.

Annie, in her sheltering niche, was filled with distress at the spectacle of the squire's son thus sacrificing himself for the likes of her. Such a thing had never been heard or thought of in Dunstanborough before.

'Oh, sir,' she protested again and again, 'do – do go home and make yourself dry. If anything should happen to you, the squire and my lady would never forgive me. *Do* take care of yourself – never mind me.'

'Don't talk nonsense,' he retorted, much gratified by her solicitude on his behalf, absurd as it was. 'What am I here for, if not to mind you? It's – it's the greatest bit of luck I ever had in my life.' She made no comment on this, and he said presently, 'Won't your father and mother be very anxious about you?'

'They will think I am at the coastguards' with Rhody,' she replied.

'I hope they will; that would be one trouble the less for us. What made you stay out at the mussel beds so long? Didn't you know it was time for the tide to come in?'

'Yes, sir, I knew, but I had forgotten. I was so taken up with some sea anemones that I wanted for my aquarium that I did not notice the time. I shall never forgive myself for having caused you. . . .'

'O bother! I like it – I'm tremendously glad – I wouldn't have had anybody else do it for the world.'

'There was nobody else, sir – only you. And you saved my life – with God's help.'

'Bosh! rubbish! you make too much of a trifle. But' – as she did not immediately protest against this view – 'though I say it that shouldn't, I believe you would have been at the bottom of the sea at this minute if it had not been for me.'

He had turned his back to the rain, and was looking at her, and as he spoke he laid his hand on her shoulder, with the idea of presently slipping it round her waist. He had been known to flirt with barmaids in his day and to kiss a pretty housemaid behind her pantry door, and, having had time to realise the present situation, it seemed to him that it afforded an opportunity for a little sentimental diversion. He almost felt as if he had a right to it after all he had gone through.

But Annie, in the midst of fervent protestations of gratitude, drew herself back, gently but resolutely, and looked at him with eyes in which he read disappointment and reproach. In a moment he withdrew his hand, and withdrew himself an inch or two, with a slight flush on his cheek and a sensation of manly respect for her in his heart. If she had been the most finished coquette, designing to lead him on to admire her, she could not have done it more effectually than by this delicate repulse.

'The rain doesn't seem likely to hold up yet, and the tide is rising fast,' he said, after a little conscious silence. 'If we don't go now the water round the point will be too deep for us to get past, and we shall have to sit here till the tide goes down again. We had better fight through it and have done with it, hadn't we?'

She assented eagerly at the suggestion of this second danger that she had overlooked, and they rose together and hurried over the rocks and into the sea again, which, though not deep enough to drown them this time, was well up to Dicky's waist.

'You had better give me your hand,' he said politely, 'so that I can steady you a bit. And don't be in a hurry, or you will lame yourself amongst these stones.'

She gave him her cold hand, which he took loosely, but soon held in a firm clasp, for she required his support. Her dependence on him in the deep water amongst the stones seemed to imply that confidence in him was restored, and he ventured to say again how glad he was that he had happened to see her in time. 'Strange to say, I had been thinking of you all day,' he made bold to remark; 'ever since I saw you at church this morning.'

He looked at her, and she was not displeased. Her teeth chattered, but her expression was not cold; it was more feminine than he had seen it yet. 'Did you see me this morning?' she murmured. The provocative question encouraged him wonderfully.

'I thought you were some beautiful young lady visitor that my cousin had scraped acquaintance with. It must be years since I saw you, Annie – I feel quite afraid to call you Annie now – for I only remember you as a little girl.'

'I spent some of my holidays in London, sir. And you were away sometimes.'

'Don't call me "sir," Annie. I say, mind that rock – there, I told you so! Lean on me, Annie – let me guide you.' He boldly put his arm round her waist this time, and, as they were in rather a deep place, he did thereby hold her up and support her; but the moment this help became unnecessary she firmly dispensed with it.

'Thank you, sir – Mr Richard – I can get along quite well now,' she said, and drew away from him with her modest dignity, that was as charming as her pretty deference, and all the more so because he saw there was no offence in it. It just kept him in his place, without snubbing him. It compelled his respect, without damping his sentimental impulse.

They had not far to wade before they came to a point where the cliff receded landward, and a little strip of shingle was left for them to walk upon. Then they gained the open beach, recovered Dicky's clothes, and turned their faces towards a flight of wooden steps that led up the cliff to the village.

'Take my arm,' said Dicky, presenting it. 'It is heavy work getting up here, and you look dead beat.'

'No, thank you, sir,' said Annie. She put one foot on the bottom step of the steep staircase, and stood, panting, to muster her strength for the ascent. Then she looked at him with her soft eyes, and he promptly drew her hand within his arm and held it there firmly as they marched up. He even laid his own palm over it, so sure did he feel that she had no inward objection to his attentions – within bounds.

'You must go to the coastguards', dear, and Rhoda Appleton will give you some of her things to put on, and I'll send a message to your mother to tell her you are all right, and I shall make Mrs Appleton give you some brandy and water and put you to bed,' he said, trying to cover his young tenderness with an elderly air.

Annie murmured something to the effect that he was too good, and he pressed the hand on his arm. Upon which she gently drew it away, but without causing him to regret having pressed it.

Separately they made their way along the footpath at the top of the cliff to a gate leading into a narrow lane, which lane had a right of way through a yard in front of the Delavel Arms (happily deserted at this moment on account of the rain), and led into a road across which, on a slight eminence, stood the tall flagstaff and neat white cottages of the coastguard station; and they brought their tired and muddy feet to a standstill on Mrs Appleton's spotless doorstone. Dicky knocked at the door, and it was opened by Miss Rhoda – familiarly called Rhody – who was keeping house in her mother's absence.

CHAPTER V

●

At The Coastguard Station

Miss Appleton, a young person whose chignon and crinoline were much larger than Lady Susan considered suitable to a coastguardsman's daughter, opened the door with an airy flourish, revealing behind her an exquisitely neat apartment, brilliant with polished surfaces, its only litter the materials of an unmade dress, upon which she had evidently been at work. On recognising her visitors and their dilapidated condition, her careless face and manner underwent a change.

'*Annie!*' she cried, with a long emphasis on the first syllable of the name, and an accent of mingled dismay and amusement – the amusement predominating – that set Dicky's teeth on edge. 'Whatever *have* you been doing?' Then, turning to the young man with an effort to be respectfully serious, but still giggling under her breath, 'Oh, Mr *Richard*, sir! – goodness gracious, what a mess you *are* in, to be sure!'

'So would you be in a mess, Miss Appleton, if you had gone through what we have,' said Dicky brusquely. 'Miss Morrison was caught by the tide at the mussel beds, and I happened to be walking on the beach, fortunately, and saw her, and fished her out. Do take her in, please, and make her dry, and get her something hot; she is chilled through and through, and will be laid up with a fever if we don't mind. I think she had better go to bed, with a lot of blankets over her.'

The young lady looked with some alarm at Annie's boots and petticoats, and the spotless floor and furniture; then thriftily pinned her own dress skirt round her waist and turned up her neat cuffs. 'And you too, Mr Richard,' she said sweetly; '*you* must be attended to. I don't know what Mr Delavel and my lady *would* say if you went home like that – and such a long way, too, and your teeth chattering.

Will you just come up to father's room, sir, and let me lend you his best suit! T'aint fit for you to put on, I know, but if you wouldn't mind that, I could dry your clothes for you in half an hour.'

Dicky thanked her, said he was ashamed to trouble her, but would be grateful for the loan of her father's clothes and a seat in the chimney corner for a little while – presently – when Miss Morrison had been looked after. But Annie would do nothing, and Rhoda would do nothing for her, until he, the illustrious Delavel, had been duly served; seeing which, he consented to mount to a little closet in the roof, there, supplied with all he wanted by the fair hands of his hostess, to make his rough but comfortable toilet. While he was washing and rubbing and clothing himself he could hear the girls moving about the house briskly. Miss Appleton's tongue never ceased going for a moment, and at intervals her voice, raised to exclaim or interrogate, reached his ear more distinctly than she imagined; on which occasions an imploring 'Hush – sh!' betrayed Annie's anxiety and distress lest, in the honour that was being done them, they should forget their duty and their manners and what was due to the squire's son. How different they were, he thought, as, guiltless of eavesdropping, he listened to their broken talk. Annie, with her modest grace, was a little lady in spite of Delavel-Pole's opinion.

He was a long time dressing himself, for the coastguardsman's uniform was not made for a tall and slender youth, and, Delavel though he was, he was not above trying to make himself look as little ridiculous as might be in the eyes of those rustic maidens. He came downstairs at last, wearing a pilot coat over a pair of short and baggy trousers, his feet in blue worsted socks and gay carpet slippers, his handsome throat bare – not such a very grotesque figure after all. The wet clothes that he had put outside his door he found in the kitchen, some hanging before the fire, and some in the washtub, being rapidly rubbed and rinsed by the young lady of the house, who well deserved to be called a 'smart gal'. A couple of flat-irons were heating at the grate, the kettle was singing on the hob, and on a deal table, temporarily adorned with the green and red parlour table-cloth, Annie (in a very old frock of Rhoda's) was setting out the tea-tray. It was characteristic of Miss Appleton's good sense that she supposed Mr Richard would rather be warm and comfortable in the kitchen than genteel and cold in the front room – where a fire was not to be thought of at this season, with the fireplace full of paper lace and roses; and very cheerful and cosy the humbler apartment looked as he descended into it, in spite of the wash-tub and the steaming clothes-horse. But he was annoyed to see Annie waiting upon him instead of receiving attention herself.

'Why, what are you doing?' he exclaimed. 'Didn't I tell you to have some brandy and water and go to bed?'

'Oh, *she's* all right,' Miss Appleton interposed, 'and she don't want brandy. There'll be a cup o' tea in two minutes. Look alive now, Annie, and make a slice o' toast for Mr Richard while I clean up. Take this seat, sir,' hurrying to the fireside to place her father's chair for him. 'I hope you are feeling more comfortable?'

Dicky declared he was very comfortable, and politely protested against the trouble she was taking for him. She assured him that trouble was a pleasure, turned the coat and trousers on the horse, hung socks and shirt beside them, and whisked out of the kitchen with her heavy tub in her arms before he had time to offer his assistance. In two minutes more she had flown upstairs to 'tidy' herself, and he was left alone with Annie.

Annie was kneeling at his feet making toast, according to orders. Some slices of bread lay on a plate on a three-legged footstool beside her, and Billy, his dog, was sniffing at them. For a moment he looked her all over to see what she was really like; it was the first fair chance he had had. And he came to the conclusion that she was charming. Her brown hair was bright and silky, with two or three pretty waves in it, and the way she wore it, without horsehair stuffing, or comb, or ribbons, simply rolled round and round in a large knot, was very becoming. Her face, though not intellectual, was refined and sweet, and her figure was as pretty as her face, her attitude just now showing all its soft and healthy curves and its girlish flexibility to perfection. She was the village maid of romance – the ideal farmer's daughter; and she had grown up here in Dunstanborough without any one finding her out – until he, Dicky Delavel, came, like the Lord of Burleigh, with the seeing eye and the understanding heart, to make the interesting discovery. As for Delavel-Pole, who could not see that she was a lady, and yet had a certain sordid and vulgar apprehension of her charms, Dicky felt that he would like to kick him.

'Get up this moment,' he said to her, having fixed the instantaneous photograph upon his memory. In a twinkling he had her sitting in the cushioned chair, which was the seat of honour, and was himself established on the three-legged stool, with the toasting fork in his hand. Annie protested in vain. 'Sir, *please* – Rhody will be so angry when she comes back to see you doing that!' And indeed the spectacle of a Delavel thus engaged, amid such surroundings, was too shocking to witness unmoved. It seemed as if the world was being turned upside down that afternoon. She could only wonder for the fiftieth time what my lady and the squire *would* say if they knew.

'And if I were to see you faint away before the fire I should be angry,' he said lightly. 'And do you suppose I can't make toast as well as you?'

At this moment the sound of a loudly-ticking pendulum in the parlour was interrupted by five reverberating strokes. The recollection of Delavel-Pole's appointment flashed into both the young heads at once. Dicky could not bear to think of it.

'Do you often go to the rectory?' he asked bluntly.

Annie answered, evidently with pride, that she often did, adding in an anxious tone, that she ought to be there now.

'You won't go to-night,' he emphatically declared. 'You must stay here and rest, and have some tea; and when the rain is over I will take you home.' He had already caught a small coastguard boy, and sent him with a message to the farm to say that she was in safe shelter, so that time did not seem of any particular consequence now. 'Do you go alone to the rectory? Or is it a class?'

She went alone, she said. It was not a class. The rector expressly desired her to go.

'And what do you do when you get there? – if it's not a rude question.'

Annie called his attention to the fact that the toast was burning, and as he scraped it rather savagely with a black-handled knife, she explained – again with an air of modest complacence – that Mr Delavel-Pole arranged the Sunday-school lessons with her, and explained the meaning of obscure passages of Scripture. He told her always to bring her difficulties to him, and when she did so he never failed to solve them. It was a great privilege, she concluded, with an air of returning thanks to the Almighty for it.

'A great privilege for him, no doubt,' said Dicky. 'And do you go often to those early services of his?'

'*Always* – when I can,' she replied, straightening herself a little, and closing her soft lips firmly. 'I would not miss them for anything.'

'Your mother says she shan't let you go when the winter comes.'

'I *must*,' she returned resolutely.

'What, when she says you mustn't?'

'We must do our duty, sir, even at the risk of displeasing our parents.'

'That's Delavel-Pole's doctrine, I suppose. Curiously enough, it's the exact reverse of the advice he gives to me.'

'It's the teaching of the Church, Mr Richard – which commands us to meet together' –

'You don't meet together,' he interrupted flippantly. 'You only meet Delavel-Pole and the almshouse people, who don't go willingly, but are dragged out of their beds, poor old souls, ill or well, wet or shine, and feel anything but like praying when they get there, I'll be bound.'

Hitherto Annie had had little to say for herself, but now she became quite animated, in her decorous fashion, as she protested against these unholy sentiments. She urged, with solemn vehemence, that the services of the Church were the great and only comfort left to the almshouse people in their old age. Life was over for them, and had been all toil and trouble mostly; they should be glad to think of the next world now, and to take these precious opportunities for preparing for it.

'Well, I'm afraid I shouldn't do much preparing under those circumstances – forced to go because I was a pauper and dependent on the parson's bounty; and then to have to hear him rattling through the service with that irreverent gabble of his, as if he were doing it for a wager.'

'Sir, you don't suppose the rector takes all that trouble for only his own pleasure?'

'Oh, as to that, I don't give an opinion. But if those old creatures don't come to church in the winter time, you'll see – they'll get no soup and blankets. And they know it. I don't call *that* worshipping God. It's just show and self-interest and make-believe – and a lot of mean tyranny at the bottom of it. Max wasn't so fond of going to church himself in the old times, I can tell you.'

Dicky was quite aware that it was not good form to talk thus of the rector to his parishioner, but he justified himself, nevertheless – as we always can when we want to. He imagined that he saw Max taking a mean advantage of his privileged position, and considered that he had a duty to Annie to perform. The girl listened to him with a kind of soft obstinacy, gazing into the fire and rubbing her hands slowly one over the other on her knee.

'It is a help to *me*,' she said firmly. 'When I begin a day like that, I feel that all the rest of it is made better.'

Then a brief silence fell upon them, while Dicky pondered over this statement and questioned its secret import. Was it the influence of the material church – the beautiful 'Early Decorated' architecture and stained windows and immemorial associations – upon a young imagination and a reverent mind? Was it the walk from the farm and back in the delicious early hours of the summer days? Or was it Delavel-Pole?

'At any rate,' he said, 'you have no business to go to the rectory in this way. If the parson wants to see you, let him call at the farm.'

Annie blushed, suddenly aware of his point of view.

'I could not give him that trouble,' she murmured.

'Trouble!' he echoed hotly. 'Is it for a lady to take trouble to save a man from taking it? That is a new doctrine.'

'It is not a case between a lady and a gentleman,' said Annie (deeply flattered that he should think it was), 'but between a clergyman and his parishioner.'

'Well,' said Dicky, rising from his stool (for the toast was made), 'all I know is, we shouldn't think of letting Barbara go to the rectory by herself – though she's his own cousin – and Max would know better than to ask her. Therefore I say he has no business to ask you, unless it is for a class. Of course, if Mrs Morrison had time to walk round with you it would be different; but even then. . . .' He broke off as he caught sight of her crimson face, and flushed the same colour himself as he realised that he was in effect accusing this innocent creature of impropriety. 'It is not treating you with proper respect,' he stammered, in a tone of apology; 'that is what annoys me.'

At this moment his hostess came sailing downstairs in her Sunday gown and a silk apron. The staircase descended into the kitchen, and from the upper landing she had a view of the young pair below before they knew that they were observed. Dicky was standing by the table, very red, and perturbed by the audacity of which he had been guilty; and Annie was standing near him, also with burning blushes on her face and with her eyes cast down. Preparations for tea were at a standstill. One glance convinced Miss Rhoda that her guests had taken advantage of her absence in the manner she believed customary with young Oxford gentlemen and village maidens when thus conveniently thrown together.

As she advanced to the table she looked from one to the other with a smile that made the Delavel blood boil. All Dicky's gratitude to her for washing his shirt for him was swallowed up in disgusted resentment of her impertinence in standing there and smirking in that abominable manner.

'Come, now, Mr Richard,' she said archly, 'I am sure a cup of hot tea will do you good, if you don't mind sitting down at our 'umble board. Why, Annie, haven't you got the tea made yet? You lazy girl, I expected to find it drawed by this time.' She fetched earthen teapot and rosewood caddy, and soon had the tea stewing on the hob; and then she bustled about to set the chairs round the table. 'I'm very sorry I haven't any cake just at present,' she said affably. 'If I'd only known you'd been coming, Mr Richard – but that was the *last* thing I ever expected.'

She prattled gaily as she tripped about the room, while Annie stacked the buttered toast in silence. Some instinct prevented Dicky from looking at the embarrassed girl, and also from making any movement to help her or wait upon her; he gave all his attentions to his hostess, who quite revelled in the excitement of the occasion and the important part she filled in her mother's absence. She thought she knew what young college gentlemen were like, and she had heard in the village and at the Hall that Master Richard was even a little more 'wild' than usual. This gave great piquancy to her enjoyment, albeit she was a perfectly proper young woman, against whose character no one had a word to say.

The three sat down when tea and toast were ready, and were chatting freely (Dicky and Miss Appleton monopolising the conversation) and apparently enjoying themselves and their repast, when a shadow fell across the kitchen window, and Rhoda jumped up with an ecstatic shriek. 'Lor!' she cried, 'I do declare there's John.'

'I suppose he has come for me,' said Annie.

John Morrison, jun., entered heavily, and with a face that did not harmonise with the festive atmosphere of the room. He was a big, solid, coarse-featured, common-looking, though not altogether unhandsome, working farmer – oh, *so* unlike Annie, Dicky thought, as he gave the new-comer a short nod. 'How strange it is that the men of that class are seldom or never superior to it,' he reflected, in the rapid moment that he compared brother and sister together. 'Well, John, how are you?' he inquired aloud, brightly.

'Good-day, sir,' John returned with perfect respect but little enthusiasm, making a movement as if to touch his forehead with the knuckle of his forefinger. Then he submitted gravely to be kissed and interrogated by his sweetheart, and laid his hand upon Annie's shoulder.

'What's this you've been doing on?' he demanded with some sternness.

Annie looked surprised at the tone, flushed and hesitated; where-upon the voluble Rhoda gave the story of the afternoon's adventure in all, and with more than all, its thrilling details – dwelling with fervour upon Dicky's gallant exploit. 'If he hadn't happened to be with her, her dead body would just have been floating out to sea at this moment,' said Rhody dramatically.

'He was not with me,' murmured Annie.

'I happened to be walking on the beach,' said Dicky, leaning back in his chair and stretching himself, 'and I only saw her after the tide had surrounded her. I never imagined it was a Dunstanborough native. I took her for a visitor.' He was driven to say this much, and yet was enraged to find himself accounting for his proceedings, and in a sense defending himself against the man's evident suspicion that he had been too much concerned in the matter. John listened coldly, with an occasional grunt, and, when he had heard all there was to tell, said that he was much obliged to Master Richard, but hoped Annie would know better than to be such a fool again. He was singularly ungracious. Dicky had never seen him like this before – he had always thought him such a pleasant, well-mannered fellow – and the lad began to remember that he was his father's son, and what was due to him as such.

'Be good enough to go over to the inn and order a trap for me, will you?' he said, with the true Delavel air, rising abruptly from his seat. 'I am awfully obliged to you, Miss Appleton, but I think I won't wait for my clothes to dry. Your father won't mind my going home in his; they can come back in the trap.'

John Morrison went at once to the Delavel Arms and brought a fly, and our hero withdrew from the scene with great dignity. He was even a little cool to Annie – until he took her hand in his to say good-bye; then he could not be cool. He squeezed her fingers until they ached. After all, they had been nearly drowned together, and it was not her fault that her brother was a boor.

CHAPTER VI

●

A Faithful Watchdog

When the fly had departed, John turned to his sister and bade her put her things on to go home also. It rained still, but he had brought the gig – an old-fashioned, two-wheeled vehicle, the possession of which had for many years conferred gentility upon the people at the farm – and the gig umbrella, a huge green cotton affair, with a bulbous yellow handle, also of the nature of a family heirloom, and well adapted to the purpose for which it was made; so that there was no risk of her taking harm from the further exposure. 'Come on, now,' he said testily. 'Let's be getting along back. Mother's fidgeting till she sees you, and well she may. You'll have to have a nuss to take you out for walks, Annie – that's what you'll have to have.'

'You have no business to speak to me like that,' she replied with dignity. 'Do you suppose I risked my death on purpose?'

'Oh, there warn't much risk, I s'pose, with people standing there ready to jump into the water after you.'

Annie turned her back on him in silence and marched upstairs, and the door of Rhody's bedroom shut rather sharply.

'Why, John,' said Rhody, with a nervous laugh, 'whatever are you so cross about?'

'I'm not cross,' said John – as people always do say when they are in a particularly bad temper; 'no more than you are.'

'Oh yes, you are, now – you're as cross as two sticks. If you weren't you wouldn't want to be running off like this, before you've hardly set foot in the house, and me all alone, and haven't seen you for two whole days. I don't take it kind of you' – bridling coquettishly. 'I suppose you're getting tired of me.'

'Don't you be foolish, Rhody,' replied her lover, unabashed. 'I've got enough to do bothering after Annie — I don't want to have you making a fuss too.'

'Oh, I shan't make no fuss – don't you flatter yourself. If you can do without my company, I can do without yours, I'm sure. And as for poor Annie, I can't see that it's any such great crime she's done – that isn't the way her mother looks at it, I'll be bound. Accidents will happen, and it's just the merest chance that she isn't lying dead and drowned at this moment. Supposing you'd ha' found her stretched out stark and stiff on that there table,' said Rhody, pointing with lurid triumph to the half emptied plate of toast. 'How do you think you'd ha' felt, then, eh?'

'There's worse things than that,' said John gloomily.

'Oh, there is, is there? Perhaps you'll tell me what's worse than losing your only sister, the pride of her father and the prop of her mother's declining years?'

'There's other ways o' losing her,' said John.

'What ways?' But Rhody now saw, in a flash, what he was driving at, and she dropped her truculent manner and looked at him with intense interest.

There was a momentary silence between them, and the man fixed his eyes solemnly on her eager face. 'Look here, Rhody,' he said, with impressive sternness, 'tell me true now – has he been about with her afore to-day?'

'Not as I know of,' she replied. 'No, he can't h' been, for he happened to say as he saw her at church this morning, and didn't know her.'

'At church? What did *he* go to church for?'

'To say his prayers, I s'pose.'

'Don't you believe it.'

'Well, at any rate, it wasn't to see her. She's been away mostly when he's been at home for the last year or two, and he didn't even know she was grown up.'

'He knows it now – worse luck. Look here, Rhody,' he repeated, this time clasping her wrist with his horny hand, 'tell me now – *was* he walking about with her this afternoon? Or did he only see her after the tide came round her, as he makes out?'

'Well, John,' said she, with earnest candour, 'I wasn't there to see no more than you. I can only go by what they say. Mr Richard declared he had no idea it was her till he got to the mussel beds after the sea had cut her off. And she says the first she saw of him was when he came running and shouting across the sands, in his shirt-sleeves and his stocking-feet, at the very moment when she gave herself up for lost.'

'I never knew Annie tell a lie,' said John, looking on the floor with his clouded eyes.

'Of course you never did,' said Rhody cheerfully, beginning to clear away the soiled cups and plates. 'You're just a suspicious old thing, and that's the best of you. I wonder whether you're going to make a row every time a man speaks to *me*? And whether you'd let me drown sooner than have me helped out o' the water by another feller, if so be I happened to get caught by the tide when you wasn't there – which I shouldn't be such a fool, I hope. If it had been an old man instead of a young one,' she went on, laughing, 'he mightn't have been strong enough to pull her out, for she's none so light, for all her slim looks – she weighs half a stone more than I do. And they couldn't flirt much while they were being half drowned, first with the sea water and then with the rain – if that's what you are afraid of.' Rhody vividly remembered the guilty looks of the young pair when she surprised them *tête-à-tête* in the kitchen half an hour ago; but, in John's present temper, she did not consider it expedient to refer to that episode.

'She's grown a very handsome girl,' said the farmer gloomily, after a brief pause.

'Oh, she's handsome enough,' assented Rhody, not with enthusiasm, by any means. 'Still I shouldn't think her the sort likely to captivate Mr Richard' – smiling to herself. 'He must see a many girls prettier than she is.'

'I'm not so sure of that,' said John. 'She's got that soft way with her; she's tender and delicate like; and I can see they all notice her. Even the rector turns round in the reading-desk to see if she's there, afore he's hardly up from his knees. I've caught him at it times and often.'

'Oh, the rector? He's what they call a celibate. He don't hold with having anything to do with women at all. He's just taking notice of Annie because she's willing to teach in the Sunday-school and give away the tracts. She's useful to him, you see.'

'Oh yes, I see,' said the suspicious brother grimly. 'I don't suppose *he's* much to be afraid of; but Master Richard is different. He's grown to be a man now, and he don't bear the best of characters, if all they say is true.'

'I daresay he's no worse than the rest of 'em,' said Miss Rhody easily; 'and I must say you think a lot of Annie if you suppose gentlemen like him and Mr Delavel-Pole must needs fall in love with her the moment they set eyes on her.'

'Men are men and girls are girls,' said John, oracularly. 'Master Richard is handsome, too, and he has a sort o' taking way with him. . . .'

'That's true,' Miss Appleton broke in, this time with no lack of enthusiasm. 'Neither Mr Roger nor Mr Keppel can hold a candle to him.'

'And he's got scent of her,' continued John. 'He come round to the house to-day, pretending it was to see father – when he hasn't been near for a matter of two years. And as soon as he hears that Annie is down on the beach, off he goes after her. He must have gone there straight, or he couldn't have been there when the tide came up.'

'Well, that was a lucky thing, anyhow, and it shows that he hadn't much time to walk about with her before it happened – doesn't it? He couldn't ha' been in two places at once.'

'But *he went after her*,' persisted John. 'And if he takes to going after her, it can only mean mischief,' he concluded, striking his knee heavily with his clenched fist.

'Nonsense!' ejaculated Rhody, with disdain. 'You ought to have a better opinion of your own sister than to suppose she's a girl o' that sort. And as for Mr Richard, he's got something better to do. If he hasn't lost his heart all the time he's been at Oxford, he won't lose it at Dunstanborough – don't you believe it; You needn't alarm yourself about *that*.' Miss Appleton had not that high opinion of her future sister-in-law's attractions that prevailed with the other sex.

' 'Tisn't his losing his heart I'm afraid of,' muttered John, with a snarling laugh. 'His heart's safe enough, I make no doubt.'

'I should think it was,' said Miss Rhody loftily. 'And I'll tell you what it is, John' – here she became as serious as he – 'if I was you I'd be a little more careful how I treated my landlord's son – let alone a gentleman as has done the family such a service as to save their only daughter's life. You hardly so much as thanked him for what he'd done, and he went away quite offended, and no wonder. I really was surprised at you. I thought you'd ha' known better –seeing who he was, and that the family's sure to hear of it. You've been at the farm for five generations, I know; but, all the same, Mr Delavel could turn you out to-morrow if he liked.'

'Let him!' retorted John savagely. 'I'll have no fine gentlemen meddling with my sister. If Master Richard tries it on he'll have to look out, though he is the squire's son; and so I shall tell him, and I shan't waste no words neither. I know what that sudden friendship for us all means – Oh yes, he may hoodwink the old people, but he don't take in *me*. He doesn't go and sit in the keeping-room, and drink his beer with father, just for the sake of cheering the old chap; them are not the ways of gentlemen's sons like him. And he don't ask himself to our wedding for the sake of drinking good luck to you and me, my girl. Don't you believe it.'

'*What*!' ejaculated Rhody, starting backward and nearly dropping the teapot on the floor, 'did he say he would come to our wedding? *Mr Richard*!'

'He'll get no invitation from me,' said John. 'I'd like him to keep his place and let us keep ours, as we've always done.'

But Rhody set the teapot gently down on the table, and stood looking at her lover, swelling visibly. Visions of the honour and glory certain to accrue to herself from such a condescension on the part of a member of the great family at the Hall thronged her active brain; and, incredible as it may appear, she did not for a moment question the integrity of Mr Richard's intentions in this particular instance. Why, indeed, should he *not* invite himself to the wedding for the sake of drinking good luck and showing a kindness to her? He had just been treating her as if she were a born lady (with much more deference than John had ever shown); and in her blue silk bridal dress and orange-blossom wreathed bonnet she felt that she should be quite competent to hold her own against Annie, or any other woman, for special and general attractiveness. John might say what he liked, but if Mr Richard had a mind to come to her wedding, come he should, or she'd know the reason why. Such a chance as that was not one to be let slip by people who had their families to consider. Oh, what *would* all the Dunstanborough folks say? And what a glorious inauguration to her reign as the new Mrs Morrison! What a position in the village it would give her!

'John, dear,' she said coaxingly, and with much sound good sense, 'don't you go for to be headstrong and rash, now. If you kick up a fuss, it will just be putting things into their heads, when very likely they have no such ideas at all. And it will set people talking about Annie, and do her more harm than ever Mr Richard would. And if the squire should hear of it, there would be bad blood for certain, and no end of trouble – and you've always got on with him so comfortably all these years. Just you wait, now, till they really *do* do something, and you really *have* got something to take hold of.'

'That would be too late, Rhody. You can't undo mischief when it's done. I want to prevent it. I'm not going to kick up a fuss, but I'm going to take care of my sister, who's too young and foolish to take care of herself. I shall just speak a word of warning to her to-night – that's all I mean to do at present – till I see how Master Richard behaves himself.'

'*All*!' exclaimed Rhody, throwing up her hands. 'Goodness gracious! and enough, too. You're just going to put into her silly head that Master Richard is in love with her, which, of course, will make her think at once that she's in love with him – that's all! Oh, go and do it, pray – it's the cleverest way of taking care of a sister that ever I heard of. Go and shove him down her throat – go and and show him that you have to tie her by the leg and keep the doors locked to prevent her from running after him – and see how that will cure them of thinking anything more about each other. Oh, you are a sharp one, John, I must say – that you are!'

John sat silent under this scathing satire, apparently quite unmoved by it. But it had its effect. It shook his confidence in his own wisdom (though he would not have owned it, even to himself) so far that he forbore to say his 'word of warning' to Annie as they drove home together. He did what was quite as bad, however – never once opened his lips throughout the journey. Annie knew what the silence meant; it was plainer than speech. And Rhody's prophecies began to come true.

CHAPTER VII

•

New Lights

On the doorstep of the farmhouse Annie saw her mother standing, when the gig and the old pony stopped at the garden gate. As Rhody had truly said, Mrs Morrison's way of taking the news of the after-noon's occurrences was not as John's way. The thought that her darling might have been 'lying dead and drowned at the very moment' was uppermost and paramount in her agitated mind; and because Master Richard had averted this catastrophe, at the peril of his own invaluable life, she was in no mood to find fault with anything else that he had done or might do, but was ready to bless him altogether on bended knees. Maternal solicitude and anxiety were evident in her round face and the attitude of her redundant form, as she stood on the threshold watching and listening, peering through the rain; and the sight of her was comforting to Annie, who did not greatly crave for comfort from that source as a rule. She allowed herself to be wrapped in the tender arms and crooned over by the foolish voice with affectionate condescension.

John went round to the yard, and there put up the gig and the pony, and attended to other matters that his errand to the coastguard station had delayed. The old father came in, heard the tale without much emotion, and hastened out again to his business of the moment, unable to picture the danger he had not seen, and troubled about his hay above everything. And mother and daughter – Annie in a shawl, with her feet on a stool, and a cup of hot spiced elderberry wine beside her – had an interesting *tête-à-tête* in the keeping-room.

Mrs Morrison, like her son, saw a possibility looming on her domestic horizon, but it did not inspire her with unmitigated dread. Mothers are daring and ambitious to any extent of folly, and women are proverbially credulous and ridiculously romantic, and some hearts keep young and soft long after the bodies belonging to them are middle-aged; and so this homely matron, who was thought to have plenty of sense, was capable of believing that her child was worthy of any distinction that an aristocratic admirer could confer. It did not seem to her warped judgment that Mr Richard's fancy – 'if so be he had one' – must necessarily mean mischief.

'And to think o' that girl giving you nothing better to put on than that old rag,' she said, scornfully regarding the borrowed dress which Annie still wore, 'and him there and all! Why didn't you ask for something better? She's got more good frocks than any girl in Dunstanborough.'

'She likes to save them,' said Annie, 'and if she didn't offer them of her own free will I wasn't going to ask her.'

'I wouldn't ha' had him seen you such a guy as that for anything,' the mortified mother went on. 'It was just a bit of Miss Rhody's jealousy. She can't abear anybody to look better than she does.'

'Mr Richard looked rather a guy himself,' the girl remarked. 'He had to wear Mr Appleton's clothes.'

'Poor dear young gentleman! Well, I suppose there was nothing else for it. I wish I had been there to attend to him I do hope he hasn't caught a cold or done himself any harm. Do you think he's all right, my dear? 'Cause Mr Delavel and my lady will blame it on to us if he isn't.'

Annie reassured her mother on this point, and the old woman went off into raptures about his manliness and beauty, his bravery and his affability; his striking superiority to the rest of his family, sacred beings as they all were. 'And I shouldn't wonder if we don't have him coming round tomorrow to inquire how you are,' she concluded, beaming upon her daughter like a noonday sun.

Annie answered, with a moonlight kind of smile, that she shouldn't wonder either.

'Then we must take care to let him see you looking respectable,' said that fond and foolish parent. 'You put on your lilac muslin with the bows.'

Annie said she would.

Tea-time was over before she reached home, and dusk and supper-time were drawing on, when, for the first time, she mentioned the rector – till now the most important person in her mother's eyes, and the chief topic of their private conversations. 'I could not go to the rectory this afternoon, mother, and I promised Mr Delavel-Pole to be there at five.'

'My pet, he's heard by now how it was you couldn't go. I suppose he'll be round by-and-by.'

'Yes. And to-morrow is Saturday. He will want me to go to-morrow, perhaps; for he likes to arrange the lessons himself.'

'Well, it's no matter if he does. You can't go trapesing down there if you feel knocked up. If he comes to-morrow, he can show you the lessons; if he doesn't, it can't much signify. If you ain't able to teach them little things out of your own head, it's a pity – that's all I can say.'

'I have been thinking,' Annie went on, 'that perhaps I won't go to the rectory again – not in that way. Though, how to get out of it now, I don't know.' She paused, and Mrs Morrison waited to hear the reason of so unexpected a proposal. Annie was eager for Church work, for that religious, or rather, ecclesiastical usefulness, which is so much more attractive than the common work of the world to young people of a serious turn of mind; and hitherto the visits to Mr Delavel-Pole had been regarded as very precious privileges, spiritual and social. 'You see,' she went on, 'the rector has no regular teachers' meeting. As far as I know, Miss Cousins and the rest of them never go to him for instruction. He just tells them what to do from Sunday to Sunday. And – and it is like making differences between us, you know.'

'So it is,' said Mrs Morrison. 'And not very flattering to you, neither. Why, you're about the only one with learning enough to be trusted to teach out of your own head – you and Miss Barbara. It's the others ought to go to the rectory for to have instruction – not you.'

'Yes. And Miss Barbara never goes. Mr Richard was talking of it,' said Annie thoughfully, and with an air of conscious dignity. 'He said Miss Barbara never went, and that Lady Susan would never let her – not by herself, I mean – and that Mr Delavel-Pole would never dream of asking it, because it would not be paying her respect. And then he said the rector ought to do the same by me as by Miss Barbara, because I was a lady, too. . . .'

'Mr Richard is mighty particular.' Mrs Morrison broke in, profoundly flattered, and fain to believe that the young man would do no less than practise what he preached. 'Had you been talking to him about it?'

'No; he knew. Probably from Mr Delavel-Pole himself. I suppose he has been talking to him about me.'

'Well, it's by no wish of mine that you go to the rectory by yourself, my dear, and I think it's just as well to stop it – not to have Miss Cousins thinking you're made more of than her, and passing remarks about it.'

'But what can I say to Mr Delavel-Pole?' inquired Annie anxiously. 'I can't refuse to go, and give no reason, and I can't tell him the true one.'

'*You* can't, perhaps, but I can. You let me see him, and I'll just say that father and me don't wish you to be going to him by yourself, because he is a young man and hasn't got a wife, and it's just as well to be on the safe side when there's such a lot of gossiping as there is in Dunstanborough. You needn't be supposed to know anything about it. I'll say it's father and me, and if he likes to take offence it'll be with us and not with you. And we shan't mind it.'

'Don't let him think I said a word,' begged Annie, with almost tragic earnestness. 'And, above all, don't bring Mr Richard's name in.'

'You may trust me,' said Mrs Morrison confidently.

Mr Morrison came in, and after him John; and the supper tray, loaded with that supper which people of their class somehow managed to digest in those days (for what I know, they may do so still), though they mostly went to bed the moment they had swallowed it – bread and cheese and beer, cold pork and pickles, cold puddings and pies, and so on – was brought in by the strong-armed maid-of-all-work, Eliza. The old couple and their son sat down to a hearty, serious meal, as was their wont, barring illness, every night of their lives; but Annie, preferring her own thoughts to their company, and wanting no food after her elderberry wine and toast, took her candle and slipped off to bed.

She slept soundly, for she was tired – 'wore out', her mother declared, when she waddled in presently to see that her darling was all right – and in the morning she awoke at an early hour, with her bodily health and strength restored, as if nothing had happened. It was a lovely day, after the rain. She sprang out of bed to open her small lattice – for, like other old-fashioned folks, Mrs Morrison would have thought it death to leave it open during the night – and curled herself up again for half-an-hour, in company with 'The Christian Year', 'The Imitation of Christ', and a little book containing a long string of questions as to the state of her spiritual health, which she had bound herself to answer night and morning. As she lay, absorbed in her devotional exercises, her mother bustled to and fro between kitchen and dairy over the rough pavement under the window, and all sorts of busy sounds rose upon the soft, fresh air – the clatter of milk-pails and hob-nailed shoes, the clear ring of Eliza's pattens on the bricks, the cluck and scuffle of feeding fowls, the grunt of hungry pigs in the farmyard, the consequential coo of pigeons and their flapping wings. The Marthas of the world were at work, distributing breakfasts and preparing for to-days and to-morrows; but she, who had been to boarding-school and was one of the elect in grace, was exempt from that homely service. They had to think of others; she needed only to think of herself. Hers was the good part, no doubt; it was likewise the easiest. So she heard all the sounds of activity in the yard below, and heeded them not. Her mind, when it was not occupied with what she was reading, was absorbed in one momentous question – Should she go to morning service, or should she not?

She was especially anxious to go to thank God for His late mercies vouchsafed to her, and to invoke His blessings upon the instrument of her deliverance, and it did not occur to her that she could do this fittingly by any other means. On the other hand, if she went she would see Mr Delavel-Pole, and he would be sure to ask her to go to the rectory – which she had almost made up her mind not to do again in her new character of a lady who should be treated with the same respect as Miss Barbara – and she was not prepared to refuse in so many words. She might also see Mr Richard; and, though not exactly reluctant to meet him, she was very shy about doing so. He was her saviour and hero, certainly, but he was also a young man whom it behoved a modest girl to keep at a certain distance. It was hardly within the bounds of reason that he should ever want to marry her, so far beneath him as she was (though she dwelt on this idea); and it was not in her to contemplate sentimental relations in any other than a matrimonial sense. She was the most strictly proper little person that ever owned a pretty face.

Seven o'clock was the farmhouse breakfast hour, and she joined her parents at the early meal without having come to a decision. Her mother was still thinking of her household cares, and therefore talked about them, and her father was still engrossed with his hay. They said little to their daughter beyond complimenting her on her good looks, and the girl wrestled in silence with the now intensely urgent question – Should she go, or shouldn't she?

At twenty minutes to eight something had to be done. She therefore put on her hat and set forth, leaving herself the interval before service began in which to decide the matter – which seemed to her of more consequence than all the hay and butter and market prices that were the objects of her parents' solicitude. It was an exquisite morning to be out in, and the walk (if she had had time to attend to it) delightful. The light spring tints were gone, and trees and hedges in full leaf and richness. Families of young birds swarmed everywhere, rooks cawing in the pastures and skylarks singing overhead. Sweetbriar scented the dewy lanes, where the pink dog-rose flowered, mixing with the perfume of beans and red clover and drying hay in the fields; and the blue sky, and the vapours of delicate mist that melted in the sun, and the colours of the landscape, and the distant glitter of the sea that was too dazzling to look at, were altogether delicious. But Annie Morrison only listened to the tinkle tinkle of the matin bell at the park gates, and only looked at the great tower that peeped above the trees.

After all, she did not go to service. Within a stone's-throw of the church she suddenly turned back, and retraced her steps to the farm. 'They will miss me,' she thought; 'they will come to see me by-and-by if they don't see me now.'

Meanwhile the rector had heard of the accident of the previous day, and at morning prayers looked out for his young parishioner with some anxiety. She was not there, but Dicky was – Dicky the scoffer and scapegrace, with a grave face and his prayer-book in his hand. Mr Delavel-Pole did not for a moment believe that his cousin had come to church for any good – like John Morrison, he scented mischief in such fair behaviour – and a little reflection convinced him that but one feature of the early service could have any attraction for a young man of his low tastes.

'If he takes to dangling after the girls of the village,' said the rector to himself angrily, as he passed from the vestry to his stall, 'it will become my duty to inform his father of it.'

To himself his duty at that hour seemed somewhat flat and flavourless. He shut his eyes and folded his hands and recited his solemn formula in the usual manner, looking very stern and rigid; but all the time he was conscious of the empty place where a fair girl's face should have been, and missed the soft and solemn voice that was wont to chime with his rapid utterance. He seemed to have no audience. The old people sat and stood like dilapidated automatons, expressing nothing but patient endurance, regarding their week-day churchgoing as a part of their hard and humble lot in life; and the antipathetic young Delavel, who alone represented the higher classes, was worse than no one. He affected the clergyman much as the presence of a sceptic affects the medium in a spiritualistic séance. Dicky looked upon the service as a formal and soulless performance, and was disgusted with himself for taking part in it. He had, of course, not done so from any proper motive, and therefore felt himself a hypocrite. He didn't want to praise and pray – how could he, in Max's company? He only wanted to see Annie Morrison and ask her how she felt. Annie was not there, and he had his trouble for nothing.

Service being over, he hurried out of church by the family door in the chancel without waiting to be asked questions by his cousin, and went home to breakfast through the delicious morning sunshine as fast as his long legs could travel. At the Hall he said nothing of where he had been. Entering the house by a back way, he found an idle stable-boy, and despatched him quietly to the farm with 'Mr Richard's compliments, and please how was Miss Morrison this morning?' about which proceeding also he said nothing, but slipped out when he had had his breakfast to watch for and intercept his returning messenger, who brought him Mrs Morrison's duty, and the satisfactory assurance that Annie was quite well. His anxieties on that head being set at rest, he took a book under his arm and went out to read all the morning under the yew trees in the garden. He would have liked to pay a visit to the Morrisons himself, but reflected that, after John's behaviour at the coastguards', it would be hardly expedient to do so. Moreover, the old people would want to thank him for saving their daughter's life, and he did not wish to put himself in the way of that.

CHAPTER VIII

—————————•—————————

A Mistaken Policy

While Dicky lay on a bed of soft grass that sloped down into the moat at his feet, half reading and half meditating, the shadow of those dark umbrellas over his head, and the bubbles and ripples made by the carp and the swans on the still waters glinting in the sunshine a few yards distant, and sending dazzling reflections into his half-shut eyes, his cousin, Delavel-Pole, was bestirring himself on his and Annie Morrison's behalf. As early as eleven o'clock the rector set forth to the farm to make inquiries after his protégée, and to learn, if possible, the facts of the affair of the accident and rescue, the story of which had come to his ears in various contradictory shapes.

Annie and her mother were together in the kitchen, making those elaborate preparations for the Sunday meals which were customary on Saturday morning – stuffing and trussing fowls, baking pastry and cakes, and so on – when he arrived. He was not accustomed to consult the convenience of his parishioners when making his calls – it was one of his ways of marking their social unimportance – and the Morrisons were used to receiving him in the midst of washing, cooking, or jam-making, or when their dinners and teas were growing cold on the table, at which, of course, he never sat down himself; so the farmer's wife merely sighed in a worried way when Eliza announced his presence in the parlour, and bade Annie see to the kitchen business while she went in to talk to him.

'Yes, sir,' she said, in answer to his inquiries, 'she's pretty well, I thank you. Not but what it was a great shock she had, poor dear, and very trying to a growing girl – first nearly drowned in the sea, and then soaked through and through with the rain. Hours she must ha' been without a dry stitch to her back, and the wind blowing all the time. I expected no less than to have her in a high fever after all she went through, for she's none so strong, isn't Annie. She's not like them hearty, bouncing girls, that takes naturally to roughness and knocking about, as one may say – she's a tender young creature, and she can't stand it. Howsomever, it might ha' been worse, Lord knows. If Master Richard hadn't happened to be there, dead and drowned she would ha' been, bless her, at this very minute!' concluded Mrs Morrison, quoting Rhody's formula, and putting the corner of her apron to her eyes.

'God would have sent some other instrument,' said the rector piously, 'since it was His will that she should be spared. Still, I am very glad that Mr Richard was able to make himself useful. He is not an ill-disposed lad, by any means, but it is not often he does anything so well worth doing as that was. He has grown sadly idle and dissipated of late, I am sorry to say, and gives his parents a good deal of anxiety. Of course, this is between ourselves, Mrs Morrison. You must not talk of it, you know. And I have no doubt he will steady down when he gets older,' said the rector hopefully.

'It was a noble act,' said Mrs Morrison, ignoring the proffered confidence, 'and I, for one, shall bless him for it to my dying day. You don't know what it was, Mr Delavel-Pole – with a frightened girl, dressed in all her clothes, clinging to him, and dragging him down in the deep water, and as much as the length o' this garden to struggle through, inch by inch, as one may say. Annie says she looks back and wonders he didn't shake her off and leave her then and there. For his life was just as much in danger as ever hers was, she says, while she was hanging to him and he trying to swim, with little kicks and jumps, and his head under half the time.'

'Oh no,' said the rector, with an amused, indulgent smile. 'You and Annie don't understand what a good swimmer can do, how easy it really is. The boy is like a fish, nothing comes amiss to him in the water. I've seen him do feats compared with which this was mere child's-play, just for the fun of the thing. It was serious for poor Annie, of course, but as far as *he* was concerned, he would simply enjoy the chance of exercising himself.'

'Well, sir,' said Mrs Morrison, 'we don't make so light of it, I can tell you. We've lived in Dunstanborough all our lives, and we know the tides, and we've Annie's word for it that he had a hard job to pull through. The best swimmer is no better than the worst when his arms and legs are tied – and they might as well ha' been. He saved our dear child's life, sir – say what you will – and we are grateful to him accordingly, and ever shall be. Heaven bless him, and send him such a friend as he's been to us whenever he wants one!' – beginning to weep in her apron.

'Far be it from me,' said the rector eagerly, 'to undervalue his bravery. His presence on the beach, in the nick of time, and when, strangely enough, no one else happened to be there, was most opportune, most providential. And though he could do no less than go to Annie's help, his promptness and perseverence were praiseworthy in the extreme. You ought indeed to be grateful for the service he was privileged to render you, and still more grateful to the Higher Power in whose hands he was but the humble instrument. I suppose Annie will like to return thanks in the church to-morrow?'

'Sir, we've been returning thanks all the time, I think.'

'But I mean publicly, properly, as the Church directs,' said the rector, with his most severe professional air.

Mrs Morrison looked dubious and uncomfortable. She was not religious enough to enjoy making a public show of her religion, she would have said, could she have expressed her thoughts. To hear her daughter's name called aloud in church, and to see all the village gossips turning round to stare at her, seemed a sort of indelicacy to this rustic woman. Annie would probably thus desire to testify to her undoubted orthodoxy, but the old-fashioned mother shrank from the idea of it. She said nothing, and, with a touch of impatience, the rector desired that Annie herself should be summoned, that he might speak to her about it.

'Well, sir,' said Annie's mother, drying her eyes and becoming watchful and business-like, 'I'm afraid I must ask you to excuse her just now.'

'Is she not well enough?'

'Oh yes, she's well enough. But she's very much engaged. She wished me to ask you to excuse her coming in. Saturday morning is rather a busy time, you know, sir.'

'Well, she will be at leisure in the afternoon, I suppose. Ask her if she will step down to the rectory at about five o'clock. Then we can talk it over, and see about the school lessons at the same time.'

The rector rose and took up his hat. Mrs Morrison also rose, twisting her apron round her fingers. He put out his hand to bid her a stately good-morning, but her eyes were fixed on the carpet, and she did not notice the gesture.

'Now that we're upon the subject, sir,' she said, as if with a sudden burst of candour, but in that tremulous, hurried, deprecating manner which told him she had long premeditated what she was going to say, 'now that we're speaking of it, sir, I think I'd better tell you that her father and me don't quite like her going down to the rectory by herself. You see' – temporising weakly – 'it's rather late when she gets home, and the roads are lonesome.'

'Let her come earlier then,' suggested Mr Delavel-Pole affably, jumping to the unfounded conclusion that the old people were afraid of Dicky being abroad on those lonesome roads – which, however, were light enough at six or seven o'clock in June. 'She can come as early as two o'clock if she likes. I have finished my lunch by two.'

'I thank you, sir. But – but, we've hardly cleared away and got straightened by that time. And, to tell the truth, that isn't the only thing. You see you don't have a class for the teachers, sir, and it's like to make Miss Cousins jealous, and to say nasty things of Annie. Especially as you are kind o' young, you know, sir,' falteringly, and with an air of cringing apology for suggesting such a thing, 'and there isn't no lady at the rectory like there used to be.'

Mr Delavel-Pole wondered whether he could have heard aright, and stiffened with offended dignity. 'Will you kindly inform me, Mrs Morrison,' he inquired, with terrible deliberation, 'whether you have heard Miss Cousins, or any one else, say nasty things as, you call it, of Annie, because she comes to the rectory by herself?'

'Oh no, sir!' – reassuringly – 'not a word. Not a breath.'

'Then may I ask who has put such a preposterous idea into your head?'

'Sir,' replied the matron, nettled, 'I have my own ideas, and I don't think it's right and proper for a girl so young and pretty as Annie – for pretty she is, though I say it that shouldn't, to go alone to bachelor gentlemen's houses. . . .'

'That will do, Mrs Morrison.' He interrupted her in a tone that made her jump and gasp. 'I don't think you mean to be impertinent, but, at the same time, you are sadly forgetting yourself – forgetting to whom you are speaking,' said he, quite pale with wrath. 'Be good enough,' he continued, 'to tell me why this insulting, this – this coarse and disgusting idea, has only now occurred to you, and then I wish to hear no more. Has Annie asked you to speak to me? I can scarcely believe she would be guilty of such atrocious bad taste – that she would take such an outrageous liberty.'

'Annie, sir? – of course not!' returned Mrs Morrison, rallying under the stimulus of these hard words. 'I don't take advice from her – nor from anybody, for that matter – as to what I think is for her good.'

'Has anybody been speaking to her about it?' he continued, rapidly and angrily, with a sudden intuition.

Mrs Morrison was ready to go through fire and water for her child, but she had scruples about telling a lie in so many words. She hung her head.

'Has Richard Delavel been meddling?' demanded the rector, with a savage intonation that savoured of pre-sacerdotal days.

'Oh, not meddling, sir – he never thought of meddling, I'm sure. He merely said that – that Miss Barbara wouldn't go and see you by herself.'

'Miss Barbara!' The rector burst into a brief and sudden laugh, a laugh that sent the colour into the old woman's cheeks. The next moment he was more majestic than ever, though still with a curl at the corners of his thin lips. 'That will do,' he repeated, making passes in the air with his hands; 'that will do, my good woman. If Annie so completely forgets both her own position and mine, it is indeed time that she should cease to come to the rectory. Keep her at home, by all means; keep her at home, pray. I should exceedingly dislike to expose myself to vulgar village tittle-tattle by receiving her again. And if you think it is for her good to let Richard Delavel amuse himself by pretending to teach her the laws of propriety, do so – do so. He is the most fitting person, since he breaks them all himself systematically. *Good* morning, Mrs Morrison. Pray do not trouble yourself to open the door.'

And, waving his hand as if to wave her back from his path, the rector marched out to the parlour, through the empty keeping-room and into the porch (where he left the farmer's wife crushed with shame and self-reproach for the manner in which she had bungled her delicate task), and took his way across the fields and the park to the Hall, to have lunch and a little serious conversation with Lady Susan.

When he was gone Mrs Morrison returned to the kitchen, dropped upon a wooden chair, and wept a few tears of mortification and anger, rubbing her eyes with her white apron. Then, while she stuffed a pair of plump ducks, she narrated to Annie the dismal details and result of the recent interview, with many apologies to her daughter for not having managed better. Annie knew her duty too well to reproach her mother, but she also was deeply mortified. At the same time she had the comfort of knowing that she had vindicated her dignity as a lady – the kind of lady that, since her acquaintance with Mr Richard, she had discovered herself to be. And Mr Delavel-Pole's equal harshness to herself and his cousin had the natural effect of rousing resentment for the wrongs each suffered for the other's sake, and other sentiments of a dangerous and undesired tendency.

In the afternoon the two women had another sensation. They were sitting quietly in the keeping-room, sewing and chatting, Annie in her lilac muslin with the bows, prepared for certain contingencies – their men folk being with the haymakers in the field – when, looking up at an unwonted sound, they beheld the Delavel carriage driving up to the gate. The visitor was none other than Lady Susan herself, and the sight of that illustrious being filled mother and daughter with a flutter of consternation. Under any circumstances the event would have been remarkable enough, but today it had an alarming significance.

'I was having my drive,' said Lady Susan, waddling in very much as Mrs Morrison would have done (there was a striking resemblance in the physique and style of the two), and sinking heavily upon the much-antimacassared parlour sofa, 'and I thought I would just come round and see how you were, my dear. We heard about your dangerous accident yesterday, and how my son jumped into the sea to rescue you. It was very fortunate he happened to be there, was it not? – and also that he is such a splendid swimmer – like a fish, as my nephew says. Happily, he is as much at home in the water as on the land, so that it was nothing to him, comparatively speaking – though the wetting might have given him a bad cold. But you must be more careful for the future, must you not? Another time you might not be so fortunate. A Dunstanborough girl ought to know enough about the coast to keep clear of the tide when it is coming in, ought she not?'

'My lady, no one can be more sorry than I am for what Mr Richard was exposed to through my carelessness,' said Annie with appropriate meekness, and in her best boarding-school manner; and then, at a sign from her mother, she left the room to get out cake and wine.

Lady Susan did not scold, like John and the rector. She was very kind and pleasant, and to judge by the way she watched the girl's face and movements, took a flattering interest in her. After the contempt that Mr Delavel-Pole had poured upon them in the morning, the gracious attitude of the squire's lady was very soothing to both mother and daughter, who, nevertheless, kept a nervous watch for some explanation of it. In their hearts they felt that she had come for a purpose – a purpose that was inimical to their peace and comfort – and might be only another adversary in disguise. And presently she betrayed herself.

After a desultory chat with the farmer's wife, during which she watched Annie's comings and goings with scarcely veiled anxiety, she suddenly remarked that shocks to the system as the girl had just undergone had often very serious consequences – though such consequences were not always immediately apparent to the eye. She cited several instances of this which had occurred within her own experience, and then proceeded to describe the treatment which alone was efficacious in such cases. 'Change of air,' she said encouragingly; 'that is the great thing – complete change of air and scene. In any derangement of the nerves, especially, it is simply marvellous in its effects. I daresay you feel all right now, my dear. Though I have known people, when they have been shaken in railway accidents, feel nothing of it for days and perhaps weeks – until a creeping paralysis came on, and they found too late what the secret mischief was. Your accident was not serious, of course. Still it must have shaken you. And if I were your mother I should just send you away for a little visit – say a month or two – to recruit you after it.'

She was a very poor diplomatist, and this little device for removing temptation out of Dicky's way was too transparent. Mrs Morrison and Annie, knowing what they knew, exchanged a furtive momentary glance; and then Annie took upon herself to reply - deferentially, of course, but still with spirit (for was she not a lady, like Miss Barbara, with whom people had no right to take liberties?) – that she was perfectly well, but that, if she had not been, there was all the more reason why she should remain at home in her mother's care. 'And besides,' she said conclusively, 'my brother is to be married in three weeks.'

'Even three weeks' change would set you up wonderfully,' said Lady Susan.

'Thank you, my lady, but I could not go just now. We have to make new things for the house. There is a great deal to do before the wedding.'

Lady Susan said, 'Oh, very well; you know best, of course,' and ceased to urge her point. But by-and-by, having thought it over and renewed her energies with cake and wine, she had a fresh inspiration.

'When Rhoda comes here,' she said, 'you will hardly care to remain at home, Annie. Rhoda will take your place and do your work, and it is only right that you should make room for her. It will be her husband's house, don't you see? – and there will be little ones coming, no doubt – and you will not like to feel in the way. Why not take a situation and earn your own living and be independent, as Rhoda herself has been for years past? If you like, I daresay I can find a nice place for you. I know my sister, Lady Elizabeth, is looking out for a superior schoolroom maid – one able to travel abroad with the young ladies and the governess, which would be very interesting for you – and I will write to her at once if you would like to try for the situation.'

To Lady Susan there was no social difference between a coast-guardsman's daughter, who was a dressmaker, and the daughter of a yeoman farmer, who had been educated regardless of expense at boarding-school; but to Mrs Morrison there was a great deal. And this ill-advised suggestion set her portly person quivering with angry agitation, like a shape of blancmange.

'Rhody Appleton is a respectable girl, and she's going to be my son's wife, and so I'll not say nothing against her – but it isn't the likes of her that'll turn my daughter out of her own home, my lady,' she protested with tremulous dignity. 'If we find there ain't room for us all, 'tisn't Annie that'll go – not while her father and me is above ground, at any rate. And we didn't give her the best of schooling to make a servant of her, neither. Much obliged to your ladyship, all the same. You mean it kind, no doubt.'

Lady Susan did mean it kind, but, like many other persons of her class, she was sadly clumsy in giving effect to her intentions when dealing with the 'common people'. She drove away from the farm-house with a sense of having impaired her popularity in the village (which was very dear to her), and a consciousness of failure in her efforts to serve the best interests of her son, which made her low-spirited and inclined to the darkest forebodings.

Reaching home, she met Dicky on the stairs, and, as he stopped to kiss her and ask her how she had enjoyed her drive, she broke down and wept, to his great dismay and surprise.

'Oh, my boy,' she sobbed, embracing him, 'if I see you taking to evil courses – ruining poor innocent girls, and our own tenants too – it will break my heart! It will kill me, I know it will!'

'What – what?' gasped Dicky, bewildered, disengaging her arms and holding her from him while he stared at her wet eyes and twitching lips. 'What *on earth* are you talking about?' Then a light flashed on him. 'Oh, I see' – his face darkening and hardening ominously – 'I think I see what you mean. This is Master Max's doing, I suppose. I thought he was up to something when he honoured us with such a long visit. I'll be even with that fellow' – setting his teeth. 'I'll teach him to insult me – and her – with such suggestions as those. I wonder you were not ashamed to listen to him, mother!'

With which he almost flung her off, in his virtuous indignation, and, seizing his hat, rushed there and then to the rectory, to 'have it out' in a deadly quarrel with Delavel-Pole.

The direct result of this all-round meddling and muddling was – as any sensible person (say Rhody Appleton, for instance) might have foreseen – to precipitate the very catastrophe that was so passionately feared, and which a policy of masterly inactivity might easily have averted.

On Sunday morning Dicky and Annie went severally to church – he to his curtained pew in the chancel, she to the benches close by, where she was accustomed to sit with her school-children; and the very first time they happened to look at each other their two young faces reddened from brow to chin. That was proof enough, had any one seen it, that the mischief was done.

CHAPTER IX

—•—

Defiance

The surface of things was calm during the three weeks that elapsed between the accident and Rhoda's wedding. In the village not much was heard of the former affair outside the circle of those immediately concerned in it; and Rhoda became of so much public importance as to eclipse all rivals for local fame. Annie stayed in the house, helping to make curtains and table-cloths and other preparations for the homecoming of John's wife. Only the call of duty drew her out. She went to the morning service in a kind of surreptitious way, slipping into a back seat and out of church the moment prayers were over; and she took her class in Sunday-school as before, teaching the children 'out of her head', unmolested and ostentatiously unnoticed by the rector, to whose house, of course, she went no more. But below the surface there was considerable disturbance, all on her account, and by reason of the incalculable temperament of her young admirer. Mr Delavel-Pole was at deadly feud with his cousin, and had laid the farmhouse under an interdict similar to that laid on the Quirinal by the Pope when Victor Emmanuel went to live there. For their independence and their presumption the Morrisons were punished by the withdrawal of his gracious favour; and he pleased himself by thinking that the deprivation would be peculiarly distressing to Annie, which certainly it was. Lady Susan had sleepless nights on account of that danger which the rector had pointed out to her; and the same cause kept John Morrison sternly alert and watchful. Dicky himself did not go to the farm, lest Annie should be made to suffer for it; and he did not go to church on week-days, because, as he said, it sickened him to see Max playing the hypocrite. He attended on Sundays, as a duty to his family and the State; and then alone did he get sight of the farmer's daughter – a luxury the more ardently appreciated because it was so rare.

Over the uncurtained doorway of the squire's pew he looked down upon the lowly benches where she sat beside her schoolchildren, and even when his eyes appeared to be fixed upon his book, he lost not one movement of her supple young figure nor one turn of her graceful head. She certainly was alarmingly pretty for a girl in her class of life, as poor Lady Susan also convinced herself by many surreptitious investigations from her own cushioned throne; and on Sundays Annie never failed to emphasise that most fatal of her attractions – a faculty for looking so like a lady that a stranger would not have distinguished her from one. During this summer weather she wore delicate muslins in pale blues or lilacs, and a little straw bonnet with white strings tied under the chin – and sometimes she added a white muslin fichu, crossed over her breast and tied at the waist behind, all edged with virginal little frills – a simple but dainty costume, that marked her out as a person of refinement and good taste. Moreover, the girl could not have sat or stood to better advantage had an artist occupied the squire's pew and posed her for his own observation. The contrasts of the dark oak, the cold stone, and the coarser specimens of humanity around her, threw her into fine relief, and the light from the stained windows, whether the sun shone or not, always seemed the right thing for her soft complexion and her burnished brown hair. Her attitude and behaviour were modest to a fault; she did nothing that could offend the most severe or jealous critic. And this scrupulousness of propriety and self-respect was more potent in its effect on Dicky than the most alluring devices of the most experienced siren of the ordinary type could have been. It inflamed while it ennobled his admiration. Every minute that he watched her, and saw how delicately and how discreetly she bore herself, his first impression that she was a lady deepened in him – the sense that she was worth to be loved by a gentleman, and that he was ready to love her upon those terms.

Yes, it had come to that, though he had only spoken to her once. He was young and of an ardent temperament, and long before she had appeared to him in her charming womanhood, he had been like a thirsty wayfarer at the public-house who is solicited by his friends 'to give it a name' – if the reader will forgive so coarse a simile. If he had not yet drunk of the wine of life, he scented its aroma, so to speak, and was conscious of a capacious appetite for its consumption. To a certain extent it did not much matter what the nectar was, or rather, to modify the metaphor a little, it did not much matter what the goblet was out of which he drank it, so long as it did not obviously discredit its sacred office. He wanted to love somebody as much as he wanted somebody to love him – indeed, a great deal more; he was impatient for an opportunity to let his young passions, that had begun to feel their strength, go free. Several times he had thought himself provided with an object for his adoration; but violent disparities of taste or sentiment had arisen at an early stage and nipped all those fair illusions in the bud; this was the first attractive woman who had captivated the man in him without immediately thereafter rubbing his aesthetic susceptibilities the wrong way. Therefore he plunged into love, not falling accidentally, nor yielding to external enticements, but like a diver taking a header into deep water – into what he imagines to be deep water. It was what goes by the name of love with girls and boys, whose claim to know all about it is so preposterously supported by novelists, poets, and other presumably experienced people who ought to know better; a very fine and vigorous sentiment certainly, but with very little bottom to it as a rule.

When the three weeks were nearly over, and he was coming home to dinner from one of his fruitless walks about the village, taken daily in the hope of getting a glimpse of his Annie somewhere, he met John Morrison and his sweetheart sauntering side by side through a green lane. Rhoda had been to the farm to inspect the new improvements, and John was escorting her home to the coastguard station.

'Good evening, sir,' said John respectfully, touching his hat.

'Good evening,' responded Dicky, with a brief nod. He had no softening of heart towards either of these two, who were so unpleasantly near to Annie, and had made themselves so objectionable to himself, and his set face did not relax a line.

Rhoda smiled her most engaging smile, hesitated, said 'Good evening, Mr Richard,' and passed on, with evident reluctance to thus conclude the interview. On rejoining John she began to talk rapidly, her distant voice sounding shrill in Dicky's ears as he strode towards his home; and presently she turned and ran back, arresting him at a door in the park wall, the convenient key of which he carried in his pocket.

'Sir,' she exclaimed breathlessly, but with all her wonted air of self-possession, 'I beg your pardon, but I believe you said something to Mrs Morrison about doing us the honour to come to our wedding.'

'Did I?' he replied. He had to think for a moment; then he admitted that he had said something about it.

'Well, sir,' proceeded Rhoda archly, 'the day is near at hand – next Thursday. We're to be married in church at eleven, and have our dinner at mother's, and in the evening Mrs Morrison is going to give a tea-party to welcome us home, and there's to be a dance in the barn.'

Dicky listened composedly; it was no trouble to be dignified with Rhoda Appleton out on the neutral ground of a village lane; then he said he would go to church to see her married with pleasure, and would bring his sisters with him.

'But' – insinuatingly – 'you said you would come *to the wedding*, sir?'

'And isn't that the wedding? But if you'll give me an invitation for the dance I shall be delighted to accept it.' And though he looked grave and cool as he spoke, he meant what he said very thoroughly.

Rhoda gave him the invitation there and then, and he did accept it, subject only to the condition that it should be endorsed by the Morrisons, who were to give the entertainment. This preposterous scruple was laughed to scorn by the bride-elect, who took upon herself to assure him that the Morrisons would be only too much honoured by his condescension; but under the circumstances he insisted upon the formal guarantee that John would make him welcome.

And the same night an elaborate invitation, indited by Annie, was brought to the Hall by John himself, who was not only willing to indulge his Rhody, and make things pleasant for the great occasion, but was gratified by the proper spirit shown by Master Richard in the matter. For John assumed that his character of watch-dog was understood, and flattered himself that, owing to his prompt measures, the squire's handsome son had abandoned his fancy for Annie, and his pernicious danglings after her. 'I've taught him his place,' said the young farmer, with a sombre smile. 'It's hands off, and he knows it. Oh yes, he may come to the dance and the supper, Rhody, and the dinner too, if you like. I don't think he's half so bad as they make out, and of course I shall keep a sharp eye on him.'

So Annie consulted her manual of etiquette, and composed a polite note, her maiden heart all a-flutter within her; and Mr Richard Delavel had great pleasure in accepting Mrs Morrison's kind invitation, and went about for some days with a sense of treading upon air.

The wedding 'went off' in the most satisfactory manner, its most brilliant feature, not even excepting the bride in her blue silk and orange blossoms, being the presence of Mr Richard in the group before the altar in the morning and amongst the guests who danced in the Morrisons' barn at night. His parents, to Rhoda's intense relief, did not object to his thus descending from his high estate and demeaning himself to the level of the common herd (because they did not know anything about it); and his discreet and affable behaviour was such that the 'weddingers', as they styled themselves in the idiom of those parts, not only felt honoured to the last degree by his company, but even at ease and able to enjoy themselves notwithstanding.

He walked across the park to the church in the morning with his sisters and their governess, the sedate Barbara carrying a little packet of half a dozen silver teaspoons and Katherine a bouquet for the bride. They went through their own churchyard gate and chancel door into their great pew, where they sat and gossiped behind the curtains until the bridal party arrived and the rector stalked from his vestry to receive them. Then, as the little procession passed up the church (as they had walked all the way from the coastguard station), two and two, Katherine, signalled by her brother, stepped from the door of the pew into the chancel aisle and held out her bunch of white flowers to Rhoda. The bride accepted them with a whispered 'Thank you, Miss', and a curtsey – for if Dicky had lost some of the divinity that hedged a Delavel, the rest of the family had not – and hesitated about passing on until she saw what direction the young lady meant to take. Katherine politely waved her on, and turned to rejoin her governess; but Dicky pulled her sleeve and said 'Stand here, Kitty – we can see better.' He did not particularly want to pander to Rhoda's vanity, and he was as exclusive for his sisters as he was eclectic for himself; but he saw an opportunity to annoy Max, and it was too precious to be thrown away.

So he stood up with the wedding party, between pretty Annie in her white muslin and pink ribbons and Katherine in her brown holland and garden hat; and as soon as the service was over – read by the rector in his most distant and stately tones – hastened to shake hands with bride and bridegroom and all the plebeian party, and to conduct himself generally as if he was their nearest and dearest friend. Mr Delavel-Pole had himself meant to unbend and be gracious, to relax somewhat the rigour of the interdict, in consideration of the occasion, and perhaps pave the way for a gradual reconciliation with the Morrison family, and a return to favour of his interesting young Sunday-school teacher; but when he saw his cousin behaving in this manner, altogether forgetting his position and encouraging the poor to forget theirs, he felt that some counteraction was necessary for the support of Church and State and of the honour and dignity of the Delavel House, and stiffened into a rigid hauteur that was enough to freeze the marrow of all around him. He did not radiate the palest gleam of sympathy for anybody – happy bride or tearful parents – no more than those effigies of his dead and gone ancestors that lay, stood, and knelt in stony stillness all about them. He would offer no congratulations; he would take no part in –he would not even appear to notice – the little flutter of pride and importance that animated the new-made wife and her relations, when the deed that they had come to do was done. He hoped Rhoda would do her duty, he said, in the new state of life to which it had pleased God to call her. That was all.

Dicky was delighted. He went into the vestry and insisted on signing the register. He introduced his sisters to Annie (though they knew her much better than he did), and instigated the kind-hearted governess to say pretty things and be friendly to the agitated and wet-eyed mothers of the newly-married pair; and he presented Lady Susan's teaspoons with a little speech in which he told Rhody that he hoped he should stir with them many a cup of tea brewed by her fair hands; and so on, and so on. When it was all over, he marched back across the park hand in hand with Katherine, in the highest spirits at having succeeded in putting Max into 'one of his infernal tempers'.

At lunch he was very lively; in the afternoon he was very restless; at dinner he was so silent and abstracted that no one could get a word out of him. And the moment dinner was over and Lady Susan had left the dining-room, he slipped from the table and dashed up the shallow, dark old Jacobean staircase that led to his bedroom, half-a-dozen steps at a time.

'Why, Dicky, what is the matter?' exclaimed Barbara – a very proper and staid young lady – who was descending from the schoolroom to join her mother. 'Where *are* you going?'

'Nowhere – to bed – for a walk – never you mind,' he replied in breathless gasps; and, leaping headlong into his chamber, he banged the door behind him.

Soon he emerged in his morning clothes – his best morning clothes

– and like one of the ghosts of the house, of which there was an assortment, flitted lightly up and down corridors and back staircases until he reached the stable yard. There he found a horse saddled and waiting for him, on which he sped forth into the night.

CHAPTER X

---•---

Danger

It was a soft, starlit summer night. Dicky observed that there was no moon, and reflected that the light – or, rather, the want of light – would be agreeable to dancers who might wish to cool themselves in the open air. He rode through the park at a speed that should have aroused the suspicious vigilance of gate and gamekeepers, but did not; and, dismounting, let himself out by that door in the wall which was supposed to be opened only at certain seasons of the year, and for special purposes of woodcraft, of the key of which he had unlawfully possessed himself. Along the white highroad for a little way, rousing clattering echoes as he went – in and out of grassy lanes, where his horse's hoofs struck the earth with muffled thuds, and where the full-leaved trees darkened the twilight over his head – he passed like a pursued highwayman; and soon arrived at the farmhouse, where lights and voices and the shrill scraping of a violin indicated that the revelry was at its height. Though the stars as yet were few and pale, and the daylight still lingered in translucent green and golden streaks in the western sky, this wedding guest was late. They had waited for him, as in higher circles we wait for the Governor or the Prince of Wales, for a long time after the tea-party had come to an end and the tea-table been cleared for supper. Then they had given him up on the supposition that his parents had interposed, and gone to the barn to dance without him. As he quietly walked his horse from the road gate to the stack-yard, which lay between the house and the barn, and was contiguous to the cart sheds and stable, he could hear the merry thump and scamper of many feet in Sir Roger de Coverley – a dance that mostly marked the climax of these entertainments. Not a soul was about that he could see. Everybody was in the barn, and was so absorbed in Sir Roger, and made so much noise with feet and voice, that his arrival was unheard and unnoticed.

He dismounted in the yard, found an empty corner in one of the sheds (the stable being full) where he put up his horse tying its bridle to a waggon wheel, and then he stood a few minutes, in the gradual darkening of the day and brightening of the stars, to take his bearings and decide whither he should bend his steps. As he stood, looking round him and listening, he saw that the window of the keeping-room, across a little corner of yard and garden, was open; that the room itself – as well as the parlour beyond – was lit up, and shadows passing to and fro within. Probably Mrs Morrison was in the house, on hospitable cares intent, while the guests were revelling in the barn. Dicky thought the proper thing would be to go to the house, therefore, and present himself to her. Lightly he turned and left the yard, passed through a little green wicket into a path bordered with dahlias and foxgloves and with clumps of Indian pinks that smelt very sweet in the moist air, and took his way round to the porch entrance. And there he stopped suddenly, while he stared before him with bright eyes and held his breath.

All the doors were open. In the furthest room a moderator lamp stood on a beaded mat in the middle of a highly polished centre-table, round which books and shells and other ornaments were disposed in the fashion of a wheel of fortune at a fair. A card-table stood open near the gaily-aproned hearth, with two candles in old-fashioned plated candlesticks at two opposite corners, and packs of cards and a cribbage-board symmetrically arranged in the middle. The piano, which was very old, high, and shallow, with faded green silk fluted into a central rosette, from which hung cord and tassels, covering the primitive and worn-out mechanism above the meagre keyboard, also stood open, its few narrow yellow keys shining under the soft glow of two more candles in two more plated candlesticks. The thrifty linen cloth was removed from the drugget that covered the floor; flowers bloomed from the vases on the mantelpiece, and bunches of dried grass adorned the yellow-gauze-swathed frames of the pier-glass and pictures. Antimacassars, freshly washed and starched, abounded in unprecedented profusion. The best parlour was in full dress for company, displaying all those evidences of gentility and prosperity which made the marriage such a recognised social promotion for the coastguardsman's daughter: but no company was there. Young and old had deserted the decorous house for the irresistible jollity of the barn.

In the keeping-room, however, two steps from the threshold on which he stood, Dicky saw the one solitary person who had stayed behind – and that one was *not* Mrs Morrison. The keeping-room was lighted only by the candles intended for the illumination of the supper-table; and the supper-table, composed of several tables joined together, nearly filled all the available space. It was loaded with fowls and hams, and jellies and pastry, and custards and creams, so that scarce an inch of tablecloth was to be seen; and Annie was busily flitting around it, like a pink and white butterfly, touching up the flowers and cut paper frills and adding little garnishings here and there where they seemed to be needed – surveying her operations from time to time critically, with her head on one side. Her sleeves were turned back over her arms, and her book-muslin skirt pinned up round her waist. Her hair was unruffled, her pink bows and pink roses uncrushed, her face calm and serious. She had not yet taken her share in the prevailing excitement.

Dicky watched her, and she did not see him for a minute or two; then a turn round the table brought him within her range of vision. The surprise was so sudden and complete (for, like the rest of the party, she had given up expecting him) that she was not able to guard herself from the betrayal of her delight at his appearance. Her lips parted; her bosom heaved; her eyes brightened and glowed. 'Oh – h!' she cried, under her breath, with a quivering sigh of satisfaction that was beyond words. It was her only welcome, but it was more than sufficient.

Human nature is human nature, as so many profound philosophers have told us, and this boy was not a saint – far from it. What he saw in the girl's aspect and manner told him that now he might venture to kiss her with the certainty of being forgiven, and such an opportunity it is not the custom of unregenerate young men to throw away. In the twinkling of an eye, and before she could unpin her skirt and roll down her sleeves – which was her first instinctive impulse – he had his arms around her and was pressing his eager lips to hers, paying little heed to her bird-like flutterings and modest struggles to escape. He had no thought of 'insulting' her by this proceeding, or of harming her in any way. He loved her, as we have said – with what young creatures, who cannot possibly know much about it, call love, and which is certainly a very ardent sentiment – and, though he was no saint, he was a true man, and had the true man's chivalry to him. But certainly he acted without any thought of matrimonial contingencies.

Annie, however, who *was* a saint, more or less, saw orange blossoms and wedding-cakes, and all sorts of fine things floating in the distance, as she protestingly, and yet not unwillingly, submitted to be hugged and kissed. 'Oh, sir,' she murmured, when at last she had collected herself a little, and got her dainty dress smoothed down, 'it is not right! You ought not to – to think of me in this way. Remember your family and position, and how far above me you are!' Duty required that she should point out this formidable objection to the fore-shadowed alliance.

'How can you talk such rot?' he returned, in tender accents, laughing at her; and he dismissed such considerations as altogether irrelevant to the business in hand. 'You dear little thing, I can't tell you how I have been longing to see you again, and looking forward to this chance. But I never dreamed of finding you alone in the house. Did you stay back here expecting that I would be coming this way. . . .'

'Oh no!' she interrupted, quite shocked at the bare idea of such a thing. 'How *can* you think I should have been so forward? We had all given you up.'

'It would not have been forward – it would have been awfully sweet of you,' he said, again drawing her to him. 'Why should you be so shy when you know I love you?' And he kissed her more boldly than ever.

How should she know he loved her when he had never spoken to her since the day he met her first? And she might have known that that sort of love was not of a matrimonial character, had not her good principles forbade such knowledge. 'I love you' was, to her right-minded judgment, equivalent to 'Will you marry me?' – as of course we know it ought to be in all cases, where a man addresses a woman who is not his blood relation. So that his careless question filled her with the most profound emotion. 'Are you *sure* you love me?' she asked him in an agitated whisper.

'My little darling,' he responded, delighted with her implied surrender, and not thinking much of terms on either side, 'you know I do. How can any one help loving you?'

'You don't know me yet,' she suggested.

'I know you perfectly – as if we had been friends all our lives,' he said, caressing her sleek brown head.

'I am not worthy of you,' she went on, discharging her conscience fully. Something in this phrase staggered him a little, and kept him silent for a moment. The ghost of an idea that she might be taking things over seriously flitted across his mind. But it vanished at once; he would not have this delightful meeting spoiled by thoughts of anything beyond it. 'Don't talk nonsense,' he said lightly. 'That's only a bait for compliments. You know as well as I do that you are worthy of anybody or anything – you dear little woman!' And again he was about to dishevel that neat white muslin and crush those pretty bows and rosebuds that were already showing the results of his embraces – only at this moment the sound of an opening door gave him a shock which arrested his attention.

Mrs Morrison came toddling into the keeping-room from the direction of the kitchen to see how the preparations for supper were getting on. And there by the supper-table she saw Mr Richard standing, propping himself against the edge of it in a stiff and unnatural manner. And there she saw Annie standing before him, head hanging down, eyes veiled with modest lashes, cheeks ruddy as the rose, occupied in picking a bit of green parsley into a hundred thousand fragments. Our worthy matron knew little of the ways of the world, but she recognised what that meant. 'What a handsome pair!' was the instant thought of her maternal heart; and then she prepared for action. Had she been the most experienced old campaigner of a dozen London seasons she could not have acted better.

'Ah, Mr Richard, have you come, sir, after all? Well, you're kindly welcome, and Rhody'll be just delighted. She'd almost given you up. Have you been here long, sir?' – warmly shaking hands with him.

'No,' said Dicky, who had been there about a quarter of an hour. 'I have only just come. I made all the haste I could, but somehow dinner seemed to be twenty-four hours long to-night – I thought they would never get done. But you won't break up yet, will you? It is not supper-time for hours, is it? I have been so looking forward to a dance in the barn. I have been asking your daughter if she will have me for a partner' – looking pointedly at Annie, who took no notice of the hint.

'Oh, she will, with pleasure, sir; she learnt dancing at school, and I daresay you'll find her as good as any of 'em. But you mustn't forget the bride,' said the mother-in-law slyly; 'I think Rhody'll want to be number one, you know – she'll look to have you ask her first.' Then she glanced at Annie, who was apparently absorbed in her business at the supper-table. 'Go and get some more parsley, my girl,' said she; 'there isn't half enough. There's nothing sets a table off like plenty o' parsley.'

A brief silence followed Annie's disappearance, and then the mother asked her young guest if he didn't think the child was 'looking well'.

'She's looking lovely,' Dicky responded with fervour. 'She has grown up the prettiest girl I ever saw.'

'Well, she *is* pretty. And I thought you'd noticed it,' said Mrs Morrison. 'But, now, you won't turn her head, will you, Mr Richard? She's only seventeen, and she isn't used to gentlemen's attentions. You won't go for to – to' – she hesitated in some confusion, and then burst out recklessly – 'You know what I mean, sir; I can't say it!'

Dicky's face flushed crimson; he did know what she meant perfectly. 'I wouldn't,' he said solemnly, 'hurt a hair of her head for all the world could give me.'

'Bless you, my dear,' rejoined the gratified woman, too much overcome by her emotions to remember to order herself lowly and reverently, as was her wont; 'bless you; I know you wouldn't! There's something about you that I can trust, and trust I will – let them say what they like.'

'Do they say I am not to be trusted?' demanded Dicky, with some heat, mentally referring to Delavel-Pole.

'Never mind what they say. I don't believe 'em. There's a look in your face that speaks for you,' said the farmer's wife, benevolently regarding him. 'And you'll not play with my girl, as some young gentlemen in your place would do – you'll not take advantage of her because you've saved her life and made her grateful – I know you won't.'

Dicky, as we have seen, was not so scrupulous as he might have been, but he had a soul that was capable of being profoundly stirred by such an appeal as this. He began to hope that he had not been something worse than a fool, and to make high-minded resolutions. 'That I never will,' he replied solemnly; 'never – on my word of honour.'

'Then I shall trust her to you, my dear. I shall trust you to take care of her, with an easy mind.'

'I will take care of her as if she were my own sister,' said he. But in thinking how he should take care of her, after what had just happened, the idea of marrying her some day necessarily presented itself to his mind. It was rather a disturbing, even rather an appalling idea at first, but he faced it promptly. A man must do his duty, he told himself, and take the consequences of his acts; and the prospect of braving the world and defying its conventional tyrannies had always possessed a fascination for him. Why should he not marry a farmer's daughter? It was nobody's business but his own, and she was good enough for any man, let him be fifty times a Delavel. 'Have no fear,' he said. taking the hand of the old mother, who had so effectually pierced his most vulnerable point; 'it shall never be said that a woman trusted me in vain. I'm not a very good fellow, I am afraid, Mrs Morrison, but at least I am not a villain. No woman shall ever say that of me.'

'Bless you, my dear,' repeated Annie's parent, wiping a tear from her eye, and even showing an inclination to kiss him, with difficulty repressed. 'You are a true gentleman, every inch of you.'

'I hope so,' said Dicky, swelling a little.

And then Annie returned, and they could say no more. But Mrs Morrison felt that she had made good use of her time – as she certainly had – and was tremulously cheerful.

'Give it to me, deary,' she exclaimed, holding her plump hand for the parsley, 'and you young folks go off and have a dance while there's time for it. I'll do what else is wanted in the house.'

But Annie was not prepared to go alone with Dicky to the barn through the dark yard and garden, though he entreated her so earnestly with his boyish bright eyes. A fit of maiden bashfulness possessed her. She looked at her mother with a look that was promptly responded to by that intelligent matron.

'Though, perhaps,' said Mrs Morrison, as if struck by a happy afterthought, 'it would please Rhody better if you went and spoke to her a bit first, without telling her as you had been into the house; and me and Annie 'll follow you in a few minutes. We've got to mind our p's and q's with Rhody, I can tell you, Mr Richard, and she'd be finely jealous if she thought we'd been keeping you all this time away from her, and she the bride and all. If you'll just go and have a dance and a bit of a chat with her first she'll like it, and so will John. You'll find the old man there too. We'll be after you directly.'

'All right,' said Dicky, 'I will – if I must.'

And reluctantly he tore himself from his blushing lady-love (who, the moment he was gone, flung herself upon her mother's ample breast, to confess that Mr Richard had told her he loved her 'in so many words') and took his way alone to the rustic ballroom, where he met with an ovation none the less enthusiastic for being respectfully subdued, and was triumphantly taken in charge by Rhody. The bride, still in her blue silk, and with a killing wreath of orange blossoms round her head, was dancing with great spirit and vigour, but had all the evening kept a watchful eye upon the doorway for his much-desired appearance. She had made such a boast of the compliment he had designed to pay her – she had stirred up so much delightful envy and jealousy thereby – that if, after all, he had failed to come, the mortification to her vanity, and to all her tenderest woman's feelings, would have been insupportable. She was just beginning to despair, and to be harrowingly conscious that furtive smiles and whispers were permeating the company, which naturally was inclined to triumph a little in her disappointment, when her quick eye caught sight of his tall figure in the dimness of the outer night. Instantly she dropped her partner, and made a rush across the floor, scattering the dancers right and left without ceremony. 'Ah! *there* is Mr Richard!' she cried rapturously. 'John! John! Stop that fiddle – tell them to leave off – and come and speak to Mr Richard.'

John obeyed his wife with an alacrity that was productive of many winks and jokes, and the pair advanced together to the barn doors to receive their distinguished guest. The festive spirit was in them, and also many glasses of punch and negus. Peace and charity and an all-comprehensive benevolence animated their lively souls, and John was ready to think every man a jolly good fellow, let him be whom he might.

'Come in, sir, come in,' he urged hospitably; 'we are only plain folks, but you're welcome to the best we've got. Come in, Mr Richard, sir; and we take it very kind of you to leave your fathers' 'all to drink good health to the likes of us – very kind indeed, we do. Here you, Eliza, where are you? Get some punch for Mr Richard Delavel – a fresh brew, mind, with plenty of good stuff in it.'

The punch was brought, and Dicky imbibed it freely, and himself began to feel that it was a world of good fellows, and to be generally pleased with himself and his surroundings. He drank Rhoda's special health with many compliments on her charming appearance, and then, careful to avoid making further distinctions, shook hands with everybody – even with Eliza, who nearly 'dropped' as she afterwards described it, under the unexpected shock. He gave his arm to his young hostess with as much deferential grace as if the barn were a London ballroom and she a new-made duchess, and paraded her about in a manner that made her dizzy with delight and pride. Then he joined the elder Morrison, who sat in a group of hilarious old farmers (himself the most hilarious of all), smoking long church-wardens and drinking brown October that was as strong as brandy; and a great tankard of beer was added to the punch. The liquors were too good to pass, and it was thirsty weather, and Dicky would not for the world seem to slight the hospitalities that were so warmly pressed upon him.

CHAPTER XI

•

Caught

Morrison was an old-fashioned farmer of the old-fashioned days, content to do as his father had done before him. The old plough turned up the stubble, the horny hand scattered the seed in the furrows, and when the corn was ripe it was the sickle that mowed it down. Even the flail was heard in the barn still, though the hum of steam machinery was not unknown in the village. Nevertheless his farm was (for an old-fashioned farm) in good order; hedges trimmed and ditches cleaned and crops well up to the average; rent paid to the day and profits accumulating – very slowly, but with a steadiness that is rarely experienced by men of his class now-a-days. His system was to save all his money, pound by pound, instead of re-investing it in the land (in the shape of improved implements, drainage, artificial manures or pedigreed stock); to let nature take care of herself, with such nursing as he could give her without expense; to be content with slow processes, and small but safe returns. In short, to walk in the benighted old paths generally. And the system seemed to suit his conservative landlord as well as it suited him. Mr Delavel was wont to hold up this comfortable old tenant as a model for the rest.

In the lifetime of the previous Morrison the present one had been but an ordinary labourer amongst the hired men, with no prospect of marrying and making a home for himself until the death of his father left him to inherit the tenancy of the farm. In like manner his son John was only a working bailiff to himself, and he never dreamed of parting with his money in his own lifetime to set up that young man in the world. 'What I done,' said he, 'he can do, and what *my* father thought right *I* think right. The place'll be his own in the course o' nature, and surely he don't want to hurry me into my grave afore my time.' This was when it was first broached to him that John wanted to get married. He could not see what a man wanted to be married for when he'd already got a comfortable home and a good mother to cook his vittles and mend his clothes. He wouldn't hear o' such nonsense. John must wait as he awaited. Plenty o' time for the cares of a family when he was ten or twenty years older. He himself had married at forty-five, and consequently that was soon enough for anybody.

But John, though a slow man, was a determined one, and he insisted on not waiting till he was forty-five. His father and he had repeated battles. All the family, save himself, objected to Rhody, for one thing; they did not consider her their equal in rank, nor eligible in any way. 'And o' course you can't expect to get one o' the right sort, while you've nothing to offer,' the old farmer argued plausibly; 'but wait till you're the master here, and then see how the gals'll run arter yer. I waited until I came in for the place, and what was the consequence? Why, I got yer mother and five hundred pounds down, with silver teapots and house linen, and a mahogany bedstead, and goodness knows what besides.' John replied that he was quite satisfied with his humbler choice, and that all he wanted was a little something to start with – a few hundreds on loan, that he would bind himself to repay in certain instalments. Upon which the old man lectured him at great length upon the iniquity of borrowing. He had never owed any man a penny in his life, and never would, no, not if he was to starve for it. Once you went into debt you were done for – ruin was a mere matter of time. John naturally proceeded to beg his father to give him a small instalment of his inheritance, if that was how he felt about a loan; and then the old man went into a passion, and declared that while he was above ground, at any rate, he'd take care o' the bit o' money he'd had such hard work to scrape together. If people chose to make ducks and drakes of it when he was in his grave, why let 'em, and he thought it hard that a father as had give his son a good eddication, and as comfortable a home as any in the land, should be turned agin' like this and wished out of the way so as others might step into his shoes.

This kind of thing continued for some time, and John used to carry the discouraging reports to the coastguard station when he went to see Rhody of an evening. At last that intrepid and resourceful young woman stepped into the breach. 'Let *me* tackle him,' said she, 'and see if I don't make him change his tune.' She tackled him accordingly, and with complete success. In a short time she was able to wind him round her little finger. Her energy, her impudence, her fearlessness, her practical view of things, her general 'smartness' captivated him – for even an old farmer of seventy is a man, and a man is the prey of the appropriate siren while the breath of life is in him. Not even she could persuade him to untie his purse strings, but short of that she could bend him to her will. And thus it came to pass that the marriage was allowed, and that patriarchal arrangement for the maintenance of the young couple entered into – an arrangement that gave father and daughter-in-law equal satisfaction. It was the latter's suggestion and contrivance, but the former believed it to be entirely his own brilliant idea, and was therefore very proud of it. It seemed to him that it answered all the requirements of the case. 'Not only costs us nothin' – for we shan't miss what the gal eats – but gives us her services free,' said he; 'and many a penny she'll make and save, I'll be bound, with that clever head o' hers.' When Mrs Morrison pointed out that two missuses in a house never *had* been known to agree, he captiously told her that it would be her own fault if she didn't get on with such a gal as Rhody, who'd brighten 'em up so as they wouldn't know theirselves. And when the jealous mother deprecated the plan on Annie's account, the old man hotly affirmed that it was just what Annie wanted – such an example of industry and practical good sense as her sister-in-law would afford her. '*She* won't lie abed or be trapesing off to church o' churning mornings, leaving her mother to do all the work,' said the farmer, newly conscious of his daughter's shortcomings. 'And when Annie sees her bustling round, maybe she'll be stirred up to imitate her a bit.'

On this wedding evening, as he sat amongst his cronies, as happy as a king, taking all the credit to himself for the joyfulness of the occasion, Rhody came behind him, put her arms round his neck, and kissed his purpling cheek with a resounding smack. 'Well, old man,' she said heartily, 'and how are you getting on? Are they looking after you as they ought to?'

He took his pipe from his mouth and returned the smack with vigour. 'Fust rate, my duck, fust rate,' he cordially replied. Then, turning to the company, he added with pride, '*She*'s the gal to take care on yer.'

'I mean to take care of you,' said Rhody, with determination. 'I'm not going to let you drench yourself in thunderstorms same as you did the other day, laying up rheumatics and lumbago for your old age. Good folks are scarce.'

'And so are pretty gals,' said the farmer, saluting her rosy cheek again. 'And they must be took care on too. Have a sup o' beer – come, do; it 'ill do yer good. She do a credit to us, Master Richard, don't she? Many's the poor young man that's broken-hearted this day, I'll be bound!'

Dicky declared that, for his part, he was ready to cut his throat for envy and despair; at which Rhody bade him 'go along', and then reminded him that, if he suffered in that way, he had only himself to blame. The jest was taken up by the circle of old fogies, who at all times deemed it most appropriate for young people, but on this occasion felt that etiquette demanded that it should have the fullest and broadest treatment, and Dicky was rallied upon the supposed state of his heart, the supposed effect of association and example upon it, at great length. He bore it good humouredly, and even entered into the spirit of the thing, admitting the hypothetical young lady and the possession of all the tender feelings attributed to him, until he found the general company gathering round to listen and to mingle their guffaws with the wheezy cackle of the old men. Then a sudden spark of irritation flashed from him. 'Why are they not dancing?' he demanded sharply.

Somebody suggested that they 'didn't like to make so bold', now that he was present, which quickly drove him from his seat, and sent him striding across the ballroom, in search of the orchestra, which had retired to a dark corner, and was silently burying its nose in the inexhaustible tankard. In a few moments he and Rhody were dancing a vigorous polka up and down the barn, and all the heavy, sheepish men in shining broadcloth and gay neckties and all the girls in their Sunday muslins and alpacas and bows of bright ribbon were dancing around them.

Rhody, by way of showing the high tone required of one who associates with the aristocracy, affected to despise the barn and its simple gauds, but it really made a very charming picture. That the floor was ridgy and rough – that the seats were mainly composed of sacks of corn tucked up in household draperies – that the light was produced by tallow candles guttering into tin sconces, and was scarcely strong enough to define the outline of the roof, or to inconvenience the white owl on her accustomed rafter – that the air was heavily charged with strong, warm, mealy, grainy odours that tickled sensitive nostrils like the smell of ripe grass inhaled by people affected with hay fever – only added to the charm of the place. The walls were hung with bunches of evergreens and flags of glazed calico; a rough stage, formed of a shutter laid upon bushel measures, precariously bore up a windsor chair which accommodated the musician, and harmonious blacksmith, whose fiddle was an indispensable adjunct to all Dunstanborough festivities. A table in a corner was loaded with bowls of punch and vast jugs of beer and negus. The rustic revellers were in artistic harmony with their surroundings, and their enjoyment was good to see. From the broad aperture of the doorway – both the great leaves being thrown back – the lovely night looked in, not quite dark yet, and full of stars and mystery. Dicky thought that, if only Annie would come, nothing would be wanting to make it the most perfect ballroom in the world.

'Why doesn't she come?' he demanded of the bride, in irrepressible impatience.

'She's helping her Ma,' said Rhody carelessly.

'And can't the others do that? Why is she drudging in the house, like Cinderella, instead of dancing with the rest?'

'She likes it,' said Mrs John; 'and she don't care for dancing. She's too religious.'

'Rubbish! Send somebody to tell her she *must* come. Everybody should dance at your wedding, for luck,' he added; for he kept most of his wits about him still, in spite of his potations.

He stopped dancing himself and immediately the fiddle stopped. Eliza came by, bearing empty jugs to the cellar to be refilled; and by her the young missus, whom Eliza was prepared to rebel against as such, sent a rather peremptory message to Annie to give over pottering after the supper, and come along to the barn. 'Tell her Mr Richard Delavel wants her,' she called after the servant, with a sharp laugh.

Seeing that he had aroused a little suspicion and jealousy in his young hostess, Dicky set himself to restore her confidence in him, and in her own pre-eminent attractions, and, of course, succeeded in no time. Annie was forgotten in two minutes, and Rhody was languishing on his arm in blissful triumph. She reminded him of what he had said in the morning about the silver teaspoons, and asked him when she might have the honour of his company to tea.

'I shall be most happy to come,' said Dicky, 'any day you like to ask me.'

'Then suppose we say next Sunday,' Rhody suggested, being a young person not given to letting the grass grow under her feet, and belonging to a class that dispenses with the formality of a honeymoon. 'By Sunday I shall be quite settled, if that would suit you.'

Dicky determined to invite himself to schoolroom tea on Sunday, and then to get the good-natured governess to excuse him without saying anything about it. 'All right,' he said; 'I'll come on Sunday.'

This readiness to pay her honour, of course, charmed and delighted the bride, but it was not of her that Dicky thought in making that promise.

Then a reel was started, and taken up with enthusiasm, the men flinging out their arms and snapping their fingers as they swung and jigged around their partners, and the girls responding with smiles and rustic antics as they twirled their full petticoats in the dusty air. Dicky flung himself into the fray with as much ardour as any of them, for he loved a reel and could dance it well, and some of the Dunstanborough maidens, who had come to tenants' and servants' parties at the Hall, had been his partners before, and were of proved efficiency. He did not, and was not required to, observe any ballroom etiquette; he was privileged to consult his own goodwill and pleasure only; so he took one girl and another as fancy dictated, dancing with each for just as long as it pleased him, and then returning her to her rightful partner, who in no case resented his temporary deprivation. In this way he gratified a great many people, found variety and interest in his own performances, and held himself at liberty to appropriate Annie as soon as she should appear upon the scene. But in fact, he did not do it of design. I am sorry to say his head was so full of the fumes of punch and old October that he did not quite know what he did.

When Annie came at last she was accompanied by her mother, and Mrs Morrison's arrival was taken as a signal for supper. At sight of her, Rhody, the mistress of the ceremonies, held up her hand; the fiddler laid his fiddle on his knee; the dancers paused, and held their sides, and panted, and flapped themselves with their handkerchiefs, and trooped laughing towards the door.

But Dicky was not to be robbed in this way. He swept them back with an imperious arm, Mrs John and all, protesting that supper was not to be thought of at this absurd hour. 'Come!' he cried with a voice and gesture that made the girls look at each other and whisper 'Well, I never!' under their breath, holding out both hands to the shrinking daughter of the house. 'Come along! What shall it be? Can you waltz, Annie? Oh yes, I know you can. Play us a waltz,' he shouted to the blacksmith, who was about to descend from his rickety rostrum.

And the musician, reluctantly returning to his windsor chair, struck up the venerable Elfin waltzes; and Annie, standing hesitatingly just within the barn doors, was taken without more ado into her lover's arms.

'We have lost nearly an hour,' he said in an impassioned undertone. 'Why didn't you come before?'

He whirled her into the room and down to the far, dark corners – growing darker and darker as one after another the candles burnt out in their dripping sockets – and mechanically she fell into his step and moved with him without consciousness of any effort on her own part. She had learned to waltz at boarding-school, and she was naturally light-footed and agile; but she did not know whether she was doing well or ill, and did not care. She was filled with emotions that transcended all trivial anxieties of that sort. Her conversation with her mother had assured her of the honourableness of Dicky's intentions, and the prospect that had opened before her bewildered her with its magnificence. She was young and healthy, she had had her dreams like other girls, and this noble youth, who had hitherto dwelt like a young god of Olympus so far above her, more than realised them. So she yielded gently when he strained her to his breast as they waltzed together, and she touched his sleeve with her soft cheek – a touch that maddened him in his present state – feeling it lawful to thus express herself now that he had told her he loved her, and told her mother that no woman should ever say he had deceived her. The other people were dancing; they had a spirit in their feet, as Shelley says, which made it impossible for them to stand still while the fiddle went on; and in the confusion and dimness about them he took her through the wide doorway into the open air, where the sweet smell of cow's breath mingled with the odour of stale straw, and where it seemed so quiet and dark – darker than it really was. The moment he found himself safe, as he thought, from observation – not remembering the conspicuousness of a white dress and the distance at which it can be seen when the stars are shining – he flung his arms round her, tightened them until she gasped for breath, and kissed her with a vehemence that made her tremble. He was intoxicated in more ways than one, and quite reckless of consequences by this time. He told her that he loved her again and again, calling her his darling, his precious one, all the tender names that passion could devise; and when she asked him whether he would love her as much as that always, swore by his honour, and all that a gentleman held dear, that he would be true to her, and to her only, to his life's end.

Suddenly into the midst of this madness, came John Morrison, himself as cool and grim as if he had taken nothing stronger than water all day. Annie gave a little shriek, and Dicky, in his fury, nearly felled the intruder to the earth.

'Steady, sir, steady,' said John, parrying the attack with more quickness than might have been expected from a man of his build and habits; and in a moment the boy's wild beast impulse passed, and he waited in a panting silence for the inevitable question. 'What does this mean, Mr Richard? What are you doing with my sister out here in the dark?'

It was Annie who spoke first. 'It is all right, John,' she said, with a note of gentle triumph in her trembling voice. 'He is not doing wrong – no more am I. We are – we are *engaged*, John.'

Silence followed this statement, which was a shock to Dicky as well as to John, but not nearly such a shock as it would have been an hour ago. Then the brother declared that he didn't believe a word of it. 'What does Mr Richard say?' he inquired, after a second pause of incredulity and astonishment.

'I say what Miss Morrison says, of course,' replied Dicky. 'We are engaged – if she is good enough to accept me.'

'And what does the squire and my lady think of it?' queried John.

'I have not asked them,' said Dicky.

'Does nobody know?'

'Not yet. And I think,' added the boy, who was sobering with great rapidity, 'that it would be just as well to keep the matter to ourselves for the present.'

'I suppose you have only just made it up between you?'

The silence of the young pair gave assent to this.

'I'll tell you what it is,' said the farmer, in a changed tone, 'the liquor has got into your head and you're excited. All the fellows are making love to-night – they don't know what they're doing, half of 'em, and they'll forget all about it to-morrow.'

With great dignity Dicky begged that he might not be classed with those human pigs who did not know how to behave themselves in ladies' company. He hoped he was a gentleman, at any rate.

'All right,' said John. 'We'll talk about it in the morning, and see what you have to say then. You'd better come to supper now. Rhody's hunting for you high and low.'

CHAPTER XII

•

The End Of The Wedding Day

The wedding day did not end well, upon the whole.

As midnight was approaching, and while the guests were still seated at the supper-table, having eaten to repletion and abused themselves with strong liquors, having made their realistic speeches and sung their time-honoured songs, a thundering knock upon the front door made them jump in their chairs and ejaculate 'Lord-a-mercy!' with great fervour. After the first moment of alarm, all eyes were converged upon Dicky's face. The boy had been joining in the rough merriment around him to an extent sufficient to cover his growing discontent with his own proceedings, the awakened sense of caste and of the anomalousness of his position, which increased with the hilarity of his companions, and as the seriousness of his escapade sobered him. He carved fowls, and pulled crackers, and made speeches with the rest, and occasional jokes that provoked roars of admiring laughter. Now his fine-cut features wore a passionate scowl that changed his aspect altogether, and at once explained the situation. An embarrassed silence was maintained while the sleepy maid-of-all-work shuffled into the entry, and more briskly returned to the keeping-room.

'Somebody from the 'all, sir, wishes to speak to you,' said Eliza.

Rising haughtily, he went out, and found a groom standing on the door-step. The man touched his cap and said, 'If you please, sir, my lady wished me to say you was to come home directly.'

Dicky asked no questions; he was too keenly conscious of cutting a ridiculous figure in the eyes of those grinning rustics behind him to run the risk of adding to his humiliations. He turned and said good-night in a stately manner, explaining that his mother was a nervous woman, and was anxious about him if he happened to be out a few minutes later than usual; and then, ignoring many friendly expressions of the generally-felt hope that he wouldn't get into trouble, and scarcely looking at Annie, he mounted the horse that his servant had fetched for him, and rode home in vengeful silence.

His mother, in her dressing-gown, came out upon the corridor to intercept him as he went to bed. 'Oh, my boy,' she wailed, in a cautious undertone, 'what *are* you thinking of to go on like this? If your father were to know what you have been doing! Fortunately, he was in the library, and I managed to keep it from him. . . .'

'How did you know yourself, mother?' interrupted Dicky breathlessly.

'Never mind how I knew. . . .'

'Has Max been here?'

Lady Susan hesitated, and then reluctantly admitted the fact. 'He walked up after dinner, as he often does, and he happened to ask for you – and Barbara said she had seen you going out. . . .'

'Damn him!' said Dicky savagely. 'I'll give him something to meddle for in earnest next time.'

His mother uttered a little whimpering wail at hearing the wicked word on those young lips that were generally so courteous to her and to everybody; it stabbed her tender heart with its testimony to the truth of the prevailing belief that this favourite son was on the road to ruin. 'O Dicky, Dicky!' she cried, with the tears in her eyes.

'Mother, I beg your pardon,' he said, with swift compunction. 'I ought not to have spoken so. But really it is more than I can bear, to have that fellow playing the spy and the informer in this way – and you encouraging him.'

'He only does it for your good, and because he feels it to be his duty,' Lady Susan protested. 'He wants to save you from evil courses, and from bringing disgrace on us and on that poor girl.'

'Disgrace!' cried Dicky, immediately breaking out again in fire and fury. 'Let him use that word to me, and I'll break every bone in his body – parson though he is.' He spoke through his set teeth, wild with rage; but in the extremity of his anger he felt a glow of comfort and triumph in the reflection that he had acted as a man of honour to 'that poor girl'; and then and there he determined to discharge the obligations he had so recklessly undertaken to the very letter. Max and the Family should be satisfied to that extent; there should be no disgrace of the kind they feared.

'You don't know what you are saying,' lamented Lady Susan, in a voice of despair. 'You have been taking too much – I can smell it,

Dicky. Oh, my boy, I thought you loved your mother better than to break her heart, as you are doing!'

'I do love you,' he said, putting his impetuous arm around her. 'And it is that lying sneak who is breaking your heart, making you believe what isn't true – not I. You didn't use to side with other people against me, mother.'

'I don't, Dicky. But you *know* it is all true – that Max is not lying. Oh, I wish – I wish you were more like him!' concluded Lady Susan, who had a genius for saying the wrong thing at the wrong moment.

'All right,' said Dicky, promptly withdrawing his arm. 'If he is your ideal it is no good for me to try to please you. I may as well give it up at once. Good night, mother. It is time for both of us to be in bed. I'm tired to death.'

She gave him a tearful kiss, which he coldly returned, and they parted – she to spend the rest of the night in tears and prayers, and he to toss through the slow hours in feverish thought, varied by demoniacal nightmares.

At the farm the bride and bridegroom, having seen the last of the guests out of the house, exchanged a word or two on the doorstep.

'It's my belief,' the former remarked in a decisive manner, 'that Master Richard was pretty far gone.'

'He'd had quite enough,' said John, 'but there was a many worse than him.'

'He'd never have carried on as he did with Annie if he'd known what he was about,' said Rhody, who, even at this momentous period of her life, could afford to feel annoyed at the recollection of the little injury that her vanity had received. 'He pushed me right out of his road as if I'd been so much dirt, and he took hold of her – in front of everybody – in a way that was quite disgusting. I really wondered how she could let him do it, and she always setting up to be so proper. You don't mean to say you never noticed it, John?'

'Oh, I noticed it,' replied the farmer slowly. 'I thought he was going it rather too strong, but afterwards I had a word or two with him on the quiet, and I found it was all right. Look here, Rhody, you mustn't say anything about it just at present – but we'll be having another wedding some of these days. I never thought it of Master Richard, but so it is – he's not playing with Annie, after all. He means honourable by her.'

Rhody uttered an exclamation that was almost a shriek. 'Oh, how can you be such a born idiot?' she burst out; and he thought they were strange words for a bride to use to her husband on their wedding night, and did not like them at all. 'To think of a gentleman like *him* meaning honourable to a girl like *her*! You must be out of your senses to talk such nonsense.'

'I know what I am saying just as well as you do,' he retorted surlily. 'And you oughtn't to call me names, Rhody. If you begin like this afore we've been so much as a whole day married, what am I to expect by-and-by? It hurts my feelins. Rhody – I didn't think it of you.'

'Well, I don't mean to hurt your feelings, old boy. But of course it *is* foolishness to think such things. He'll no more marry Annie than he'll marry me – goodness, no! I should think not.'

In her own mind she determined that he should not, if she could prevent it; it was not likely that she was going to have Annie set over her head in that way.

'Why, it's as plain as the nose on your face that he's amusing himself, because she lets him, and because it's dull being at home for the holidays with nobody but his ma and sisters. 'Taint his fault. It's what all young gentlemen do, if girls let 'em.'

'I wasn't aware you knew so much about young gentlemen's ways,' said John, still unappeased.

'Oh, I hear people talk, of course, and they all say that he's just as fast as he can be. Why, only last Christmas his ma caught him kissing Alice, the young ladies' maid.'

'Under the mistletoe, I reckon.'

'No, it wasn't under the mistletoe – it was behind the schoolroom door, and it was *in the dark*.'

'Well, he's open and above-board as far as Annie is concerned. He never made no bones about it. He up and said he was engaged to her the minute I asked him.'

'Poor boy! – for after all he's nothing but a boy – is that how you take advantage of him when he's so drunk he doesn't know what he's doing?' Rhody spoke bitterly, for the bitter thought possessed her that – supposing such things possible – *she* might have had that golden chance; and her envy and jealousy knew no bounds. 'Well, there's one thing certain – he'll tell a different tale to-morrow, you'll see. And if he don't, you've got the squire to reckon with. I think I see his face when he hears who's to be his daughter-in-law!'

'It's Master Richard we've got to do with, not the squire,' said John; 'and he'll be his own master in a few months. And he can play the man, though he is a young 'un. I think the squire'd have a tough job to make him do what he hadn't a mind to. He's not one to be forced.'

'Poor boy!' ejaculated Rhody again, with passionate fervour.

'He was not so drunk that he didn't know what he was doing,' proceeded John. 'He knew as well as anybody. And, drunk or sober,' he added grimly, 'he's got to behave honourable to my sister, or I'll know the reason why.'

'You think a lot of your sister,' sneered Rhody.

'She deserves to be thought a lot on. She's as good as he is.'

'Better than I am, of course: I'm nobody!'

'Now, Rhody, it isn't kind of you to speak so – today of all times. I did think,' he added disappointedly, 'that you and Annie'd be happy together – that you'd be fond of her and think well of her.'

'I'll be fond of her if she behaves herself,' said Rhody. 'But if you expect me to go down on my knees and worship her as if she was an angel out of heaven, why, I can't do it. She's no more an angel than I am. She pretends to be so religious and so proper, and she's the greatest flirt that ever walked. She's led Mr Richard on – she's laid herself out to catch him – from the first. Why, on the very day he saved her at the mussel-beds – I never told you at the time, 'cause I was ashamed to, and I thought you'd be so mad about it – I left them alone in the kitchen for a few minutes, and when I came back there they were a kissing and hugging' –

'That's a lie,' said John quietly.

'Thank you. If I am accused of telling lies – and by my own husband – and afore I've been a day married' –

Here Rhody broke down and wept. She was overwrought by the excitements and fatigues of the day, and fevered by the liquid refreshment that she, in common with her guests, had too freely indulged in, and her nerves at this moment were beyond her control. John put his arm round her, and presently she laid her head on his shoulder. It was the end of the first matrimonial quarrel, but the beginning of many of which Dicky and Annie were the cause.

CHAPTER XIII

●

Dicky Plays The Man

Dicky awoke with a headache and in bad spirits next morning. He saw quite clearly what he had done, and would not for a moment admit to himself that he regretted it; but he knew that he would not have done it (just in that fashion) had he not been carried away by the contagion of excitement and foolishness. He had a heavy sense of having been precipitate, and having got himself into a mess generally; and he thought how men of the world, how his Oxford contemporaries, would scoff at his callow boyishness if they knew. He also thought, with considerable consternation, of his father and brothers, and how they would deal with him if *they* knew. Nevertheless, his resolve to play the man, as John Morrison had phrased it, was fixed and firm. What was done was done, and what remained was to make the best of it. The skies might fall, but he would stand to his word of honour. All his prospects in life might go, but Annie would stay; and that gain, he told himself, would cover all his losses.

Soon after breakfast, which he took in the schoolroom, a message was brought to him that John Morrison wished to speak to him. He summoned his future brother-in-law to the little room which was his private den, supposed to be devoted to study, and there met him with a frank hand outstretched – a kind of greeting that caused the young farmer to sink his truculent air – as of one come to force terms from a strong adversary taken at a disadvantage – to a manner which suggested a desire to make things as comfortable for all parties as the circumstances allowed.

'Well, Mr Richard, sir,' the visitor began, almost in a tone of apology, 'I thought as how I had better walk round and have a word with you – as between man and man, you know, sir.'

'Certainly,' Dicky cordially responded. He liked that phrase, 'as between man and man', and he liked John's attitude, which implied a respect for both of them. 'I am very glad you have come. But if you hadn't I should have gone to the farm myself.'

'I suppose you know what I have come about, sir?' John rather diffidently inquired.

'About my engagement to your sister,' replied Dicky. 'I understand.'

'You hold to it that it's a real engagement, Mr Richard?'

'As far as I am concerned, of course. I hope Annie has not changed her mind since last night?'

John took no notice of this query; he was looking with intense, solid earnestness at the alert, flushed face before him. 'You really mean it?' he said slowly. 'You are ready to act honourable? You promise to make her your lawful wife?'

Dicky's flush deepened. 'I don't know that I've ever done anything to make you think me a villain,' he replied, with the Delavel air.

'No, sir. But still it's hard to believe that a gentleman like you can be serious, when the girl belongs to another walk o' life. Not but what,' he added promptly, 'I consider that Annie is any man's equal, be he who he may.'

'So do I,' said Dicky.

'You've only seen her a few times, sir.'

'Only twice – to speak to.'

'Only twice! You don't mean to say that's all?'

'That's all. But you see it was enough.'

'Would you – would you like another chance, sir?' asked John, after a thoughtful pause, and evidently with an enormous effort. 'Maybe if we hadn't been all merrymaking and foolish it wouldn't have happened as it did – maybe you were carried away through being excited and having had a little drink. And though I don't mean to let my sister be took liberties with – not if it's the king on his throne – I don't want you to feel as if you was caught in a trap and we wouldn't let you out. 'Twouldn't make Annie any happier to be married that way.'

In silence Dicky held out his hand, touched to the quick by this generous offer, which he could not for a moment entertain. 'No,' said he, 'I don't want another chance. It's quite true that I was carried away last night. If I had been cool and sober I should have remembered that it was my duty to wait until I had something of a home to offer her – some prospect in life to go upon. But if it hadn't happened then it would have happened later. And if Annie and her family are satisfied for her to take me as I am, I am only too glad that I spoke. And I pledge you my word of honour, John Morrison, that I will be true and faithful. She has given me her love, and you shall find me worthy of it. No woman,' added Dicky solemnly, 'shall ever say that she trusted me in vain.' This was the dearest aspiration of his heart – the foundation of his moral code – the whole duty of man as he understood it.

John took his offered hand, and wrung it warmly. 'Sir,' said he, with something like emotion in his voice, 'you are a gentleman.' It was the highest compliment he could pay, though, as a matter of fact, he had but a poor opinion of gentlemen.

Then Dicky went to find the housekeeper, and shortly returned, followed by a servant bearing a tray of refreshments. The two young men poured out two tumblers of beer, and looked at each other as they raised them to their lips.

'Your health, sir,' said John, 'and may you be as happy as you deserve to be.' He drained his glass, set it upon the table, and remarked, with some compunction, that his host was over young to undertake the cares of a family.

'Well,' said Dicky, 'I'm afraid I shall not be able to undertake them for some time yet. I must set to work to make a home before I can marry – and I have everything to do.'

'I thought you was to be made a parson now directly, sir, and be put into a family living like Mr Delavel-Pole.'

'Never, John, never! I'd break stones on the road first.'

'That's what they all say, sir – that the squire means to make a parson of you.'

'I believe the squire does mean it, but I don't – and, after all, that's the main thing. One can't always fall in with one's father's views, John.'

'No, sir. I've found that out myself. But if you go against the squire he'll be hard on you, won't he?'

'He will, no doubt.'

'He won't like your marrying our Annie?'

'No.'

'He'll cut you off with a shilling, as like as not?'

'I am quite sure he will, without the shilling.'

'And you feel as you ain't afraid to face it, sir?'

'Oh, I can face it. I have foreseen it for a long time – before I thought of Annie. She won't make any difference. When he realises at last that I won't enter the Church he's sure to kick me out.'

'It's almost a pity that you can't make up your mind to it, sir.'

'Do you think so?'

'Well, not if it goes against the grain, of course. But it would make things easy and comfortable.'

'I don't know that life is any the better for being easy and comfortable,' said Dicky.

'I'm thinking o' my sister,' said John. 'It's what she's counting on. To be a parson's wife, with a parish to look after, would be Heaven to her. That's what she's looking forward to.'

'I'm sorry for it,' said Dicky, 'but I hope she would rather have an honest man for a husband than a hypocrite.'

John was silent for a few minutes, trusting that Dicky was not by implication accusing himself of being the black sheep that Mr Delavel-Pole described him. Then he made so bold as to ask the young man how he proposed to make a living and a provision for his wife if he cut himself off from the natural source of supplies.

'I will work,' said Dicky, 'as other men work. I am only waiting till I am twenty-one. When I am of age I shall have 500 pounds, my godfather's legacy; it isn't much, but it will give me a start – it will give me freedom. I think of going to Australia, John, and I mean to make my fortune there.'

The home-staying farmer was rather shocked at this audacious project, but was brought to see some wisdom and promise in it when it was unfolded to him in detail. At any rate, he was glad to recognise that the boy's scheme of life had something practical and definite in it. That was enough to satisfy him for the present.

'But I must wait till I am twenty-one,' repeated Dicky. 'I don't want to come into open collision with my father until I am free – unless it is impossible to prevent it.'

John agreed that it would be wise to avoid being kicked out in the interval of helplessness, and offered to let his sister's engagement remain undiscovered to the family until the twenty-first birthday had passed and the legacy became available. 'Nobody knows anything about it yet except mother and Rhody – and Rhody don't know much. I'll undertake that mother holds her tongue; and as for Rhody, why, I must just bamboozle her a bit,' said the bridegroom, with a touching faith in his new powers.

Dicky accepted the convenient concession gratefully, though he would not have condescended to ask for it, and, with another friendly glass of beer and a warm hand shake, the young men parted, on the best of terms with themselves and with each other.

This was on Friday. All the rest of that day and throughout Saturday Dicky stayed at home and thought. Then on Sunday, having in a measure adjusted himself to the responsibilities of his new position, he became eager to enjoy the contingent privileges. Seeing Annie at church in the morning, prettier than ever, with her conscious, down-cast face, and reflecting as he looked at her that she belonged to him, induced a strong desire for closer intercourse. So remembering Rhody's invitation, he laid his little plans, and announced at luncheon that he should take his tea in the schoolroom if agreeable to Miss May, the governess. To his surprise Mr Delavel raised his head, and said sternly, 'You will do nothing of the kind, sir. You will dine with us as usual.'

Miss May looked uncomfortable; the girls stared, surprised; Lady Susan sighed loudly.

'Have you any particular reason for desiring my company to-night?' asked Dicky, with ill-concealed impertinence.

'Yes, sir, I have,' replied his father promptly.

'And may I ask what it is?'

'No, sir, you may not. It is enough for you that I do desire it. And I expect you to obey me.'

Dicky bowed in silence, and continued to eat his lunch with elaborate deliberation. He thought he saw the hand of his enemy in this move, and naturally determined that he would not give that young man the satisfaction of outwitting him. When the meal was over, he accompanied governess and pupils to their schoolroom quarters, and offered to escort them to afternoon service as a compensation to them for the loss of his company at their evening meal. 'I know it must be a bitter disappointment to you,' he said, 'but I am ready to make such compensation as is in my power. I'll go and listen to two of Max's sermons in one day – there! Could I give you a greater proof of my affection than that?'

Miss May, who shared the prevailing impression that he was a black sheep, though she loved him none the less for it, replied that it would do him good to go to church a little more (which was also a prevailing impression), and that she therefore accepted his offer gladly. And at half-past two the little party set off. There were morning and afternoon services at Dunstanborough; in the evening none, as the old church had no apparatus for lighting, and 'after tea' on summer Sundays, from time immemorial, had been devoted by the villagers to family walks and saunters on the beach and the cliffs, and in the green lanes

– a habit as firmly established as that of church-going itself. From the Hall Mr Delavel and his family attended in their curtained pew in the morning, and in the afternoon their servants filled another pew at the opposite end of the church. The Delavel sons, as they grew to man's estate, followed their parents' custom of staying at home at ease after the forenoon expedition; but governess and children were expected to attend a second time. To them it was of the nature of discipline and educational routine, and it was an equal surprise and gratification to them that Dicky should choose to accompany them when he was not obliged to do it.

He was very agreeable and entertaining, and they greatly enjoyed their walk with him across the park, although Miss May did have to remind him once or twice that it was not quite decorous to talk of the rector and other sacred institutions as he talked – at any rate, not before his sisters; and during service he behaved himself with the most irreproachable propriety. But when service was over – when Annie Morrison had filed out with her school children at one door, and the occupants of the great chancel pew had emerged upon their private footpath through another – then Dicky drew Miss May aside, and opened her unsuspecting eyes. 'I am not going back with you, if you will excuse me,' he said hurriedly. 'The fact is, I promised to go and see John Morrison's new wife this afternoon, and she would feel hurt if I did not. I shall be home in time for dinner.'

'Ah, now, Richard!' the poor woman protested, knowing enough of what was going on to be aware that she had heavy responsibilities at this moment. 'What am I to say to Lady Susan when she asks me for you?'

'Nothing,' said Dicky sternly, holding up his forefinger; 'not a syllable. Now, look here, Miss May, if you say a word to any of them. I'll never speak to you again.'

'And would you have me tell a lie? – with my prayers upon my lips?' she inquired pathetically.

'Certainly not. If they ask you where I am, say you don't know. Because you don't know, you know.'

'You have just said you were going to the Morrisons' – the place of all others that they wish you not to go.'

'Then I'll say I am not going,' said Dicky cheerfully. With which he strode off, singing a lively tune under his breath, while the distressed and helpless governess gathered her brood around her, and slowly turned her face in the opposite direction.

Half-way between the church and the farm he came up with Annie Morrison, who had dismissed her children in the churchyard after service, and was walking home by herself. Rhody and John had, of course, accompanied her in the morning, the former in her bridal dress and bonnet, the cynosure of all eyes; but they had stayed behind to enjoy their wine and fruit, their little arm-chair nap, and their lovers' *tête-à-tête*, in the afternoon, as befitted people of their position, who had partaken on a hot day of a very rich and heavy dinner.

'Are you running away from me, Annie?' asked Dicky, as he over-took the farmer's daugher, who was quite aware that she was being followed, and by whom.

She stopped and turned, with a glowing face and downcast eyes. 'Mother will be looking for me,' she said, with the sham modesty and pretended ignorance that sacred convention demanded of her at such a moment, as he took her hand.

'Nonsense,' he reasonably retorted, his own young visage as red as hers. 'She's got Rhoda to wait upon her now.'

Annie's face changed a little; she lifted her eyes; her soft lips hardened. 'As to that,' she said, 'I think mother will want me more, and not less, now. It has been a mistake to have Rhody to live with us – we always knew it would be. It's early days yet to be finding fault, but I can see she means to be mistress and turn mother out of her place and make a nobody of her. She has taken her chair at the head of the table. Mother gave it up to her – though I told her not to. And it isn't right, is it?'

'Right!' echoed Dicky indignantly. 'It's the most confounded cheek and impudence I ever heard of. I shall set my mother to talk to Mrs John if she doesn't behave herself better than that. I say, Annie, come and have a little walk with me and tell me all about it. Come through the woods' – turning towards a stile that was nearly hidden in the brambly hedge. 'It isn't half a mile farther, and you will be out of the sun and dust.'

Meanwhile, Mr Delaval-Pole had taken note of Dicky's unaccus-tomed presence at afternoon service, and had made up his mind, long before beginning the exhortation to his 'dearly beloved brethren', that he would take a walk to the farm himself when the congregation had dispersed, for the double purpose of holding out the olive branch to the Morrisons in general and to Annie in particular, under the guise of a complimentary nuptial visit to Mrs John, and of keeping a watch upon his cousin's movements. Accordingly, when he emerged from his vestry, uncassocked as well as unsurpliced, and saw Miss May in the distance alone with her young charges, he set forth in the direction that Annie, and Dicky after her, had taken, with the certainty that he should find that guilty couple (for he had begun to suspect that one was as bad as the other), up to mischief of some sort that required his counteracting interference.

His fears were more than realised. The first glimpse he had of Annie, whom he recognised by her blue muslin and white bonnet, and the neat unbroken outlines that her slender person presented, was just after her lover had overtaken her, and while they lingered to talk of Rhody's misdoings. The Rector was prepared to advance and disperse them, but while on his way to do this they turned aside, evidently without seeing him, and went over the stile into the woods that skirted the road; and then he did not know what to do. There was something very vulgar in the idea of following them now, and yet he was strongly impressed with the sense that he had a bounden duty to perform − to his kinsfolk and the Delavel House, to his erring young parishioner, and to that misguided boy who was leading her astray. After a moment's hesitation he walked to the stile, and with some trouble, tracked the lovers to their retreat. He stood a moment to stare at them, petrified with horror (for they were locked at that moment in each other's arms), and then turned and hurried back to the Hall to tell his aunt and uncle what he had seen.

CHAPTER XIV

•

The Son Proposes: The Father Disposes

The culprits sat on a fallen log, arm round waist, head upon shoulder, hand clasped in hand, and were quite happy – blissfully unconscious of the rod that was in pickle for them. Grasshoppers hopped about their clothes, and beetles crawled over their boots with impunity; unnoticed bees, and even wasps, hummed and buzzed around them; unheard ringdoves cooed through the woodland solitude, where the evening came so much sooner than elsewhere. The mythical first lovers in their enchanted garden could not have taken things of this sort more completely for granted than did our young pair just now.

'I don't know exactly what is best to do,' said the lad thoughtfully, caressing her smooth hair, from which he had removed her bonnet, with his smooth cheek, 'but I think – and John thinks – that we had better say nothing about it till I am of age. There is no use in shutting our eyes to the fact that there will be a trememdous row about it, and, until I am my own master, I shall have no power to protect you. After that,' said Dicky, with a thrill of pride, and thinking of his 500 pounds, 'after that we shall be all right.'

Annie asked him how long it would be, for she burned to have her glory known, at any rate to Rhody, and he told her. In three months more he would be twenty-one. She pondered silently for a few minutes, while he kissed and caressed her, and she sweetly submitted. Then she remarked earnestly that, above all things, and at no matter what personal sacrifice, they must do their best to propitiate 'Mr Delavel and my lady', and to avoid making a permanent breach with the family. To this end she suggested that it might even be desirable to keep the engagement from their knowledge to a still later period – in fact, until the young man was 'settled'.

'As to that,' said Dicky, 'the breach is inevitable. It doesn't matter whether we tell them sooner or later – so it may as well be sooner, and have done with it. My father would never forgive me – not if I waited for a hundred years. I know him too well.'

Annie coloured with wounded pride. 'He would think me too much beneath you,' she murmured.

Dicky coloured in his turn. 'You mustn't mind what he thinks, my darling – I don't – for he's quite as often wrong as right. He thinks my brother Keppel ought to marry an ugly widow, old enough to be his mother – I believe Keppel will do it too – just because she's rich, and has got a pedigree. I call that wrong, not to say idiotic to the last degree, for Keppel hates her as it is, so that when he's married to her there'll be catastrophes for certain.'

'I wish I had a pedigree,' sighed Annie.

'So you have,' said Dicky. 'Everybody has.'

'But not the right sort.'

'Made up of robbers and king's mistresses?'

'No, of Norman knights and. . . .'

'Pooh!' interrupted the boy, contemptuously. 'A lot of scamps, you may depend on it. You have something better than that, my pet; honest blood for as far back as you can trace it, and a sweet little body that many a fine lady would give money and pedigree and everything for. Wouldn't Keppel like to change with me, that's all!'

'I don't think I have ever spoken to Mr Keppel,' remarked Annie, with a little flutter of pleasure at the idea presented to her – the idea of another gentleman of the Great House and the great world having possibly been attracted by her charms.

'He's a stupid fool, and he'll find it out,' said Keppel's brother, who was inclined to think himself a wise man. 'Far better marry the girl you love and trust to Providence.'

'Yes,' said Annie, yielding herself to a fresh series of caresses. She approved of this sentiment in the abstract, but the instincts of her prudent little soul condemned anything like recklessness. 'Still – still,' she said with grave earnestness, 'perhaps, if we are very careful – if we wait for our opportunity and do things quietly and gradually – in time Mr Delavel might be persuaded to see things as we do.'

'Never, my dear child, never! Best not flatter ourselves with any such false hopes.'

'Oh, but I think so,' she insisted, with a pretty woman's confidence in her own weight when it is upon a man that it is to be brought to bear. 'When he sees that I am educated, and that I am not – not common, as he might think; when he sees how suited I am to be a clergyman's wife, and when we are living at a distance, not mixing up with Rhody and all these people, that will make a difference, won't it?'

She spoke very sweetly, but what she said gave her young lover a chill, a dim sense of inadequacy in her, an obscure foreboding of the future that he was making for himself. 'You don't want to cut yourself off from your family!' he said. 'I would never ask you to do that, Annie.'

'We should be in a different class of life,' she gently responded.

'I don't know about that. . . .'

'Oh yes, the husband always raises the wife to his level. And I am not like Rhody — it goes against me with Mr Delavel and my lady to see me mixed up with her.' Annie tingled at the recollection of Lady Susan's offer to get her a place as schoolroom maid to Lady Elizabeth's daughters. 'But if they were to see me in your house — in your parish, amongst gentlefolks — and what I could do. . . .' She broke off, quite overcome with the glorious vision that rose before her of Sunday schools and parochial meetings at which she would preside as the vicar's wife and deputy, a model of all that was excellent and refined.

'My dear girl,' said Dicky with the faintest coolness in his voice and an imperceptible relaxation of the muscles of his arm that clasped her waist, 'I shall never have a parish. I am not going to be a clergyman. I thought you knew that?'

She heard the announcement in silence. She had known something of his intention from John, but had given no importance to it. She had refused to admit that such a disappointing thing was possible.

'Oh, you don't mean that,' she murmured, with a caressing, persuasive gesture.

'I do mean it. Why shouldn't I mean it? What should make you think I say things that I don't mean?'

'When you have thought it over you will feel differently about it. You will see what a grand and noble career it is — the highest in all the world. . . .'

'That may be,' he interrupted, withdrawing his arm from her waist unconsciously. 'But I have no vocation for it. If I went into the Church, it would be for the sake of getting a provision for life without working for it — that's all my father wants me to go into it for — in the same way as Keppel will marry his widow and I should like it just about as much as he will like her. You wouldn't wish me to be so mean as that, Annie?'

'No, dear,' she said, modestly leaning towards him, so that he again put his arm around her. 'But – but if you would only think it over. . . .'

'I have – I do, and I can't do it. I am not good enough – or bad enough. It's out of the question. I'm sorry if you are disappointed, Annie. I thought you'd rather have an honest man for a husband than a hypocrite.'

'Oh, don't speak so,' she pleaded, and this time she put up her charming face in such a way that he kissed it with a sudden rush of passion, a sudden outpouring of his sympathy-craving heart.

'My darling, I will do my best for you – I will be as good as I know how,' he said, with a tremble in his voice; 'and you'll trust me, won't you? You won't care what I am, or what becomes of us, so long as we love each other? I wonder if you love me enough, Annie, to face things for my sake, as I am ready to face them for yours? I don't believe you do.'

'Oh,' she protested, with soft reproach, 'how can you say that?'

'Do you?'

'You know I do. You are everything to me.'

Whereupon he hugged her to his breast and kissed her a thousand times. And after that they spoke no more of the comfortable provision that he would not have, but of the alternative career that he had sketched for himself. He told her how he meant to take his money – and her, if she was not afraid to venture – to Australia, and there build himself a fortune, as so many others had done. 'It may be hard at first,' he said brightly, as if the hardness was the charm of it (as indeed it was); 'and perhaps you ought not to risk it – perhaps you ought to stay behind till I have made a home that is suitable for you. . . .'

'No, no,' she murmured. 'I don't mind anything to be with you.' She knew that the hardest life with him would be softer than the softest life with Rhody.

'My precious one! Then I will take you, and we will make our fight together. That is how it should be, Annie – that is my idea of marriage. We will make our fight together, and we won't care for anybody. I shall have to delve, like Adam, and earn our daily bread by the sweat of my brow, and you will probably have to bake it, for we shall not be able to afford servants – at any rate, not at first. But we shan't mind that, we shall like it; it will be delightful!'

He went into raptures over his scheme, which to Annie's mind had so much that was 'low' about it, while she was silently tormented with visions of that dear conventional parsonage house, with its white-aproned maids and its graceful proprieties, which represented the things that *her* soul loved. Oh, it was hard to exchange that splendid position, that elegant home, for the kind of life that Dicky was proposing; she could have cried to think of it. But she hoped still that it might not come to that, and in any case the man she was to marry was a Delavel. So she stifled her regrets.

No visit was paid to the bride that afternoon. She spread a bounteous tea table, and put her silver spoons into her mother-in-law's best cups, and sat in state, with a temporary apron over her blue silk dress until half-past five. Then Annie appeared alone, bringing a message that Mr Richard was very sorry he was not able to come as he had promised.

'And why not?' Rhody tempestuously demanded, stung with mortification and disappointment.

'Because his father wished him to be home to dinner.'

'At half-past six! And we have tea at five!'

'He couldn't have got back in time, Rhody.'

'Now look here,' said Mrs John, 'he was coming along this afternoon, as he said he would, and you met him and stopped him.'

'I did not,' retorted Annie indignantly.

'Didn't you meet him?' The girl was silent. 'And wasn't he coming this way?' Silence. 'And haven't you been alone with him all this time when he might have been with us here?' Still silence. 'I'll tell you what it is, miss, if you go on in this way I shall just walk straight over to the Hall and tell my lady about it. I won't stand by and see that poor boy hunted into a scrape that'll be his ruin, after all the kindness we've had from the family.'

'Drop it,' said John, who was standing by. 'I won't have Annie spoke to like that, and I won't have her interfered with neither.'

'Oh, won't you?' cried Rhody, with quick breath and expanding nostrils. And then there was a quarrel.

Meanwhile Dicky went home, elate and satisfied, full of his enterprises, inspired by the near prospect of adventure and difficulty, and by the generally picturesque and definite aspect of life. He did not at once seek the company of his parents; indeed he avoided them as long as possible, until the punctual dinner-bell compelled him to join them. Then he saw at once that he was in disgrace, though whether for old sins or new ones did not appear. His mother was dejected and lachrymose, his father coldly rigid as a graven image; and both were studiously careful to take no notice of him. Seeing this, he assumed the air of taking no notice of them, and entertained himself with his own thoughts until the cheerless meal was ended. The moment he saw an opportunity to slip away he seized it, but before he was out of the room his father sharply called him back.

'Richard!' thundered the stern old gentleman, in a tone that was like the sudden report of firearms.

'Sir,' responded Dicky haughtily.

'I am going to London in the morning, and I wish you to go with me. Be good enough to have your things packed by ten o'clock.'

The boy looked at his mother. She was looking at the table-cloth and she did not raise her eyes, but she said, in a low voice, 'Sarah will do it for you.' Sarah was her elderly maid.

'Will the visit last long?' he inquired, addressing his father.

'It will last until the vacation is over,' said Mr Delavel significantly.

Then Dicky saw the state of the case. For a few minutes he stood silent, battling with a rising torrent of passionate words – telling himself how critical was this moment, and how necessary it was for Annie's sake that he should be calm, while the temptation to break out was almost irresistible. In the end prudence conquered, and he restrained himself. 'Very well, sir,' he said quietly, and went out without another word.

CHAPTER XV

•

Dicky Stands To His Word Of Honour

Richard's last term at Oxford was drawing to a close, and the merry days of his youth were numbered. It was the last week in November, and he had not seen his Annie since August; and in the interval he had attained his majority and come into possession of his estate. He had also spent some of it. As Dunstanborough did nothing to celebrate his coming of age, which under the circumstances was not considered an event to make a fuss about, he celebrated it himself; and when he did give an entertainment he liked to do things handsomely; and when you do things handsomely you must be prepared to pay in proportion. Moreover, on his refusing to let his father invest his money, Mr Delavel had promptly intimated that a man who desired to be so entirely his own master could do no less than pay his own debts; and Dicky, whose allowance was meagre for a Christchurch man, and whose disposition was generous, had liabilities to the amount of a full third of his legacy, though they were trifling compared with the college debts of his brothers. So that in the first month of his legal manhood he got rid of about 200 of the 500 pounds which were to make his fortune.

But he had had a good time. He had borne the long separation from his sweetheart (after the first few weeks), not only with fortitude, but with cheerfulness. In point of fact, though periodically reminded of his engagement by a beautifully written and carefully composed letter – which was generally answered in most affectionate terms by return of post – the nature of his passion for Annie was not what it once had been. He had not, to his knowledge, ceased to love her – not at all – but he had ceased to remember her for the mere pleasure of remembering her; it required the postman to bring her to his mind. And her letters, though models of good grammar and penmanship, had no charm or flavour – few people's letters have, for that matter; they did nothing to fix the impression she had made on him. So the impression waned. He forgot to transfer her photograph from pocket to pocket when he changed his coat, until it drifted to the back of a drawer, and he could not find it one day when he wanted to show it to a friend. And other pretty girls attracted him and interested him, just as she had done when he first saw her at the church porch. And in a general way he was quite happy without her. Alas! alas! But such is life, and such is youth, in spite of the poets and novelists.

He had had a good time, as I have said, in the two months that had passed of that Michaelmas term – never a better. Those were the days when stately academic Oxford kept herself to herself, before fellows got married, and undergraduates got businesslike, before the Spirit of the Age had poked its intrusive nose into her affairs. Her young barbarians played a great deal more than they do now, and if they played Tom Fool the most of the time, they certainly had plenty of fun out of it. And fun is a pleasant thing, though the modern reasonableness may be better. Dicky had had good fun, with money in his pockets and a personal popularity that was independent of money; he had hunted, and boated, and fished, and shot, won tennis and billiard matches, had wild fights in the street, and midnight larks in the quadrangle, and never a heartache the whole time, though occasionally a headache in the morning. But now his fun was coming to an end, though he did not know it.

He came out of his bedroom one day, fresh from his ice-cold bath, bright and handsome and in the liveliest spirits, to entertain a couple of friends at breakfast. The friends had already arrived, and so had the devilled bones and the omelette, and so had the post. There were several letters on the table, and he glanced at them one by one as he chatted to his guests, tore some across and threw them on the fire, stuck others in the oak panel that framed the glass over the chimney, and put one into his pocket unread. The one he put into his pocket was from Annie.

Now he had not heard from his sweetheart for a whole fortnight, and yet this is what he did. He had a long and merry breakfast, eating a prodigious quantity of game pie and bread and marmalade; then he went to lecture; then he joined a friend in a tandem-driving expedition, which came to an untimely end by the smashing of the dogcart; dined at a country inn; got home as gates were closing; played cards till two and went to bed. And he clean forgot the letter he had put into his pocket until he awoke next morning. He had been dreaming of running off to Gretna Green with a young lady (I think it was the barmaid of the inn where he had been dining), and that the chaise broke down on the wrong side of the border, with John Morrison in full pursuit behind; and that put him in mind of it. He reached out of bed for his coat, found the neglected missive, broke the seal, and as soon as the grey dawn lightened sufficiently, read it. And this is what he read:

My dearest Richard, I am afraid you will be feeling anxious at my long silence, but you will forgive me when I tell you the sad cause of it. My dear mother had a stroke of paralysis ten days ago. She seemed to rally from it, but a second one followed, after which she gradually sank, and breathed her last on Friday. I am thankful to say she had no pain, and Mr Delavel-Pole was most attentive to her in her last hours. She received the sacrament on Thursday, though we did not think then that her end was so near. It took place on the following morning at three o'clock, and she was buried yesterday beside Grandmamma Morrison under the south wall.

Dear Richard, this sad event makes a great difference in my circumstances. While she was alive and well she always stood up for me with Rhody, and would not let me be put upon; but now I am without any protector, for my father thinks everything right that Rhody does, and if John interferes he gets into trouble himself and does me more harm than good. John says I ought to be allowed to live in my own home, but my father and Rhody want me to go. At least Rhody wants me to go, and my father never takes my part against her. She feels me in her way, and she says I ought to be earning my own living and not eating the bread of idleness. She has talked over Lady Susan, who has never seemed to understand the difference between me and my sister-in-law, and classes us together, as if we had both been brought up alike. A fortnight ago her ladyship came to see mother, to tell her of a situation for me and to persuade her to urge me to take it, and I feel sure it was the worry and trouble of this that brought on dear mother's illness. Even Mr Delavel-Pole seemed to think it quite reasonable that I should become a national schoolmistress to please Rhody, though otherwise he has been most kind.

You can understand, dear Richard, in what a painful position I am placed. I have no one to protect me now, and the home where

I have been made so much of all my life will soon be mine no more. At present, of course, Rhody lets me alone and next week I am going to stay with a schoolfellow in London, who saw mother's death in the paper, and thought it would be good for my health to have a change, and I dare say I shall be allowed to eat my Christmas dinner under my own father's roof. But after that I am sure I shall be turned out – my life will be made so unbearable that I shall be obliged to go – unless in the meantime you proclaim our engagement, and show them that I still have some one to take care of me. While mother lived I did think it better to keep the matter to ourselves, hoping you would see your way to take orders and please your father, who in that case would certainly use his influence to get you a living; but now that she is gone, and I am situated in this way, I feel that we ought not to hide the true state of the case any longer. I think that is how you will feel too. Dear Richard, I rely upon you – I have no one else to look to now. I am sure you will not let me be thrown upon the world, homeless and friendless, if you are able to prevent it.

Mother was not able to speak after her second seizure, or I am sure she would have left you a message. She was so fond of you, and always said she trusted you with her whole heart. She would never hear a word against you.

Hoping you will write soon, and with much love,

Believe me, my dearest Richard, your devoted and sorrowing

Annie

P.S. – My school friend, Mary Greenwood, with whom I am going to stay, lives at Hammersmith. I do not care for her very much. Her family are tradespeople and dissenters. But it will be better than being with Rhody.

Our young Oxonian read this letter again and again, as he lay in bed, staring hard at the beautiful handwriting, and gnawing the ends of his moustache as if anxious to gnaw them off. Then he dressed himself thoughtfully, went to chapel, ate his breakfast, lit his pipe, and sat down to think things over. After thinking them over for the best part of the morning, he seized pen and paper and wrote as follows:

My poor little girl, I need not say how much I grieve for your loss and trouble. Why didn't you tell me before? Of course you have a right to look to me to take care of you, and you don't suppose for a moment that I am going to let you be thrown upon the world. There is only one thing to be done, Annie dear. I dare say, when I tell you what it is you will be dreadfully shocked, and say that it is impossible, but circumstances alter cases, and as you put yourself in my hands, darling, you must leave it all to me. Come up at once to your friend, Miss Greenwood – I am sure she must be an awfully nice girl to have thought of asking you just now – it is just one of those considerate things that only a real kind woman thinks of, and bring all your little belongings that you care for with you. I will meet you at Shoreditch and take you to her house, and I will make arrangements for our marriage before you leave it. Say nothing to any one, dearest, till all is over. Leave everything to me. I will find some hole and corner church in Hammersmith where our banns can be put up without a soul knowing it, and I shall have a free week before Christmas to get a lodging ready to take you to as soon as you are my wife. Be as quick as possible, so that we may have it over before Christmas. I am my own master now, and I promised your poor mother that I would take care of you, and this is the only way of doing it, my darling. So don't make any objections, but get ready at once and come to me. Write and tell me your train, and I will meet it. Tell the Greenwoods not to come to the station, as a friend will be there. And we can settle everything in the cab as we drive through London.

The rest of the letter was merely this part of it over again, only expressed a little more strongly, as his delightfully simple plan for the removal of Annie's domestic difficulties unfolded itself to his young mind, and it concluded with a further injunction to her to trust all to him and fear nothing. He was quite confident that he was right, and therefore feared nothing on his own account.

His iron-clamped door admitted no visitors that day. When he had posted his letter, he hunted up the photograph of his beloved, and looked at it (through a cloud of tobacco smoke) long and earnestly, by way of stimulating the old passion that could no longer be allowed to sleep. She was represented in outdoor costume, with a curtain to her bonnet and a large shawl over her full-skirted gown; and the simple elegance of her attire was most grateful to his aesthetic sense. So was the charming face, framed in the narrow bonnet-cap – the soft, grave mouth – the soft, smooth hair – the modest downcast eyes.

By long looking and thinking he brought himself to feel in love with her again, and stimulated his natural pleasure in the idea of immediate matrimony to an almost intoxicating enthusiasm.

What was to happen after the marriage he was not very clear about; he did not look so far as that. Only he felt it was no use sitting down to his reading again, since he would be certain to have to leave Oxford before he could take his degree.

CHAPTER XVI

•

His Last Wild Oats

Had Annie been free to choose how she would be married we may be sure that everything would have been done with the strictest regard to decorum and the sacred customs of society; but circumstances alter cases, as her lover had justly pointed out, and, under the circumstances in which she found herself, she felt she could do no better than accede to his proposal. Its audacity certainly dismayed her for a moment, and the thought of a wedding only a month after the funeral of one's nearest relative was very shocking to her highly proper notions; but she was not a young person to allow her feelings to run away with her judgment, as Dicky was, and knew what was for her own advantage much better than he knew what was for his.

So she packed up at once, and set forth on a long visit to her London friend. Rhoda bade her a cordial good-bye, and recommended her to utilise the fine opportunity she would have for picking and choosing to get a real nice place to go to after Christmas; her father gave her her railway fare and two pounds to spend; and John drove her and her neat canvas-covered boxes to the great town where he went to market once a week, and put her in the train. Not one of them had any idea of the important enterprise to which they so lightheartedly committed her.

No difficulties in the shape of university regulations prevented Dicky from being on the Shoreditch platform when that train came in. Wild horses would not have held him from his Annie now that she was in his charge – a helpless woman dependent upon his protection; chivalry demanded that he should be rusticated and ruined, if need be, rather than she should be left to the tender mercies of possibly uncivil porters or exposed to any similar discomfort from which a man could shield her. So there he was, his long form wrapped in the Inverness cloak which was the fashionable overcoat of the period, his keen, clear-featured face making, like Una's, a noticeable spot of brightness in the gloom and grime of those shabby precincts. What an unmistakeable aristocrat he was, she thought, as she watched his quick eyes flashing into window after window as the carriages drew past him, and waited to meet that eager glance with a welcoming smile. To think that this princely young man was to be her husband – that she would be Mrs Delavel for the rest of her life – was enough to make her for the moment as indifferent about other future circumstances as he was. Whatever happened after she was married, nothing could happen that would take her precious title from her. The thought lent a sweetness to her smile that enchanted him. And if she had looked charming in her blue and lilac muslins, she was quite beautiful in that colour which, so sombre in itself, is so pre-eminently becoming to fair women; and its pathetic suggestions all helped towards the vivid new impression that he had prepared himself to receive.

At any rate, they had a most cordial and tender meeting. He took her out of her second-class carriage and bestowed her in a four-wheeler – the porters waited on her as if she were already a member of the family – and sat with his arm round her waist as they drove through the city, pouring out the thousand details of his delightful scheme. It was indeed a most elaborate and finished programme by this time. There was only one fault to find with it; it ended with the wedding – or, rather with the honeymoon – instead of beginning with it, as it should have done.

'And *then* what?' Annie diffidently inquired, as they were approaching Hammersmith.

'Oh, then – then we must think what is best to be done,' he responded lightly. 'Of course, we can't decide on anything till we see how my father takes it. I must write to him and John the first thing; and it's no use meeting troubles half way. We'll fix things up somehow when the time comes. We shall be all right as long as we are together.'

As the cab passed through the street where Mr Greenwood conducted a thriving grocery business, and turned into the neighbouring road, where he dwelt with his family in a neat house called Byron Villa, Dicky begged to be allowed to present himself to Mrs Greenwood.

'As they don't know anybody in Dunstanborough, they can't tell tales, and I want to be able to get at you when I have a chance to run up,' he urged; for Annie did not seem willing to grant his wish. 'Besides, I'd like to see that friend of yours – I'm sure she's a jolly girl, and she might be of the greatest use to us just now.'

'Oh, she's not my friend particularly,' explained Annie. 'We were at school together – that's all. And they are quite common people. Not the sort you are used to at all.'

'What does that matter?' he returned, with an inward twinge. 'I shan't care whether they are common or uncommon, if they are kind to you. And we shall have to mix with many commoner people than they are before we have done – if I'm not mistaken.'

'I don't see why that should be necessary,' said Annie.

'Beggars can't be choosers, my dear.'

'I don't think you'll need to be a beggar,' she said gently, 'unless you like.'

The cab stopped at Byron Villa, and, before either occupant could get out of it, a round and rosy-cheeked damsel, in a warm red frock that pleasantly relieved the murky colours of the street and atmosphere, came flying into the road to meet them. She was plain, and no doubt she was common, but the moment Dicky looked at her he felt that his instinct had not misled him. He had been sure she would turn out to be a jolly girl, and she was a jolly girl. Her character was written all over her so that a child might read it at a glance. Quickly he sprang out of the cab, lifted his hat, and smiled that pleasant smile of his which never failed to dispose the female heart towards him.

'How do you do, sir?' said Miss Greenwood, frankly giving him her hand. 'You have brought her to us safely? Ah, Annie dear' – receiving the descending figure into her arms and hugging it cordially, though it was in the open street – 'I can't tell you how sorry I am for you! But come in – come in. We are going to cheer you up and do you good. Come in to the fire, dear, and get warm. The cabman will bring your things. Come in, Mr – Mr' –

'Mr Delavel,' said Annie, rather coolly, and with the composure of the lady-like young person who has made a study of manners – a composure intended to correct the effect upon Dicky of Miss Greenwood's noisy welcome.

'Come in, Mr Dellaby, and have a glass of wine. Mother'll be so pleased to see you. We were so glad for Annie to have a gentleman to meet her, for father is busy all day at the shop – not but what I'd have met you myself, Annie dear, with pleasure. Come in now to the fire – you must be nearly frozen.'

She led Annie into the little garden, and Dicky, having paid the cabman, accompanied them with the greatest alacrity. There was nothing vulgar to him in Miss Greenwood's vivacity, and her hospitality was irresistible. And he clearly foresaw that she would presently be a party to the great scheme, Annie's bridesmaid in due course, and, perhaps, a support to her in the wrath to come when wedding ceremonies were over.

A comfortable family sitting-room, a buxom hostess, cordial as her daughter, a big fire and a well-spread table, kept Dicky at Byron Villa longer than he should have stayed, seeing that he had other business in London and was bound to get into his college before midnight if possible. He made himself at home with all the domestic circle, down to the baby, who sat on his knee and blew the case of his watch open. Mrs Greenwood felt, she said to Annie afterwards, as if she had known him for years, and the little boys and girls all asked him whether he was coming again – to which he replied that he certainly was, if they would let him. He kissed the children when he went away, and shook hands with Mary and her mother as if they had been his aunt and cousin at least, accepting their invitations to return quite as if he were grateful for them. All which misplaced familiarity vexed the soul of his fiancée who would have preferred to see him stand upon his dignity with people so far beneath him.

'Good-bye, my sweet, for a few days,' he said to her, as he was hurrying away. 'I shall be up again soon to see how you are getting on. I am so glad to be leaving you with such nice kind people. Your Mary is delightful. Make a friend of her and tell her all about it – won't you? I must be off now to see the parson about putting up the banns on Sunday. What a blessing the Greenwoods are dissenters! Whatever you do, don't go to church, for they'd be sure to want to go with you – they're so kind. Go to chapel with them for the next three weeks.'

'That,' said Annie gravely, 'is a thing I *couldn't* do.'

And she did not do it. She went to church regularly, and her friend accompanied her. Nevertheless, no hitch occurred in the elaborate arrangements which might so easily and so often have been upset. Fate willed that our hero should, at the early age of twenty-one, marry the least suitable woman he could find, and repent it ever afterwards. A toothless old clergyman, who mumbled his words, and who showed that he had never heard the illustrious name of Delavel by pronouncing it with the accent on the second syllable instead of on the first, published the banns of marriage between the young couple for three Sundays running, without attracting anybody's attention to the fact. The Morrisons at Dunstanborough deluded themselves with the belief that Annie in London was looking for a situation; and the family at the Hall supposed their scapegrace son to be reading or pretending to read at Oxford; behaving himself neither better nor worse than usual. Not until he failed to come home at the end of the term, and wrote from London that he was engaged about a matter that would detain him there till Christmas, did the idea (suggested by Mr Delavel-Pole) that he was pursuing Annie Morrison trouble them; and then, though they peremptorily commanded his return, and he neither returned nor wrote to say why he didn't, they had no prevision of the impending catastrophe. They waited for him to appear, and watched for the postman, and told each other that Christmas was near, and that, at any rate, he would certainly come home for Christmas. Thus they did nothing to check the paying-out of that long rope, the possession of which seems to make it necessary that one should hang one's self. Dicky had a long rope this time, and the proverbial consequences ensued.

Having made several flying trips to London, regardless of expense, and done nothing worth doing at Oxford in the intervals between them, he at last set off with his bag and baggage to return no more. He gave a great supper party before he left, at which men got drunk and played high jinks, as their manner was; and that was his farewell to youth and liberty and the merry days of life. The next morning he took the train to London, and three mornings afterwards immolated himself upon the hymeneal altar, making a burnt-offering for his sins that was cruelly in excess of the requirements of justice, a sacrifice more costly than he had the least idea of.

In the brief interval he was desperately busy, first looking for a lodging in which to instal his bride, and then suitably preparing it for her reception. After much hunting he found the place he sought in peaceful Chiswick, in an old world house, that looked from under a canopy of trees across a quiet road upon the river, a place that seemed to him artistically appropriate, as well as convenient and comfortable. The trees were bare now, and the river, full to the brim, was mostly veiled in mists. By four o'clock in the afternoon the opposite shore was indistinguishable, and the boats going up and down were like phantoms in the grey fog. But the prospect from the windows of the old house, though it might become melancholy if looked at for a whole winter at a stretch, was quite to the taste of our young man, who desired one that should be as different as possible from the vulgarly commonplace; and behind the windows were a couple of wainscoted rooms, furnished in flowered chintz, and presided over by a widow who had seen better days, which – rooms, chintz, landlady and all – charmed his susceptible fancy the moment he saw them. It did not take twenty minutes to conclude an arrangement whereby he became the widow's tenant at three pounds a week; and it did not take half-an-hour to develop business relations into friendship – to inspire her with a maternal interest in the youthful bridegroom, and him with cordial gratitude and admiration for the widow's kindness, good manners, and good looks.

'She's no ordinary landlady,' he said to Annie, when triumphantly reporting his proceedings in this matter. 'I never saw a more well-bred woman. And she's got beautiful dark eyes – rather sad eyes, as if she'd had a lot of trouble, poor thing. And so she has. Her husband was a sea captain, and his ship was reported missing fifteen years ago. Fancy waiting and hoping against hope for fifteen years! No wonder she looks worn and sad. She must have been,' he added thoughtfully, 'a wonderfully handsome girl.'

'And how old is she now?' his sweetheart naturally inquired.

'About forty-five, I should think.'

'I'm afraid she's an artful old creature,' Annie rejoined, with a playful air, 'and knows how to get round unsuspicious young men.'

'I'm sure she's nothing of the kind,' declared Dicky warmly; 'and I'm not one to be "got round" either, I can tell you.' His feelings were hurt by these two misapprehensions, neither of which was removed by time and a better knowledge of the circumstances.

However, his vexation was but momentary, and he continued to believe in his landlady, and in his own penetration. He and she worked together to prepare the rooms at Chiswick for the bride. The landlady offered furniture and conveniences from her own apartments – so little like the ordinary landlady was she, so demoralised by the fascinations of her open-hearted young lodger; but of course Dicky would by no means allow her to incommode herself for him or his. He preferred to purchase what was necessary out of his own pocket, which was as open as his heart.

A good deal of money from that pocket dribbled away in the course of those three days. The cupboard in the wainscoted parlour was stocked with wine and choice delicacies of various kinds. Flowers were ordered in; multitudinous wedding presents were bought – jewellery, furs, little knick-knacks that tempted him in the shop windows – for the beloved one who had so few to give her presents, and for the family which had been good to her in her hour of need. But this was not a time to think of sixpences and shillings, and he certainly had a large amount of pleasure for his money.

When the eventful morning came, and he stood in his Inverness cloak, with his hat in his hand and the ring in his pocket, to survey the preparations he had made, and pictured his young wife's happy recognition of all his tender thought for her, his heart swelled with emotions that brought a mist to his eyes and a lump into his throat. In that moment he had entrancing dreams of a blissful wedded life; dreams that were not going to make the very faintest attempt to come true, of course, but which filled his soul with a solemn sense of unworthiness.

The landlady – Mrs Carthew was her name, and she really was the nice woman he believed her, and not a designing creature – put out her white hand to him as he was leaving the house.

'I wish you every happiness,' she said earnestly.

'Oh, thank you, *thank* you,' he returned, wringing her hand with passionate gratitude. 'I do think I am going to be happy.'

Alas, poor young idiot! He was going to cut himself off from his chances of happiness as completely as human ingenuity could do it.

CHAPTER XVII

·

The Irrevocable Deed

It was near Christmas, but it was a beautiful morning. It began with a cold fog that completely hid the river – a fog that could be felt and breathed; but after breakfast the woolly atmosphere became suffused with the sunshine it failed to smother, and distilled great drops from the twigs of the bare trees and the eaves of the old house, and slowly thinned and lifted, until, at the hour when Dicky went forth to be married, all London stood fresh and shining in the radiance of a winter day such as Australia need not have been ashamed of.

The boy walked to Hammersmith, and was met at the appointed place and time by an Oxford friend who had promised to see him through the ordeal of the marriage service; a good-natured, wild-oat-sowing son of a strait-laced Clapham family – a black sheep in his way – not deeply dyed in vice any more than our hero, but loving whatever was most at variance with the principles of respectability and evangelicalism in which he had been brought up. The pair stood on the steps of the cold, empty, fusty church for half-an-hour, the bridegroom suitably impressed by the gravity of his position, the best man making fun of it, and full of curiosity to see the young woman for whose sake a good fellow like Delavel was ready to go these extraordinary lengths; and then came Annie and Mary Greenwood, the bride in grey merino under her long crape-trimmed cloak, the bridesmaid in the cheerful colours that befitted her face and character.

'I couldn't let her be married in black,' said Mary, when, the best man having been introduced and the snuffy pew-opener sent to see if the old clergyman was in the vestry, the little party grouped itself before the chancel rails. And she drew from her pocket a pair of white shoes and a little scarf of white lace. 'Annie, dear, take off your bonnet and boots. Yes, take them off this minute. The least bit of black is unlucky, and you shall not be unlucky if I can help it. Tell her to take them off, Mr Delavel, please, before the clergyman comes.'

Dicky blushed; and the best man turned aside to look at a tablet on the wall. Annie was the colour of a peony, feeling herself ridiculous in the eyes of the strange gentleman; but, as she shared the prevailing superstition, she allowed herself to be divested of the forbidden colour. With great dexterity she slipped off her boots and slipped on the white shoes, and got rid of her mantle and crape bonnet; then she threw the lace scarf over her head, and the bridal costume was as complete as circumstances permitted. That it was so far from being as complete as it should have been, and had to be arranged in this indecorous manner, caused her keen suffering; but Dicky thought she looked lovely, and so did the best man when he ventured to turn his eyes on her. And, at any rate – as Miss Greenwood presently pointed out – there was the satisfaction of knowing that if ill luck came it would not come by their fault.

The feeble old man who had published the banns, came shuffling out of the vestry with the pew-opener at his heels; they looked terribly pinched and withered when contrasted with the blooming young folks composing the wedding party. No spectators were present. The clergyman, who had a bad cold, blew his nose irritably, and opened his book with a depressed and suffering air; the dank atmosphere made him shiver, and all his anxiety was to get his job over and get back to his study fire as soon as possible. The old woman hovered about the pews and did a little dusting while the function proceeded.

It took but a few minutes. The vows were spoken, the troth was plighted, the fatal ring was in its place, the young pair were blessed and duly exhorted; and, Annie having resumed her boots and bonnet, the party retired to the vestry to register the irrevocable deed. That done, Dicky took his bride in his arms and kissed her; and, being a good deal carried away by the excitement of the moment, bestowed a similar salutation upon the bridesmaid. The best man had confidently expected to enjoy the privilege of kissing the bride, but there was something about her which made him feel – what he seldom felt – shy, and he only ventured to shake her hand warmly and wish her happiness. After which he supposed he had better, now that nothing more was wanted of him, make himself scarce.

'And I too,' said Mary Greenwood, as she took his arm to be escorted out of church, the nuptial ceremonies having been concluded by the payment of fees, the amount of which was a pleasant surprise to the recipients. 'I must go home and tell my mother that I have deceived and cheated her for the first time in my life.'

Dicky heard the words and wheeled round, with his wife on his arm, unheeding the slight pull she gave him. 'And it is my fault,' he said impetuously; 'I have made you do it. But I am not going to let you take the consequences all on your own shoulders, Mary dear. We three will just go straight back to your mother, and I will tell her all about it and take the blame that properly belongs to me. You don't mind, Annie? We needn't stay ten minutes. And I shouldn't feel happy if I hadn't done it. She has been such a brick, and all against her own conscience, for the sake of helping us. It would be the most disgusting meanness to let her go home alone.'

Annie objected very strongly, but consented to his wish, as he made such a point of it. So they parted from the best man at the church door, and walked towards Hammersmith till they found an empty cab which conveyed them to Byron Villa.

'Perhaps you'd rather sit in the cab, darling,' Dicky suggested to his bride, 'and wait for me?'

'Oh dear no,' she replied with soft composure. 'I have done nothing to be ashamed of.' And she walked up the garden path beside him, holding her pretty head quite an inch higher than had been her wont. She was Mrs Delavel now and the approval or disapproval of grocers' wives had become a matter of very small importance.

Poor Mrs Greenwood was summoned from the kitchen, where she was preparing dinner, and came with her smiling face, in no way anticipating the shock in store for her. She did not know that Annie had gone out for a walk in a gown of grey merino, or that her boxes were packed upstairs, or that anything had happened out of the ordinary way. Dicky wrung the plump hand outstretched to welcome him, and plunged headlong into his confession.

'Mrs Greenwood, I'm afraid you'll think me an awfully mean fellow – it looks as if we had just been making use of you – we wouldn't have kept things secret if we could have helped it; but – but – well, the fact is, Annie and I are married. We have been engaged a long time, and when she lost her poor mother, her sister-in-law made things so miserable for her at home, that I persuaded her not to wait till her mourning was over, but to marry me at once, so that I could take care of her. And we were married this morning, and I've got lodgings at Chiswick, where we're going to live till we can turn ourselves round. Really, it was the only thing to do,' he urged persuasively. 'I hope you will forgive us for keeping our little secret from you – forgive me, rather, for it has been all my doing.'

He had imagined that it would be an easy task to mollify that amiable matron, and was greatly surprised and shocked when she turned upon him and upbraided him with acting as no gentleman would have acted. And she was much harder upon Annie than upon him. A three weeks' acquaintance with that churchy and genteel young lady had not endeared her to the chapel-going grocer's wife, who had, moreover, discovered the great disparity of rank between the two young people. 'You had no right to mix my girl up with your under-hand doings,' she said to Annie severely, 'teaching her to deceive her mother – she that was always as honest as the day. I'm ashamed of her for what she's done. You ought to have told me, being in my house and all. Mary, you, at any rate, ought to have told me.'

'It was all my fault,' said Dicky, 'that she didn't tell you. If you had known, Mrs Greenwood, you would probably have felt it your duty to communicate with our friends. That was what I feared.'

'I *should* have felt it my duty,' Mrs Greenwood admitted. 'It would have been anybody's duty. And what then? Why should you be afraid for your friends to know it?'

The young husband made an elaborate and plausible statement of his reasons, but even as he did so felt that they had lost a good deal of weight and value since he had last considered them. Mrs Greenwood waved them aside as not worth answering. 'Stuff and nonsense!' was all she said. And then she assured him that no good ever came of hole-and-corner doings of that sort, and prophesied that he and Annie would rue the day before they were a week older. 'And when you're my age, and have sons and daughters of your own,' said she, 'I hope they won't do as you've been doing, and bring a judgment on you – that's all.'

Annie listened to this censure with dignity and calmness, making little signs to her husband to bring the interview to a close, but Dicky was deeply concerned and shocked at the turn affairs had taken. With a man who had dared to reproach and criticise him he would have been furious, but he was never furious with women, and Mrs Greenwood's denunciation of clandestine proceedings was too much in harmony with his own ideas not to raise the most painful doubts in his erewhile complacent mind. Disregarding Annie's steadfast gaze, he appealed to the indignant matron not to cloud the first hours of his married life with such dark forebodings.

'It's done now,' he said, 'and can't be undone. I've acted as I thought, for the best, and we're not going to rue the day if I can help it. Do wish us good luck, Mrs Greenwood – won't you?'

Mary looked at her mother imploringly. What was the use of taking off the black bonnet and boots as if that careful precaution against ill omens was to be frustrated in this way? 'Do you wish them good luck,' she repeated, as earnestly as if it were for herself that she asked it; for she was an unselfish creature, and the romance of the secret marriage had interested her deeply.

'Oh,' said Mrs Greenwood, 'I'll wish fast enough if wishes are of any use. But wishing won't bring good luck to people beginning their lives together in this way – in deceit and disobedience to parents, and making trouble for everybody belonging to them – so don't expect it.'

It was evident that she could not be talked over. Annie rose with an air of decision. 'Richard, I think we will take my boxes with us instead of sending for them, if you don't mind,' she said.

Her tone indicated an intention to shake off the dust of this plebeian house forthwith.

'Where are they?' he returned, pale and grave, all his enthusiasm quenched. 'I will take them to the cab.'

Mrs Greenwood sent the maid-of-all-work to fetch them downstairs, but even a maid-of-all-work was not allowed to burden herself while he stood by, and on the stairs he took them from her and carried them out to the vehicle standing at the gate. Mary was weeping, and when he took her aside to thrust into her hands a packet of presents for herself and her brothers and sisters she sobbed aloud and kissed him without waiting for the invitation to do so, which would certainly have been given a moment later. Mrs Greenwood did not say she was sorry to part from her guest, but said she was sorry to part from her 'in this way', and sorry it wasn't somebody else's house from which such a marriage had taken place. She made an effort to express good wishes, being a benevolent woman, but her good wishes took the form of deprecating misfortune rather than of invoking happiness. 'I hope you won't rue it, my dears,' were her last words.

Thus inauspiciously did our young pair commence their married life. Silent and crestfallen, they entered the humble chariot that bore them forth into the wide world. The sun still shone brightly; the wide world looked kind and cheerful; but Dicky's buoyant spirit was depressed with a weight of misgiving and foreboding – the wettest of wet blankets had fallen upon his nuptial fervours, and for the moment

quenched them. He supposed that Annie was suffering in the same
way as himself, and his first impulse was to comfort her.

'Never mind, my darling. We did for the best, and we shall be all
right, you'll see. Don't let it make you miserable.'

'I shall certainly not allow myself to be made miserable by anything
a woman of that sort may say,' Annie calmly answered. 'A tradesman's
wife and a dissenter — what right has she to dictate to us?'

'She's a good woman,' said Dicky gravely; 'and I don't think she
was so far wrong, somehow. We might have managed better — at least,
I might. If I had been open about it — and it is best to be open — I
should have spared you this unpleasantness, at any rate. Poor little
girl!' And he drew her hand under his arm and caressed it between
his muscular palms.

'If you had been open, and my family had objected, you would have
had to wait for me for three years,' said Annie. 'Would you rather
have waited for three years?'

The possibility of her family objecting had all along been too remote
for serious consideration; yet Dicky brightened visibly at a suggestion
which seemed to justify him. 'I couldn't have waited for three years,'
he assured her, and at the moment he actually believed what he was
saying. 'And I'm glad I've got you safe, in spite of Mrs Greenwood
and everybody. And I'd do it again under the same circumstances.'

The cab was in a quiet street; the windows were closed, and a film
of congealed breath overspreading the glass. So he put his arm round
her and kissed her. 'We've got one another,' he whispered, 'and that's
the main thing. And it rests with ourselves whether we rue the day
or not. We're not going to rue it, are we?'

'No, indeed, dear,' assented Annie, in her sweet soft voice. And
the wet blanket seemed to lift, and the damp feathers of his soaring
spirit to get warm and dry again. He was just beginning to feel as a
bridegroom ought to feel when she spoilt it all by saying, with an
attempt at airy archness which was most inappropriate to such a
solemn moment, that she hoped he would alter some of his 'ways'
now that he was a married man.

'I hope you will remember that all your kisses belong to *me*,' she
said.

'Why, of course,' he answered, staring at her.

'I don't like to see you giving them to all sorts of people,' she
continued, gently but firmly. 'And right under my nose,' she added,
laughing.

'Are you thinking of Mary Greenwood?' he inquired, with no responsive smile. 'Do you call her all sorts of people? She's like a dear, good little sister – I'm sure few sisters would have done what she's done. Surely you didn't mind my kissing her – just for once – now it's all over and we are parting from her?'

'It wasn't once – it was twice. And then all those dirty children. . . .'

'They were not dirty at all. And – what! mustn't I even kiss children, now that I'm a married man?'

'Nobody but me,' said his wife; and she leaned caressingly towards him and put up her pretty mouth.

The window panes were opaque by this time, and he stooped and laid his lips on hers. But it was not such a kiss as the last he had given her.

CHAPTER XVIII

---•---

Swift Repentance

No, he could not feel that it was the ideal wedding-day. When they arrived at the little home he had so carefully prepared for her, he expected to see her face light up with a pleased recognition of his taste and thoughtfulness, and was hurt that her first remark should take the form of a fear that such lodgings were too expensive for their means. The wainscoted parlour had never looked more charming than when he led her into it. The old-fashioned, recessed window was full of the pale but cheerful sunlight, full of shimmering reflections from the river; and the other side of the room glowed with the ruddy warmth of a deep-hearted fire, whereon big coals had been heaped with an unsparing hand. Between the window and the cosy hearth stood a round table spread for lunch; it had hothouse flowers upon it, and the finest linen and silver and glass that a lady who had seen better days could furnish, and the most tempting little festive dishes that her ingenuity could devise. There were two seductive old chintz-covered arm-chairs drawn to the fireside – there was, in short, every-thing in the way of graceful welcome that a bride of taste could wish for. Ane yet this bride looked round with an anxious look, and hinted that her husband might have been more economical. So he might, of course; so, no doubt, under the circumstances, he ought to have been; but it jarred on his sense of the fitness of things that she should mention it, and mention it at such a moment.

Then there was her behaviour to Mrs Carthew. When that kind lady, having spent herself in voluntary and unremunerated labours for their benefit, met the newly wedded couple at the door with her sympathetic maternal smile and outstretched hand, Annie was cold and stiff and distant – insomuch that in two minutes Mrs Carthew retired in a huff, sending a housemaid to represent her. Young Mrs

Delavel was not going to allow herself to be made free with as if she were Miss Morrison still, and she persisted, in spite of Dicky's protestations, in regarding Mrs Carthew as the landlady and nothing more. Landladies and husbands, respectively, were to be kept in their place, if possible.

This severity was very grievous to our easy-going and overflowing young man. When he saw his charming new friend, who had been so good to him, snubbed by his wife – the captain's widow by the farmer's daughter – the mature matron by the girl of eighteen – and because of social distinctions which he blushed to recognise, he felt more humiliated than he had ever been in his life. His ears grew hot and his heart grew cold, and his manner to his bride changed so much that she presently noticed it, and asked him the cause. When he told her she very sweetly pointed out to him that Mrs Carthew was nothing to her, and that he was too much given to 'spoiling' people, but offered, if he pleased, to make a point of thanking the landlady for having done so much to make them comfortable.

'I really wish you would,' he said earnestly, 'I wouldn't for the world have her think us ungrateful. Nor have her think we forget she is a lady because she lets lodgings.'

So, when Mrs Carthew appeared, Annie thanked her for having made her and her husband comfortable. But though she did it politely, in well chosen words, it was with an air of affability and condescension that caused Dicky's ears to burn more hotly than ever as he listened to her. She would only recognise the landlady in the person of that superior woman with the beautiful eyes and the white hands – a common landlady, patronised by the upper classes. He wondered why he had never seen this spirit in Annie before – his gentle Annie, who had always seemed so modest and meek. It did not occur to him that her sudden rise in the social scale had effected the transformation.

'Mr Delavel is quite welcome to any little services I have been able to render him,' said Mrs Carthew, in answer to the bride's gracious commendations. 'While he was alone I was glad to do what I could for his comfort.' She looked at him with a friendly smile, as she pointedly implied that he was the only person she had considered.

'I'm sure I shall never forget your – your angelic goodness,' he burst out, answering her look with one eager, fervent, full of deprecation and appeal, that touched her heart. And he held the door for her as she left the room, hung about her and waited on her as if she had been a queen.

But after that they saw very little of Mrs Carthew, and the arrangements were strictly of the lodging-house pattern, and nothing was as comfortable as it had been.

Then a further disappointment awaited Dicky when the wedding breakfast was disposed of. He had bought some champagne for the occasion, and he and Annie had shared a bottle in the proportion of seven-eighths to him and one-eighth to her – all he could induce her to take, even for the sake of pleasing him; and with the generous wine warming his heart, dissolving his cold doubts, suffusing the general aspect of things with that light which never was on sea or land, he very naturally desired to enjoy himself in loving *tête-à-tête* with his bride – to prove to himself as far as possible that he was really as happy as he felt. And what did Annie do? She said she must go and put away her things before she could feel comfortable to sit down.

'Oh, what does it matter about your things, *now?*' he cried impatiently, trying to draw her to one of the big chairs by the fireside, where he wanted to nurse her in his arms, and talk to her of the great event that had made them one. 'You can surely leave them for a little while?'

'No,' she said gently, but with a firmness that he had no power to shake. 'I always do it the first thing, and it is better to do it by daylight than with a candle, especially in a strange place.'

She was a little person of most exquisite neatness and orderliness, and to see the way she unpacked her clothes and laid them in the empty drawers, all mathematically folded without a single crease in the wrong place, would have delighted the soul of a mother or a schoolmistress; but the young bridegroom fretted and fumed while the work went on, until all his radiant good humour departed from him. He went to her at intervals to see what progress she was making, and each time found her gravely absorbed in her task. She did not tell him to go out of the room when, in the character of a lawful husband, he diffidently appeared there, but she looked at him with an air that discouraged him from walking boldly in and sitting down to watch her – which, for lack of anything better, he would have liked to do. So the afternoon that he had designed to spend so differently – first in that luxurious fireside *tête-à-tête* – then, perhaps, in a stroll by the river in the peaceful twilight – wore on slowly, and all the enjoyment he had in it was due to a surreptitious pipe. And as he sat alone and smoked, the rosy colour faded from his dreams as the daylight from the sky. Annie had to light candles to see to finish her job, but he sat in the gathering darkness, and the dim red shine of the fire, which touched his keen-featured, brooding face; and by the time she rejoined him he was as sober, in every sense of the word, as ever bridegroom was at that hour of the fateful day.

She looked very charming when she appeared at last. She had done up her beautiful brown hair afresh – the two or three ripples in it took the light like satin – and she wore her best black dress, with an immaculate little white frill round her soft white throat. Of course, she had a crinoline, like other people, but it was of moderate dimensions, and in those days she would have been thought to look supremely ridiculous without one. Altogether she was an exquisite little person, and her husband's eyes acknowledged it. But I think it was at this moment that he began to feel her excessive neatness irksome – began to feel what its daily maintenance was to cost him in more precious things. If she had come out with a few hairs straying from the rigid hairpins, and in the half-worn dress in which she had married him – for the sake of saving time to spend in his company – it would have been more human, and he would have liked it better.

Nevertheless, he held out his arms to her. 'Come, darling, come. Oh, what an everlasting time you have been!' he cried.

'But now it is finished,' she answered, with an air of satisfaction, 'and I can sit down comfortably. Dear Richard, I put your coats and things in the left-hand cupboard, and your boots at the bottom, and your hat-box on the wardrobe. . . .'

'You might have thrown them under the bed or out of the window, for what I care,' he interrupted. And then he drew her to him closely, lifted her chin, and kissed the soft fresh lips. There was not much passion in his kiss, but a great yearning for something – something that he knew he should have had, and that was missing – a yearning for comfort and reassurance. His face, with his eyes closed, had quite a tragic gravity as he stood over her, motionless in this embrace, with his mouth pressed to hers.

She rested in his arms for a few seconds, submissive and affectionate, but not in the least understanding or responding to the dumb appeal he was making to her; then she suddenly pushed him from her, not with force, but with a firmness to which he yielded instantly, and sat down on the opposite chair, demure and composed, as if nothing had happened. Dull as her perceptions were in some things, compared with his, she had heard the step in the passage which indicated the approach of the housemaid with the lamp, while he was lost to all sublunary matters outside the limits of the hearth rug. It disconcerted him to have his kiss thus broken off in the middle – good reason as there was for it – and to witness her self-control, which seemed almost unnatural. He remembered how she had blushed and fluttered when he kissed her first on Rhody's wedding day, and wondered if it had been all in his imagination, like so much else.

The nuptial banquet having been of a solid and satisfying description, their evening meal was light tea at seven o'clock. Dicky had ordered it two days ago, the muffins and the cream and the little confections that were so appropriate to youth; and he had delighted in the thought of seeing her pour out his tea – a function as symbolical as the sewing on of shirt buttons. And very charming and domestic she looked as she was doing it, and very nice and refreshing was the tea she made. But tea does not act upon the brain like wine; it throws no magic glamour over the facts of life. And therefore Dicky did not recover his enthusiasm any more.

He sat by his fireside in the evening, and allowed his wife to sit down opposite to him, as if the honeymoon that had barely begun were over; and the sense of misgiving and foreboding that champagne had temporarily dispelled oppressed him more and more. Mrs Greenwood's prophecy that he would rue the day rang in his ears like a witch's curse in the ears of a mediaeval rustic; his budding hopes shrivelled under it as spring flowers blighted by a frost. All those considerations of reason and prudence that he had refused to entertain while it was of any use to entertain them crept into his undefended mind and filled it, driving out the sentimental dreams.

'I think I have been selfish,' he said, staring into the fire, over which he leaned with his elbows and his palms outspread to the cheerful blaze. 'I doubt if you have done a very good thing for yourself in marrying me, Annie.' It was the only way in which he could express the feeling of disappointment that had been creeping over him all day, and would no longer be ignored.

'Why do you say that?' she returned gently. 'You remember your own words this morning; it rests with ourselves whether we are happy, whether we do well or not.'

There was a little pause, and then she rose from her chair, crossed the hearth rug, and knelt down beside him, laying her hand on his shoulder and her cheek on his coat sleeve. It would have been natural for him to meet such a caress half way, much more than half way, but some instinct warned him that it was not a demonstration of pure love, and he did not move, nor withdraw his sombre gaze from the fire.

'Richard, darling,' she said, in a tone of earnest appeal, 'you will – oh, you *will*, to please me – to make me happy. You said you would do the utmost in your power to make me happy. You *will* be dutiful to your father, and do what we all want you to do? He would forgive us then. Our future would be assured. Such a noble, useful, splendid future, dear! It is for your own sake as well as mine that I beg and entreat you not to be wicked and wilful, for I am sure you would repent it so dreadfully afterwards. O Richard, dear, you won't refuse me, will you? He'll forgive your marrying me if you tell him you will enter the Church – I am sure he will. And this is our wedding-day, and it's the first thing I have ever asked you. And it has been on my mind all day, and I have set my heart on it. I have prayed for it night and morning from the first. And – oh, my dear husband, you *will* make me happy, as you promised you would, won't you?'

Dicky did not answer at once, but the grey eyes, staring at the fire, suddenly shone with a film of bitter tears. He knew now, beyond the possibility of ever doubting it again, what a ghastly blunder he had made and what an incredible fool he had been.

CHAPTER XIX

A Last Chance

On the following day the letters were despatched which announced the marriage to the families concerned. They were answered promptly. Rhody wrote, on behalf of Annie's relatives, to say that Mr Morrison senior was heart-broken at the wicked behaviour of his daughter, who had always been considered a respectable and virtuous girl; and to intimate, on her own behalf, as a matron of unblemished reputation, a desire to be spared the necessity of ever again associating with such a person. 'When peeple marres in that hastey and undurhand maner,' wrote Mrs John, 'it is done for resons that I won't demene myself to menshon'; and therefore she washed her hands of her sister-in-law, and prophesied, like Mrs Greenwood, that Mr Richard would rue the day that he had let himself be led away by "dissolution and artfulness."

This letter was followed by an evidently independent one from John, laboriously regretting that he had not been taken into the confidence of his sister and her husband, whom he had always wished well, and hoping Mr Richard knew what he was about, and saw his way to keeping his wife now he had got her. John was aware, he said, that Annie had not always been comfortable at home, but he would never have allowed her to want for anything, and she could not expect to go through life without troubles any more than other people. All he hoped was that she had not married in haste to repent at leisure, nor Mr Richard either; and he wished them all good wishes, and bade them remember that they had always a friend in him when they wanted one.

'John is a splendid fellow,' said Dicky, with his ready enthusiasm, as he folded the letter. 'And I wish we had told him. And I wish we could see him to explain things – I don't like him to feel hurt that we shut him out.'

'But you would not allow me to go near that – that *creature*, again?' said Annie, using the strongest feminine expression for a loathed object of her own sex that language supplied, with a set look on her face that gave it the fullest emphasis. 'You would not give her another opportunity to insult me, Richard?'

'No, my dear, of course not,' he replied promptly. Then he added, to his wife's deep but unexpressed displeasure, that, though Rhody was a low-minded little vixen, he didn't suppose for a moment that she meant what she said, and that it wasn't worth noticing. She had a bad temper, he thought, rather than a bad heart. For he couldn't bear to hear a woman called a 'creature'. From his point of view, a woman – simply because she was a woman – must necessarily be good somewhere.

Mr Delavel's answer was short and to the point. 'In reply to your communication, I beg to say I have done with you' – that was the substance of it. Richard was no longer to consider himself a son of the house, whose doors would be closed to him henceforth, nor to hold communication with any member of the family whose noble name he had disgraced. To them (Mr Delavel spoke for the soft-hearted mother, the careless brothers and the affectionate sisters, as a matter of course) he was to all intents and purposes dead; they had ceased to recognise his existence. He was desired to take himself as far away from Dunstanborough as possible, and never to let them hear of him or see his face again.

'It is only what I expected,' said Dicky, pale and proud, as he handed this letter to his wife. But, in fact, he had not expected anything so cruel as the terms in which his excommunication was set forth. He knew his father's temper and prejudices, and had expected to be 'kicked out'; but this cold-blooded repudiation for an offence that, after all, was not a deadly crime, went far beyond the just bounds of parental severity. It was an outrage upon nature. All the ancestral spirit rose in the young man's breast.

'It is the first shock,' said Annie. 'His anger will cool in time – especially if you humble yourself to him, Richard dear.'

'Never,' said Richard, his pale eyes shining and his teeth set. 'I will take him at his word – I will obey him to the letter. He shall never see my face again.'

Annie attempted to beseech and persuade, but this time she was silenced with a peremptoriness that taught her the limits of her power, and the fact that her husband was not so wax-like as she had supposed.

To humble himself was the very last thing he was likely to do under the circumstances. No, indeed, he would starve first. And when Annie delicately suggested that he should think of her, for whom he had now become responsible, as well as of himself and his own headstrong pride, he responded by at once putting an end to their drifting honey-moon life, and hastening preparations for the voyage, and those enter-prises in a new world which were to make his fortune. He collected the remainder of his money, sold his books and unnecessary luxuries, gave Mrs Carthew notice, and set to work at packing with a passionate energy that made a great commotion in the quiet house. They should all see, he was determined, that he had the stuff of a man in him, and was able to fight his way through the world without anybody's assistance. Yes, they should see what he could do. And some day he would be in such a position that even the family which had cast him off should be proud of him.

'Never fear,' he said to his wife, again and again. 'Where there's a will there's a way. We are young and strong, and all we've got to do is to put our shoulders to the wheel.'

He put his own shoulder to the wheel certainly, but Annie had no heart for helping him. The prospect that inspired him with so much enthusiasm was hateful to her in every detail; it would have been so even if there had not been the delightful alternative to contrast with it – the possible that he was determined to make impossible. What would be the use of being Mrs Delavel in a wild country where the name had no significance? And was it likely that a man who had idled and squandered all his life would suddenly become thrifty and industrious? And oh, to think that she must go forth into the wilder-ness, when the gates of Paradise stood open and she had the right to enter them! She dropped tears into her boxes as she packed her clothes; she went about with a languid step and a despondent mien; she seldom spoke to her husband, and when she did, it was in a tone of hopeless melancholy, the effect of which upon his highly-strung nerves can be more readily imagined than described.

One day, when she had been unusually dismal, and he was falling into a momentary despair over her impracticability, she asked him suddenly if she might go home to Dunstanborough to say good-bye to her family.

'Surely, dear,' he answered, melted into tenderness at once by so touching a request. 'Of course you may. Why didn't you mention it before? I thought you did not mean to go near Rhody again?'

'I want to see the others,' she said.

And so he pulled out his purse and gave her money for her journey and a brief sojourn at the Delavel Arms, took her to the station, tucked her up in the carriage with rugs and wraps, and saw her safely off to Dunstanborough, having written to John to arrange for her being met and taken care of at the other end. And when she was gone, and he returned by penny 'buses through the city to his little home at Chiswick, there is no doubt that he was conscious of a pleasant sense of relief and freedom, though he had only been married for a fortnight.

He found his way to Mrs Carthew's sitting-room that evening, and poured himself out to her in a delightful talk, that lasted until she put an end to it at midnight by an inadvertent yawn. He told her of his Australian schemes and also of that other scheme which his conscience had prompted him to discountenance at so great a sacrifice of his worldly interests; and he entrusted her with some of his crude opinions in respect of human responsibility, his young ideals of life, the secret aspirations of his soul, such as his chosen partner never had a glimpse of in all the years that she lived with him. And Mrs Carthew, though only an ordinary kind woman, assuaged his hunger for sympathy, and sent him to bed consoled and encouraged, with a stronger if not a lighter heart.

And then, next day, his brother Keppel came to see him. Keppel was a brilliant young man of fashion, about to marry a middle-aged widow for her money, having no conscientious objections to such a course, which he regarded as an unpleasant necessity; and no particular sympathy was to be expected from him. But the handsome guardsman was a good-natured fellow; he came not to upbraid, but to extend the hand of friendship to the outcast, whom he considered to be hardly done by. He certainly told his brother in so many words that he was a greater fool than ever a Delavel had shown himself before or since, but all the sting was taken from that remark by his cordial recognition of the pluck and spirit that had characterised the boy's proceedings. The bride being absent, much to his disappointment (for he remembered the pretty girl, and had intended to give her a surreptitious brotherly embrace), Keppel bore the bridegroom off to town with him, entertained him at dinner at his club, and took him to the theatre afterwards, in defiance of the parental ukase, the terms of which had been duly communicated to him. And all this was very grateful and soothing to our young man.

Also he enjoyed being alone for a little while with his own thoughts. He enjoyed a solitary ramble in the foggy twilight of a calm winter day, a walk that he took to rest himself after a hard morning's work; a last gathering ofmemories – the river, veiled in slate-grey mist, dimly reddened with the sun – the ancient churchyard, with Hogarth's tomb in it – the quaint and quiet nooks and ways that were full of old-world associations, not yet disturbed by the new – memories to be hoarded up for the years to come and the land of exile, where picture galleries were supposed to be unknown. And he enjoyed going to see the Greenwoods and discharging his soul of the debt of gratitude he conceived himself burdened with, so far as words could do it, and feeling himself reinstated in the goodwill of that amiable family. In short, he enjoyed the interval of Annie's absence, in one way or another, more than he had enjoyed the time spent with her, though quite unaware of that melancholy fact.

But he worked much more than he amused himself. His preparations for colonial life went on with unflagging vigour, and he took the keenest interest in them. He ransacked London for those time-honoured utilities wherewith the amateur emigrant persists in burdening himself, and packed his parcels of gunshot and garden seeds, his hammers and nails, his Garibaldi shirts and cooking-utensils, with the tender care one gives to precious articles which, if damaged, can never be replaced. And the ships he went to look at, the cabins he measured, the agents and outfitters that he consulted – their name was legion.

But before he had quite decided on the ship he had a message from Annie, begging him to join her at Dunstanborough. She said his mother wanted to see him before he sailed, and that started him off post haste by the next train.

The railway was brought to Dunstanborough many a year ago, but at that time it stopped short of the village by about a dozen miles, in deference to Mr Delavel's strong prejudice against it. He thought it vulgar and levelling, and the ruin of landscape scenery. It was not until young Roger came to the throne that the sacrilegious innovation was permitted, whereby the little hamlet was turned into a fashionable watering place and much wealth accrued to the lord of the manor, who had not been a citizen of the world for nothing. On the day of Dicky's last visit to his native place such things were not so much as thought of. He hired a gig in the town where the train landed him, and drove the twelve miles through as peaceful a country as any to be found in England. The quiet road traversed a sleepy village now and then, passed under the shadow of a great castle in ruins, skirted wide park lands and miles of woodland, enclosing the seats of half-a-dozen county magnates, and finally reached the sea without offering any suggestion of modern times whatever. 'As it was in the beginning, is now, and ever shall be,' was the general belief and aspect of things at that date.

The afternoon was still and cold; the frosty road rang to the stroke of the horse's hoofs. There was snow under the leafless hedges and ice on the ditches and wayside pools. It was naked and cheerless winter time, and yet Dunstanborough looked pretty enough in the fading light to make the heart of the prodigal ache as he gazed at it, and reflected that he should see it no more. He was full of thoughts of his mother, who had wanted to see him. His impressionable heart was warm and soft, though his fingers were frozen and his nose blue with cold. He was just in the mood to be managed, if any one had known how to manage him.

But no one knew, or else no one cared. When the gig stopped at the door of the Delavel Arms, Annie came forth to meet him, and kissed him affectionately. It was such a very tender greeting that it made him as delighted to get her back as he had been relieved to let her go. 'Well, my darling,' he cried, pressing her to his breast in full view of the landlady and the ostler, 'you see I have come as quickly as I could. Is my mother here?'

'N – no,' replied Annie, who was flushed and agitated, 'She is not here herself, but she – but they – they have sent somebody – they have sent you a message. . . .'

She turned to the open door of her sitting-room and walked in without finishing the sentence. Dicky walked in after her, and found himself face to face with Delavel-Pole.

All the softness and warmth went out of his heart at once. He had hated the sight of his cousin before, when there was no particular reason for it, but now he found the presence of that arch-enemy, presumably triumphing in his downfall, unendurable. Guessing the true object of Annie's visit to Dunstanborough, and seeing that the two were in league together against him, did not tend to soothe his perturbation.

'May I ask,' he inquired, with stately fury, 'to what I am indebted for this – this unexpected honour?'

'I am here as an ambassador, Dicky,' said Mr Delavel-Pole, who, to do him justice, behaved with dignity and gentleness, and showed no sign of triumphing. 'Your family are, of course, deeply shocked and grieved – that you know. It is impossible they can be otherwise. Indeed, I don't think they will ever get over it. But they consented to see your wife, who' – looking at Annie – 'seems not to have been so much to blame as we imagined, and at her urgent intercession they are willing to give you another chance.'

'You are not my family,' said Dicky, 'and you have nothing to do with my affairs. If my family have anything to say to me I will hear it from them – not from you.'

'You cannot hear it from them,' returned the clergyman quietly; 'your father forbids them to hold any intercourse with you, and he especially commissioned me to be the bearer of his message.'

'Where is my mother?' asked Dicky of his wife. 'You told me she wanted to see me. Is that another deception?'

Annie stood apart with flushed face and downcast eyes. The Rector answered for her, 'Your mother does want to see you, Dicky, but whether she will do so or not entirely depends on the result of my errand. She is most anxious about it, but unless you return the answer they expect of you she will not be allowed to have her wish.'

'Then state your errand, if you please,' said Dicky haughtily. 'But before doing so understand distinctly that I did not authorise my wife to intercede for me with my family – that for myself I ask no favours from them, and desire none.' He was in a mood now to do anything rather than return the answer expected of him, no matter what it might be.

'My errand is,' said his cousin slowly, 'to lay before you a proposal – to offer you a last chance of retaining your connection with the family and the position of a gentleman.'

'Yes, go on.' Dicky smiled an unpleasant and portentous smile, and Annie watched him with an imploring gaze that was meant to soften him, but had precisely the opposite effect.

'If,' said Mr Delavel-Pole, 'you will go quietly back to Oxford, and work and take your degree, while your wife remains with her relatives – she is quite willing to do this, or anything, to leave you free – and will afterwards give your mind to the plans that you know have been made for you, and which – if you have any spark of good in you, as we believe you have. . . .'

'Thank you,' interrupted Dicky, with a deep bow.

'Which,' continued the Rector, flushing, 'you could make yourself fit for if you liked to try – well, in that case your father will allow you a small sum for your expenses, and, when the time comes, assist you to obtain a living in some quiet place at a distance from Dunstanborough, where these matters are unknown, and – and, in short, recognise you as his son, in spite of what has happened.'

'I'm sure it is awfully good of him,' said Dicky. 'And awfully good of you to take so much trouble on my account. But . . . .'

'O Richard, think – think!' wailed Annie. 'It is the last chance! Don't throw it away and break my heart!'

'It is really the last chance,' said the Rector earnestly, 'and one you may think yourself lucky to get – one that no one ever expected would be offered you. I'd strongly advise you to give it a little consideration, Dicky – for your wife's sake if not for your own.'

'But,' proceeded Dicky, ignoring these interruptions, 'we have made our plans, and have no intention of altering them. You may thank my father for his kind offer, and tell him I prefer to keep to the first arrangement – to the terms of his letter, which were so very explicit.'

His tone was icy, but his eyes were full of fire; he stood like a rock, with his fair head thrown upward, immovable in his Delavel pride, and his sense of being at bay before his enemies. For Annie was his enemy too – Annie, for whose sake he had sacrificed himself. That was the bitterness of this tragic moment.

She began to lament and weep, with more passion than she had ever shown before about anything. 'You don't care for me,' she cried. 'You don't care what becomes of me! You said you would do your utmost to make me happy, and you do your utmost to make me miserable. I cannot go to Australia – we are certain to starve there, with hardly any money, and neither of us brought up to work. I will not go – my father says I am not to go. He says I am not fit for such a life, and he will not allow it – Mr Delavel-Pole will tell you how set against it he is. The first moment I told him he said he would not hear of such a thing.'

To Dicky's surprise, this proved to be the case. Old Morrison, who had never been taken into the calculations at all, turned up at the inn door almost as she spoke, not in the least broken-hearted, as Rhody had described him, but ready to assert his rights as a father with all his characteristic obstinacy. He didn't hold by the marriage, he said (though evidently as proud of it as he could be), and hoped as how the squire wouldn't lay it at his door, as knew no more about it than the babe unborn. But since married she was, it was his duty to see as his daughter was took care on, and 'twouldn't be takin' care on her to cart her off to a desert island where she'd be et up by cannibals. If Master Richard wanted to go to Australia to seek his fortune, why, let him go; but let him leave his wife at home, where she'd be safe, till he'd found it – provided, of course, that he 'kep' her in the meantime, as a husband was in duty bound to do.

John then appeared upon the scene, and backed up his father's arguments. 'You go, sir, if you want to,' said he. 'I can see you're keen for it, and if you're so dead against being a parson, why, it's the best thing you can do. But just leave Annie here for a bit. She can go to you when you've made a home for her, or perhaps you'll not like Australia and want to come back yourself. Anyway, get the first struggle over – it'll be easier for both of you if she's out of it – and I'll keep an eye on her while you're away. There's them as says,' concluded John, evidently referring to Rhody, 'that if we let you go to Australia alone, we'll never hear of you again, and Annie'll be left on our hands. But I can trust you, sir – I can trust you.'

'If that is Annie's wish,' said the young husband, in a vibrating voice; 'if she cannot feel safe in my charge – if she prefers to live with others rather than with me – of course I have nothing to say. It must be as she pleases.'

'You can stay with me, if you will,' sobbed Annie.

'No, dear, I can't stay,' replied Dicky. 'But if you wish to do so, you can. I will leave all the money I have with John – all but my passage money and perhaps a five-pound note to start with, and leave him to make you as comfortable as he can with it until I fetch or send for you. It's not the way I meant us to begin life,' he added, after a pause, during which he swallowed down a big lump in his throat; 'but perhaps it's the best we can do under the circumstances.'

And thus ended the brief honeymoon.

CHAPTER XX

•————

Goodbye

That night Dicky visited his home for the last time. He did not go inside its doors – nothing would have induced him to do that, in the face of his father's prohibition; but he went over the bridge that spanned the moat, under the great gateway and into the courtyard, and there skulked like a burglar in the black shadows thrown by the wintry moon from the gigantic masses of masonry. Max, he knew, had long ago delivered his reply to his father's ultimatum, and the sentence of banishment had been finally pronounced; but his mother had wished to see him, and he could not go without saying good-bye to her.

After he had waited for some time, watching the lighted windows of the drawing-room, Alice, his sister's maid, crossed a corner of the quadrangle on her way to keep tryst with the head gamekeeper. It was the pretty Alice whom, in his gay young days, that were all over, the young master had kissed behind the schoolroom door (according to Rhody), and she, in common with her fellow-servants, adored the charming scapegrace as she had never adored the well-behaved members of the family. As soon as she was aware of his presence and errand she wept and begged to know how she could serve him, being ready to shed her blood if that would do him any good; and she eagerly undertook to carry a surreptitious message to Lady Susan, who was lying down in her room with a headache.

A few minutes later the mother and son sat in an arbour of the old garden, and half-a-dozen servants, who in the interval had crept out into the courtyard to offer their humble sympathy, constituted themselves a guard to secure the pair from interruption. The poor mother seemed to have been weeping continuously for a length of time, for she was quite broken down and shattered. She had no reproaches now; only tears and kisses. Dicky wrapped her fur cloak round her stout form, and then wrapped his arms round the fur cloak, and made her lay her head on his shoulder, and caressed her extravagantly in his passionate compunction. He would not bend his proud neck at the command of the family in its sovereign capacity and as represented by its clerical ambassador, but he bent it to her and owned his human fallibility and besought her forgiveness for all he had done to disappoint and grieve her.

'I don't know how it has come about,' he said, 'but I have not meant to do wrong – I have not, indeed, mother. I have been a fool, no doubt – I am sure I must have been a fool – but I have not done anything that should make you ashamed of me. Oh, do trust me – do believe in me a little! Don't *you* cast me off, whatever the others do.'

'My boy, my boy,' sobbed Lady Susan, who, poor dear woman, could not think of more than one thing at a time, 'you will be starved in that dreadful country – I know you will – I shall never see you again!'

'Oh no, I shan't be starved. I shall be all right. You wait, dear – you wait and see. I am going to do great things yet, and surprise you all. If only I knew you would think of me sometimes – you, at least, mother – my own mother!' And he broke down himself as he thought how little would be left to him if his mother's love were lost.

She promised she would think of him, and pray for him, and love him through evil report and good; and he promised to come back to her a successful and prosperous man, to be the pride and prop of her declining years; and then they kissed a long time without speaking, and he led her, sobbing, back to the house.

It was the last she ever saw of her boy, that dim glimpse of him as he stood in the moonlit courtyard, waiting to answer her last wave of the hand as she passed indoors. She died about a year afterwards, while he was still far enough from the realisation of his dreams. Mr Delavel said it was the misconduct of her Benjamin that killed her; but it was not, for she would never believe him wrong, but only unfortunate and ill-used, from the day that he was turned out of his father's house. What killed her was apoplexy, simply.

The next morning Dicky parted from his wife, for it was decided that she should remain in Dunstanborough now that she was there, and he was feverishly anxious to get out of the place as quickly as possible. Annie was installed as a lodger in a pretty cottage belonging to a widowed aunt, who was the village post-mistress, an arrangement that satisfied her very well under the generally unsatisfactory circumstances. She could defy Rhody, and at the same time enjoy amongst her own people the distinctions of her new rank. That she had been tacitly recognised by the family was an unspeakable consolation to her – a state of things that implied the most beautiful possibilities. She expected, though her expectations were not realised, to have some intercourse with the Delavel circle as a humble member of it. And she expected that some day before long Dicky would return, cured of his fancy for Australia and penniless independence, to fulfil his natural destiny and make her completely happy. In the meantime she would be a link between him and his people, keeping the way of reconciliation open. That was her idea.

The parting between the young couple was a very emotional piece of business, but it did not wring Dicky's heart like the parting with his mother. To the last, and in her most loving demonstrations, Annie maintained her look of sad reproach and suffering resignation, and of disappointment too deep for words; and it was but natural that he should feel a certain relief when it was all over, and that accusing face confronted him no more. He left her crying on the sofa of her little parlour – left her with her own eyes wet; but long before he reached the town, whither John drove him to catch his train, he was reconciled to his widowed condition.

'Don't you fret about her,' said John, on the railway platform. 'She'll begin with her Sunday schools and churchgoings and things, and that'll make her happy; and I'll look sharp after her to see that she comes to no harm. You take care o' yourself, sir, and keep up your heart. And goodbye and God bless you' – thrusting his horny hand into the carriage window.

'Good-bye, dear old fellow,' said Dicky, wringing that hand with all the fervour of his grateful nature. And the train moved out of the station, and the last he saw of his Dunstanborough life was John's heavy, common face gazing wistfully after him.

Arrived in London, it did not take him long to clear up his affairs. He engaged his berth the same day – a second-class berth, in order that he should have the more money to leave his wife – and the day after shipped the bulk of his own baggage and despatched Annie's belongings to Dunstanborough. He kissed Mrs Carthew, and he went to Hammersmith and kissed all the Greenwoods; he wrote farewell letters to his sisters and to the young attaché at Vienna; and then he went on board his ship, and in due course vanished into the unknown

– effacing himself from the records of his distinguished family as completely as if the ship had been his grave.

Keppel went to the docks to see him off – which was really very fine of Keppel, when you come to think of it. Moreover, though he was always in straits for cash, he brought twenty pounds that he had scraped together with him as a parting gift. It was an odd thing to see the two young men in the sordid little cabin which Keppel declared was not fit to house a dog. What a contrast in the fate of the brothers – the brilliant guardsman, popular in his regiment, petted by society, and about to marry half-a-million of money, and the nearly penniless second-class passenger, bound for a land where he would have to work like a common labourer or starve, without a friend to help him. Keppel keenly felt the painful force of it, and was ashamed of his own prosperity.

But call no man happy till he dies – or unhappy either. What befell Dicky in the later years we shall presently see. What befell Keppel was this: his elderly spouse, whom he hated, first took to drink, and then lost all her wealth in the crash of the mercantile house that created it. He fell in love; he sank deep in debt; he yielded to divers temptations to which this condition of things exposed him; and finally, having got his life into what seemed to him an inextricable muddle, put an end to it summarily by putting a bullet through his brain. So that there was no such great disparity of fortune after all.

This was the last goodbye – the parting of the last strand between our hero and his home and kindred and his familiar life. Keppel went off to pay a duty call on his fiancée, and to dine at the Guard's Club on the fat of the land; and left his brother to the companionship of illiterate emigrants and an evening meal of hard ship-biscuit and nauseous tea. The vessel dropped down the river in a murky twilight of smoke and fog, and Dicky saw the last of his native country a few days later through a veil of falling snow.

CHAPTER XXI

●

Five-And-Twenty Years After

Five-and-twenty years after all this happened a young girl walked one day out of a house in Sydney – one of the many charming houses of the well-to-do that overhang the bay at Darling Point – and looked up and down in search of a city-wending omnibus. She was a tall, well-grown young woman, straight and graceful, with an intelligent, eager face; not handsome at all, but decidedly attractive. Her mouth was large, her nose was not all it should have been, and her complexion showed the want of parasols and veils; but the look of health and wholesomeness that pervaded her whole person had the effect of beauty upon those who observed her. She was most simply dressed in dark serge, with a leather belt round her waist, and wore an unnoticeable hat and dogskin gloves; but in this plain costume there were evidences of money and a position in life which no female eye failed to recognise at the first glance. This was Richard Delavel's daughter and only child. 'Susan,' her mother used to say, on introducing her to a new acquaintance, 'after her grandmother, Lady Susan Delavel.' Susan she was named, in memory of her titled ancestress, and she was called Sue – except when her father called her Sukey, which he was fond of doing, but never did in Mrs Delavel's hearing unless he forgot himself.

The girl, who was a little over twenty and looked thoroughly a woman, did not wait for the invisible bus, but walked quickly along the road until it came up with her. Then she took her seat, kept it until the vehicle stopped at its city terminus, and walked from that point to her destination. All the way she had an air of being full of business and economical of time, but in the end she did nothing – nothing, that is to say, which seemed to justify so much trouble for the sake of doing it. She went to Dawes Point, and there sat on the broken end of a stone wall and looked at the bay – which, of course, she could see at any time from her own verandahs and garden terraces at Darling Point. The prospect was a most interesting one, certainly, but not usually so to those who had been all their lives accustomed to Sydney Harbour views. Rather to the casual stranger, in the course of his first discovery that Australia has a spot so unique in beauty as the ramifying inlet of the sea on which her chief city is built. To him Dawes Point has its own fascination, as showing how the charms of nature and the utilities of modern civilisation may blend in such a way as to heighten the significance of both. A native of the place, used to this aspect of things, seldom cares to study it.

It was the usual Sydney winter day, which is lovelier than words can describe, and Susan Delavel seemed to bask in it. The clear water was as blue as the deeply azure sky, the shadows of the warships at anchor trembling on the shining surface amid the delicate webs of foam spun by the bay steamers – water and sky marking out in grand relief the green promontories, dark with their rich vegetation, which sheltered the peaceful harbour from the restless sea outside. And though this was the fag end of George Street, and adjacent to the wharfs and offices and huge vessels of the great merchant companies, there was no suggestion of the toil and moil of traffic, such as one knew must be carried on amongst them. The funnels of the P and O and the Messageries and the North German Lloyd boats smoked gently side by side almost under her nose, while the current Orient liner, in a noble company of fellow voyagers, spread her gigantic length along the opposite quay; and they were as dignifiedly quiet – or seemed so – as the old Nelson in Farm Cove. No noise, no dust, arose from that busy neighbourhood, which was a mart for the world's wares. There was just the sense of strong and stirring human life underlying the outward serenity of things, enhancing the charm of it, as the mighty unseen forces at rest in their long hulls enhanced the impressiveness of the tranquil ships. On the two little grassy tongues of land immediately enclosing the inner port no moving thing was visible. Fort Macquarie, so dwarfed by contrast with the mighty ware-houses close by, was as blank and silent as an old tombstone. Fort Denison, islanded in the placid waters, was an inert mass of sandstone rock again. Over the way beyond the warehouses, the battlemented walls of Government House rose from the beautiful gardens of the Domain; and on the opposite point the Admiral's roofs and flagstaff, and the terraces from which he could overlook his anchored fleet, nestled in shrubs and trees – each place as quiet as if miles of park encircled it. Further down the bay a dozen vessels, big and little, were going out and coming in, their sails gleaming like white satin against the dark background of Bradley's Head as they rounded northward on their course, their smoke dissolving like a breath in the wide expanse of light and air.

Surveying this scene, Susan Delavel sat on the broken wall at the edge of the street – which at this end was a 'low' thoroughfare to most people of her class – from three o'clock to five. Then she jumped up, briskly walked back to the omnibus stand, and took herself home as she had come.

In the pretty house on Darling Point Mrs Delavel waited tea for her daughter until it was dark, and her husband returned from town – usually a sign of its being time to think about dinner – and he found her in a state of subdued but implacable anxiety about Susan's absence.

'Where can the child be?' she asked him in the same gentle, level tone with which she had made the inquiry fifty times before. 'Hannah does not know; none of the servants have seen her; she is not in the house or garden. Surely she cannot have gone to the camp again, after all I said to her about it?'

'No,' said Susan's father promptly, 'if you made a point of her not going there you may be sure she has not gone.'

'But she knows what my objection was, Richard. Not to the camp, of course, but to a girl of her age and position being out alone. And she is certainly out alone now.'

'Well, my dear, I really don't think she'll come to any harm if she is,' said Richard (he was never called Dicky now). 'She is as capable of taking care of herself as anybody I know.'

'Sue! There never was a human being over five years old less capable. She's incredibly childish – in some things.'

'She's more of a woman than many who are double her age.'

'You say so only to be different from me,' said Mrs Delavel, smiling resignedly.

He shrugged his shoulders and smiled too. 'Yes, yes, of course. The desire to disagree with you is the ruling passion of my life, isn't it?'

'I truly think it is, Richard.'

'I know you do, my dear, and therefore it is no use in the world for me to deny it.'

She was moving gently about the room, inwardly restless, though outwardly serene, and pausing by her husband's chair, she laid her plump hand on his shoulder. 'But surely,' she said, 'you cannot think it is proper and seemly for our daughter to be wandering about the streets alone?'

'About the propriety of it I'm no judge,' he returned. 'All I say is she is a girl who can take care of herself, whereever she may be.'

'Only the other day,' said Mrs Delavel, 'she was accosted by a person – a perfect stranger, whose very name she could not tell me. They had a long talk together, sitting side by side on a bench in the Domain. Mrs Blundell saw them there, and told me of it.'

'Man or woman?' inquired he quickly.

'Woman. And who can tell what sort of woman? If she had been any one of our own class – any one of repute – Mrs Blundell would have known her. And, unfortunately, it is always the least reputable people who attract Sue most. It is there where she shows her incapacity to have the care of herself – shows how young for her years she is.'

'I wonder who it was,' mused the father, gazing thoughtfully at the carpet, 'and why she didn't tell me.'

'She kept it a secret,' said Mrs Delavel. 'I should never have known it but for Mrs Blundell. So now' – with a gentle sigh – 'I cannot tell *what* she mayn't be doing when she is out of my sight.'

'Don't fret yourself, Annie,' said her husband kindly. 'She's as honest as the day; she will never deceive you. There isn't a bit of bad stuff in her – only a little drop of wild blood perhaps – something that makes it harder for her to keep herself corked up than it is for most girls. We must make allowance for temperament.'

'Where should she get wild blood from? Not from me, I am sure.'

'Oh no, my dear, not from you – certainly not. And yet I remember the time when you used to go about alone and think of nothing of it.'

'That was very different,' returned his wife. I only did so when I was in our own land and amongst our own people. I was at home anywhere within miles of the house, and every one I met belonged to us. I was quite safe. No one would have dared to show me the least hint of disrespect.'

Annie might have been a Delavel from the beginning, in her own right, for all the recollection that remained to her of the real character of her bringing up. She believed as firmly as did her daughter and friends that the late Mr Morrison (John and Rhody were to her nonexistent) had represented an 'old family'), and inhabited a 'seat' in the Delavels' county, and that Richard did not marry her without a fierce struggle with his brother Keppel and his cousin Max for her possession. Years and certain circumstances will often affect a woman's memory in that way. A man, somehow, manages to keep a better grasp of facts.

Her husband was accustomed to this theory of her social origin, and never attempted to dispute it.

'If any one had dared to be disrespectful,' he remarked, with a twinkle of his eye, 'he'd have caught it, wouldn't he? No coals and blankets for him! No port wine and flannel petticoats?'

'I know you like to jeer, Richard' – and she looked at him with her soft, resigned expression – 'but I only wish we had our own poor round us now.'

'Our own poor!' he echoed, with an ironical laugh. 'O Annie! can't you find a better wish than that, at this time of day?'

'And that Sue had the same protections for her youth that I had,' she continued, disregarding his, to her, irrelevant question.

'Poor Sue,' he ejaculated, with another and broader laugh. At which his wife looked hurt, shut her lips and seemed determined to say no more.

In middle age our old friend was – what she had been from her youth – the evenest-tempered woman that ever a well-meaning husband found it difficult to get on with; an orderly, conscientious creature, governed by principles that were as correct as her manners and costume, and as firmly established as the everlasting hills. No Delavel of them all had a more profound and ineradicable belief in the authority of the past and the divine right of landed gentry. She had conformed to the customs of a country wherein birth was disestablished like its ancient friend the church, and had no dependent 'lower orders' to take off the loyal hat and drop the humble curtsey to it, as in the good old times; but she had done so as under the direction of an over-ruling providence, and from a high sense of wifely duty. Those customs, and all the fundamental changes in the social state that they implied, had never ceased to be repugnant to what she called her instincts – the inherited bias of her plastic but unimpressionable mind. People and things might change with changing times and circumstances, but she never changed. She was always the same, rooted and grounded in the faith that her forefathers had bequeathed to her; a gentle and complaisant being, soft and smooth, apparently yielding to the touch, but dense, square and solid as a well-dumped wool bale. In person she had become comfortably round and stout, of a dignified presence, upright in figure, and with no furrows in her refined and placid face. Her pearly teeth were white and even as ever, her brown hair glossy and abundant, without a silver thread in it, her neck and arms as creamy fair as her daughter's. A good conscience and a tranquil mind had preserved her youth and beauty in despite of time.

Richard Delavel, on the contrary, had become lean and grey. He had warred with life and bore the scars of his battles – lines on his bronzed forehead and in his hairy cheeks and crows' feet in the corners of his light blue eyes. But it was a more intellectual head than hers that that keen-cut face belonged to, and a finer spirit that looked through the shining paleness of those deep-set eyes. The soul within him was not as a white lamb browsing in green pastures and by still waters, as hers was, but as a caged lion that dreams of desert freedom while vulgar little boys poke it up with sticks. He had the power to rend and tear, but also the power to control this propensity where its exercise would be futile and out of place. A strong man, full of strong human passions, that the discipline of long restraint enabled him to hold in check, but which, when roused, could be seen all aglow behind the bars of his iron will like a furnace fire. He had a great look of 'blood' about him, something that was more impressive than physical beauty, an air of distinction that Annie was beyond measure proud of. She thought there was no man in the world to be compared with her husband – in some things.

When Sue came into the room, just as the gas was being lighted, it was easy to see where the father found an outlet for the pent-up forces of his heart. His eager face lit up at sight of her, as did hers at sight of him. It was evident that they were not child and parent only, but equal comrades, understanding each other thoroughly. She was not a true Delavel, with that mouth and that nose – even her mother reluctantly admitted it, though she was sure that the virtues of the old race would have all appeared under the proper conditions. Nevertheless, Sue was essentially her father's daughter. From him she had inherited that drop of 'wild blood' which individualised them both and set them apart from family and class. All the hereditary influence of the house had failed to destroy it in him, and no amount of similar cultivation could have cultivated it out of her.

'I am very sorry, mother,' she said, hastily drawing off her gloves.

'I am later than I meant to be. I hope you have not waited for your tea.'

'Of course, I waited,' said Mrs Delavel calmly, ringing for the teapot. 'Where have you been, my dear?'

'I have been – out,' replied Sue.

'So I see. But where?'

'Into the town!'

'O Sue, into the town! Alone?'

'Yes, mother.'

'And what for?'

'For nothing – as it happened.'

'Susan,' said Mrs Delavel solemnly, 'tell me exactly what you have been doing.'

'Well, I have been sitting on a wall at Dawes Point watching the ships.'

Annie looked at her daughter, then shut her soft mouth and turned away. 'I am afraid you are not telling me the truth,' she said coldly.

An indignant flush crimsoned the girl's face. She looked appealingly at her father, who, not trusting himself to interfere, got up and left the room. 'Mother, I don't think I ever told you a lie in my life,' she said, with passionate earnestness, 'and it is cruel of you to suspect me of such a thing. I may not tell you *everything*,' she added conscientiously, 'but whatever I do tell you is the truth.'

'Half the truth is as bad as a lie,' said Annie. 'And you have deceived me in that way before today.'

'Never, mother, never!'

'Yes, Sue. You remember that person you met in the Domain, of whom you told me nothing. And don't you call it deceiving me to slip off in this manner when my back is turned for a moment? Why did you not tell me you were going into town?' Mrs Delavel paused for an answer.

'I suppose,' said Sue, after a brief silence, 'because I knew you would be certain to forbid it.'

'Exactly. You knew I would not have allowed you to go out alone – that it was contrary to all rules, and against my express wishes. But, my dear, you ought to have known also that I am ready to do everything in reason to give you pleasure. Had you told me, I would gladly have gone with you. I would have had out the carriage, and taken you properly.'

The girl drummed with her fingers on the top of the piano against which she was standing, and responded but stiffly to her mother's propitiatory manner.

'Now,' said Mrs Delavel, laying a soft hand on her daughter's shoulder, 'promise me, Sue, never to do this again. Give me your word of honour that you will not go out alone any more. I only ask it for your own good, and it is not much to ask – that you should do such a little thing as that to please me – is it?'

Sue lifted her head and looked at her mother with a tragic earnestness that seemed out of all proportion to the requirements of the occasion. 'Mother,' she said solemnly, 'it is *not* a little thing – it is asking more than you have any idea of. I cannot – I *dare* not – promise. If I did I should be bound to keep to it, and I know I couldn't. The very feeling that I was tied would make me long to do it all the more – I couldn't help it. I will try my best – I really will try, mother dear; but don't ask me to promise in so many words.'

Mrs Delavel removed her arm and walked away from piano. 'Very well,' she said, with gentle implacability. 'Then I have only one resource. Henceforth I – or some one – must keep you always in sight.'

'*Mother*!' she burst out wildly, 'are you going to make a prisoner of me – by main force?'

'I am going to make a lady of you, my dear, if possible. Now go and take off your things if you don't want any tea. You had better have a warm bath before dinner – considering where you have been to. And ask Hannah to give you some of my lotion for your face; it is burnt black with the sun.'

Sue, snatching up her hat, flung out of the room, and, I grieve to say, slammed the door behind her.

CHAPTER XXII

●

In The Next Generation

Hannah was that exasperating but cherished treasure, an old servant. She had lived in her master's house since it was first prepared for her mistress, when it consisted of but four slab-walled rooms; herself at that time having been deserted by a bad husband, who had left her to go to the diggings and never been heard of more. She began as maid-of-all-work, her original position in life having been that of a respectable tradesman's daughter, but as the family she served increased in social consequence, so did she; until now she ruled over the large establishment with a not less absolute control than did Mrs Delavel herself. She wore silk dresses on occasion, had her own sitting-room and meals apart, and was a generally privileged person. She had no definite post, and did only what she liked to do, but in point of fact she worked from morning till night to the limit of her strength – which was very considerable for her years – and excellently discharged the duties of housekeeper and ladies' maid combined, with those of cook and butler, governess, nurse and needlewoman frequently thrown in. The foundations of the domestic order rested upon Hannah, without whom it was supposed that the whole structure would collapse, and she rejoiced to know her value and to demonstrate her authority and power – as what old servant does not? She had a particularly arbitrary fashion of dealing with Sue, whom she had nursed from her birth, but the high-spirited girl could bear the rough words of her nurse, which seldom meant much, better than the soft implacability of her mother's speech. She and Hannah were comrades at heart while outwardly at war, and she and her mother tacit adversaries when apparently at peace.

'You be a reasonable girl, now,' said Hannah, as she tied a yellow sash round her young lady's white gown, 'and don't fly out all over the place like a gas explosion because you can't have everything just as you like.' For the old woman knew all that went on in the house as well as if she had been one of the family.

'I don't want to have everything just as I like,' retorted Sue, who was certainly in a temper; 'I only want to *breathe*.'

'Pooh!' said Hannah, 'you are so well off that you don't know what you want. And if you can't bear a little restraint now, how will it be by-and-by when you've got a husband to order you about?'

'I will never have a husband,' said Sue.

'Oh, won't you? We shall see about that. *You* are not cut out for an old maid, whoever else may be.'

'Not one who will order me about – most certainly.'

'As to that, you'll have to take the woman's lot, my dear, like the rest of us. It's Hobson's choice.'

'Never – never!' the girl protested passionately.

'It's impossible,' proceeded Hannah, 'to tell how any man will turn out till you try him. There's meek and mild young fellows, that you'd think butter wouldn't melt in their mouths, become regular fiends when once they get a poor woman into their power. And on the other hand, there's your father – a man with a will and a temper fit to kill anything that crossed him – there's him, that I made sure would be a tyrant, turned out a perfect lamb.'

'*I* don't call him a lamb,' interposed his daughter.

'For a husband he's a lamb,' said Hannah. 'But then he's one by himself. You mustn't expect to find another like him.'

'If I don't,' said Sue vehemently, but with a dancing light in her dark eyes, 'if I get a man who doesn't treat me properly I shall have an easy remedy. I shall pretty quickly leave him.'

'You'll find that easier said than done.'

'Yes, I shall soon put an end to it. No man or woman either shall ever make a slave of me.'

Hannah laughed cheerfully, but shook her old head.

'You don't know much about it *yet*,' she remarked, grimly amused; 'but you'll be wiser some day. Take my advice, my dear, and learn to give in while you're young. It's the very best lesson your mother can set you.'

All this seemed to show a want of comprehension and sympathy on Hannah's part, but its effect – or the effect of something underneath the words – was to send Sue back to the drawing-room in a much better temper than when she left it. She looked almost pretty and quite charming in her simple dress, with her golden brown hair – her mother's hair – in order, waving back from her alert and characteristic face, and hanging in a soft coil at the nape of her long neck. Those hereditary physical qualities for which Mrs Delavel was always so anxiously watching seemed to reveal themselves a little when she had been under Hannah's hands, and the mother's heart rejoiced within her as she looked upon her daughter and saw what an unquestionable lady she was in spite of herself.

Mrs Delavel, for her part, looked simply beautiful in a dress of black lace, with a diamond cross resting on the white cushion of her satin neck; the model of a gentlewoman in the ripe autumn of life – autumn in its early prime before decay begins. And all her surroundings were in harmony with her person. Her drawing-room was delightful – renowned in Sydney society for the perfection of its taste. There were some things in it that might have appeared, not exactly vulgar (which was a word that no one thought of associating with Mrs Delavel for a moment) but just the least trifle significant, to the ideas of a common person. There was a large painting of Dunstanborough Hall hanging in front of the door, and there were photographs of the family standing about on the tables. The Delavel arms were embroidered on a banner screen, and again on a sofa cushion; and the ancestral tree, with all its kings and queens and knights and earls, hung in a recess where it could easily be referred to in the course of conversation. But, after all, Annie had a right to these insignia, and did not unlawfully attach them, as some folks do. And, for the rest, no person of any culture, common or uncommon, could find reasonable fault with the furnishing of her room, which, in colour, in comfort, in artistic arrangement and refined simplicity, was, like herself, a model for the imitation of all who desired to be well bred. The dinner-table over which she presently presided was equally tasteful in its appointments. Silver and china and glass of the best, freshest linen of the finest quality, flowers – but not too many, and no complication of irrelevant ornament – and well-cooked delicate dishes, selected to suit each other with an art that might almost be called scientific. And this simple but dainty order was adhered to under all circumstances, whether the party consisted of one, two, or three; whether the family were alone or entertaining company – in total defiance of hereditary precedent. The unalterable person at the head of affairs administered her system like natural laws, which in a world of change can always be depended on.

Tonight the family dined alone, and afterwards they repaired to the drawing-room together. Mrs Delavel got out some knitting and settled herself in her favourite chair. Sue took a stool at her father's feet, and Mr Delavel, who was accustomed to read aloud to his wife and daughter at this hour – solid works, for the improvement of the latter's mind – brought out the volume that was then in hand. It was Mill's *Political Economy*, and after several weeks of it they had now reached the seventh chapter of the fourth book.

'Now, Sukey,' said Richard, as he drank his coffee and regulated his reading lamp, 'listen well, for this is going to be interesting.'

'Still about labour and capital, father?' asked Sue.

'Not so much about labour and capital this time as about men and women.'

The alert face at his knee kindled at once, but Mrs Delavel looked up anxiously. 'Is that fit for her, Richard?' she asked in a warning tone.

'Perfectly fit,' returned the father promptly. 'I don't know anything fitter.'

With which assurance Mrs Delavel was satisfied, and went on with her knitting.

' "The observations in the preceding chapter had for their principle object to deprecate a false ideal of human society," ' began Richard, in a clear, cultured, sympathetic voice that gave every word its due. And then he described, in the writer's firm and muscular sentences, that time-honoured theory of the relation between rich and poor which was held as a matter of revealed religion by his wife. ' "It should be amiable, moral and sentimental; affectionate tutelage on the one side, respectful and grateful deference on the other. The rich should be *in loco parentis* to the poor, guiding and restraining them like children. Of spontaneous action on their part there should be no need. They should be called on for nothing but to do their day's work, and to be moral and religious. Their morality and religion should be provided for them by their superiors, who should see them properly taught it, and should do all that is necessary to ensure their being – in return for labour and attachment – properly fed, clothed, housed, spiritually edified and innocently amused." '

He looked at Annie, sitting before him in the shaded lamp-light, so placid and handsome; but she was unconscious of his look. At the moment she was absorbed in wondering whether the Miss Delavel mentioned in the last *Court Journal* (her favourite periodical next to the *Church Times*) was old Barbara or one of Roger's daughters.

Richard proceeded to dissect the theory to which she was so much attached, but to the statement of which she had paid so little attention. ' "Like other ideals, it exercises an unconscious influence on the opinions and sentiments of numbers who never consciously guide themselves by any ideal. It has also this in common with other ideals, that it has never been historically realised. It makes its appeal to our imaginative faculties in the character of a restoration of the good times of our forefathers. But no time can be pointed out in which the higher classes of this or any other country performed a part even distantly resembling the one assigned to them in this theory. It is an idealisation, grounded on the conduct and character of here and there an individual. All privileged and powerful classes, as such, have used their power in the interest of their own selfishness." '

Here the reader broke off suddenly, and flashed a quick glance across the hearth rug. 'Are you attending, Annie?'

Mrs Delavel lifted to him a serene and meditative face, and he answered his own question with a smile. 'Not she; she's never heard a word. Are you wondering whether you'll give us puddings or flapjacks for dinner to-morrow, Annie?'

'No, Richard. If you must know, I was thinking of the new flower-beds.'

'I thought so. Well, go on, my dear. Don't let us disturb you.'

And she did go on, unheeding the awful heresies that fell upon her ears. She heard it stated in the most incisive language that the social virtues which she revered above all others belonged 'to a rude and imperfect state of the social union', and had ceased to be efficacious or desirable; that 'the so-called protectors are now the only persons against whom, in any ordinary circumstances, protection is needed'; that 'the working classes have taken their interests into their own hands', to the great increase of well-being and well-doing amongst them; but her ears were like the doors of a house where the master has gone to bed, and the words that asked for admission were not let in. Night after night she listened to these serious readings perfunc-torily, as the Northern Farmer listened to the parson, and 'niver knwa'd whot a meän'd' any more than he did; keeping to her own little circle of orderly interests, outside of which her attention seldom strayed, and feeling comfortably and conscientiously drowsy after her dinner.

But father and daughter were wide awake, with all their mental faculties in exercise. The region of these great world questions, long familiar to the one, was native to them both, and in it their souls expanded like lungs dilated with mountain air. They liked nothing better than to climb over the heads of the petty, every-day trifles that crowded around them, and take a look at the distant landscape.

Presently, in the course of the chapter, mention was made of that 'change which lies in the direct line of the best tendencies of the time' to which the philosopher so especially called attention; and the reader paused again. This was one of the passages which Sue's mother would not allow her to listen to. To Mrs Delavel the very word 'sex' was improper, and the subject, howsoever treated, unfit for feminine ears. So, though the father felt that he held the key to many of the perplexities of social life and longed to furnish his daughter, already grown to womanhood, with the knowledge that would fit her to understand her place and power, the force of habit and the sense of having the other parent at a disadvantage restrained him. Looking across the hearth rug, he saw that his wife was tranquilly asleep, and he shut the book abruptly.

'You are not going to leave off yet?' exclaimed Sue. 'We shall never get through at this rate.'

'If you like,' said he, looking thoughtfully at her vivid face, 'you can take the book and go on with it by yourself. I can pick you up anywhere – I know it all already. Let us go out on the verandah for a bit and see what the night is like.'

CHAPTER XXIII

●

Moonlight Confidences

It was a divine night. From the verandah fell the lovely garden, dropping from terrace to terrace down the slope of sandstone to the sea; and it was full of trees and ferns and flowers that were glorified by the broad moonlight in a wonderful manner. Beyond this foreground of delicately patterned shadow the placid bay spread into the mystical distance, gleaming like quicksilver where it appeared open to the sky, the darkness of its surrounding coast and of the forms of anchored ships and travelling ferry-boats set with a thousand stars, that spilled little trickles of fire upon the water here and there – yellow as topazes against the cool blue-white diamond radiance of the few electric lights. There was, as usual, no sound but the faint throb and swish of the little steamers plying to and fro, the dip of unseen oars, the lap of the tide against the lowest terrace balustrade – all as soft as the whisper of leaves around the house, rustling together in the gentle airs of the scarcely breathing night. Father and daughter stood for several minutes silently inhaling the beauty of the scene to which they were so well accustomed, but which never lost its charm for them; then Mr Delavel said abruptly, 'Who was the lady you met in the Domain, Sukey?'

She had no objection to being questioned by him, and never the slightest hesitation about telling him all he asked. With her two hands clasped round his elbow, and her cheek laid upon his coat sleeve, she replied frankly, 'I haven't the least idea. I was so stupid as never to think of asking her name.'

'What was she like?'

'Old, rather. A widow, I fancy. She had the look of a widow in her face, though her dress was just like other people's – only neater. I don't mean that she looked miserable, but – well, I can't explain it.

It was a lovely face – for an elderly woman. Do you remember that engraving of Sister Dora in Miss Lonsdale's book? Well, something like that.'

'How old was she, do you suppose?'

'I should think forty, at the least.'

'Oh, so old as that? And did this ancient beldame use a stick to support her failing limbs? Or was she trundled in a Bath chair?'

'She walked beautifully, with her head up, like a queen. But no – I don't imagine real queens are anything like so dignified, or have such sweet manners. It was quite striking, the way she carried herself.'

'In spite of her weight of years. White hair, of course?'

'No, only a few threads at the temples. It was dark hair, and just put back, with a knot behind. She did not wear a fringe – it was not curled like everybody else's.'

'No, of course. Frivolities of that sort would have been quite out of place. Do you think she's what your mother would call a lady, Sue?'

'I don't know, father. I don't fancy she's very rich.'

'Would *you* call her a lady?'

'A lady of the first water,' replied Sue with immense energy. 'A lady through and through, from the crown of her head to the sole of her foot. I only wish you could see her, and you would say so, too.'

'I wish I could, I'm sure. Don't you think you might manage to introduce me?'

'I'm afraid I mayn't see her again. I went out this afternoon in the hope of coming across her – I have been three times – and all for nothing. She lives – or did live a week ago – in a dark little street up on the rocks, above Argyle Cut. It looks a respectable house, quite as nice as a house wants to look, but of course it isn't where gentlefolks live.'

'Did you go there to look for her?'

'No; I didn't like to take that liberty. I went to Dawes Point because she said she often sat there. I thought it would be a likely place. Though it is almost in the street, you have no idea how quiet it is; and the wall is broken in such a way as to make a most comfortable seat and footstool. And the view is charming, you can see such a great deal all at once.'

'Yes; but about this mysterious lady. It was in the Domain, I think, that you met her for the first time. By the way, *was* that the first time?'

'Yes; the first and the last, too. Yesterday week.'

'And what made you speak to her? Is it your habit to accost strangers when you are out walking by yourself?'

'As to that,' said Sue impartially, 'I don't see why one shouldn't if one is thrown into contact with them and they look nice people. You know you do it yourself continually – when you haven't mother with you. But in this case I didn't accost the stranger – the stranger accosted me. I was sitting on the grass, with my book, and she came by and said, "My dear, I think the ground is too damp to sit on." That was how it began.'

'You didn't think it was impertinent of her to interfere with you and to call you "my dear"?'

'No. It was her voice and way of saying it. In all my life I think I never heard such a lovely voice – like music. And the way she pronounced her words – you knew her for a lady, just by that, without looking at her. Some people,' the girl continued, 'have a sweet way of talking, because they train themselves to it, but her voice was sweet because she was. It was natural – it was just herself.'

'Yes,' said Mr Delavel thoughtfully, 'I understand the difference. I knew a woman once with that kind of voice – every note of it true – true as she was. Go and get my cigarette case off the study chimney-piece, and a wrap for yourself, and let's go down to the lower bench.' He was growing interested in the conversation and wanted to continue it at a further distance from the drawing-room and chances of interruption.

She whisked into the house, and in two minutes returned with the cigarettes and a shawl over her white dress; and together they descended by steep asphalted paths and flights of steps – between banks of ferns on the one hand and low stone balustrades on the other – to a strip of green lawn about a foot above high water, and some two hundred feet below the verandah floors. At one end of this little plateau were the boat and bathing-houses, screened with flowery lattices and the ever present ferns; in the middle, piercing the balustrade on the sea wall, an iron gate and a flight of landing steps outside; and at the other end a comfortable wooden bench. On this bench Mr Delavel sat down and lit a cigarette, and his daughter sat down beside him. Though it was an August night, the fresh air was mild, and the peacefulness of this little nook, so exquisitely contrived, with only that white bar dividing it, like a ship's bulwark, from the bay, had its effect upon the springs of talk. The sympathetic hearts opened, and delicate confidences that would not have ventured into public places crept out

– drawn by the shining moon and the tender shadows that it cast, by the smell of the salt sea and of unseen violets on the ferny banks around by the sound of the near water lapping against the wall.

'We went from one thing to another,' said Sue, with her head on her father's shoulder. 'It was only the weather at first and the ships; and then somehow we got on to John Stuart Mill and religion and things of that sort.'

'Rather a long jump to start with, wasn't it?'

'Yes, I know. But it happened quite naturally – we seemed to understand each other's thoughts – and she wasn't the woman you would talk society gossip to. Besides, we must have sat together for an hour and a half at least. And then I walked home with her.'

'What did she say about Mill and religion?'

'Oh, I was telling her what we were reading at night. I asked her questions – I wanted to know what she thought about things. And she was so clear – so quiet and strong! She wasn't a bit worried about the mysteries that are always worrying me. She said you got over it like the measles, and that it wasn't of any consequence, one way or another. There was no necessity for us to believe things or to disbelieve them – you did as well without a creed as with one – but only to attend to our own conduct and do the best that was in us to be unselfish and true.'

'An Agnostic evidently, pure and simple. I don't think, you know, it was quite the thing for an old lady of forty to talk in that way to a casual young innocent like you.'

'She did not until I told her that I was used to it – that you and I always talked of everything – that you had brought me up not to be afraid of what people said, and to find out what I felt and thought for myself. And she helped me, really. She gave me at least one new idea.'

'What was that?'

'Well, you know, the trouble with people who are not – not like other people – is the want of a distinct plan to live by. I told her that, and she said, yes, she quite understood; and then she said the simplest plans were best, and that a very good one was to apply the ordinary rule of honest dealing in small things to big ones, and make it our business to pay back to the world what the world did for our advantage – don't you see? – not to take all and give nothing; not to moon about, and be vague and self-indulgent, but to be always reckoning our debt and discharging it. Nothing about money and ministering to the poor and afflicted, you know – at least, not that more than anything else – but in an all-round way to improve life in general, according as our own lives have been improved. I'm afraid I'm bad at explaining,' confessed Sue; 'but *she* was quite clear. And it really is a help to have that idea that one would be dishonest if one lived all for one's self. One cannot permit one's self to be dishonest, you know, though one is ready enough to be selfish and idle. I shall always think of that now, and it will be a great help. It is so hard to be good when you can't see a right down plain reason for it, isn't it?'

Her father threw away the stump of a cigarette and proceeded to light another. 'Yes,' he said, 'yes, my dear, it is. And more than that, it's hard to be good without getting something for it. At least that's what I feel. It is wrong, I know.'

'*Quite* wrong,' said Sue; 'we must be good for the sake of it – to be worthy of ourselves as we have been made. We know quite well, she says, what is the noble life. The knowledge is born in us, or, at any rate, it is not put into us by sermons, and we can live it if we like, for we have the power. She says we *have* the power, and I think she knows it by experience, by the manner of her.'

'It looks simple, Sukey, and it may be easy for women. But I have never been able to be good for the pure sake of being good. I do want something for it. If I could have what I want' – there was a thrill in his voice suggesting the momentary opening of the furnace door behind which the fires of his manhood burned so strongly – 'if I could only have what I want; well, it seems as if it would be easy to be good then.'

'You're quite as good as anybody wants to be,' said Sue.

'I'm a black sheep,' said Mr. Delavel, striking a match and beginning to suck and puff, 'painted to look white. I have a fair and innocent appearance, I know, but if you were to turn the wool over you would see the dark colour at the roots. All is not good that looks good, my dear.'

She laid her cheek upon his sleeve. 'You are just the one person in the world who never pretends to be what he isn't,' she said quietly.

'Not in words, perhaps.'

'Nor in deeds either. If you judge yourself otherwise, I am sure you must judge by a totally wrong standard.'

'Old girl, the heart knoweth its own bitterness. You don't.'

She was silent for a few minutes, not understanding him, and prevented by the delicacy of her nature from asking him what he meant. In the interval they watched the steamers' lights moving over the water, and the thoughts of both wandered from the point at which they ceased to speak of them.

'It's easier for women than for men,' said the father at last; 'women can make sacrifices – they like it; but a man, if he's flesh and blood – a man may make himself *seem* to conform, but he can't make himself do it. "I will be good," he says, and he makes believe to be good, but it's only the outside after all.'

'Well, it's something to make believe so well that nobody knows the difference,' said his daughter. 'And it is the outside that matters, not the inside. We can't help our thoughts.'

'It's not that I haven't tried,' he continued, as if speaking to himself. 'But the worst of it is it's all trying and no succeeding. I don't think women know the hardness of it as men do.'

She did not answer, for she felt that he was not dealing with the general question, but with some particular case – presumably his own – that was in his mind. 'I don't know anything about it, but I don't think you ought to speak for women, father,' was all she said.

'Perhaps not. There are women and women, of course. I was thinking of one – a woman of whom your friend reminds me – who found it no trouble to be good. She would have made a first-class martyr – she'd have been canonised if she'd lived in the old days. She would have gone to the stake smiling, and never faltered at the sight of the faggots and torches.'

'I don't like *that* sort of goodness,' said Sue; 'it isn't human.'

'Oh, she was human enough. It wasn't fanaticism – she didn't pose. It was just the natural straightness of her soul. It had to go the right way like the needle of a compass. You might shake her up all you liked, but back the needle would go – always to the old point.'

'Did I ever see her?' asked Sue, after a long and thoughtful pause.

'No. It was before your time.'

'Was she the lady you spoke of just now – with the voice?'

'Yes.' He puffed at his cigarette for full three mintues. 'When I came out to Australia,' he continued, 'I was alone. I had hardly any money – I got into no end of scrapes – it was the great struggle of my life. And she – she helped me through it. She was only a girl like you – not so old as you – but she was the best, the bravest, the truest woman! If I am worth anything today' – he flung the remains of his cigarette into the sea, and rose impetuously to his feet – 'if I am even good on the outside, it is her doing.'

'And it is long – since?'

'About two-and-twenty years. I have not even seen her for two-and-twenty years. But that makes no difference.'

Sue asked no more questions. She slipped her hand into his, and he drew it through his arm, and held it tightly to his breast, where she could feel his heart beating strongly and quickly; and they stood in that attitude, looking at the calmed waters and the spangled shores and ships, until Mrs Delavel sent a servant to inform them of the lateness of the hour, and to call them in to bed. Then they climbed the dark paths and steps, hand in hand, with obvious reluctance to face the lights and conventionalities of the house.

'Shall we go to the camp tomorrow, Sukey?' said Richard in a quick whisper, as they mounted the verandah.

'Oh *yes*, father!' she replied, in the same low and eager tone.

CHAPTER XXIV

●

The Camp Of Refuge

They broke it to Mrs Delavel at breakfast time that they wanted to have a day at the camp.

'What, *again*?' she sighed, with an aggrieved air.

'My dear girl, I hav'n't been over for more than a week,' said her husband, 'and it's as well to look up the old Bo'sun occasionally.'

'Don't take Sue, then. She is really too old now to run wild at that place. And I want her this afternoon to pay calls with me.'

Sue looked at her father with a quaking heart, but he did not abandon her. 'I want her too,' he said, 'and you must let me have her today. It will do her more good than paying calls, and we shall be quite by ourselves – unless you will come too. Will you?'

Mrs Delavel declined, as she always did. She had no taste for 'that place' nor for the sort of people she heard of as being occasionally entertained there – people of no 'repute' who, by gaining unauthorised access to her unguarded daughter, had given the camp a bad name in her ears. She said, 'No, thank you,' softly and coldly, and without another word went off to her housekeeping.

'I suppose we may take it that I am allowed to go?' queried Sue, when left alone with her father.

'Oh yes,' he replied shortly. 'She washes her hands of us.' He looked gloomy for a moment, and then the light of enterprise returned to his face. 'Shall we take the boat across, Sukey, or shall we go by the steamer? It's a lovely day; we've got it all before us; don't you think the walking would do us good?'

'Yes, father, certainly. We'll walk and trust to the Bo'sun to find something for our lunch.'

'Oh, I forgot about that. Don't you think we ought to take some provisions in case he's short?'

'Perhaps so. We can buy something as we go through the town,' said Sue.

So they did. Mrs Delavel not being there to see them, nor Mrs Blundell either, Richard filled one pocket with chops wrapped in paper, and the other with rolls of bread, and he carried a bag of cakes in his hand and Sue a bag of bananas. Thus loaded they walked down to the Quay and took the boat to Mossman's Bay, walking thence over the hills to their camp in Middle Harbour. In their own boat they could have reached it very quickly, coming straight across from Darling Point, but, with leisure and fine weather, they generally preferred the more circuitous route, for the sake of that walk over the hills.

On this particular August morning, which was fresh and sunny, full of delicate suggestions of spring – a Sydney August morning, which at its best nothing can match, the whole world over – it was a walk calculated to purify and inspire the most sordid soul. The path from the landing-stage climbed at once up the soft and ferny sandstone, for some way overhanging an arm, or rather a finger, of the bay, which penetrated into a green glen to the foot of an unseen but audible waterfall, and then it wound over heathy heights, covered with the rich vegetation of the harbour shores, those marvellous wild flowers that one must see to believe in, and the shrubs and ferns that seem to love the sea breeze. And then it dipped again, more and more steeply, a shadowy woodland path by this time, showing sudden wide views of the intense blue waters, all overspread with the twinkling dazzle of the reflected sun; and at last it dipped down to the shore, a quiet, lonely, sheltered shore, with a narrow strip of white beach on which little wavelets broke and bubbled, faintly echoing the sound and fury of the ocean surf outside. And here was the camp – a cluster of tents, a little garden, a woodstack, a water tub – almost hidden in the trees and bushes until one was close upon it; and the camp looked out upon the great gateway of the Heads, and saw all the ships that passed through, voyaging to the distant world and back again. But the ships did not see it. Nothing was visible to them except a little wisp of bunting fluttering above the tall scrub, or the lantern that the old Bo'sun hauled up in its place at sunset, in case – as had been known to happen – his master should want to find his way there on a dark night.

Here was the shelter that Richard Delavel had contrived for himself – his refuge from fashionable society, from all the boredom of conven-

tional life for which nature had so ill fitted him, from the fret and
chafe of the matrimonial bondage, to which years of conscientious
endurance had not reconciled him. It was his own camp – his own
place – his real home, where he was free. Once Annie had had an
afternoon party there, taking over boat-loads of carpets and furniture,
servants, flowers – all the apparatus of fashion *en fête*; but that was
long ago. The experiment did not answer; the place was too much
out of the way, and the guests did not know what to do without tennis;
and nothing of the sort was repeated. Since then she had been there
with her husband and daughter, and had had a cup of the Bo'sun's
tea; but that, too, was long ago. Carriageless expeditions, and the air
of 'running wild' that the camp suggested, were repugnant to her
taste, and after the third visit she went no more. Then she heard that
people whom she did not admit to the house – people not in their set
– had 'dropped in' upon Richard at Middle Harbour, and been
entertained with whisky and conversation in the tent, and that some
of those persons had been allowed to scrape acquaintance with Sue;
and from that time she was not merely indifferent to the camp – she
hated it. She would have liked a bush fire to burn it up, or land
buyers and builders to oust it. Every time her husband went there she
assumed that he did it on purpose to vex her, and every time he
took their daughter with him she considered herself furnished with a
grievance that justified her in refusing to speak to him till the next
day. Nevertheless the camp remained, and Richard could not give it
up. The more difficult it was to steal away to it, the more did he enjoy
it when he got there; and this, naturally, was the case with Sue also.
They had the feeling of escaped prisoners, secure from pursuit, when
they had put those few miles of water between themselves and Darling
Point.

   The girl was warmly welcomed by the old sailor who represented
the permanent establishment, and who adored her attractive womanhood in the true old sailor fashion. Sometimes they found him drunk,
and sometimes playing the truant, but today he was at his post and
sober, and ready to do anything in the world for his young missus.
The stove in the little shed that served for kitchen was piled with
wood, the kettle was set on for tea, the black pot for potatoes; and he
ladled out flour for new bread with his horny brown hands, and
was most anxious to make a currant cake, which was his proudest
achievement. To all these impulses of hospitality Sue gave the
expected encouragement, and when he was fairly absorbed in his

cooking went off to inspect the premises and generally follow her own devices.

The large tent was in apple-pie order – it always was; and a pleasanter sitting-room it would be hard to find, though it had little enough in it. The floor was raised a few inches from the sand, and boarded and matted; at the back stood a big chest of drawers, at one side a table covered with red cloth, at the other side a narrow iron bedstead (the white bed ready for use under its mosquito curtain), and a few folding and wicker chairs, homely but comfortable, occupied the middle space. This was all the furniture, with the exception of a lamp on the drawers, some pipes and books on the table, and ship-cabin looking pockets on the walls. The whole of the front of the tent was open, and 'gave' upon a mathematical little garden, in which a few homely flowers grew luxuriantly, as if the sea were a hundred miles instead of a half-a-dozen yards away. A little ridge of hard sand, banked against the roots of the wild bushes, protected the neat beds and paths; and just over the ridge was the strip of smooth beach and the bubble-fringed water. There was an unobstructed view of the bay and the Heads, the tumbling ocean outside, the passing ships, from the tent door – from the pillow of that bed within, where on rare occasions Richard slept, or lay awake, with the salt night air pouring over him, and the broad beam of the electric light from the South Head opposite playing at minute intervals upon his face. But there was no view of the great city from this quiet cove – no glimpse of Darling Point. Near the big tent was a little tent for washing and dressing in; another little tent, with another little bed in it, for Sue or a casual guest; a tent with a plank table and benches for meals; a tent for the Bo'sun, and the kitchen shed already mentioned; and these were intersected with paths and a backyard that were as beautifully tidy as the decks of a man-o'-war. It was a delightful place. Sue rambled over it and revelled in it, rummaged drawers, mended chair cushions, set out plates and tea-cups, and wished she could live at the camp always. But, of course, its greatest charm was that it could be lived in so seldom.

Meanwhile her father, who was ordinarily a busy man (shipping business was his business, and he had an office in Pitt Street), took his spell of idling, as a busy man should do. He furnished himself with a pipe and a pillow and went out and lay down upon the beach. His head and shoulders he propped comfortably upon the ridge under the bushes, the cushion keeping the sand from his neck and hair, and his feet he stretched out seawards; and there he lay, with his soft hat pulled over his eyes, and looked at the sparkling ripples from under the brim, and thought his secret thoughts in peace for the best part of two hours.

Sue came to look for him when the chops and potatoes were ready for dishing up. 'Have you been here all the time?' she asked, sitting down beside him; 'are you tired, father?'

'No, my dear,' he answered, 'I've been thinking.'

'What of?' She questioned him as freely as he questioned her, it being quite understood that he need not answer her questions unless he liked.

'Of many things,' he said. 'But at the moment when you disturbed me I was thinking of Mrs Taylor – J. S. Mill's Mrs Taylor.'

'Mrs Taylor seemed to make a great impression on you when we were reading the autobiography,' remarked Sue. 'She was a little too perfect for me.'

'There are perfect women in the world,' he rejoined; 'just one or two. But I wasn't thinking of her perfections. I was thinking of all she was to Mill through those best years of his life – what a different man he might have been without her – how much the world, as well as he, might have lost.'

'I don't believe it would have lost anything,' said Sue. 'It was just his arrogant humility and overweening self-distrust that made him imagine she was the author of his great thoughts.'

'She was twenty-three when they first met, and she was forty-three when he married her. And he loved her then fifty thousand times more than he could have done when she was young.'

Sue was silent. Naturally she could not realise the idea of a great passion in connection with a person of forty-three. Moreover, she had a dim sense that her father was associating some other memory with that of Mrs Taylor, and so he was. It was a great breach of parental etiquette to allow her to feel it, however dimly; but propriety, as we know, was never his strong point. He had a habit of talking to her as if she were a man and a brother rather than his child, and it led to her hearing things occasionally that were not intended for Annie's daughter. At the present time a crowd of old memories, revived by their conversation of the previous night, thronged his mind, and he could not – if he spoke at all – hide them altogether from this close companion. He pushed his hat up from his forehead and gazed at her earnestly. 'Sukey, is your friend tall, with beautiful eyes – very serious and looking straight into you?' he asked.

'Yes, she is tall, and her eyes are like that.'

'And a lovely figure?'

'It might have been lovely once. It's too thin now.'

'I want to see her,' he said, lifting himself into a sitting posture. 'I wish you could find her.'

'Do you think she can be the lady you used to know?'

'Oh, that isn't likely – I don't think it's possible. Still – I wish you knew her name.'

The old Bo'sun came along to tell them their lunch was ready, and they at once became aware that their appetites were in the same condition. With great alacrity they repaired to the dining tent (which consisted of four stout posts and a canvas roof) and fell upon the homely dishes like a couple of schoolboys. It was another of the charms of the camp that it induced the most delicious sensations of hunger and thirst and gratified them in the most delightful manner. None of the daintinesses of the pretty table at Darling Point were to be compared for a moment, in the estimation of these savage-natured creatures, with the Bo'sun's chops and tea, partaken of with the piquant sauce of the free salt air after a walk over the hill from Mossman's Bay. 'A crust of bread and liberty' – that was their motto. Even the Bo'sun's bread, which was of close grain and solid consistency, and which they ate instead of the delicate loaves they had bought of the confectioner in order not to hurt his feelings, was sweet under these circumstances.

In the afternoon they went to sit under the hedge by the seashore again. Richard lit another pipe, and Sue opened a little volume of Sydney Dobell's poems which had been left behind on a previous visit. She read 'Home Wounded' aloud to him, at his request; its meditative spirit seemed to harmonise with the more restful mood that came upon him after his dinner.

My soul lies out like a basking hound.

That pretty line, which the reader paused to dwell on, seemed to describe his condition at this moment, stretched on his back on the sloping sand in the warm late-winter sunshine, away from his business and the petty worries of his life, and alone with the sympathetic companion who never bored or misunderstood him. But under his superficial sensations of peace there were depths of unresting trouble that, like subterranean volcanoes, were beyond the reach of soothing influences. It was only his body that was like a basking hound; his soul did not enjoy a corresponding tranquillity. He listened to his daughter's voice; every word of the poem he heard and understood, but the thread of his secret meditation unwound with the unwinding verse, as the words of a song follow the music – part of it and yet separate; and his thoughts were the same that he had been thinking for two-and-twenty years. And they pained him, as they had pained him all that time, like an unhealed wound.

Suddenly Sue broke off in the middle of a line and uttered a disgusted exclamation.

'O *father*! here's somebody coming!'

They rose to their feet together and looked up the hill side. There, descending the wooded path that led to their retreat, they saw a long light-grey figure, surmounted by a battered wide-awake and a yellow beard.

'It's Mr Rutledge,' said Sue; and the frown passed from her face.

'So it is,' said Richard. 'I'll go and meet him. You get out the whisky and tell the Bo'sun to make some tea. He'll be thirsty after his walk.'

Evidently Mr Rutledge had been to the camp before today, and was a guest to be made welcome.

CHAPTER XXV

•

Noel Rutledge

He was a large fair man, with an amiable fresh face and frank blue eyes; to all appearances quite a commonplace, every-day fellow, whose battle of life would be on the tennis lawn, and his highest satisfaction a champagne supper at his club. But appearances are deceitful, as we know, and they were particularly so in his case. He was as far as possible from being commonplace. Otherwise he would not have been in a position to walk uninvited into the camp, as he did this afternoon.

Once he had been a clergyman, little as he looked like it. But the artificial skin fastened on him by the church when he was young and undeveloped, speedily became too tight. Long before he was thirty he had expanded beyond the limits within which it could bind him without splitting like the shell of a chrysalis in spring. This, by the way, is an experience that must be much more common than appears; the inadequacies of that inelastic integument to the growing soul that inhales the outer air in spite of it must be felt by a great number who carefully conceal them. Noel Rutledge was the unusual man who set principle above self-interest and local expediency. A fine intellectual rectitude, the habit of a mind trained to precision of thought, withstood the degenerating process to which it was subjected, and carried him by the straight road of honour out of the false position into which family influence and youthful inexperience had led him. It was in England that he trod the first steps of this rough and painful road, in ever increasing difficulties with parents and bishops and authorities in general; then he came to Australia with the idea of relieving himself of the most galling of his chains – of possibly reconciling professional and personal scruples in the comparatively untrammelled activities of primitive missionary work. Needless to say, his expectations were not realised. The aggrieved parishioner and the pugnacious churchwarden awaited him here, and proved as much more formidable than those he had left as the Australian mosquito is more formidable than the English midge. He found no primitiveness about the colonial arch-deacon, and no sign of episcopal powers being attenuated in the free air of a young country. Quite the contrary. And so, happily for him, he was soon called upon to define his position once for all; and he did it as a man of such simplicity of mind and integrity of soul was bound to do. He preached a farewell sermon, in which he said exactly what he thought, confessed his shortcomings, explained his scruples, made an open renunciation of the vows that he was unable to keep with honour. It was a very plain sermon, but its effect was that of a fizzing bombshell, scattering all before it. It gave that congregation such a shock as was, perhaps, never suffered by a congregation before or since. It created a scandal in the church that the respectable folks have not got over to this day. And it effected the social ruin of the preacher as thoroughly as the most orthodox could have desired.

Mr Delavel and his daughter happened to hear that sermon. The hubbub that had already arisen over the heresies of Mr Rutledge had drawn Richard's attention to him; since singular independence of character in a man of his profession seemed to imply a black sheep, in whom our hero felt he might possibly find points of likeness and sympathy. He listened one day to a dialogue between his wife and her pet priest – they were heaping upon their nonconforming brother that virulent abuse of which only very good people are capable – and straightway fetched his hat and went forth to pay the first call he had made upon a clergyman for many a long year. The interview lasted for two hours, and laid the foundation of a substantial friendship. Rutledge was upon the eve of his recantation; the historic sermon was preached on the following Sunday. Richard, who had an inkling of its purport beforehand, went to church – also for the first time for many years – on purpose to hear it and to give his moral support to a brave man; and, like the reckless father that he was, took his daughter with him. He did it, not by accident, but of *malice prepense*.

'She has heard all the old platitudes till she's sick of them,' he said to Rutledge, when that conscientious person expressed his hope that he had not unsettled the peace of mind of one so innocent and so young. 'I thought it would do her no harm to have a lesson in common honesty, for a change. She's not a child, and her innocence is in no danger from people like you. That kind of "youngling" virtue which my dear wife is so anxious to cultivate in her I believe, with Milton, to be "but a blank virtue, not a pure" – only useful while we keep her out of the world like a nun in the convent. I want to fit her for the realities of life. I take upon myself to let her see what she's got to face – it's the best plan. Oh, you needn't mind what you say before Sukey – she'll settle or unsettle things for herself without your help.'

Certainly the hearing of the sermon did Sue's religious principles no harm. But it had another effect, which her father had not foreseen. People fall in love in many curious fashions, and she fell in love – not, of course, knowing it at the time – while watching and listening to the preacher. The impression of his upright form, and his calm straightforward countenance as he fronted the restless congregation, and of that direct and simple exposition which revealed a character so much in harmony with her own, was as strong and deep as it was sudden. His voice stirred hitherto unsounded depths within her.

'I have searched for wisdom and knowledge with all the powers of my mind, reverently, sincerely' – thus he apostrophised the unsympathetic faces so variously expressing the fact that he was misunderstood; and he closed his manuscript. 'I don't say that I have found what I have sought. I suspect it takes many more years than I have lived for that; but I have found that no simple, ready-made key unlocks the mysteries with which I am confronted ... I will not say to others, "This key will suffice for you", when it has not sufficed for me. I will not pretend it has sufficed for me when I have found it utterly useless. ... Many things are dark to the human understanding, but one thing is as clear as day – that a man's first duty is to be true to himself and to deal faithfully with his fellow-men; not judging others, nor trusting his own judgment too much, but standing to his colours, whatever they may be – honest before God and before the world, however much mistaken. To be sincere – that is the greatest service he can render to his generation, no matter how frightfully he may seem to blunder.'

His eyes met those of the young girl, and he knew that she, at any rate, understood him, and she saw that he knew it. A subtle warmth diffused itself through both of them – a quivering sense that something important was happening all in a moment. When he paused impressively, having said all he wanted to say, she drew a long, deep breath. 'Father,' she whispered, 'that is a man worth calling a man.'

At the conclusion of the service, when the rustlings and murmurings of the dismayed congregation swelled like a gathering storm around them, father and daughter pushed their way to the vestry to offer their camp of refuge to Mr Rutledge, who seemed in urgent need of shelter. Richard bade him repair thither as soon as he could get free of his immediate parochial entanglements, promising to join him in the afternoon. And the three met a few hours after, and had a long talk by the sea-shore, and Sue made the acquaintance which was a friendship from the first and became love in no time. From writing admirable sermons the ex-priest took to writing for the newspapers, and found his society amongst pressmen and artists, cultured Bohemians like himself; but there was seldom a week that he did not spend an hour or two at the camp with that interesting pair who soon had the largest share of his affections.

He appeared there now, in his secular grey tweeds, a poor man living from hand to mouth, and with no prospects to speak of – the very last person whose acquaintance a prudent father would have encouraged; and the smile that overspread his wholesome face betokened one confident of a welcome! 'I thought I might find you here,' he said to Richard, palpably happy in the realisation of his hope; and then to Sue, who strolled slowly from the tent to meet him, 'Miss Delavel, I hope I don't disturb you too often.'

'No,' she replied, giving him her warm brown hand. 'We don't want everybody at the camp when we come here to enjoy ourselves, father and I – but we never mind you.'

'It's awfully good of you,' he murmured; and he held her hand in his large grasp more tightly than he would have held another person's, and looked extremely grateful.

'Come along and rest yourself, old fellow,' said the cordial host; 'come and have some whisky and soda.'

'Or tea,' said Sue. 'The kettle is on and I'm going to have some.'

She briskly set out cups and saucers, cakes and bread and butter, upon the round table in the large tent, flitting to and fro with her unobtrusive, capable, womanly air, intently watched by the new-comer. She might not be beautiful to the vulgar eye, but every time he saw her she seemed more beautiful to him.

When she went to the kitchen to make the tea, the whisky and soda was discussed, along with other matters that were not paraded in her presence. Richard inquired, in the tone of the man of business, whether pecuniary affairs were improving with his friend, and Mr Rutledge presently revealed an anxiety on their behalf which had not previously seemed to trouble him. To be 'his own man', able to pay his way at the rate of two or three pounds a week, had sufficed for his contentment hitherto; but now it appeared that bed and board and liberty were not enough. Mr Delavel thought it desirable to get on in the world, but could not see that it was worth while to make a fuss about it, as long as a fellow had only himself to think of.

'It will all come in time,' he said. 'Happily, you have no wife and children to complicate the case.'

'No,' said Rutledge slowly; and he mused for a minute or two. Then he looked up, as if moved by a sudden impulse. 'But I'll tell you what I am feeling, Delavel – that I *might have had* – if I could have conducted myself like other people. By taking these erratic courses – by making myself a slave to conscience – I have deprived myself of my wife and children. I am just now feeling it – feeling it very badly.'

He laughed, but not in the whole-hearted manner that was usual with him, and his friend looked at him quickly and keenly. Here was the old, universal trouble; it was easy for one who knew it so well to recognise it.

'I don't see why,' said Richard; 'I don't see why.' After a silence he continued, gravely and firmly, 'If any one has given you up because of what you've done, you are well rid of her. Of all the consequences that can follow from your step that is the very best of them, you may depend on it – the very best thing that could happen to you.'

'She hasn't given me up,' said the ex-parson, 'because I haven't asked her to have me.'

'You think she won't have you?' queried Richard, wondering who in the world that she could be. 'Then don't bother yourself about her. I am morally certain she isn't worth it.'

'Oh yes, she is.'

'Not if she hasn't sympathised with you.'

'But I think she has.'

'Then what have you to fear – beyond having to wait?'

'Well, you see, waiting isn't easy, especially if you can't see an end to it. And the immediate difficulty is the beginning. Socially considered, I am a heathen and an outcast, without a rag of respectability. I am sure I have no faculty for making money, and I haven't a penny of my own. Can I go and ask a woman to marry me under those circumstances?'

'It depends on the sort of woman she is.'

'A girl accustomed to every luxury in life.'

'She mightn't care for luxuries so much as she cares for you. I suppose you know whether she cares for you or not?'

'I haven't the least idea.'

'Does she know that you care for her?'

'No; I am sure she doesn't.'

'Oh, well, if that is the position of affairs, I think you ought to try to put her out of your head for the present – until your prospects open a little. Don't you?'

'One can *try*,' said Mr Rutledge, looking up at his host with his frank smile, 'but perhaps you know that it is not always easy to succeed – in a case of that kind?'

A sudden gleam from the hidden fires flashed into Richard Delavel's pale, bright eyes. 'My God,' he ejaculated, 'if any one should know than I should!' The sudden and almost fierce earnestness with which he spoke gave his visitor a momentary shock, but at the same time assured him that his confidence had not been wasted upon unsympathetic ears.

CHAPTER XXVI

●

Sue Shows Her Defective Education

Sue returned from the kitchen with an earthen teapot smoking in her hands, and stood at the table between the two men. Mr Rutledge, who drooped forward in his basket chair, looking down on the floor, was scrupulously careful not to lift his eyes to look at her; and her father, who watched her movements with his usual interest, had no idea that it was she who had made the difficulties of his friend's position so much more difficult than they need have been.

She poured out the tea, and he rose to take his cup from her hands. Then he looked at her with some intentness, and said abruptly, 'Your father advises me to go to another country, where I am not known, Miss Delavel. What do you think about it?'

She shot a quick, questioning glance at her father. 'Why?' she exclaimed, dissentingly. 'What should you go away for? You have nothing to be ashamed of. I have always thought how fine it was of you to stay in the place and face everything. So has he. You have said so, daddy, a score of times.'

'He has vindicated his courage,' said Richard, 'but he hasn't managed to make a living. His character is against him here. In another place he would have a better chance.'

'What does he want with a character?' demanded Sue vehemently. 'What does he want with a better chance? The newspapers don't concern themselves with his private affairs, and if I could write articles like you,' she added, looking at her guest, '*I* should be satisfied.' She sat down with her cup of tea, and he sat down beside her with his. 'Why are you not satisfied?' she asked him, with evident concern.

'Because I don't get enough money,' he answered.

'*Money*!' the young heiress echoed, with unspeakable contempt. She drained her cup, set it down with a clatter, and threw herself back in her chair. 'Well, I should have thought you were the last man in the world – the very last of all – to care about *that*.'

'One is obliged to care, Miss Delavel, to a certain extent.'

'Oh, to a certain extent, of course. You must have food and clothes, I know; but you earn enough for all your real necessities. I did think,' she added, after a pause – and the ring of disappointment in her tone was unmistakable – 'that there was *one* person in the world who was absolutely free from the taint of that vulgar vice.'

'What vice?' he asked, in no way abashed by her plain speaking, but wholly regardless of the dangerous angle at which he held his teacup.

'The love of money.'

'But I don't love money,' he protested, gravely smiling. 'Don't you think I did something to prove that a year ago?'

'Yes; and that's why I can't bear to think – why I don't like to see you' –

'What?'

'Well, becoming *common*, like other people.'

Richard laughed, but Noel Rutledge's blue eyes fixed themselves with a look of intense interest on her face. 'I am afraid I am common,' he said gently, 'but not quite in the way you think. I don't want money for money's sake – not for any vulgar luxury. The only luxury I would like to see my way to is – a home. I am thirty-two, Miss Delavel, and life is short. I would like to be common in that respect – to have a home of my own, like other men. And to get any chance of that I must do something better than I am doing now.'

'A home is not made with money,' she said severely. Both the men laughed at that statement, and the colour sprang into her face. 'You know what I mean,' she urged. 'You can have all the comfort of – of sympathy – of help and companionship – all you want – as you are.'

'Not quite all,' he returned.

Richard had been quietly smoking and listening. At this point he broke in. 'Don't you see he wants to be married, Sukey? And marriage means tables and chairs, and butcher's meat and bonnets and gowns, and all sorts of things, for the providing of which money – vulgar as it may be – is indispensable. I hope I'm not indiscreet in mentioning it,' he added, seeing a strange look on his guest's face. 'You don't mind her knowing, Rutledge? She's as safe as the bank.' But he saw in a moment that he had blundered.

Rutledge did not answer; he only stared at his boots, and she became suddenly crimson, and then as suddenly pale. There was a brief silence, which she broke by coldly remarking that she was not aware he was engaged.

'Nor am I,' he protested, with ludicrous eagerness. 'Far from it. I told your father it was the dimmest, the vaguest hope – hardly so much as a hope, indeed. It is all in the future, Miss Delavel – and I may never realise my dream' – He broke off in confusion, with a reproachful glance at his host, who, after wildly puzzling for a few minutes over the mystery presented to him, began to see the clue dimly. And Sue rose with a business-like air to clear the tea-table.

'Under those circumstances,' she said, in a tone that was as business-like as her manner, 'I think you are right to go away. Of course, you will have better chances of making money in a place where you have no enemies. I suppose you will leave off writing and take to trade. Trade is the only thing that pays.' Her cold and scornful accents trembled a little. 'You will probably get rich very soon if you give yourself to it. I hope you will – I hope you will realise your dream. Father, you don't forget that Mrs Blundell and her globe trotter are coming to dinner tonight? We must take care not to miss the boat.'

'I think we ought to be going,' her father returned gravely, consulting his watch.

They all rose. Sue carried out the teacups, Mr Rutledge following her with the heavier articles that had to be returned to the kitchen. Conversation was at an end. The Bo'sun was interviewed in the back-yard, final instructions given and farewells exchanged; and in thoughtful silence the three friends left the camp together. With a sense of changed relations, they mounted the hill down which they had so lightly stepped just now, winding round trees and boulders, threading the bracken and flowering bushes, stepping over little fissures and runnels, climbing steep pinches by the aid of each other's hands. The rosy afterglow lingered yet, but the moon was rising over the North Head – they turned round to look at it whenever they reached a point that gave them a clear view. The great cliff was black as blackest night, but the waters of Middle Harbour were softly shining and twinkling, every moment growing whiter and brighter. And the shores were veiled in that exquisite pinky-blue haze which never seems so ethereal and dreamlike anywhere as in Sydney Harbour at the close of a sunny day.

'I should think,' said Sue to her younger companion, as they stood side by side for a moment, drinking in the beauty of the scene, 'I should think you will miss this when you go away.'

'I am not going away,' he returned promptly.

'No! I thought it was a settled plan.' There was a shade of brightness in her voice and manner, and it was not lost upon him.

'Nothing would induce me to go – now,' he repeated steadily, fixing his gaze upon the distant sea.

She said no more, but the healthy colour in her cheeks slowly spread and deepened to a blush that made her for the moment beautiful. Her father came up beside them, and laid his hand on his friend's shoulder. 'Don't decide in a hurry,' he said. 'Second thoughts are best. You might feel it a sort of duty to go on thinking it over – Eh?' The tone was light and easy, but Noel Rutledge thought he discerned a hidden seriousness under it. He turned quickly, and the two honest men looked into one another's eyes. In that look each saw that the other understood him.

'Do you mean at once?' asked the younger, in a low voice. Then he added hurriedly, 'I suppose you are right. It is for you to decide. I must do what you think best.'

'We'll talk of it another time,' said the father. 'Sukey, my dear, if we're to catch that boat and get home in time for dinner we must step out.'

'Then I'll say good night,' said Noel, holding out his hand to Sue. 'I have no engagements, and it's so pleasant out of doors – I think I'll stay here a little while. Good night, Delavel.'

Richard had had time to make up his simply-constituted mind. Half-a-dozen seconds sufficed. 'Good night,' he responded, with impressive cordiality. 'Go back to the camp and make the Bo'sun give you some dinner. Why not? It is a charity to me to find that old scamp something to do to keep him out of mischief. I wish you'd go there whenever you feel inclined, Rutledge, really. The place stands empty, doing nothing, and it would be quiet to write in.'

The recipient of this handsome invitation seemed too much affected to speak. He wrung his friend's hand with excruciating force, lifted his hat, and turned away and left them without another word.

'Well, he might have said "thank you",' remarked Sue, when he was out of earshot.

'He did,' said Richard, with a curious laugh. 'Though I doubt if he's as grateful as he ought to be.'

Father and daughter walked quickly over the hill and down the other side to Mossman's Bay. The immediate fear of losing the boat and not being dressed when the dinner-bell rang temporarily occupied their minds, and it was all they spoke of when they spoke at all. But once safely on board, and quietly sitting on the steamer's upper deck, with the lovely evening around them – the tranquil water, the hazy shores, the delicate moonlight that shone through the yet rosy air – their more personal interests came to the surface of thought again.

'Father,' said Sue, after a long silence, 'do you know who the lady is that Mr Rutledge wants to marry?'

'I think so,' he replied; 'but I'm not sure.'

'Who do you think it is?'

No other father in the world, perhaps, would have answered as he did under the circumstances. But then he was quite different from all proper and prudent people.

'I think,' he said deliberately, as though making a casual remark upon the weather, 'that it's you.'

'Nonsense,' she ejaculated, in a deep shaken voice.

'Well, it *is* nonsense, of course,' he rejoined calmly. 'That is, if it is so. It's only my guess.'

'You must be mistaken,' she murmured, in great agitation.

'Do you think I am mistaken? You ought to know better than I. What do you think yourself, Sukey?' He laid his hand on her knee.

Her only answer was to seize and clasp that hand in both her own, very tightly. But hands can be as expressive as tongues sometimes, and hers seemed to admit that he might possibly be correct in his guess.

'Accidents will happen in the best regulated families,' he said lightly. 'I am sure he hasn't done it of *malice prepense*. He didn't mean to let it out – not at this stage of affairs, at any rate. He knows how preposterous it is quite as well as we do.'

'I don't see what there is *preposterous* about it,' said Sue.

'Don't you? You must be a very dense young person then.'

'I suppose you mean because he is poor, and we are not? The advantage there is altogether on his side,' she said loftily. 'I detest rich people, and especially rich young men; and I hope I shall be an old maid to the end of my life before I sell myself for money.'

'There's a fashion of giving yourself away that's as bad as any selling.'

'Oh!' she said, letting go his hand, 'it's not like you to talk so! I thought *you* were above that worldliness. I'm not saying that I want

Mr Rutledge – far from it – and I don't suppose he wants me, but if
– but if it were so – is he not a man worth all the rich men of our
acquaintance put together?'

When Richard heard that, he knew where he was. 'Yes, if you think
so,' he said, drawing her to him. 'At first I thought he was not; I
wanted him to go straight off, before he could make trouble; but
afterwards I reflected that he was good enough to be let alone. I
thought I might leave him to his own guidance – and yours. But be
careful, my girl. You little know what a terrible business it is if you
mismanage it. Don't be in a hurry, whatever you do.'

She took his hand again and leaned to him as closely as the publicity
of their position allowed, her heart gushing over with love and gratitude. 'I think it's you who are in a hurry,' she said with tender banter.
'It is just an idea of your own invention and nothing more.'

'Perhaps so – very likely. I shall be quite content to find myself
mistaken. But, anyhow, I am not going to interfere with you – further
than to advise you, to the best of my ability, out of the fulness of an
experience that has been more considerable than you think. You'll let
me advise you, won't you? You won't be afraid to tell me things?'

'Afraid!' she echoed, crushing his hand against her breast. 'You
have never given me a moment's cause to be afraid of you in the
whole course of my life. And now less than ever.' After a pause she
added, as a testimony to the truth of her statement, 'I do love him,
father, I don't want to hide it from you.'

'Dear old girl,' he replied, 'it is only what I expected of you – that
you should make such a choice. But it's the beginning of troubles,
Sukey – it's the end of all our peace and quietness! What do you
suppose your mother will say?'

'Oh, poor mother!' sighed Sue.

Poor mother, indeed! She met them when they entered the drawing-room with her sweetest smiles, little dreaming of that last and
greatest treachery for which the hated camp was responsible. All the
coldness of the morning had disappeared from her face and manner.
Her guests had just arrived – Mrs Blundell, who was the daughter of
a judge and the grand-daughter of a baronet, and herself of the very
cream of Sydney society, and her latest globe trotter, Lord Boyton.
The latter was a stout youth with a chubby face and an eye-glass.

'My husband,' murmured Annie, with pride in her aristocratic
spouse, who looked like a prince in his dress clothes; 'my daughter
Susan – named after her grandmother, Lady Susan Delavel. Mrs

Blundell tells me Lord Boyton knows our family well, Richard; he met Katherine in London only two months ago.'

'Charming woman, Mrs Delavel-Pole,' interposed Lord Boyton affably, dropping his eye-glass after a brief stare at Sue. 'She was taking her niece out – one of the Dunstanborough girls. Charming little thing – I danced with her twice at the Lumley-Cavendishes. But not so charming as her cousin' – bowing to the young lady before him. He had all the self-confidence proper to a lord, and thought he knew how to please Australians.

'That would be Roger's second girl, Nancy,' said his hostess, softly radiant. 'Beatrice, the eldest, was married last year to the Duke of Cork's nephew, and Ethelberta can hardly be out of the schoolroom.'

Mrs Delavel was in her element now, rustling about in black velvet and diamonds, conscious of a perfect dinner in process and of a perfect house, and with what she called congenial people around her, to whom she could converse of 'our family' and the affairs of the great world. Mrs Blundell, who was a society woman to the tips of her toes and fingers, was always entertaining, and liked nothing better than a battle of words with 'that queer man,' as she styled her host – who, for his part, could be brilliant in his queer way with very little trouble. Lord Boyton prattled freely, evidently laying himself out to be agreeable: and it would have been a most successful evening if Sue had only behaved becomingly. But she was silent; she was indifferent; she was rude; she snubbed the illustrious globe trotter with all her might. Never before had Mrs Delavel been so disappointed in her child. 'What *am* I to do with her?' she cried in despair, when alone with her husband after her guests had gone. 'Mrs Blundell was sure he was struck with her, and you saw how pleasant he made himself even when she yawned in his face. When I wanted her to show him the garden and the moonlight on the bay, how eager he was to go. He has fully twenty thousand a year, and could give her her proper place in England – the position to which her birth entitles her. And such a nice fellow with it all! I don't know when I have met a man who charmed me more.'

'Don't call him a man,' said Richard, as he calmly wound his watch. 'An unlicked cub like that – an impertinent young ass, with no more brains than a tom cat.'

'Oh, of course!' ejaculated Annie, suddenly freezing into her displeased reserve, 'I might have known you would set yourself against it. I might have been sure you would frustrate me, if you could.'

CHAPTER XXVII

•

An Old Story

The next day was Sunday. At twenty minutes to eleven Mrs Delavel's pretty landau and satin-coated horses came round to the door at the back of the house, which was necessarily the front entrance, and she and her daughter stepped into it and were driven to church together. This was a regular custom, which had only been deliberately broken on the one occasion when Richard had taken Sue to hear Noel Rutledge's recantation; and not a word of protest was ever raised against it. Enough had been said and done, when positive action was demanded, to exonerate both husband and child from the hypocrisy of feigning assent to opinions and practises wherefrom their consciences dissented. Annie knew, as well as they did, that they were very bad church people at heart. But the main thing, to her, was to ignore this family secret as far as possible, and to preserve the outward semblance of conformity; and as a matter of good taste and dutifulness her wishes were considered as far as possible. She had an idea that by taking Sue to church she was counteracting the influence of the father's heretical teaching, but nothing did so much to strengthen it as the discourses she was there obliged to listen to.

'If it were not for the sermons!' she sighed, when, having taken off her best bonnet, she went into the garden with her father for a chat before luncheon. 'Why aren't sermons suppressed by Act of Parliament?'

'Oh, they'll suppress themselves,' said Richard easily, 'in time.'

'They were all very well in the old days,' continued Sue, whose nerves had been irritated, 'when the priests had all the learning and the congregations none. But now the position is reversed – the priests seem the only class that never learns anything. And, oh, the nonsense we have to listen to – we who do know better! I am like Mrs Lee in

"Democracy", who didn't go to church because it gave her unchristian feelings. Nothing ever makes me feel so wicked as one of Mr Pilkington's sermons. We had Joshua and the sun this morning – after having Jonah and the whale last Sunday.'

'Oh, well,' said Richard placidly, 'it pleases him and it don't hurt us.'

'It doesn't hurt *you*, because you never go to hear him: that's one of the advantages of being a man and independent,' sighed Sue enviously.

In the afternoon the pair went out for a walk, according to their vulgar Sunday custom, undeterred by the fact that Tom, Dick and Harry did the same, while Darling Pointers, as a rule, didn't. Annie never went out on Sunday except in her carriage to church, and had no idea what devices were followed by her husband and daughter when they had shut the front gate behind them. They rode in penny trams, and threepenny 'buses and steamboats; they bought bananas and ate them; they sat in public places with artisans and shopkeepers; in short, they did everything that Delavels would have been expected not to do. It was their way of counteracting the ill effects of the morning sermon.

'Where shall we go today?' asked Sue, as they set forth.

'To Dawes Point,' said her father promptly. 'I want to look at the place where you sat the other day to wait for your friend.'

'All right,' said Sue. 'And perhaps we may see her.'

Accordingly they took the 'bus to town and walked to the north end of George Street, which was a little less attractive on Sundays than on week days when the shops were open. The wall that was so quiet when the streets and wharfs were busy they found in the occupation of miscellaneous idlers, the toiling fathers of the quarter, enjoying their peaceful pipe and yarn on the day of rest. Under the shade of the Moreton Bay fig-trees in the old enclosure near were boys playing marbles, and more boys were disporting themselves on the grassy promontory below.

'She will not be here today,' said Sue, as they paused for a moment to survey the seaward prospect.

'Come on, then,' said her father, 'and show me the house.'

She took him in and out and up and down the quaint rockhewn streets of that picturesque part of old Sydney until they came to a sort of cul-de-sac – a quiet corner, all in shade, where the houses had an air not only of present respectability but of bygone dignity, as different from the modern elegance of the fashionable suburbs as from the sailor's boarding-house aspect which generally characterised their own. Plain and unpretentious as they were, they evidently dated from historic times, and the building of them had cost money. And while neighbouring dwellings exhaled their internal poverty and shabbiness, these had a self-respecting neatness and cleanliness in their windows and door handles and bits of front garden that refreshed the eye of the spectator, not looking for such charms in such a quarter.

'This is it,' said Sue, nodding towards one of them, 'but I don't think it is her home. I think she was just lodging here, and I am afraid she is gone.'

The man's quick glance roved over the sombre brick front and the plain sash windows, searching for a sign of life. But there was none. They passed closely to and fro for some minutes, until they found themselves attracting attention from other windows, and then they continued their walk in disappointed silence. There was no way out of that shadowy end of street save by a steep and narrow flight of rock-hewn stairs descending to the wharf-side lanes, and down these they went, and back to the Quay, where the great liners lay side by side, and where the bay steamers were going out and coming in the whole day long.

'Shall we go to Watson's Bay and sit on the cliff?' said Sue, who loved nothing better than to look at the open sea.

But her father did not respond to the suggestion. He was attracted by the neighbourhood where the mysterious woman dwelt, and was reluctant to leave it.

'Suppose we go up the Cut to the Observatory Hill,' he suggested. 'We have not been there for ages.'

'All right,' said the cheerful Sue. And thither they bent their steps. Up the Cut – that curious tunnel in the natural rock, with houses above and below – and then up and up the zig-zag road in the flower-curtained rock face, they climbed to the Observatory Hill; and there they sat on a bench to rest and talk and to look at the ever-present harbour view. There were people here too – plenty of them; young men sprawling on the grass, young women sitting beside them, mothers with children, old creatures sunning themselves on the warm benches. But none amongst that Sunday crowd had the appearance of gentlefolks save themselves.

'What an idiot I was,' said Sue, 'not to tell her I wanted to see her again. But I made sure she would guess, and would look out for me.'

'You don't expect a venerable lady of forty to concern herself about a chit like you? I expect she never gave you another thought,' said her father, taking out his pipe.

'Perhaps not,' sighed Sue. And thus they dismissed the subject and turned to others that were of more immediate interest. No reference was made to yesterday's events, but the conversation on the steamboat had strengthened the tender bond of comprehending sympathy between them, and all topics had become more fruitful because of it. They drifted into talk of Richard's early days in Sydney – days that were much in his mind just now, but which, in deference to Annie's feelings, were seldom alluded to. He tried to point out the crowded quarter of the city where he had lodged as a young man, and had had the strange experience of hunger and broken boots and empty pockets, and a flinty-hearted landlady who had taken no account of his position in life.

'There was one night,' said he, 'that I came home in a state of despair, not having found any employment, and without so much as a copper to bless myself with. It had been a pouring day, and I was wet to the skin and had a bad attack of bronchitis coming on, and that old harridan met me at the door and told me she had let my room to another tenant. I was a fortnight in arrears for rent, and so she turned me out without a moment's warning. Nobody would believe such a thing could have happened in this hospitable country, but it did. I suppose there are creatures like that in all countries. I paid her her money about two months afterwards, and I think she was never more surprised in her life.'

'Wretch!' cried Sue, who heard this story for the first time; and the tears sprang into her eyes. 'Poor darling! and what did you do? Oh, how I wish I had been there!'

Her father laughed at this aspiration. 'You were in spirit land at that period, my dear. However, you had a substitute in the flesh, and she did for me all that you would have done. I went to the house of a neighbour, a young man whom I had been able to do a little service for – well he fell off a ship's gangway into deep water, and I fished him out – it was nothing, for I could swim and he couldn't – but I knew he was grateful, and thought he would let me sleep in his outhouse, as it was such a wet night' —

'Oh, poor, poor darling!' cried Sue again, her heart wrung by the recital of this tragic bit of history; and she took his hand and vehemently kissed it.

'However, he was not there, he had left to go to a distant goldfield; but his mother and sister were. And they knew me, and took me in, and made me a bed in a little back room, and gave me some hot tea, and dried my clothes – did everything they could for me, as if I had been their own.'

'Bless them! I hope you were able to do something for them after you got rich, father. Were they poor people?'

'Poor, but genteel. The mother was a clergyman's daughter, and her husband had been an Imperial army officer – came out in command of troops in the early days; but he was dead, and the son was the head of the house. There was a little income from street property, but they lived in a small way.'

'And was it the mother or the daughter who was a substitute for me?'

'The daughter. The mother was a cripple, tied to her armchair. Poor thing, she died not long after. It was the daughter – Constance.'

'Constance what?'

'Constance Bethune.' He roused himself from his lounging posture, and his pale eyes gleamed at the recollection of her. 'My attack of bronchitis got very bad – it ran into inflammation of the lungs. I was as near going off the hooks as ever I was in my life, and she nursed me through it all. She was an angel – she was better than that – she was the best, the truest woman – but I can't describe her,' he concluded abruptly, drawing violently at his pipe.

She was silent for a while, putting two and two together; then she asked how long he had stayed with the Bethunes. 'I stayed with them until – until your mother came out to me,' he replied, with a sudden heaviness of manner. 'Soon after I got well we heard that young Bethune had died at the diggings, and then I tried to be a son and brother to them in his place. Thanks to their goodness, it was a turning-point in my luck – I mean as regarded my worldly circumstances; I got a situation in a shipping-office, and my affairs began to go well. I became their boarder – and I think I was able to make my self a comfort to them. Constance and I read German of an evening' —

He broke off again, and smoked hard for a few minutes.

'And then,' said Sue gravely, 'mother came – *we* came.'

'Yes. Your grandfather Morrison died and left your mother a little money, and I was in a position to give her a home, though it was but a poor one at first. So she came out to me. And you were not very long in following her.' After another pause he said, 'It was while she was on her way out that Mrs Bethune died.'

'While you were still in the house?'

'Yes.'

'And Miss Bethune was left alone?'

'Quite alone. She had no one in the world except an old seafaring uncle – and me.'

'And what became of her?' asked Sue with great seriousness.

'I don't know. I wish I did.'

'When did you see her last?'

'Twenty-two years ago.'

'Then she is the lady you spoke of the other night?'

He nodded. And then he began to feel that it was time to change the subject, and, giving himself a great shake, remarked cheerfully that there seemed to be as many yachts out as if it were a summer Sunday.

She remained silent. She did not follow this lead. She looked with unseeing eyes at the yachts and the ferry-boats, weaving their spider's web tracks over the sheet of silver water, and thought of Constance Bethune with profound interest and anxiety – trying to picture the life she had shared with her father in those young days of his before she, Sue, was born – dimly conscious that in the sketch he had given of it a great deal had been left out. Suddenly she lifted her eyes, and exclaimed, 'Why, there she is!'

'Where?' cried her father, springing upright, as alert as she, and knocking the half-consumed tobacco from his pipe. He followed the direction of her gaze, and saw an approaching figure – a tall and rather stately woman, with a grave, thoughtful, finely chiselled face – sauntering slowly over the grass, deep in reverie, apparently as unconscious of her human surroundings as a sleep walker. Her dress was very plain, neither dowdy nor fashionable, neither rich nor shabby, and her whole air and carriage was dignified and well-bred. She looked about forty, but was far from looking old. 'It is,' said Richard Delavel, in a deep, thrilling voice. 'My God, it is! After all – after all!'

'What?' whispered Sue, with a pang of instinctive jealousy and fear. 'Not Constance Bethune?'

The lady drew near, saw them, stopped short, and made a gesture as if she would have hastily turned back. But she, too, was fascinated, apparently, looking at the man who looked with such fiercely eager eyes at her. She grew white to the lips, which parted and quivered, powerless to utter a sound; she faltered and failed in every limb, as a rabbit in the presence of a boa-constrictor. The spell of shocked silence lasted for a moment, and then Richard sprang towards her with both hands outstretched.

'Constance!' he cried, in a tone that pierced his daughter's heart. 'Constance! Is it you indeed?' It was all he said in words, but every name that love could give her sounded in his voice.

Neither of them remembered the existence of the girl who watched their meeting with such sombre eyes. She got up from her seat and walked quietly down the hill, leaving them alone together.

CHAPTER XXVIII

———— • ————

A Sequel To The Story

It was not such a very public place as it had been an hour ago. By this time the bulk of its Sunday loungers had gone home to their early teas and to put their children to bed. On the slope where these lovers stood, re-united for a moment after a separation of two-and-twenty years, only a couple of harmless old men and a small boy remained to spy upon them. But the Observatory Hill might have been a desert island for all they thought about it.

Richard Delavel held his Constance's hand in a grip that was almost cruel, and devoured her delicate face with his eyes as a beggar in the agonies of starvation devours his unexpected crust. He was off his head with excitement.

'Where have you been? What have you been doing? Why did you leave me without a message – without a clue? I went to look for you, to tell you I was going to keep my word, and found you gone – not a trace of you left! Not even so much as a note to tell me you were safe, not dead, or kidnapped, or starving in a gutter somewhere. I was simply frantic about you. I hunted for you all through the city, I advertised, I should have set off on a search through the world, and gone on searching to this day, if I had not been tied like a chained convict – I would never have rested till I found you. As it is, I have had no rest – I have been looking for you all the time – fretting to think what might have become of you, wandering alone about the world. Why did you do it, Constance? Couldn't you trust me?'

'I couldn't,' the lady replied; 'nor myself, either. I saw that something must be done, or you would never have had a chance, Dick. And I should have given way, too – I could not have borne it.'

'Oh, *you*!' he rejoined, with a touch of bitterness. 'You never gave way – you were always safe – you might have helped me, as you were used to helping me, without any risk to your own immaculate goodness.'

She smiled faintly. She had recovered her self-possession, though he had not. 'You talk as if you were young still,' she said, 'but you must know better now. Anyway, I did for the best. It seemed the only possible course to take for everybody's sake. And I thought you would soon get over it, Dick.'

'I am sure you never thought that, Constance.'

'I hoped so.'

'You had no business to hope so, considering what we were to each other. Do you remember those old days when I was ill, when you nursed me, and read to me, and taught me to be a better man than I had ever had a chance of being – and how you helped me when I began to work and make my way? Do you remember that night, when your mother died, and we were left alone? Do you remember. . . .'

'Oh, hush!' she interrupted. 'I don't want to remember. All that should be buried and forgotten now.'

'I have not forgotten it,' he said, looking down at her with eyes full of the passion of that old time; 'and you knew I never should – you knew in your heart that I should not get over it. It was unjust to me to think it or hope it – if you really did – knowing what you knew. Oh, my dear, it was cruel of you! It was cruel and cold-blooded, and barbarous and unnecessary – yes, unnecessary, because I should have kept my word. I have been nursing this scolding for you for over twenty years, and now I find you at last I must ease my mind of it. It was cruel to go off like that, without a word, without even a note, as if I were a wild beast you were escaping from.'

'Anyway, it was right,' she replied. 'I see now, even better than I saw then, how right it was. And if I had never come back again,' she added with a quivering smile, 'it would have been more right still.'

'No, no,' he protested, with quick alarm and eagerness. 'You must not think that – you must not judge me as I am now – upset by this surprise so that I don't know what I am talking about. I'll say no more about old times, Constance – forgive me, and don't imagine it necessary to run away again to escape from annoyance. I should not have let my tongue run so freely, but the habit of the old days is still strong – I never could have reserves with you. But I'll try – don't be afraid. Tell me about yourself. Sit down on this seat and rest – rest yourself beside me. And tell me what sort of life you have been able to make of it. What did you do when you went away? Where did you go?'

'I went to England,' she said, seating herself where Sue had been sitting. 'My uncle's ship was in port when I made up my mind, and I asked him to give me a passage. He refused at first, because of having no accommodation for women, but afterwards he consented, and he made me very comfortable, and he enjoyed having me with him.'

'I should think so! And what did you do when you got to England?'

'I stayed with him a little while, and then I got a situation as governess.'

'Governess! good Lord! To think of you drudging at that work – a slave to another woman, and to a pack of ill-conditioned brats!'

'It was not slavery. They were pleasant little brats, and their mother was very kind to me.'

'I am sure it must have been insufferable. And how long did it last?'

'About two years.'

'And what then?'

'Then I went into a London hospital and became a nurse.'

'Ugh! What possessed you to do that?'

'Well, I wanted some kind of definite work, and I wanted to be my own mistress. And I like nursing; I think I have a talent for it.'

'I know you have – a heaven-born gift such as I should think few women can boast of. But it is one thing nursing your own – nursing those you love – and living morning, noon, and night in an atmosphere of blood and horror, as you must have done in a London hospital.'

'I got used to that, and I think I made a very successful nurse. The poor creatures used to brighten up when they saw me coming. They had great faith in me, and the doctors trusted me almost as if I were one of themselves. I used to wear a white cap and a big white apron with a bib.'

'You must have looked beautiful in them – I can imagine you; and I can imagine the patients brightening up at sight of you, even in the agonies of death. Well' – with a deep respiration – 'how long did that last?'

'Seven years and three-quarters.'

'And what did you do then?'

'Then I married.'

'*What!*' He nearly jumped from his seat. If she had confessed to having murdered somebody he could not have been more astounded and shocked – more tragically disappointed in her. Like a man (who must have a mate for himself, of one sort or another), it was the last thing he expected to hear of in connection with the woman who had loved him, and who had been to him the incarnation of all that was true and faithful.

'I married,' she repeated quietly, ignoring his concern. 'It was one of the doctors at the hospital – Dr James Ellicott. He had a large practice in the East End afterwards. When we married he would not let me nurse any more, professionally, but still I did a great deal amongst his private patients.'

'And you were awfully in love with him, I suppose?'

'He was a good husband,' she replied gently.

'Was? Is he in the past?'

'Yes. He died several years ago.'

'Thank God!' Richard ejaculated fervently – almost savagely. After a pause he continued, in a calmer tone, 'I'm sure he never cared a straw for you, nor you for him. Wasn't it so, Constance? I know by your voice.'

'Oh no, it wasn't so, Dick. We did care – we had a true affection for each other. We were as happy together as – as nine-tenths of married people are.'

'Just so,' he said, with a note of satisfaction, almost of exultation, in his voice; 'I know exactly how happy that was.' And he began to feel as if he might possibly in time forgive her for marrying Dr James Ellicott. 'And after your husband's death, what then, Constance? Did he leave you well off?'

'Not very. But there was enough. My wants were never many or extravagant. I left London and went to live at Lausanne with the children.'

'The children!' he echoed, again in that shocked and reproachful voice. It was horrible to think of another man having had possession of her (who could never have belonged to him), but the thought of children – hers and his – was quite intolerable. 'How many?' he inquired gloomily.

'Two,' whispered Mrs Ellicott, with averted face.

He looked round as if he expected to see them appear on the Observatory Hill. 'Where are they!' he demanded.

'They are dead,' she answered, with all the anguish of the bereaved mother in her quiet voice.

He gazed at her in silence for a minute or two after she told him this; then he took her hand and folded it in both his own, drawing her as if he would have drawn her into his arms. 'My poor little woman,' he murmured – the words full of tender compassion that was like music to her ears and strong wine to her blood – 'what troubles you have had while you have been away from me! And how different it might have been – O Constance! how different it *might* have been! How I would have taken care of you and cherished you. . . .'

'Don't! don't!' she protested, freeing her imprisoned hand. 'Don't make me feel how mistaken – how wicked it was of me to come back. I thought I would like to see if you were alive and well – when I had no longer any ties to bind me to one place – and I thought I had found you living bravely and honourably, living calmly and happily, in your home – all those old feelings dead and done with. . . .'

'Dead and done with!' he echoed, interrupting in his turn. 'They'll be dead and done with when I am, and not before.'

'We are old people now, Dick,' she went on, touching his sleeve with her hand, which he immediately seized again. 'We have lived the best part of our lives since then' —

'Oh no, Constance, not the best part, by any means.'

'The largest part – the part that should have been useful and fruitful – that should, when it was over, have left us wise and strong, capable of resisting the temptations that were too much for us when we were young. And I know,' she added in a tone of conviction, 'that if I had not come back it would have been all right. You were happy as you were – until this afternoon.'

'Who told you that I was happy as I was?'

'I saw it for myself. I have been here some months, and I have seen you several times.'

'You can't see through my clothes and my flesh. You can't see through brick walls.'

'No. But I have talked with your daughter.'

'Did you know she was my daughter when you talked to her?'

'Yes. I had seen you together.' Mrs Ellicott looked at him with a tender encouragement in her womanly eyes. 'Only to have a child like that should make you happy,' she said. 'She can be nothing but an unqualified comfort and resource to you.'

'She is – she is,' he replied, with a momentary lightening of his passionate melancholy. 'She's the best child that ever was born. I don't know what I should have done without her.' Then the cloud fell again, and his head drooped towards his knees, where he rested his forehead on his hands, that still grasped hers. 'But oh!' he broke out, with a sort of groan, 'it has been such a life of emptiness! It has been such a desert-waste of loneliness – that no child could fill! A man wants his mate, Constance. I can't help it that I'm made of flesh and blood, and not of ethereal spirit – I can't help it that I'm not a saint, like you. I've tried all I know to make the best of things – to suck nourishment out of the stone that's been my substitute for meat – but I've been hungry all the time when I haven't felt dying of starvation. It's my nature – I'm made so – I can't change myself into another man. Another man might have forgotten that he had once found his perfect counterpart – found the fulfilment of all his dreams, of all the longings of his body and soul – and lost her as soon as he had found her; but I could never forget it. Another man might, when his yule was cold, have warmed himself at little fires, as Tennyson says; but not I – not I. There has not been a day, nor a night, that I haven't cried for you in my heart, as a baby cries for its mother. And now that you have come back – even now when I can see you and hold you – even now, after two-and-twenty years, I must not ask, I must not hope for, one moment's real consolation! O my God' – sobbing heavily – 'how am I going to bear it?'

Sue waited a long time at the gate below the hill, and the thoughts that kept her company were exceedingly bitter. For the first time in her life bitter thoughts were associated with that beloved father who, she had fondly imagined, could do no wrong. There had been no mistaking the nature of his emotion when he recognised his friend, and the fact of having dimly guessed a sentimental secret in connection with the long ago past did not lessen the shock to his daughter of seeing that the illicit passion which only youth and the peculiar circumstances could excuse, had survived through two-and-twenty decorous years, and now blazed as high as ever. He had not even tried to disguise it. He had considered nothing but his own lawless feelings, just like any common man – like the agnostic of ecclesiastical tradition, who, having no fear of eternal punishment, lives for his selfish pleasures only, and counts duty and honour as nothing. Oh! how had the mighty fallen! and what a tragedy that fall was! With all the severity of young and untried virtue, Susan Delavel judged her father, and felt that she could never again look up to him as she had done. And under the bitterness of this high-minded disappointment there was the bitterness of personal jealousy, alive and full-grown all in a moment where such a feeling had never before existed. The world seemed to have suddenly clouded over. Everything was changed by this dire catastrophe.

CHAPTER XXIX

•

Love and Duty

When the culprit appeared at last he was alone. She did not look at him, nor he at her. 'Come along,' he said, with a sort of hard sternness that sufficiently indicated his state of mind, as he sharply opened and shut his watch; and he hurried her down the zig-zag road back to the familiar streets, and hailed the first hansom he came across. 'Look sharp,' he shouted to the driver, conscious of offending against the domestic regulations, which was an urgent matter, even in the face of the higher tragedies of life. And then he sat and stared at the side-walks, half turned from his daughter, and spoke not a word till they arrived at Darling Point.

In the hall Mrs Delavel met them, with the face of an avenging angel, mild but terrible. It was three-quarters of an hour past the time for that cold meat tea which was the Sunday substitute for the week-day dinner. 'How are the servants to get to church?' she demanded with sad severity. 'How can we expect them to be punctual with their duties if we set them such an example? How am I to keep any proper order in the house. . . .'

Her husband put out his hand, and quietly, without touching her, swept her from his path. He was not in a condition to bear this sort of thing just now. He made straight for the library, which opened off the upper hall, and entering that room, which was peculiarly his own, sharply shut the door behind him. He was a complaisant husband as a rule, but there were times when even Annie understood that he was dangerous to meddle with, and she saw that this was one of them. But, as usual at such times, his demonstration of independence and of indifference to her possible sufferings was very galling to her feelings. She felt that her paramount rights as a wife were disregarded, which to her, as to a great number of married ladies, was the deadliest of deadly injuries. And, therefore, a slow resentment and indignation hardened her soft mouth and eyes, and hardened her heart against him. She followed his vanishing figure with a still, set look, that those who knew her understood to mean a long continuance of grievous, if silent, displeasure, her lips compressed, her nostrils dilated, offended womanhood manifested in every line of face and form.

As the shutting – I might say, banging – of the library door echoed through the house, her daughter's arms were thrown round her neck, and she was kissed with warmth on her comely cheek.

'Mother, darling,' said Sue, with unwonted tenderness, 'I am so sorry! We went farther than usual – we forgot about the time. We made as much haste as we could when we found how late it was. I will leave my bonnet here' – putting it and her gloves on the hall table – 'and we can sit down at once.'

Annie returned the rare embrace perfunctorily, with a stiff and bitter smile. 'I am glad only *you* are here to see how your father treats me, and not the servants,' said she, with a vibrating voice; 'I think he forgets that I am his wife – that he is a gentleman.'

Sue would have flown out at these words yesterday, but they struck her now with a kind of painful truth. Still she felt bound to defend her comrade, even in his disgrace.

'He meant nothing, mother, dear. I am sure he never intended to be rude to you. But he is tired – I think he isn't very well. You know he gets a little impatient at times. Let us go and have tea.'

They went to the dining-room together, and Annie sat down behind her silver kettle, with the settled resolution of a martyr. Her daughter helped her to cold chicken and ham, to bread and to salad, to butter and to salt, hovering round her with a loving attentiveness that was not at all in the usual order of things. She thought it was intended to deprecate the reprimand which had been so justly incurred; and that reminded her of the girl's complicity in the father's offences, and rendered her unresponsive to the latter's blandishments as a rock to summer waves. It was her habit when she was displeased to 'set' slowly and steadily, like a cooling blanc-mange, and she had reached that point of stiffness now at which displeasure ceased to flow in words; but, as in the case of the blanc-mange, it acquired substance as it set, and Sue, in common with all the members of the household, knew that the less she was scolded the more in disgrace she was. She felt herself repulsed by her mother's manner – felt the breath of the Arctic atmosphere as a ship sailing in the dark feels the neighbourhood of icebergs, and knows that it must steer with caution; but she remained gentle and warmly tender herself in spite of it, full of her new-born sympathy, her profound pity for the parent who had been wronged so much more deeply than she knew. They ate and drank mechanically, for the most part in a silence that was only broken by the tinkle of a teaspoon and the noise of scraping butter upon toast. The father did not come to his waiting chair, and the mother was much too proud to call him. If he wished to show his temper in a way that would certainly set all the servants gossiping, it was for her, she considered, to bear it with what dignity she could, not to descend to vulgar remonstrance. But as the minutes passed, and he made no sign, her smooth-faced anger deepened, her cold resentment froze.

Suddenly she jumped up. 'I will take him a cup of tea.' she said. 'He must want something after his long walk, and perhaps he doesn't feel well enough to come out. May I, mother?'

Silently Mrs Delavel pushed an empty cup towards her daughter, who filled it from the teapot and cream jug. Sue cut a sandwich and put it on a plate; she added a buttered scone, then a wafer of toast, then a little cake, with that womanly and indeed human instinct for the right treatment of mental suffering which transcends reason and moral principles; and, placing cup and plate on a tray taken from the sideboard, carried them to the library.

The large room, that was richly sombre in the brightest day, was now in darkness, save where the rising moon made a white mist about the writing-table in the window and on a strip of book-lined wall, and its lonely occupant lay in a corner out of the light, stretched at full length on a sofa, with his arm thrown over his eyes. Sue knew where he was, and knew her way amongst the masses of oaken furniture that stood between him and the door, She stole with the footstep of a ghost over the Turkey carpet, pulled up a chair beside him, set her burden upon it, and then said gently, in a flat, colourless voice, 'I have brought you a cup of tea, father.'

Softly as she moved, he had heard her approach, and when she spoke he slowly put his arm down and looked at her. She could not see his face in the darkness, coming out of the lighted hall, though he could see hers; but she presently saw his two arms outstretched, his two strong hands lifted to reach her – an appeal of which she understood the whole meaning, and which she could not resist. Dropping on her knees, she leaned forward and was clasped to his breast, where, after a moment of passionate silence, she broke into sudden sobs.

'Old girl, what's the matter?' he whispered, knowing well what the matter was. 'What are you worrying yourself about?' He stroked her hair and patted her shoulder with a hushing gesture. 'Are you finding out that I am a bad lot, and not worth caring about any more?' As she still wept without speaking, he continued, a little bitterly, 'I told you I was a black sheep, didn't I?'

'O father!' she moaned at last. And the two little words – all she could articulate – bore a volume of meaning to him.

'But I am not an unmitigated rascal, Sukey; I don't commit crimes of *malice prepense*. I don't, so to speak, lay myself out for villanies. You believe that much, don't you?'

He raised himself into a sitting posture, and made her sit beside him. He laid his haggard grey face on her drooping head, still holding her in his arms. In this position, on the edge of the sofa, regardless of the spoiling tea, they kept silence for a little; and then he spoke again, more collectedly than before. 'Yes, that was Constance Bethune,' he said. 'Odd, wasn't it? – when I had just been telling you about her for the first time. I don't know what possessed me to talk about her. I have never talked about her before. I no more expected to see her rise up before me like that than I expected to see her ghost. The shock was too sudden, my dear – the surprise was too great; if I had had a little preparation I should have borne it better. I suppose,' he continued, 'you have guessed the truth – you have found out what we used to be to each other?'

'Yes,' whispered Sue, with burning cheeks. 'But, even then you were – you were. . . .'

'I know – I know. It was all wrong, of course. But there was literally no choice. She was too sweet and good – I was too much with her – and, indeed, it happened before I knew it had happened, and before *she* knew that I was not free. That was the only really bad thing I did – I did not say I was married when I knew them first. All the rest was my misfortune, not my fault. And we really did "behave well", as people say – we did, indeed; you must believe that of us. Constance was simply a saint incarnate. I wasn't, but it was all the more credit to me that I did what I did. I fought a good fight, my girl, though I say it that shouldn't – a harder one than you can have any idea of. I have done my level best. No man can do more.'

'But you love her still?'

'Yes.' He drew a long breath. 'That is a dispensation of fate – it is from no will of mine. I have tried to bury and forget it, and, since it wouldn't be buried, I have shut it up, so that no one should see it – my skeleton in the closet – my closet, which was like a secret chamber in a panelled wall, unknown to everybody but the master of the house. Haven't I kept it well? But today there was an earthquake, and the earthquake burst the closet door open. One can't provide against earthquakes.'

'And mother?' breathed Sue, almost inaudibly. 'Was she nothing to you, from first to last?'

He gave a sort of shiver as she put this hard question – Annie's child, who was so innocent and true. 'God is my witness,' he said solemnly, 'that I have done my duty by your mother to the best of my power – I have never forgotten that I was her husband.'

'And *now*?'

'Oh, now the skeleton is being put back again. It is not quite disposed of yet, but it will be soon. I am at this present moment engaged in a hand-to-hand struggle with it – for it is much livelier than skeletons usually are – and am, I think, rapidly getting the best of it. Try and trust me, my little girl,' he pleaded, tightening his arms round her, as he felt her creeping closer to him. 'Try and believe that I want to do right – and *will* – to the very limit of my strength.'

She lifted her face, and they kissed each other, sadly but sympathetically, both of them comforted by the strange confidences that had passed between them.

'I think,' said Richard, 'I will go into the dining-room now and make my apologies to your mother.'

So they left the untouched tray on the library chair, and returned to the dining-room, where Annie still sat at the head of the table, finishing her own comfortless meal. 'My dear, I'm very sorry I'm so late,' he sid gently, laying his hand on her shoulder. 'Have you another cup of tea in the pot?'

Mrs Delavel drew herself away from his touch and rose with a calm air. 'You must ask Sue to attend to you,' she replied, in tones that were calculated to chill the blood in their veins; and then she passed from the room and left them to their own devices.

Sue did attend to her father assiduously. Her mother's hardness to him melted any hardness that might have lingered in her own heart, and disposed her to be altogether pitiful. She made him some fresh tea, buttered him another scone, knelt on a stool beside him while he ate and drank, which he did perfunctorily, and more for the sake of showing her that the routine of ordinary life was uninterrupted than because he had any sense of hunger; and when he pushed away his cup and plate advised him, in the manner of a mother to a sick child, to go and rest himself on the library sofa. 'And don't fret,' she whispered. 'Remember, you have got me.'

'I shan't have *you* for long,' he returned.

'Oh yes, you will. I am not going to leave you while you want me – upon any consideration. No one can ever be what you are to me.'

'Ah, my little greenhorn, I thought you didn't know much about it!' he retorted with a laugh. 'You think you do, don't you? But you haven't learned the A B C yet. You're a perfect infant – a baby in swaddling clothes, my dear.'

'I hope I shall never grow up, if that means that I am to grow selfish,' she said gravely.

'Is that meant for a reproach? Wait till you are a little older, Sukey – a little more developed than you are now – before you set yourself up as a judge of other people, especially of an old man who has been through the whole campaign. It looks an easy matter to win battles that other folks have to fight – an easy matter not to be selfish till you've tried it – till the temptation comes to you in its full strength.'

With that he left her and returned to the dark library. And she went slowly upstairs, with her bonnet in her hand.

She had a spacious apartment of her own – bedroom at one end, sitting-room at the other – with two French windows opening upon a balcony and overlooking the Bay. It had Persian carpets and Morris-chintz covered armchairs, and all the daintiness that wealth and taste can gather about a young lady of position; altogether, it betokened habits and customs that made her choice of a partner in life seem singularly inappropriate. A little fire burned on the tiled hearth, near which stood her slippers, and her dressing-gown hanging over a chair back. At the opposite end of the room Hannah was turning down the bed, and Hannah began to scold with her usual vigour.

'Now, Miss Sue, you did ought to know better than to put your mother out in this way. You know how particular she is; and, after all, it's not much to do to please her. You've got a watch, haven't you? You know she can't bear to have you late to meals. She's that put out that she won't be herself again for days. His lordship came to call this afternoon, and he stayed right till dark, hoping you would come in' —

'Oh, bother his lordship! I wish he'd go back to England.'

'I think your mother wants you to marry him,' said the plain-spoken Hannah.

'She may want. I'm not going to marry a muff like that.'

'Well, Miss Sue, seeing what wretches husbands are – all except your father, who's the exception to the rule – and seeing that you must marry somebody, I think a muff is the best sort to choose. Then you may have a chance of managing, and of getting your own way a bit.'

'I should think a muff would be the worst sort of all to manage. He'd most likely be an obstinate mule that you could neither lead nor drive.'

'Lord Boyton isn't a mule – he's a real nice young man. Mrs Blundell's maid says it's quite a pleasure to have him in the house, he's so easy and pleasant spoken. And it would be something to be Lady Boyton, and not just a common Mrs I believe your father would like it.'

'Father would put him outside the door very quickly if he attempted to make love to me. He's not at all in father's style, I can tell you, any more than he is in mine. And you needn't take to match-making on my account, Hannah.'

'*I!*' cried the old woman indignantly, 'I am the last person. But if you've got to marry – and you're full old enough now – you may as well be thinking of it.' Her hatred of husbands as a class was combined with a fatalistic notion that they were necessary evils by no means to be evaded. 'And I don't want to see you take up with a common colonial.'

'The person I take up with, though he may be a colonial, shall not be a common one,' said Sue, smiling into the mirror of her wardrobe, as she shut up her bonnet. Then she added abruptly, 'Hannah, when was it that you first saw my father? Was it before mother came out to him?'

'A little while before. Why?' Hannah paused in her ministrations and looked earnestly at her young lady's back hair.

'Was it while – while he was living with the Bethunes?'

'What do you know about the Bethunes?' the old woman questioned sharply.

'Oh, nothing. Father happened to mention them this afternoon – that's all. And I wondered if you knew them.'

'I knew who they were,' said Hannah cautiously.

'You never told me,' said Sue.

'Why should I tell you? It was no business of yours. I knew a heap of people before you were born that I don't concern myself about now. Are you going to sit up here, or are you going downstairs?'

'I am going to sit here.'

'Then I'll put you on another log,' said Hannah.

Which she did; and then retired to her own quarters, wondering what could have possessed her master to speak to his daughter about the Bethunes.

CHAPTER XXX

---•---

Sue Takes A Message

Sue sat for some time by her fireside, deep in troubled thought. Then she began to wonder what her father was doing, whether he was very miserable in his solitude, whether he might not be comforted by her companionship; and she turned down her shaded gas-lamps and descended again to the library. On her way she passed her mother's room; the door was ajar, and Mrs Delavel could be seen sitting at *her* fireside, reading; but it no more occurred to the girl to go in and attempt to stir that impassive figure than it occurred to the aggrieved matron to call her offending daughter to her side. Full twenty-four hours would have to elapse before liberties of that kind could be permitted. The upper corridor, staircase, and hall were lighted in the profuse fashion of houses in which the cost of gas is not considered, but the library was still illuminated by the ineffectual moon. Sue made her way to the sofa with outstretched hands, and stooped to feel for a recumbent form. Her fingers touched only emptiness and morocco leather.

'Father,' she called softly, 'are you here?'

He was not there. She went the round of the dark corners and the arm-chairs, to make sure that he had not fallen asleep in one of them; then she looked into the lighted drawing-room, into the dining-room, into the morning-room, into the billiard-room, into the smoking-room, into the schoolroom, into the porch, and round the spacious verandahs. Finding all deserted, she searched the garden, peering into every alcove and summer-house, and every nook that held bench or rustic chair, until she reached the little lawn by the water's edge where they had sat and talked together on Friday night. This seat was also empty. Had he stolen away to the camp – his favourite place of refuge and rest when domestic life became more than commonly irksome?

She looked into the boathouse and saw the boat hanging there. No, he could not have gone to the camp, unless by the city and the steamboat, and he was not likely to have done that – seeing that he could hardly have returned that night – without warning somebody beforehand.

It was cold out of doors, and, after leaning upon the low balustrade and gazing over the moonlit water until her teeth began to chatter, Sue slowly climbed to the house again and returned to her fireside. She felt terribly forsaken and lonely. 'He doesn't want me,' she said to herself. 'He has no room for me in his thoughts now.'

Hannah came in at nine o'clock with the hot water, and of Hannah she was impelled to ask the question, 'Where is father?'

'Gone out,' said Hannah.

'Where to?'

'My dear, how should I know? Do you suppose I take upon myself to question him about his comings and goings? To the club, most likely, or to see somebody. When you sit upstairs in one room and your mother in another, and leave him alone downstairs, no doubt he finds it dull. Naturally he goes out for cheerful company if he can't have it at home.'

Hannah was devoted to the whole family, but there were degrees in her affection and favour, and the master of the house had the first place in her heart. Mrs Delavel was dear, Sue was dearer, but he was the dearest of all. Though a man and a husband, one of a class which she regarded with unrelenting animosity, he could do no wrong in her eyes, and his rights and interests were paramount.

Sue asked no more questions, and the old woman left her to her meditations. And as she sat and gazed at the fire in dismal solitude it suddenly flashed upon her where her father was. He had gone back to that house in the blind street on The Rocks – gone back to Constance Bethune. She was as sure of it as if she had been there to see. And with this conviction the bitter thoughts that had uprisen in the afternoon returned – the horrible feeling of disappointment, of separation, of jealousy, of wreck and ruin to all the peace of life. She had meant to sit up for him, wherever he was, but now she would not sit up. What would he want with *her*? She would only be in the way. So she undressed and went to bed, and lay awake and listened for him. Long after the household had retired to rest she heard the sound of his latch-key in the side door underneath her windows, and heard him come quietly upstairs to his dressing-room and shut himself in. She struck a match and looked at her watch; it was a quarter to one.

The next morning she knew that her conjecture had been correct. She went early to her sea-bathing house for a salt bath – to that stone-walled basin at the bottom of the garden which gave her room to swim in, protected from sharks by an iron grating, through which they occasionally peered longingly at her; and as she remounted the terrace stairway, fresh and rosy as the morning itself, she found him lying in wait for her.

'Sukey,' he said gravely, when they had exchanged their customary greeting, 'I wonder if you will do me a great favour?'

'What is it?' she inquired, vaguely apprehensive.

'Will you take a message for me to – to that lady we met yesterday?'

'No,' she replied quickly, flushing all over. Then immediately she said 'Yes'; then she asked, in a temporising tone, why she should be made a go-between? 'It is not a thing I ought to meddle with, father. Can't you say anything you want to say through the post?'

'I can. But I am in a hurry. I want to communicate quickly.'

'Telegraph then.'

'No. A telegram would hardly do. Never mind.' And he turned away from her, preceding her to the house.

She ran after him and caught his arm. 'Do you really wish me to go?' she asked earnestly. 'I don't mind – if it's anything important. Only mother has expressly forbidden me to go out alone again.'

'You could come with me when I go to the office – I would take the responsibility.'

'Very well. What is it?'

'Tell her,' he said slowly – and he looked at his daughter with a drawn grey face that seemed to her to have aged several years since yesterday – 'tell her to have no uneasiness. Tell her she may rely on me to keep my promise. I made her a promise – a promise not to try to see her any more – and I'm afraid she won't trust me to keep it. I made the same promise years ago, and she did not trust me – she sneaked away from her home and vanished, without leaving a trace; and that's what I'm afraid she will do again. It is borne in on me that's she's making preparations at this moment. I want you to stop her. You know I'm a man of my word, Sukey; you can answer for me. If I say I'll do a thing, I'll do it whatever it costs – you can assure her of that. I don't want her to go – I don't want her to be hunted about the world, just because I can't let her alone, or because she thinks I won't. She is with her old uncle now; he's over seventy, but he's as hale as I am, and he's all the belongings she's got now, and he's fond of her and able to take care of her. It's a quiet life up there in that old house; it suits her – it's good for her, after all the knocking about and the trouble that she's had. I want her to stay there and to feel herself at peace. You tell her that. Tell her if she doesn't show that she trusts me, I – I shall never get over it – I will never forgive her.'

Sue thought his friend would do well not to trust him, but what she said was, 'Am I supposed to know what has passed between you?'

'Yes,' he replied. 'That's all right. She will understand, and – and I want you to see her, though I can't.'

'I don't want to see her,' said Sue.

'You wanted badly enough last week.'

'Last week was different.'

'Well, she'll like to see *you*, at any rate. Go and give her that message' – he repeated it all over again, in stronger terms – 'and see that she understands it. Ask for Mrs Ellicott; that is her name now.'

'Where is Mr Ellicott?'

'Dead, long ago – of course.'

'Wouldn't it do if you put it in a letter and I left it at the door?' she suggested, still shrinking from the task. Then as he looked at her in silence with those haggard eyes, she added impulsively 'Oh, I'll go – I'll go; I'll see her and tell her. I don't like it, but I'll do it for you.'

And so she did.

It was with very strange feelings that she found herself, as early as ten o'clock, climbing the rock-hewn stairway to the blind street on The Rocks, and making her way to the door she had looked at with longing eyes but yesterday. With her bright face set and pale, as of one who had nerved herself to interview the dentist, she awaited admission to the presence of the lady whom she had sought so long and eagerly little dreaming of the trouble she represented. A surly old woman, presumably the uncle's housekeeper, answered the door-bell, and showed the visitor into a dark parlour, plain to primness in its simple furnishings, and devoid of all conventional knick-knacks save a silk-lined work-basket and an Indian brass pot containing freshly-gathered flowers; a room that was in perfect harmony with the exterior of the house, severely unpretending and substantial, and altogether out of date. Portraits of old-fashioned men and women and old-fashioned ships adorned the pale old walls; a telescope and sheathed sword hung over the chimney-piece; ancient crimson damask festooned the windows, and worn but still-enduring leather and solid mahogany composed the chairs and sofa. A little faded grandmotherly needlework on a quaintly-carved screen betokened an aunt as well as an uncle – an aunt who, Sue thought, must have died many years ago. The whole atmosphere of the place, albeit strongly impregnated with the freshest perfume of soap and beeswax, was of a bygone time.

Into this old room came Mrs Ellicott, an 'elderly' woman in the girl's eyes, but modern enough in comparison with those surroundings. She had the air of a duchess, or rather, the air that a duchess ought to have – in her plain black gown, and a look of fine quality generally that was more noticeable in the house than out of doors – probably the effect of uncovering her hands, which, though not small, nor particularly slender, were the most beautiful hands Sue had ever seen. One glance at her discovered that she was greatly changed since the day of the meeting in the Domain. She looked more than forty now. Her delicately-moulded face was hollow and pale; her eyes were sunk and worn, either from crying or from want of sleep. Evidently the suffering that attended the revival of the old romance was not all on one side. But she met her visitor with a proud and gentle composure that said, more plainly than words could say it, that she had nothing in the world to be ashamed of.

CHAPTER XXXI

●

How The Message Was Answered

Sue did not offer to shake hands. She bowed in response to the earnest questioning of Mrs Ellicott's grave eyes, and then delivered her message at once, with conscientious accuracy, and as much as possible the air of being a disinterested party.

'He says he once made you a promise, and you did not trust him to keep it, but he hopes you will trust him this time. He said I could speak for him, as being a man of his word and I can; I know him better than anybody. He is afraid you should go away from your home, where you are perhaps happy and comfortable, on his account; and he told me to beg you not to do that – to let him feel that you can rely on his word of honour,' said Sue in short, abrupt sentences, her face aflame, but set with a determination to discharge her errand faithfully.

Mrs Ellicott waited in silence until she had quite done, and then said gently, 'Won't you sit down, dear?'

'No, thank you,' the girl replied. 'I just came to say that – because he wished it; that's all.'

'Your father has been telling you – some of the circumstances. . . .'

'Not till yesterday. He never breathed a word till yesterday – not even your name. He never would have done, of course, if – if nothing had happened. He is one of the best of men; he does not profess much, but in practice he is the soul of goodness and honour. Only he is very impetuous – his feelings are stronger than most people's. And he did not expect to be – disturbed – so suddenly. He says himself that if he had had a little warning he would have behaved differently.'

A faint colour came into Mrs Ellicott's face. 'What happened yesterday was pure accident,' she said. 'It was as great a surprise, and as painful a one to me as to him. I had been very careful, as I thought, to avoid all chance of such a thing, and the Observatory Hill on a Sunday afternoon certainly seemed the least likely place.'

'You ought to be free to go about Sydney as you choose,' said Sue; 'and it ought to make no difference to him whether he meets you or not.'

'It ought to be so,' said Mrs Ellicott, 'and I wish indeed it were so.'

Then Sue's heart spoke. 'He has never, to my knowledge, done a dishonourable thing, or thought a dishonourable thought, till now,' she burst out; and her lips quivered and her eyes filled with tears. 'I can't help feeling it,' she added, with increasing emotion, covering her face with her hands.

Her hostess gently pressed her into a chair, and stood over her. 'Dear child,' she said, 'you ought to have known nothing about it, but, knowing it, you would be unworthy to be his daughter if you didn't feel it. At the same time, don't be unjust to him. Dishonour and he are as far apart as the poles – as much to-day as yesterday – as last year – as when he was a baby in the cradle. *I* know that, if you don't.'

'Can I help seeing what he feels?' cried Sue.

'What he feels – that is not his fault. What he can't help he can't help,' said Mrs Ellicott, her own voice full of tears, resolutely kept back. 'It is not dishonourable to suffer. It is giving in that is dishonourable – and he has never given in. He never would – any more than I would. I can trust him, if you can't.'

'Then you are not going away?' the girl exclaimed quickly.

'Yes, I am. I am going to America.'

'At once?'

'On Wednesday. I am getting ready now.'

'Even after what he says?'

'Yes; and I want to go without his knowing it until I am gone. Will you help me to keep the secret for two days?'

'I never keep secrets from him,' said Sue, with melancholy pride. 'He will want to know everything – he will make me tell him.'

'Try not to tell him. It will be better for him – for me also, if you can think of me – that he should not know it until it is too late for remonstrance. I – I can't bear any more,' she faltered, and a sudden sob broke from her.

Hearing that, Sue rose from her chair, and by a mutual impulse they kissed each other. The girl recognised the heroism of the woman whom her father loved – and who, it was only natural, should therefore adore him – in thus resolutely effacing herself because it was the best service she could render him. The daughter had the father's impetuousness, and in the gush of quick sympathy even went so far as to murmur something in deprecation of such a bitter sacrifice.

But Mrs Ellicott had the stuff of a martyr in her, as he had said; when she saw her course before her she stuck to it. She set aside at once any suggestion for a modification of her plan. 'It is the only thing to do,' she said simply. 'Don't you see yourself – you who know him so well – that it is the only thing?' And Sue agreed that it was the only thing. 'He might keep his word,' she said; 'I truly think he would. But it would be too much for him to bear. The constant effort would wear him out.'

Having come to the point of making these strange confidences, the two women talked long and freely. It astonished them both afterwards, when they recalled the conversation and remembered the curious relationship in which at that time they stood to each other, to think of the things they said without embarrassment or offence. The situation seemed to transcend all conventional considerations. They had the solemn feeling of those whom the grave is about to part.

Towards noon Sue said good-bye, and returned to her father's office in Pitt Street. She was extremely depressed and thoughtful, and disinclined to talk.

'Well?' he inquired, in a light tone, but with an agony of inward anxiety. 'Well, Sukey?'

'Well, father – I gave your message.'

'And what did she say?'

'She said she knew she could rely on you – that she trusted you perfectly.'

'Did she – did she? How did she say it, Sue? Did she seem quite sure about it? Did she say it as if she meant it?'

'Yes. I am sure she meant it.'

'You were there a long time. Did you have much talk?'

'Yes; a good deal.'

'How was she?'

'I think she was very well. She looked rather tired.'

'You are not sorry I sent you, Sukey?'

'No, father; I'm glad I went – on the whole.'

He looked at her with dumb entreaty to be told more; but she sat silently in a chair by his office table and took no notice of his look.

'Haven't you anything more to tell me?' he asked, after a long pause.

'No, father,' she replied, rousing herself at the direct question. 'No, I haven't anything more to tell you now. By-and-by I'll talk about it. It's past twelve o'clock,' she added briskly, 'and we'd better be starting home to lunch. We must take care not to be late for meals again for a long time to come.'

That evening and all the next day she devoted herself to her mother. At first Mrs Delavel would not appear to see it, but by the time Tuesday afternoon came round it was evident that the thaw had set in. She took her daughter with her for a long round of calls, and drove home in peace and charity with the world; and on Tuesday evening the *Political Economy* was brought out, and the little family returned to the serene condition in which we first found them. The father was gentle, cheerful, even gay in his demeanour – though his gaiety, to one critical pair of ears, had rather a hollow ring about it – resolutely setting himself to 'be good', as he had promised and vowed he would. He did not allude to Mrs Ellicott after Sue had expressed a wish to avoid the subject. He seemed to try to hide the whole affair away as remotely as possible.

But all the time the secret which that lady had confided to her lay heavily on the girl's mind, and the more admirably her father behaved – encouraged by his groundless confidence in her sincerity – the more she suffered in betraying him. This feeling grew and strengthened with each hour of his companionship, until at last she could bear it no longer. When the evening reading – to which she paid not the slightest attention – was at an end, she signed to him to come down the garden with her; and, sitting on their favourite bench by the waterside, she told him what was going to happen next day.

She broke it to him as gently as she could, delicately touching upon Mrs Ellicott's motives – which was quite unnecessary – and laying stress upon the fact that the step was not prompted by distrust of him; but she did it with a quaking heart, in mortal dread of the way he might take it.

He took it with extraordinary quietness. He sat quite still and listened without interrupting her, and when she had said all she had to say he continued silent and motionless for a minute or more. Then he drew a long breath, which exhaled in a deep groan. 'I knew it – I knew it,' he said, with the calmness of defeat and despair. 'I knew it, even while I thought I was believing what you told me. After Sunday night I knew she would go – I knew she wouldn't trust me. She is like a rock. I might beg and pray – I might dash myself to pieces like the breakers against the North Head – and it would be useless to think of moving her. She has made up her mind to do it, and she'll do it. I know her – I know her of old; if she says it is to be it will be. Kismet!'

'Father, dear, she is doing what is best,' said Sue, 'and I think when it is over you will be glad she did it.'

'No, I shan't be glad. It will break my heart – it will drive me to desperation. I shall just go and cut my throat and have done with it: and I'd better do it at once, then she needn't go to America – then she needn't put herself to any trouble to get out of my way. She would be at peace – I should be at peace – everybody would be at peace.'

'O father!'

'Go to bed, Sukey; go to bed, old girl, and don't mind me. I'm talking nonsense, of course, but it's nonsense you oughtn't to listen to. Your mother says I am a bad father to you; so I am, or I should have kept you out of all this. Go to bed now, and leave me to myself for a bit. I feel bad, Sukey – I feel as wicked as I ever felt in my life; but I shall be better presently.'

'Father, I can't leave you when you talk of killing yourself. You are not fit to be left.'

'Have no fear,' he replied. 'I've got you, as you reminded me the other day; you are an anchor strong enough to hold me fast to *terra firma*.'

'You don't think much about *me*,' she cried reproachfully.

'Don't make statements that you can't verify,' he said. 'And don't worry me, for pity's sake; I've enough to bear without that.'

'Promise me not to think of such a dreadful thing again,' she implored, with tears, as she stood up to leave him.

'I'll promise not to *do* it,' he answered. 'I can't answer for my thoughts – nor my words either – just now. Go to bed, child, and don't concern yourself about me. I shall be all right by the morning.'

To her great relief, and quite contrary to her expectations, he did seem all right in the morning. He came to the breakfast-room with cheerful greetings and remarks upon the fineness of the weather, read his newspaper at the table, and complained because the eggs were boiled hard. After breakfast he walked with his wife round the garden, gave orders to the gardener, looked at the horses, and then brushed his hat and went forth to town as usual. Sue had fully expected to be asked to go to The Rocks with a last message, but he made no sign that he remembered the existence of such a place. He returned punctually to lunch, and discussed that meal with the same unnatural commonplaceness. But after lunch he abruptly demanded his daughter, and then Sue knew that the event of the day was not going to be altogether ignored.

'You are not going to take her to the camp *again?*' Mrs Delavel inquired, with symptoms of the gathering of the clouds that had so lately dispersed.

'No; not to the camp this time,' he replied. 'I want her for – for something else.'

'*I* wanted her,' said Annie. 'It is my afternoon at home, as you know, and it is not pleasant to be *always* left to entertain my guests alone.'

'Well, you shall have her every day for a fortnight, if you like, provided I may have her now. Go and put your hat on, Sue, and be quick about it.' He opened and shut his watch impatiently.

She did not wait to ask questions, but ran upstairs as he bade her, and in five minutes returned booted and hatted and drawing on her gloves. They left the house without a word, jumped into a passing omnibus, and in silence made their way to the Pitt Street office and to the senior partner's private room. There, in a tumbler of water on the table, stood the most beautiful bouquet that money could buy or the earth produce, all of rare white flowers and delicate ferns, fit for a princess or a bride – a bouquet that was evidently the result of special influence and arrangement. Richard took it out of the water, wiped the stalks carefully with his handkerchief, and placed it in his daughter's hand. 'You can give it to her,' he said. 'She'd rather have it from you than from me. Come along' – looking at his watch again and taking up his hat. 'We'll go and see the last of her.'

'O father!' protested Sue, standing still. 'Are you really going to see her again? After all her trying to avoid it? What will she say to me? I ought not to have told you when she asked me not. Do let me go alone. Don't disappoint her at the last.'

'What!' he cried. 'Am I not to be allowed even to put a flower upon her grave? Look here, Sue, from this day she will be dead and buried – for me. I know her – I know her too well; she will take precious good care never to come across my path again – never to let me cross hers. She will disappear when that ship goes through the Heads, and I shall see her no more. I shall never be able to look at her face, to hear her speak, to touch her, to feel sure that we are in the same world together after this. It is my last chance – my very last and only chance, and I can't and I won't miss it. It is little enough. And if there's any harm done – there won't be, but if there is – why, we shall have the rest of our lives to get over it. Besides, she'll be alone. Her old uncle is tied to his chair with rheumatism. And I'm not going to sit quietly here while she's muddling for herself, hustled by the crowd there's sure to be, without a man to help her. Come, don't let us waste time talking. I could have gone alone, but I thought it would be better for you to go too. Still, if you would rather not go don't let me persuade you.'

'I would rather go,' said Sue. And they set forth together.

CHAPTER XXXII

●

The Skeleton Is Locked Up

The waiting-room of the steamers plying to and from the New Zealand and San Francisco boat, which lay out in the harbour, was already crowded when they reached it; so was the wharf beyond. Passengers and friends of passengers, bouquet and fruit sellers, newsvenders and miscellaneous idlers elbowed each other in the very limited space at their disposal. But Mrs Ellicott was not amongst them, as Richard, from his altitude of six feet two, ascertained at the first glance. He found a seat for his daughter, and, standing beside her, watched the doorway through which fresh arrivals continually entered from the street, without moving or speaking; while Sue nursing her bouquet, watched on her own account. At the end of half-an-hour he sprang forward and took a bee-line through the crowd; he was so tall, and his movements so powerful and impetuous, that it gave way as one man to let him pass. Mrs Ellicott had scarcely crossed the threshold of the waiting-room when he met her with outstretched hand and a strange kind of reckless smile that recalled old memories to her mind.

'Well, Constance,' he said, 'so you were going to play Jane Eyre to my Rochester again, were you? But Sue can't keep secrets from me, and I thought you'd allow me to come and see you off – to offer my good wishes for a pleasant voyage. Where is your luggage? Tell me what you have and I'll see after it for you.'

She was very white, but she kept the agitation into which his sudden appearance had thrown her to herself; the habit of self-control had become a second nature with her by this time. Turning to a cab filled with bags and wraps, in charge of her uncle's housekeeper, she told him this was all the luggage she had, except what was already on board.

'Then send that woman home,' he said peremptorily. 'I'll look after you – Sue and I. You need not wait,' he added aloud to the servant. 'My daughter and I will take care of Mrs Ellicott.'

The old woman was not agreeable to such an untimely parting with her charge, but she had to acquiesce; neither of them could withstand the force of these unexpected circumstances. They exchanged a tender but brief farewell, and then Constance was hurried through the waiting-room to the wharf, and deposited on the bench by Sue's side.

'Take care of her, Sukey,' said Richard, 'while I fetch her things.'

And the girl did not need that prompting. She took her friend's hand and held it tightly, at this moment feeling nothing but sympathy and compassion for her.

'I am afraid you will be angry with me,' she said, when they were left alone. 'But I didn't dare not to tell him. And – and it's well that somebody should be here to take care of you. It would not be fit for you to be alone in such a crowd as this.'

Mrs Ellicott pressed her hand in reply; she did not seem able to speak. And in two minutes Richard was back, with all her shawls and bags; and shortly after they went on board the steamer lying alongside, before the decks were crowded, and seated themselves in the bows to watch the other passengers embark. As usual at such times, when hearts are full to bursting, the conversation was limited to the trivial incidents around them. Who was this? Who was that? Was he or she bound for America, they wondered, or only for Auckland? And was anything more absurd than to go to sea in a blue silk dress? And so on and so on.

The whistle sounded presently, the gangway was taken up, and the boat hauled off from the pier towards the great ship lying round the corner in Lavender Bay. A gentle breeze blew from the water; the lovely shores opened out, one green promontory after another, backed by the glowing sky above, and shadowed in the silver mirror below. It was a perfect day and a charming scene as an ocean wayfarer could wish to look upon. But amongst the chattering crowd were women were handkerchiefs to their eyes – many a little tragedy in process besides that with which we are concerned – pain and pathos that the beauties of nature could not lighten. To the silent man and woman who did not weep, the sweetness of the world around seemed a mockery of the trouble that was their portion in it. It suggested wedding journeys and happiness, the youth that was past, the enterprise that was dead, the brightness that might have been.

When they reached the ship Sue led the way up the crowded

gangway to Mrs Ellicott's cabin, which was an airy little room on deck, with a wide bed in a recess, curtained with bright chintz, and a long velvet sofa under the sliding windows; like all the arrangements of the Union line, as comfortable as could be devised under the circumstances. Decks and passages were swarming with people, so that it was with difficulty they reached this haven, and having reached it, it was not possible for Sue to consult her feelings or those of her companions by leaving them to enjoy a *tête-à-tête* in solitude. The only one who could leave was her father, who, noting Mrs Ellicott's extreme paleness, shouldered his way to the bar for champagne and biscuits wherewith to revive her. He also went to see about a number of parcels that he had sent on board in the morning, and which he directed to be delivered to the lady they were intended for after the ship had sailed. He also went to find out such stewards and stewardesses as would be likely to have the remotest opportunity for ministering to that lady's comfort on the voyage, and to prepay their services at about fifty times what they were worth. He also went to interview the captain, whom, of course, he knew, as he knew all the captains frequenting the port, and to make certain arrangements that not only covered the voyage, but might possibly lessen the difficulties of a lone woman beyond the point of disembarkation. Having thus done all that a rich man and a potentate of the shipping world could do on her behalf, he returned to her cabin, somewhat comforted for the moment. The champagne was opened, and she was gently forced to swallow the best part of a tumbler, which gave her a frightful headache afterwards, but upheld her through the trials of the immediate half-hour better than all the resources of a strong mind could have done.

'It is no use drinking to our good luck,' said Richard, lifting a glass of the foaming wine to his own lips, 'nor yet to our next meeting. We can only do like the old Waterloo veterans, and toast the memory of the dead, Constance – the days that are no more!'

'We can wish her good health and a prosperous voyage,' said Sue, who was moving about, trying to 'fix up' the articles they had brought into the cabin.

'Yes; we can wish, we can wish,' he rejoined. 'Wishing is a luxury that the poorest can indulge in. Here's to your good health and a prosperous voyage, Constance. What are you going to do when you get to the end of it?'

'I don't know,' she said, 'till the time comes.'

'Have you friends in America?'

'No.'

'Ever been there before?'

'No.'

'What is the attraction then?'

'I don't know that there is any particular attraction, except that I have never been. The other lines I know; this will be a change.'

'The attraction of this line is that it sends a ship on Wednesday instead of on Friday or Saturday. If you had waited a couple of days, you could have gone straight home to your own friends.'

'There is no reason why I should go straight home. No one expects me.'

'But you *are* going home, I suppose?'

'Yes; eventually.'

'To London or to Lausanne?'

'To London, I think. But I have not made up my mind.'

'Have you no plans for your future life?'

'Yes; I have one plan. I intend to take up nursing work again.'

'Oh, no – no,' he protested, 'you must not do that. You are not strong enough for it; you will only catch fevers and cancers and all sorts of dreadful things yourself. You look just in a state of health to catch the first thing that comes near you.'

'Cancers are not catching,' she said; 'my health is much better than it looks. I must have work – I must do something. And that is the thing I can do best.'

'And it is a splendid thing,' said Sue, who was taking off Mrs Ellicott's bonnet and cloak. 'And nothing could make you happier than such work. Don't try to dissuade her from it, father. She knows what's best.'

'It's no use my trying to dissuade her,' he said; 'I know that well. But at least you might let us know where you are, Constance, and what becomes of you. Won't you write a line to Sue sometimes? I will not even look at the letters if you don't wish it.'

Before she could reply the bell rang for strangers to leave the ship. They rose to their feet together and looked at each other. 'Leave it all to her,' said Sue; 'she knows where to find me.' Then she threw her arms round the elder woman, hugged and kissed her for a moment with all her might, and dashed out of the cabin, shutting the door behind her and placing her back against it. At the same moment the sliding window that stood open to the air was shut, and for a few minutes of silent passion and agony the parting lovers were alone in the world together.

People crowded through the narrow passage, half the width of which was filled by the girl's well-developed form, hustling and squeezing her as they passed; and hundreds of noisy feet and voices clamoured from the deck outside the window; but there was not a sound within. Richard Delavel, for – as he thought – the last time in his life, took into his arms the woman whom nature had intended to be his mate, but whom circumstances had denied to him, and forgot everything but that he loved her and held her; and Constance Ellicott also at that overpowering crisis acknowledged herself human – a woman of flesh and blood; with the natural passions of her kind. They had neither words nor tears in this extremity; speechless, motionless, almost breathless, they stood together locked in that wild embrace – taking just seven minutes of freedom after twenty-two years of bondage and exile – one deep draught of anguish and ecstasy, such as young lovers with whom the world goes well never know or dream of. At the end of seven minutes Richard joined his daughter, and he also closed the cabin door behind him. Sue did not look at his face; she promptly obeyed the propulsion of his hand on her shoulder, and began to struggle through the crowd pressing towards the gangway. Around the puffing ferry-boat at the ship's side were a few smaller craft awaiting customers or the chances of an engagement, and to the owner of a smart little steam-launch Richard made a signal.

'How long will it take you to get to Watson's Bay?' he inquired.

'We'll be there before she goes through the Heads,' the man replied, seeing what was wanted of him.

Richard nodded. And he and Sue hurried down the gangway, and jumped into the little boat, which set off at full speed down the harbour. Before the big ship stirred from her moorings they were landed on the jetty at Watson's Bay, and just as she moved into the fairway they reached the head of the gap, and set themselves down on the brow of those stupendous cliffs at the foot of which the *Dunbar* was dashed to pieces. The grandeur and peacefulness of this airy outlook – the solemn headlands rising sheer out of the surf, the great Pacific stretching to the far distant horizon – so enhanced the pathos of the occasion, that Sue was fain to take out her handkerchief and indulge in a weakness that was more unusual with her than with most young women; but her father sat stern and still as a figure carved out of granite, staring steadily at a certain point, and gave no outward indication of the fierce emotion that consumed him.

Soon they saw a whiff of smoke above the cliff and heard the faint sound of a churning screw below; and out from behind the great Heads stole the Pacific mail-boat, looking like a toy from where they viewed it. They did not cry, 'There she is!' nor wave their handkerchiefs after the customary fashion. They knew pretty well that Mrs Ellicott was lying on the recessed bed with her face to the wall, beyond the reach of signals; and the passage of the great vessel that bore her from them was as the procession of a funeral, to be witnessed in awe and silence. They watched it creep out into the open – the long slender hull and smoking funnels, representing so much, yet looking so little, in contrast with the vastness around, and watched it pass over the great plain, with its white wake behind it – pass and lessen and fade and disappear into that beyond which was like a yawning grave to one of them. When there was no longer the faintest breath of smoke upon the shining azure of sky and sea, he rose and led the way down the gap to the little launch, which had waited for them, and they returned to the city, still without speaking of what had happened or of what they felt about it. Only when they found a cab, and Sue had taken her place within it, did her father break through the stony silence.

'Go home,' he said, 'and tell your mother not to expect me tonight. I am going to the camp.'

She nodded, not attempting to dissuade him, and did as he bade her. She went home and bore the brunt of her mother's revived displeasure, sheltering him all she could and keeping his secrets safely. And he hurried away to the camp, gave the bo'sun twenty-four hours' leave, and allowed himself the relief that his whole soul and body ached and craved for – the luxury of letting poor human nature have all its own way for a little while.

He lay on the beach under the bushes till midnight, then he lay on the small white bed within the tent till morning, and moaned to himself like a sick child, knowing that there was no one to listen and pry upon him. The whole front of the tent was open as usual, and his wet or burning eyes reflected the broad moonlight that poured all over him and the weird intermittent glow of the electric beam from the lighthouse. Every sense was awake to feed his suffering. He heard the ripple of the little waves that broke almost upon his threshold, and the solemn boom of the breakers outside the Heads, and the *whish-sh-sh* of the cool wind in the trees and the bushes. He smelt the salt freshness of the sea that had taken her from him – tasted the delicious brine upon his lips – felt all the beauty of the wide night that overached and encompassed her, all the profundity of the solitude to which she had left him. He had no sleep or rest, save rest from the life-long effort to ignore and resist his pain, but cried from hour to hour, and groaned aloud through his shut teeth like a wounded animal rather than a man.

But the next afternoon Sue, racked with anxiety lest he should have committed suicide, contrived to evade her mother, and went to the camp to look for him; and he came forth from the tent to meet her, with his hat on the back of his head and his pipe in his mouth, and saluted her with his habitual composure.

'What, Sukey? – time to go home to dinner?' he called cheerfully. 'All right. I'm ready.'

CHAPTER XXXIII

Three Months Later

It was hot weather – Sydney hot weather – and people with money and leisure were going or gone to the mountains, to New Zealand, to Tasmania, anywhere to get away from it. Mrs Delavel still lingered in her own house, partly because she disliked the comparative disorder of other places and had no taste for wandering, partly because Lord Boyton had returned from the Melbourne Cup to stay with Mrs Blundell till after Christmas.

Sue was wholly in her mother's hands. Her father did not neglect her, but neither did he claim her for his separate enjoyment, as he had been in the habit of doing. If he went to the camp he went alone; and it was generally supposed, when the after-dinner readings were over and he was not to be found upon the premises, that it was the club which so frequently allured him from the domestic hearth. Five times in the week he would finish the evening somewhere other than on the verandah or in the garden where Sue had been wont to finish it with him; and the late hours that he kept became a serious grievance to the mistress of the house, who saw in them not only a further proof of those propensities which had made him the black sheep of his family and deprived him of so many of the distinctions of his rank, but a deliberate device for slighting and wounding her. In the ordinary household intercourse he was considerate and amiable, gentle to his wife and affectionate to his daughter; but he was dull and abstracted, performing his little duties and courtesies perfunctorily, without putting a spark of spirit into them. Annie did not notice this difference from his usual bright interest in the details of his life, but Sue saw and understood it. She felt a little hurt at being set aside now, after having been so close a confidante; and she felt a little hurt by his apparent forgetfulness of her own not unimportant affairs; but she did not feel resentment. She sheltered him and aided him with all her native tact and magnanimity, chiefly and most effectually by drawing off her mother's attention from him and concentrating it upon herself.

In these days she was a pattern young lady. Day after day she put on smart gowns and bonnets, took her place in the carriage by Mrs Delavel's side, and devoted long afternoons to those uncongenial social duties which were the object and the end of the elder woman's existence. She sipped tea and smiled, and made inane remarks upon the weather and the current events of interest to upper circles, all in so natural and proper a manner that even her fastidious parent was satisfied – satisfied that the child on whom so many hopes were set was turning out a true lady after all. Balls had been going on of late, and afternoon dances on the warships in the harbour; and at these Miss Delavel had danced prodigiously, and received a great deal of attention. For though, unfortunately (as Annie was frequently heard to remark), the taint of trade, for the first time in the history of the family, rested upon her, and though she was entirely out of that sphere to which by divine right she belonged, still she was an interesting girl, full of frank vivacity and naturalness (and men do like naturalness, though women don't seem to believe it), and she was also an heiress – a fact which, the taint of trade notwithstanding, enhanced her attractions in the eyes of almost everybody. And in these mixed assemblies, where a chaperon of Annie's rank had need of all her vigilance, there was usually some presentable and unobjectionable person to whom a mother could trust her child with an easy mind, and concerning whom she could permit herself to indulge in matrimonial speculations. Indeed, some dozens of young men had, one at a time, enjoyed Mrs Delavel's special favour as potential sons-in-law, most of them being aristocratic young A.D.C.'s or titled globe-trotters like Lord Boyton. Just now Lord Boyton was the object of her maternal solicitude, and he was to be met with everywhere. If he was not able to come to a party in the first instance, the party was put off until he could; and thus our old friend, taking her daughter to miscellaneous entertainments, seldom missed the happiness of seeing his chubby face amongst the guests. Lord Boyton, for his part, paid marked attention to Sue. Being mostly in doubt as to the social eligibility of his Australian acquaintances, he felt a sense of safety in the family of a man who was unquestionably a Delavel of Dunstanborough. That was one reason. Another was that she marked herself out from other young ladies by treating him with cool indifference. He was not accustomed to cool indifference, and it exercised over him the fascination of novel things – filled him with curiosity and surprise, and a haunting anxiety to find out the meaning of it. Thus he attached himself to her whenever he saw a chance, and laid himself out to be agreeable – laid himself out so very plainly that it was noticed and talked of; and a strong desire to keep her mother in a good temper induced Sue to treat him with more toleration than she had shown at the beginning of the acquaintance.

This led to his becoming troublesome. Annie gave him a standing invitation – 'Drop in when ever you feel inclined' – with a cordial smile and pressure of the hand, and he took it quite literally, so that the house was hardly ever free of him. He lounged a great deal in the soft armchairs, displaying the sole of his shoe and a liberal portion of his socks and he talked incessantly, taking the lead in conversation as by prescriptive right. Occasionally his tendency to over-indulgence in the pleasures of the table led to his saying things that would have been better left unsaid. After luncheon or dinner, when his unquenchable thirst had been temporarily allayed, he would become noisy and overpowering or familiar to a degree that caused Sue to quake with apprehension as to how much further he was going to relax himself; or else he would suddenly fall asleep and snore. To all which little manifestations of a lordly temperament Annie turned the same smiling and approving face.

'Poor, dear fellow,' she would say, 'it is pleasant to see how thoroughly at home he is with us. He evidently feels that we are his natural friends – the only people he can associate with on his own level.'

'I hope not,' Richard would remark. 'I'm not proud, my dear, as you know, but I do hope we are a little above Lord Boyton's level.'

At which Mrs Delavel, with a smile and a sigh, would express her patient acquiescence in the fate that invariably befell her friends and her opinions at his hands.

But the master of the house bore this new domestic infliction with surprising equanimity. Probably it was a comfort to him to have something to bear; it lightened his marital conscience of a fraction of its load. If anything, he bore it too well. Knowing that Sue was in no danger, he ignored Lord Boyton's presence and behaviour as he might have done that of a gambolling kitten. High-bred gentleman as he was, he could, as Annie often told him, be as rude as any ploughman;

and in this case he justly merited the reproach she was not slow to cast at him of showing discourtesy to a guest under his own roof. But it was negative discourtesy – not the positive kind that would certainly have been exhibited under other conditions of his mind. He took his armchair and his magazine or newspaper, and entertained himself in silence as if there had been no guest. Only sometimes, when it grew late, or the guest was in that state which would have been advanced intoxication in a meaner mortal, he jumped up with a peremptory face and a sharp opening and shutting of his watch, that had the effect of immediately scaring the noble globe-trotter from the premises. Then he would look at his wife and say mildly, 'Well, my dear, doesn't your young man pall upon you yet?'

And Annie would reply, with calmness and dignity, that, on the contrary, the more she saw of him the more she esteemed and admired him.

Thus poor Sue became a victim to Lord Boyton. In a perfectly ladylike way Mrs Delavel flung her daughter at his head, and the girl had to submit, or to revolt in a manner that would have been more unpleasant than submitting. That he was extremely amiable and an excellent tennis player somewhat mitigated the irksomeness of his constant company; but there were times – as when she was left to entertain him single-handed while her mother invented business elsewhere, or when she found herself stranded with him in the dark on a garden terrace after dinner – that her weariness of the sight and sound of him changed to a much more active sentiment. There were times when she felt that she could not stand him any longer – that revolt was justifiable and necessary – that she must rid herself of him somehow, whatever the consequences might be.

One morning, very soon after breakfast and her father's departure for his office, she was going upstairs, and saw the approach of the young man from the landing window. On the spur of the moment, and impelled by a sense of desperation, she ran into her bedroom, snatched up a hat, plunged headlong downstairs, out of the house, and down the garden to the boathouse, and put herself beyond his reach on the harbour waters. It was a thing she had never done before, and a thing calculated to set Mrs Delavel's every separate hair on end when she heard of it; but in fact this impetuous young person did not stop to think of that, or of anything except getting away from her persecutor. The small boat chanced to be lying on the water ready for use, and the opportunity was too tempting to be resisted. She was accustomed to rowing her father about the bay, while he lolled at his ease and criticised her style, and was as capable with the oars as he was; and to cast off the little craft, to shut the boat-house doors, and to spin out into the open, was only to do what she did half-a-dozen times a week in fair weather.

But when she had done it without her father, when she found herself alone in the midst of the shipping, rather embarrassed for want of the usual steering apparatus – when she looked back at her home, 'bosomed high in tufted trees' above the terraced garden, and thought of her exploit in its conventional aspect – she was a little inclined to that sober reflection which is so much more useful before rash action than afterwards. However, it did not occur to her to turn back. 'I will row quietly down to the camp,' she said to herself, 'and leave the boat there, and return by the steamer.' Thus she proposed to enjoy her liberty for the whole morning, with as little outrage to her mother's feelings as was compatible with doing so.

She rowed down to the camp accordingly, glancing over her shoulder continually as she went, an object of much curiosity to a great many people; and she was very glad when she reached her destination. The little strip of planking that formed the landing-stage of the camp was hidden from camp view by a screen of bushes; and she shipped her oars, tied up the boat, and went ashore unobserved by the Bo'sun, who was usually on the lookout.

'I am afraid that old fellow is playing the truant again,' she thought. 'He will do it once too often, and father will pack him off. And we shall never get such another.' With all his faults, she was as much attached to the Bo'sun as he was to her. And then she remembered how hungry she was after her severe exertions, and how tiresome it would be if he had gone off without leaving anything to eat behind him.

She skirted the low fence within which tents and gardens and neat paths were enclosed on all but the seaward side, and went direct to the kitchen. This little shed was tidy, with its black pots on the hob, and its slab walls hung with cooking utensils; but the fire was out, and no Bo'sun was there. 'Perhaps he has been drinking,' she thought; and she looked round the yard and peeped into his tent, expecting to find him – as he had been found more than once before today – sleeping off the effects of a clandestine debauch. But there was no sign of him, drunk or sober. Evidently he had left his post. She stood still a minute, not much liking her solitary sensations amongst such associations of life and companionship – a solitariness that would not have oppressed her at all in the open bush; and then she lifted up her fresh young voice and called loudly –

'Bo'sun! Bo'sun, ahoy!'

While the echoes still quivered in the hills above her her cry was answered. She had not expected an answer, and certainly not such an answer. In the big tent there was a noise like a chair falling on the boarded and matted floor, and a man rushed out of it – a tall, fair-bearded man, in his shirt sleeves, whose face at the sight of her – as likewise her face at the sight of him – was a picture of astonishment and consternation. It was Noel Rutledge, who was keeping house while the Bo'sun went to town to buy groceries. And he was the only living creature within a mile of her.

CHAPTER XXXIV

•

A Camp Meeting

They said 'Good morning' to each other, with flushed faces that struggled to smile, but were not allowed to do so; and then proceeded to explain the circumstances that had led to their unexpected meeting.

'Your father was so kind as to ask me to make use of the camp sometimes,' said the young man, 'and I have taken him at his word, you see.' He did not say that Mr Delavel had warmly repeated that invitation since the day when she heard him make it, and had even joined his guest at the camp on several occasions. 'I was writing in the tent when I heard you call. The Bo'sun has gone into Sydney.' He looked quickly around. 'Is your father not with you?'

'No,' said Sue, 'I am alone. Of course, I did not know – I thought I should find the Bo'sun, as usual – I did not tell my father I was coming – he never told me you were here.'

She was exceedingly embarrassed for such a self-possessed young lady, but it was not because she felt any awkwardness in her unchaperoned condition. She was as free from conventional prudery, and as indifferent to social prejudices, as a daughter of Annie Morrison's could possibly be, and if this young man had been any other young man she would have thought no more of finding herself alone with him at the camp than of casting herself forth alone upon the public waters of the harbour, as she had just done. It was the too sudden and excessive gratification of her long-frustrated wish to see this one particular young man which upset her self-command. Mr Rutledge was himself keenly conscious of giving occasion to Mrs Grundy, but it was not for him to mention it. And, after rowing from Darling Point to Middle Harbour in the hot hours of a November morning, the strongest woman would need a rest before making fresh exertions.

Sue was strong enough, but bore evident traces of having taxed her powers heavily.

'Why, you must be quite done,' he said, when she had confessed her exploit.

'I *am* rather tired,' she admitted, stretching the aching muscles of her young arms; 'and hungry, too,' she added with a laugh.

'Hungry? Oh, you must let me get you something. Come and sit down for a bit – come into the tent and rest while I go and rummage the Bo'sun's stores. There's some bread, I know, and some salt junk, and a currant cake; and I think I can find a tin of sardines.'

'Get me some cake,' said Sue; 'a good big piece.'

'Yes; and what will you have to drink? I suppose you don't like whisky and water?'

'No, not at all.'

'That's all we have, except tea. I'll make you a cup of tea.'

'You can't; the fire is out.'

'I'll light it in two minutes.'

'I don't believe you know how.'

'Oh, don't I? You wait and see.'

All their embarrassment melted away in the consideration of these prosaic matters, giving place to a secret exhilaration, which almost rose to exultation, such as might warm the hearts of truant schoolboys on the spree. They went to the kitchen together to make the fire and collect materials for lunch, she resisting his persuasions to rest while he waited upon her; and they had never been so intimate as they were in the fun she made of his domestic incapacities, and in his simple manifestations of his hospitable zeal. There was a charm in the situation that youth and human nature had no resource but to yield to – especially when the human nature was so unsophisticated as in them. There were homely suggestions in it that were delicious and irresistible. When he bungled over his fire-making, and she swept him aside with playful contemptuousness, and even went so far as to call him a duffer, she did more than she knew to precipitate the accident that presently befell her.

While the kettle boiled she ran into her own little tent to wash her face and hands, and look at herself in the glass. She was not much given, as a rule, to looking in the glass, and perhaps this was the first occasion on which she did so with any particular anxiety as to the result. She took off her hat, and took down her pretty hair and twisted the long braids into a careful knot; and then she touched up the natural rings on her forehead, which stood her in place of the fuzzy mass made by heated curling tongs that ninety-nine out of every hundred young women were wearing; and she 'settled' her white gown, which had considerably lost its freshness, pulling down the bodice and shaking out the skirt; and she turned her head from side to side while she studied her features from different points of view – all as the vainest of vain coquettes might do. She returned to the large tent, carrying her hat, and found Mr Rutledge setting out the tea and cake, himself newly washed and brushed, and clothed in immaculate tweeds; and he thought as he looked at her that he had never before realised how pretty she was, and she thought as she looked at him that she had never done justice to his good looks till now. And each felt at this moment the forecast shadow of the near event – the meshes of fate winding closer and closer about them. Out in the kitchen they were like flies buzzing at the edge of the web – they could escape it if they liked; but here they perceived that the subtle threads were drawing them very strongly. Sue began suddenly to wish she had not lingered so long, and Noel Rutledge began to tell himself sternly that he must on no account betray her father's trust in him by taking advantage of the position in which she had inadvertently placed herself.

The back of the table was piled with sheets of manuscript – the work on which he had been engaged when she interrupted him – pens and ink, books and newspapers; the front part was spread with her frugal meal. As she entered he drew up the largest and easiest of the basket chairs.

'Oh,' she said hastily, 'I don't think I have time to sit down. I must be getting home again.'

'But you must drink your tea,' he urged, 'and you may as well do it sitting as standing. And you have not rested yourself at all – you must rest for a few minutes.'

Of course, she had to sit down; it would have been absurd to do otherwise. And when she took her seat he put a pillow at her back, and brought a little box for her to set her feet on, and a chair on which she could place her cup without having to reach or lift. 'Last time you made tea for me,' he said; 'this time I will make it for you.' And he proceeded to pour it from the brown pot with anything but a steady hand. She watched him with a fast-beating heart, and tried to think of some harmless subject to talk about, but could not for the life of her.

The stillness that was the evidence of their isolation was intense –
almost aggressive. Not a breath of wind stirred the trees and bushes,
and the harbour waters were so tranquil that the little wavelets on the
threshold of the camp were a mere fringe of bubbles, and the sound
of the surf outside the Heads a whisper no louder than that of a
summer breeze. The sense of their solitude and proximity was like a
spell upon them, and every moment of silence strengthened it.

Sue took her tea and sipped it, and munched her currant cake. She
forgot that she was hungry, and only desired to dispose of her lunch
as quickly as possible. Mr Rutledge stood by the table, propping
himself against the edge, and looked down at her. The inevitableness
of the impending crisis became apparent to him, good resolutions
notwithstanding. Human nature is human nature, and when a man
very much in love finds himself thus confronted with his opportunity
– and such an opportunity! – and sees that his beloved also appreciates
the situation, what is he to do? He has, indeed, no choice. There is
but one thing he can do.

The girl made her little modest effort to avert the catastrophe by
jumping up before she had nearly satisfied her healthy appetite,
shaking the crumbs from her dress, and declaring again that she must
set forth immediately. But it availed nothing. Before she could get out
of the tent – neither understood exactly how it happened at the last
– she was caught in his arms, as she had almost known she must be
from the moment of walking in. For an instant she struggled and
thought she would be angry with him for thus taking advantage of her
defencelessness and imprudence, but the next instant her own arms
were round his neck and her willing mouth lifted to receive the
unspeakable first kiss. There was no coyness about Susan Delavel, and
no pretences. Whatever she did she did thoroughly, and in moments of
strong feeling, she paid no heed to manners.

When Noel Rutledge felt the sudden relaxation of her protesting
muscles, and then the warm, responsive impulse, wholehearted as his
own, his rapture was something that can be better imagined than
described. The world was all forgotten – fathers and mothers and
social distinctions, pride and prudence and poverty, and practical
considerations of every sort, and he was as contented with his lot as
any mere man could be. He gave vent to his feelings in a long,
tremulous, deep-chested croon, like the croon of a mother over a lost
and recovered child. 'Oh-h!' he murmured, when the hammerbeat of

his heart and the singing blood in his ears would let him speak, 'I wondered if it could be true! It seemed too good to believe in.'

'Yes,' she whispered back. 'I was afraid it was somebody else – not me.'

Half-an-hour later, and while poor Mrs Delavel was still hunting house and garden for her daughter at Darling Point, working herself into a paroxysm of silent wrath that would take her the best part of the week to get out of, Sue was still at the camp in her lover's company. She had some more tea and some more cake, and he knelt by her chair and fed her; and when she was not eating and drinking she was having that rest which she had refused to take at an earlier stage of the proceedings – supporting her weary frame upon his arm and shoulder. The Bo'sun had not come back; the desert island solitude was unbroken. They talked of their position and prospects, and took no count of time or of Mrs Grundy.

Now that it was too late the young man blamed himself for what he had done, though exhibiting no appearance of remorse. 'Your father will despise me,' said he, 'and everyone who hears of it will cry shame on me – situated as I am – and as you are.'

'Who cares what people say?' retorted Sue. 'It is nobody's business but our own. And my father is not like ordinary fathers.'

'He is not, indeed – any more than you are like ordinary daughters. But still I think he will jib at this. Being a father, he must think of your welfare a little.'

'Exactly. That is what he will do. He knows that you are my welfare.'

'How does he know?'

'I told him.'

'When?'

'When we left the camp the other night.'

'O!' and there was an eloquent pause in the conversation.

'But, mother,' continued Sue, when it was presently resumed, 'mother will never allow me to have you – never! So don't expect it.'

'O Sue! Never? And why?'

'For a thousand reasons.'

'Tell me some of them, love.'

'I can't; you must find them out. But she will be implacable.'

'For a while, perhaps – we must hope for the best. I shall not ask for you till I am better qualified to take care of you than I am now.'

'What are you going to do to qualify yourself?' she asked rather gloomily.

'I must go away and work, and make a position. Didn't you know it was for your sake I wanted to get more money, when you were so angry with me the other day for being mercenary? Your father thinks I should get on better anywhere than here, where I have incurred so much unpopularity. I think so too. And I should have gone away at the first if it had not been for you.'

'And you would go *now*? And without even letting them know of our engagement?'

'Good heavens, no! They shall know of *that* before they are a couple of hours older. I shall take you home now and tell them.'

'Both of them?'

'Certainly.'

'Hadn't you better see father first? I will tell him, shall I? And he will walk over here and see you. And we can break it to mother after. If it came upon her all at once, I'm afraid it would be too great a shock.'

He shook his head, with his slow, easy smile – with that indolent and indifferent manner which covered so much unsuspected determination. 'Best get it all over and start fair,' he said quietly.

'Very well,' she responded at once, recognising the master spirit. 'I am not afraid if you are not.'

'If I haven't to be afraid of *you*, there's nothing left to fear, so far as I'm concerned.'

'Ignorance is bliss,' she retorted lightly. 'You'll be more humble-minded when you come home again.'

'I don't think so. I take it that, whatever the result of my interview with your mother, *you* won't go back on me?'

'Certainly not.'

'You'll wait for me – you'll want me to wait for you – however long it may be.'

'I shall want whatever you want,' she answered simply.

'Just so. Well, on that basis, I can face all that comes.'

'Except one thing,' she continued earnestly. 'I don't want you to go away. What do we want with more money? I shall have plenty. And if you are so – so *vulgar* – as to make a fuss about sharing with me, as I should share with you if you had it, I shall be too, *too* disgusted with you.'

'I am afraid I am vulgar, dear.'

'Then let me be poor with you' – looking at him with her candid and truthful eyes. 'I shall like that best – far, far best. But in any case don't go and leave me just as I have got you.'

'I won't, love, – I won't; at any rate, not yet. When we have time to think things over we may find some other alternative. Heaven knows that I wouldn't go for anything less than to try to make the time of waiting shorter.'

'Whether short or long, I can never go away,' she said earnestly. 'I must stay with my father, or very near him, as long as he lives.'

He had risen from his knees beside her, and she had risen from her chair. Standing by the table they took a long embrace and kiss, and then they went out into the sunshine to the boat. He fixed the tiller in its place, took the oars in his hands, and rowed her home to her mother.

CHAPTER XXXV

Her Father's Daughter

He took the little boat along with powerful sweeping strokes – his Oxford strokes – while she held the tiller ropes round her waist, and steered it with the precision of long practice; and the voyage was made in half the time it had taken in the morning. His eyes dwelt on her face for the most part; hers on the course ahead of them and the obstacles it was her business to avoid. But now and then she answered his look frankly with one that, while it seemed not to disturb the tranquil intentness of her expression, suffused it with a radiance of satisfaction that left him in no doubt as to her state of mind.

The nearer they approached to Darling Point the more silent and serious they grew, the more impressed with the gravity of their immediate undertaking.

'Is your father likely to be at home, do you think?' the young man asked.

'Certain,' answered Sue. 'When he finds that I am out of bounds and in disgrace, he will stay till I come back to see me through it. But, as I told you before, it is not *father* you have to do with.' She added – smiling suddenly, after a little thoughtful pause – 'You don't happen to have ancestors, do you, Mr Rutledge.'

'I've got another name,' he said, 'besides Rutledge.'

'But do you?'

'Well, I suppose I've about the same number as other people. Why?'

'If you had ancestors that Burke and the Heralds' College could answer for. . . .'

'Oh, I've none of that sort, that I know of. My father was a doctor; my grandfather was an auctioneer. That's as far as the records go.'

'What a pity!'

'Do *you* think it's a pity?' he asked quickly, resting a moment on his oars.

She smiled at the absurdity of the question.

'*I*! It doesn't affect me. Your grandfather might have been a chimney-sweep – for the matter of that, you might be one yourself – for all I should care about it. But if you had had a pedigree it might have weighed with mother.'

'I wish I'd thought of that before. I might have found one by hunting for it. My grandfather, the auctioneer – he was in a large way of business – wrote books. And my father had a big practice in London. He was once President of the Royal College of Surgeons. Will that weigh anything at all?'

She shook her head. 'I'm afraid not.'

He rowed in silence for a minute; then he announced suddenly that his mother's father was a bishop.

'That's better,' Sue hopefully responded. 'What bishop?'

He told her what bishop, and her face fell again. It was, alas! a bishop who was himself without a pedigree – a nobody whatever outside his bishopric; nothing but a scholar and a schoolmaster, who, like the auctioneer, had written books.

'She knows them all,' sighed Sue, 'and where they all came from, and what their arms are, and whom they intermarried with – everything.'

'I suppose her own family is a very old one?' he ventured to remark.

'Very,' replied Sue, promptly and in all good faith. 'The Morrisons came over with the Conqueror.'

'Well,' said the young man, making a little grimace expressive of the hopelessness of his case, 'I must just stand upon my own merits, such as they are.' The poorness of his merits, however, seemed to strike him with fresh force, and he fell into a grave and self-reproachful mood. With every appearance of right and reason, he assured his sweetheart that he had committed an unpardonable crime in asking her to marry him, and that nothing her mother could say to him would approach the measure of his deserts.

Sue listened to these arguments with quiet complacency, steadily watching the boat's course, and apparently giving all her attention to business. But when he had done she turned to him with a look that took all reality out of his words.

'Look here,' she said, with a clear directness and self-restraint of manner that was very odd in a young girl who had just been immersed in all the sensations of a sudden betrothal, 'let us understand each other about this matter. If I know anything of you – as I hope I do – you don't mean all that nonsense. And if you know anything of me – as I also hope you do – you know what utter nonsense I think it; just pure conventionalism, and nothing more nor less. You are the only man I have ever met who wouldn't have been certain to put a stop to all my ways of living – all the ways I want to live – the moment I had married him. Whatever others may think – and in the long run it doesn't matter what they think – I am satisfied. I don't want you to be in any way different from what you are. If you were rich – well, if you were rich I wouldn't have you. For then I should *know* you were not worthy of me.'

He smiled at the characteristic conclusion of this speech, but his heart swelled within him. 'What I was thinking of,' he said, 'was that by marrying me a stop would be put to a good many of your ways of living.'

'I know. But what of that? I dare say I am absurd and ridiculous, but the fact is I really don't care for money – beyond a modest competence – not one little bit. I should be equally happy without it – happier, for I should be more in my own hands, more free to do things, less weighed down.'

'You have not tried it, dear.'

'Yes, I knew you would bring out that stupid platitude. Everybody does. I have not tried it, of course. But I know what is in me and what isn't – what I really want and what I don't care a straw for.' They were passing a great ship that had just slipped her moorings, homeward bound, and was rocking the little boat in the wash she made, and Sue paused for a few moments. When they came to quiet water she went on talking. 'I'll tell you what I think of that money question,' she said. 'It is what my father thinks too – only he gets a little slack sometimes – he is preoccupied, his energies have been drained in different ways, and he has to consider others. We believe that the time is coming when people will be *ashamed* to be rich – I mean rich for merely their own purposes. It will be vulgar, it will be selfish, it will be mean; people will look down on the rich person instead of up, as they do now. And wealth will go out of fashion amongst well-bred people, and all that gross kind of luxury; and life will be more simple and sincere, more intelligent and refined; and the poor man will cease from the land then, without any bloody revolutions – if he will only be patient in the meanwhile. You are laughing at me and thinking me a visionary,' she exclaimed, laughing a little herself as she met his sympathetic eyes.

He declared that he was not laughing; that it simply made him glow to listen to her.

'Well,' she said, 'what people in general will feel some day, I feel now. I should be ashamed – I *am* ashamed – to be rich when so many are poor. If ever I have money – I suppose I shall have it some day – a long day yet, I trust! – I shall take enough for myself and those belonging to me, but not more than enough. I don't mean that I shall use the rest to found institutions – I hate institutions – but I shall sprinkle help round me wherever I go. I don't care what political economists say – selfish, hide-bound creatures! I will not be governed by them. I will just pay my debt to the world direct, without employing middle-men, and above all things else I will stop hunger and physical pain whenever I see it – as far as my means will go. There are plenty to attend to minds and souls. I'll go no further than bodies. Bodies are the chief thing, and they are always neglected. Well,' she concluded as she steered towards the boathouse at Darling Point, 'no husband in the world would let me do all that except you. But you will.'

'Yes,' he said, with solemnity, 'I will.'

'I don't want to be nursed up, and choked and smothered. I want to develop myself. I want to work. I want to *live*. The hope of my life has been that I might have something to do in it – something real and not sham. I want to use myself – don't you understand? But I know you understand. That is why you are so – so peculiarly appropriate.'

'To me,' said Noel Rutledge, drawing in his oars, 'to me work and life are synonymous terms. Some people, I know, only think that part of life worth living which is rescued from work, but I think the other part the best. I never want to be pensioned off while I have strength for active service.'

'Exactly. I knew you were like that, and therefore. . . .' They were within the boathouse. Noel had landed, and she was stepping on shore after him. Therefore the sentence remained uncompleted.

They stayed in the boathouse for about ten minutes; then, with a natural trepidation, heroically disguised, they ascended the garden to the house. One bit of the way was up a steep path and a flight of winding sandstone stairs overarched with a creeper-covered trellis and tall ferns on either side, a place that went by the inappropriate name of the North-West Passage. Here it was dark in the sunniest noonday, and no sooner had the darkness enveloped our lovers than the man's arm found its way round the girl's waist as a matter of course. 'Let me help you up,' he said; and she allowed him to help her up, though she had the strength and the elasticity of a young antelope, and could have helped him quite as well. And thus they dawdled along the path, crawlingly mounted the rock-hewn steps, and, turning a corner, came suddenly upon her father, who was standing quietly at the mouth of the green tunnel waiting for them.

'Good morning, Rutledge,' he said gravely. 'You have brought the truant back.'

'Good morning, Delavel. Yes, I have.' His arm had been withdrawn from his sweetheart's waist like a flash of lightning. 'I – I'm afraid you'll blame me very much.'

Sue ran up to her father, and flung herself upon his breast – an unusual demonstration in broad daylight, and in the presence of a third person, which told its tale. 'It is my fault,' she whispered hurriedly. 'I went to the camp without knowing he was there. I stayed a little while, not thinking. He has come to tell you and mother.'

'What, already!' the father ejaculated with dismay. Then he thought with satisfaction of the suitor's impecuniosity, and the length of time that must elapse before he could claim her, and he felt easier – easy enough to smile in a rather grim fashion, and even to shake hands with his visitor.

'Are you going up to call on Mrs Delavel, Rutledge?' he asked, with a curious look at the intrepid young man.

'Yes – if I have your permission,' was the quick reply.

'Oh! You have my full permission, certainly.'

'You know what I have come for, Delavel?' – very earnestly.

'I guess,' was the laconic response.

'Have I – have we – your consent? I am not asking for anything in the present, of course – until I am better worthy of her than I am now. But may I. . . .'

Richard waved his hand upwards in an airy manner. 'Go and talk to my wife about it,' he said, chuckling for a moment in what struck Sue as a surprisingly heartless fashion, totally at variance with his sympathetic behaviour on board the steamer the other night. 'And Sukey, my dear, did you leave the boat where it can be got at?'

'O father! you are not going away! You are not going to leave us!' cried Sue, aghast and reproachful. 'I counted on you to help us with mother.'

'Be content if I don't hinder you,' he replied. 'That's as much as you can reasonably ask of me. Isn't it, Rutledge?'

'Quite,' said the young man, 'and more.'

So the lovers went up and the father went down. This time the father was suffering from a paroxysm of that jealousy which had torn the daughter's heart when she first recognised that he loved another as well if not better than he loved her. He was pleased to think of the bad quarter of an hour that his rival in Sukey's affections was going to have, and that was the only pleasure he enjoyed that afternoon.

CHAPTER XXXVI

●

The Court Of Final Appeal

Mrs Delavel sat in her drawing-room, knitting. She looked the picture of luxurious tranquillity in the depths of her soft chair, with palms and flowers and artistic elegancies all around her; but the face she lifted at the sound of the opening door did not impose upon her daughter. It was calm and comely, the face of a dignified, reasonable, well-bred matron – quite reassuring to Mr Rutledge, who had the ordinary man's dulness of perception in such matters; but Sue saw what she had expected to see in the steady brown eyes and firmly shut mouth – the rock-like, ice-like displeasure against which their appeals would break, like waves against granite cliffs, in vain. 'Though it would have been all the same,' she said to herself, 'whatever the mood in which we found her.'

Across the pretty, spacious room the girl marched straight to her mother's chair, and her lover followed her half-way and paused, waiting for the lady of the house to look at him, that he might make his bow. He was a pleasant figure to look at, tall and broad, with his wholesome, kindly face; but Mrs Delavel carefully excluded him from her cold gaze. She fixed her eyes upon Sue, divining a more than usually serious escapade; and a dim sense of its nature caused her cheek to redden and her nostrils to dilate.

'Mother,' said Sue, with the courage of desperation, 'here is Mr Rutledge – father's friend, Mr Rutledge. He has come to see you – he wants to speak to you.'

Then Annie had to recognise Mr Rutledge's presence, and he bowed with amazing self-possession. 'I don't think I have the pleasure of knowing Mr Rutledge,' she said with a stiff and ghastly smile. She had known the clergyman of that name – had even discussed burning questions of ritual with him in the days when he was fairly respectable; it was the renegade in the tweed suit whose acquaintance she desired to repudiate. Certainly no lover, courting maternal favours, ever found himself in a more unpromising or uncomfortable position, and his constitutional imperturbability never stood him in better stead. It enabled him to maintain his dignity and his grasp of the situation, which were great advantages to him.

'I have come to tell you, Mrs Delavel, that your daughter has promised to marry me,' he said, seeing the futility, under the circumstances, of beating about the bush; 'to marry me some day – when I have prepared a suitable home for her. I know I am not worthy of her, I am ashamed to ask for your consent – indeed, I know I shall not get it; but it is right to let you know at once what has happened, and to tell you – to tell you that I will strain every nerve to make myself worthy of her; not only that, but to work myself into a position that shall not discredit her choice in the eyes of her family. As for her, she is not ashamed of me as I am. And – and a man can do a woman no higher honour than to love her with all his heart and soul. But I know how ineligible I am, as I stand in every way except in being her choice – she has chosen me as I have chosen her, otherwise I should have nothing to say – and I will leave no stone unturned to better my position for her sake. I will do all that is within the power of human effort to do. I won't ask for her until I have qualified myself to take proper care of her; and I don't wish her to feel bound by anything that has happened today. She is young – there may be a long waiting – she may think better of it' –

Here Sue, who had been standing apart breathlessly watching and listening, took a step to his side and slipped her hand in his; and Mrs Delavel, who had allowed him to run to this length because she was too stunned to speak, suddenly found her voice.

'Susan,' she said in a cold fury, 'go to your room, if you please.'

Susan didn't want to go; she wanted to stay and see the matter out. 'Mother,' she pleaded, 'it concerns me more than any one.'

But Mrs Delavel sternly pointed to the door. The girl looked at her fellow-culprit; he returned the look with an almost imperceptible nod; they squeezed each other's hands violently for a moment, and then she walked out of the room, leaving him in sole charge of their joint interests. She did not, however, go upstairs; she went to sit in the garden – in a cunningly-contrived nook amongst the trees, whence she could see, without being visible from the road herself, the gate through which her lover would pass presently when his trial was over. Her intention was to lie in wait for him, with a little store of oil and wine for the wounds he would have received; to assure him of her fidelity through all vicissitudes – her determination to be his, some day or other, no matter how circumstances might fight against them.

She sat for what seemed an hour, but was perhaps twenty minutes, and imagined the dreadful battle going on within the house. Her mother was not a scolding woman – all the blood of all the Delavels could not have made her more of a lady in that respect – but she would be more overwhelming than any termagant of the back slums in her polite implacability. Sue was not without a dim pity for that poor mother – with whom all mothers must sympathise – but she was, naturally, most concerned for her lover's tender feelings. And how cruelly would these be outraged! His poverty and his ill repute would be impressed on him as they never were before; he would be told that he had taken a dishonourable advantage of a girl's innocence and ignorance of the world – had entrapped her by secret strategems for the sake of her fortune; he would be denounced as a wicked atheist and soul-destroyer, bound to effect the eternal ruin of his victim should she be delivered into his hands; and all that unpretending high-mindedness and unworldliness which made his rare and excellent quality would be as utterly unrecognised as the girlish aspirations of which they were the correlative. He would be spurned with courteous words, but still with contempt and contumely, and the door of hope would be shut against him as fast as any one human hand could shut it.

In the midst of these painful and exciting reflections she heard the click of the front gate, and, looking round in alarm, beheld the checked suit, the pot hat, the eyeglass of Lord Boyton. He wore his clothes loose and his hat on the back of his head, which showed his stout form and his chubby face to the best advantage. His eyeglass flashed in the sun; he walked with an assured step that betokened him quite sober; he was making for the house with an air of purpose that filled Miss Delavel with dismay. Her first impulse on seeing him was to hide herself; her second to intercept him before he could reach the drawing-room and disturb the important business going on there; her third to make a straight appeal to him as a man and a brother to help and not hinder her in her time of difficulty.

She called him by name as he was passing, and he paused, turned, and hastened to join her in her green nook, evidently as much surprised as pleased by the unexpected invitation. After welcoming him with astounding cordiality, she led him away from that now inconvenient spot, giving up the chance of seeing her lover for that day; and she descended the garden to a bench on a midway terrace, hidden from view of the house windows, and there took a seat and made room for her companion beside her. He interpreted these signs of goodwill as a swell young lord was bound to do. He asked her where she had been hiding all the morning; he declared he had found himself unable to get through the day without seeing her; he reproached her with snubbing him; he showed such a dangerous tendency to put his arm round her waist, and otherwise to assume repentance and responsiveness, that she was fain to plunge at once into plain statements.

'Lord Boyton,' she said, 'did you ever love anybody very, *very* much indeed?'

The question naturally staggered him. His amiable countenance became overspread with blushes and perplexity. 'Well, I dare say I have admired a lot of girls,' he admitted, in a doubtful and apologetic manner. 'In a sort of way, you know. But until I met you. . . .'

'Oh, nonsense!' she interrupted. 'Don't be silly. I want you to talk seriously – not to pay absurd compliments.'

'But I assure you, Sue – may I call you Sue?'

'No, you may not.' She made a hasty gesture to fend him off. 'Just listen to me. I was going to tell you that I – that *I* love somebody. And I am rather in trouble. And – and I thought you might perhaps help me a little.' And – with a most engaging candour and frankness, she sketched a delicate outline of the situation, while he sat and listened, looking rather sulky and a good deal taken aback. 'I was in hopes it might have been me,' he said, when she had told her little story.

'Oh no, I am sure you never hoped anything of the kind. You never had the least reason to hope it. Come now, did I ever give you any reason?'

'Your mother did. Your mother has been encouraging me like anything.'

'Mother has been very kind to you. That's because you are a stranger, and she likes you.'

'She said only this very morning. . . .'

'Well, never mind what she said. You see she didn't know I had already made my choice; and look how unsuitable it would have been! You must marry a great lady, of course, as lords are expected to do.'

'I'm sure I have never seen a great lady who'd do me more credit than you would,' he protested.

'Thank you,' she responded; 'that's very handsome of you; but you are mistaken, all the same. I should be the most dismal failure imaginable. Don't talk of any such nonsense; be what I want you to be – be my good friend, won't you?'

She laid her warm brown hand on his; and the action and her frank appeal stirred all the gentleman in him.

'Tell me what I can do,' he said, lifting her hand to his lips. 'Do you want me to plead that fellow's cause with your father and mother? If so, you must tell me what to say, and I'll do my best, though it will be a hard job, I can tell you.'

'Oh no,' she said, smiling; 'I don't want you to do that. What I want is. . . .' But when she tried to explain it she could not find words.

'Look here,' he said, with a discernment that was very creditable to him. 'Your mother asked me to dine here tonight; do you want me to come?'

'Yes,' replied Sue promptly.

'And to play tennis with you tomorrow?'

'Yes.'

'And go on as if nothing had happened?'

'Yes.'

'All right,' he said heartily. 'You may depend on me.'

'It would be so much easier for me,' said Sue, 'if you wouldn't desert us suddenly, just at this particular moment. . . .'

'I know. I won't desert you. I'll stick to you and see you through it,' said Lord Boyton valiantly. He quite understood the part he was to perform – that of a buffer between Miss Delavel and the impact of her mother's wrath, and he very shortly came to the conclusion that it was much better fun to be the young lady's confidential friend than her unfavoured lover. In fact, he had not particularly cared to be her lover; he would not have thought of it if she had not snubbed him.

Sue did not see her parents until dinner time. She went into the drawing-room two minutes before the gong sounded and found her father standing on the hearth-rug, as he would stand to warm his coat-tails in winter, the sole occupant of the apartment. He was looking towards the door when she opened it, and he held out his hand. She flew across the room, and the next moment was clasped in his arms. He did not utter a word of congratulation, and she did not think of asking for his good wishes. It was quite unnecessary. When she spoke it was to whisper, 'How is she?'

'She's in an awful way,' he whispered back. 'You'll have to be patient, old girl. But never mind; you've got plenty of time before you – you can afford to wait. It will be good for him, too; give him his opportunity to work.'

'How did she treat him?'

'I don't know. I can only guess.'

'What is she going to do about it?'

'She's going to take you straight off to New Zealand for the whole summer. And if that doesn't cure you she's going to take you to Europe.'

'I won't go.'

'I think you'll find you'll have to go.'

'Without you?'

'I'm afraid so.'

'O father! I couldn't!'

'Well, don't make a fuss, old girl. You'll gain nothing by that, and you might lose something. Just take things as they come.'

Like lovers surprised in a clandestine meeting, they suddenly separated at the sound of approaching voices. The door opened to admit Lord Boyton and his hostess, whom he had met in the hall as she descended from her room. Mrs Delavel was endeavouring to unbend to her fascinating guest, but not succeeding very well, though better than could have been expected. Lord Boyton was in the highest spirits. He beamed upon Sue through his eyeglass in a familiar and encouraging manner that puzzled her father extremely.

'Good evening, Miss Delavel,' he said, cordially shaking hands with her, as if he had not seen her before – which, Sue thought, was rather overdoing it. 'Awfully sorry to find you out when I called this morning. I thought we might have had a little tennis perhaps. But we'll have a game tomorrow, shall we? May I come over after breakfast tomorrow?'

'Certainly, if you wish,' said Sue.

Annie would not speak to her daughter, or look at her. She was truly in 'an awful way,' as the girl could see; all the accustomed symptoms of displeasure were intensified to the point of rage and violence – or what would have been rage and violence in a less perfectly-mannered person. On the surface she smiled graciously and assumed a polite interest in various topics introduced by her guest; but her nostrils were all aquiver, and her white breast, that was like a soft satin cushion, rose and fell, and her lips were compressed over her shut teeth, by reason of the inward commotion of her mind which had not yet had time to settle. The host was dull and silent; the daughter of the house was silent also, and looking just a shade haughty and mutinous. In short, the atmosphere of the dinner-table was such as to spoil the appetite and damp the spirits of the most case-hardened globe-trotter. But Lord Boyton was not damped in any way. He surpassed himself in the exuberance of his conversation and good-humour, insomuch that his host felt grateful for his presence for the first time, while thinking that the young cub was more of a cub than ever. 'Anyone but a born fool would see that something was the matter,' thought Richard; 'but that young ass sees nothing.' Which was a mistake and an injustice on Richard's part.

Lord Boyton had an idea of his own, which he thought a great improvement upon Sue's. He would continue to delude Mrs Delavel with the belief that he was a candidate for her daughter's hand, and Sue's changed attitude to him would give colour to the assertion he intended to make, that she would get over her fancy for the vagabond she had taken up with, and allow herself to be won by the worthier suitor in course of time, if judiciously left to her own devices and his. This plan might – who could tell? – be really as successful as it pretended it would be; but if not, it would make things pleasant for him and easy for the poor girl for a good while to come. So when Mrs Delavel, in a would-be careless tone, announced that she would be off to New Zealand in a few days, he was quite equal to the occasion.

'Will you?' he exclaimed. 'Well, it's getting time to go somewhere, I suppose. I had some thoughts of New Zealand myself. We might join forces, eh? I might help Mr Delavel with the luggage and things. I'm a capital courier.'

'I'm afraid my husband's business will compel him to remain in Sydney,' said Annie, who had quite determined this time to have her daughter wholly in her own hands.

'Then you'll want me all the more. Eh, Miss Sue? I could look after you and keep you out of mischief, eh?' He was half-way through his dinner by this time, and his not abundant wits were beginning to fail him a little, or he would not have ventured upon this pleasantry, which disconcerted himself as much as it did the rest of the party as soon as he had uttered it.

'I think,' said Mrs Delavel, with a stern, portentous smile, 'that I shall be able to keep my daughter out of mischief.' Then she added, not wishing to throw cold water on his really welcome proposal, 'But we shall be very glad to have you to take care of us, all the same.'

'It might end in your having to take care of him,' remarked Richard. Which seemed extremely likely.

After his little slip, Lord Boyton made really heroic efforts to keep sober, or, at any rate, not to get more drunk than he already was; for he felt the responsibility of his position as Sue's champion and protector, and was most anxious to serve her faithfully. It was touching to see, when the bottle came to his elbow, his wistful look at it, his momentary wavering, and the noble air with which he said, 'No, thanks,' and let it pass. And during the rest of the dinner he devoted himself to the task of pleasing his hostess with a determination that deserved the highest praise. He chattered about the duchesses and countesses of his acquaintance, calling them by their Christian names; related anecdotes of the Prince of Wales and of Roger of Dunstanborough; described the goings-on of the professional beauties, and roundly asserted that not one of them could hold a candle to Miss Sue – which latter was an impudent statement, because Sue was not a beauty at all. And Mrs Delavel thawed under this treatment – while it lasted – in a wonderful manner; she seemed for the moment to forget her maternal cares.

After dinner Lord Boyton remarked that it was a jolly night, and asked Sue to take a turn in the garden with him. Greatly to the surprise of both her father and mother, the girl rose at once and allowed herself to be led away into the darkness. As soon as the pair were out of earshot of their elders, Lord Boyton began to praise himself and to seek to be praised. 'I know how to manage Mrs Delavel,' said he, with that fine taste for which he was remarkable. 'She's awfully fond of me – I can do anything with her. You see if I don't bring her round in no time.'

'You'll overdo it,' said Sue, 'to a dead certainty.'

CHAPTER XXXVII

—•—

How Lord Boyton Overdid It

When Sue went up to her room that night she found Hannah sitting there, like a patient maid waiting to undress her mistress – an office that was never required of her. The old woman sat under one of the shaded lamps, with her spectacles over her nose. She had been sewing, but her work had fallen to the floor. Her head lay on the back of her chair; her cap was awry. At the moment of Sue's entrance she was in the land of dreams. The first creak of the door, however, roused her to wakefulness and activity.

'Well,' she said, by way of greeting, 'and what is it that you've been up to now?'

'Who told you I'd been up to anything?' retorted Sue.

'Oh, you needn't pretend. I know *that* much, at any rate.'

'How do you know? Has mother been telling you?'

'Your mother hasn't told me a word – except that I'm not to let you out of my sight for a moment when she's not with you.'

Sue's face grew fiery red. She stood rooted to the floor, glaring at the old woman with indignant eyes.

'There,' said Hannah, 'you needn't look at me as if you'd eat me. *I* can't help it, can I?'

'I'm ashamed of you, Hannah,' the girl burst out, when she could find words in which to express her sense of the treatment to which she was being subjected. 'If anybody had told me that you would descend to such work I wouldn't have believed them.'

'Well, I don't like the job, I can tell you, and I told your mother so. In fact, I told her plump and plain that I wouldn't do it. But she said if I didn't somebody else should, and I thought you'd rather it was me than a common servant.' Hannah, of course, was not a common servant.

Sue was silent for a minute, battling with her rage and mortification. She saw the injustice of being angry with Hannah, yet she still regarded the old woman resentfully – as the innocent policeman always is regarded by the enemy of the Government which he represents. 'And how long is this to last?' inquired the young lady haughtily.

'Till you go to New Zealand next week.'

'And what is mother afraid I should do in the meantime? What is the danger to be guarded against?'

'I suppose she's afraid you should want to meet somebody.'

'Meet whom?'

'I don't know. A sweetheart, most likely.'

'Does she suppose I've got a sweetheart hidden in my bedroom? Am I to be watched by night as well as by day? Are you to sit here while I undress myself, for instance?'

'No, my dear,' said Hannah, gathering up her work. 'I won't intrude on you any longer. I'll sit outside the door until your mother comes up.' She went out a little huffily, for her feelings were hurt by her young lady's tone, and shut the door behind her. Sue heard her drag a chair on the landing, and knew by certain rustlings and coughings that Hannah meant to be faithful to her trust, however much she might dislike it.

In a few minutes Mrs Delavel's trailing skirts were audible on the stairs. Sue was standing before her dressing-table, taking down her pretty hair; and she paused, hearing her mother's hand on the door, and turned to receive her. She had not spoken to the culprit since the latter was ordered out of the drawing-room at the beginning of the momentous interview. Sue braced herself for a painful discussion of that event, supposing it was the object of this visit.

But Mrs Delavel had not come to talk. Her displeasure was too hard set to flow in words at present. What she did was to walk with stately composure across the threshold, draw the key from the inner side of the door, and, leaving the room again without regarding her daughter any more than if she had been a piece of furniture, reclose the door, reinsert the key, and shoot the lock on the outside.

Sue's first impulse, on realising the measure of the indignity put upon her, was to fly across the room and rattle the door handle furiously. 'Mother!' she cried sharply; and then, changing her tone, 'Father! father! father!'

Mr Delavel, however, was mooning in the garden with his pipe, thinking of his little girl's troubles, but out of reach of the sound of her cries. His wife calmly disregarded them; Sue could hear the rustle of the maternal skirts along the softly-carpeted corridor, dying away in the distance. Hannah had already been despatched to her bed at the farther end of the house. And in a moment the girl's paroxysm of rage – the unthinking impulse of a wild creature suddenly realising captivity – passed. 'No, I won't drag him into it, poor daddy!' she said to herself. 'And what does it matter! It can't alter things. It can't hurt me now.' She walked restlessly round and round the room for a few minutes, until she had regained her lost self-control; then she undressed herself; then she sat down in her nightgown and wrote a long letter to her lover – a process that soothed her spirit wonderfully; and she went to bed at last in a state of simmering happiness such as she had never known in her life before, and had the most beautiful dreams, though settled sleep was impossible.

It was Hannah who unlocked her door in the morning. Hannah had served her mistress with the early cup of tea, and was now put on guard again till breakfast-time. She came to the bedside with Sue's little tray, and was surprised at the tranquil smile which greeted her. 'Well, I'm glad to see you're all right,' said the old woman sourly; but her sourness was not for Sue. She patted the soft shoulder uplifted from the pillow, and smoothed the rumpled hair. 'I should like to know what's the matter, that you're treated like a convict,' said she questioningly. 'It isn't for nothing that your mother puts you under lock and key – and you a grown woman. I quite expected you'd have made a rope of your bedclothes and let yourself down out of the window, and gone off while we were all asleep.'

'With my sweetheart? Thank you for the hint, Hannah. I'll do that tonight if I'm locked up again; and, by the way, I've got a letter for him. Will you post it for me as soon as you go downstairs?'

'Where is it?' asked Hannah eagerly.

'Oh, you want to see the address,' said Sue, who had it under her pillow. 'I won't show it to you unless you promise to post it for me.'

'Well, I can't promise that. I've got orders not to post letters for you; and what's more, to see that nobody else does.'

'I suppose you can't prevent my father from posting letters for me if he chooses?'

'*I* can't; but your mother will, unless I'm much mistaken.'

'Very well; I'll give it to Lord Boyton. He's a free agent, at any rate. And now what am I to do, Hannah?' – for by this time Sue had emptied her cup of tea and eaten her wafer of bread and butter. 'Am I to get up, or am I to stay in bed?'

'To get up, of course. And if you'll promise not to stir out till breakfast time I'll leave you to yourself till then.'

'How good of you! Do you mean I'm not to stir out of the house, or not out of my room? Because I should like to have a bath, if I might be indulged so far, though if I'm risking handcuffs and leg-irons by walking down the corridor to the bathroom I'd better go dirty, unpleasant as that would be?'

'Don't you be silly now,' said Hannah testily. 'Go and have your bath, of course. And then stay in your room till the gong sounds for breakfast. You're not to go downstairs and talk to your father, remember; that happened last night, but it's not to happen again.'

'Hannah,' cried Sue passionately, 'you're an old wretch!'

'I can't help it,' said Hannah. 'I must obey orders, and if you don't like it, you've only yourself to blame.'

Sue, angry as she was, felt herself upon her parole, and also went in great dread of having a 'common servant' put over her in Hannah's place, so she kept in her room till breakfast time. She did not even go down at the summons of the gong, but sat on the edge bf her bed till she was specially sent for after fish and omelette were cold. She walked into the breakfast-room with a severely composed air, and saluted her father only. 'Good morning, father dear.'

'Good morning, Sukey.'

They did not dare to look at each other while they exchanged these formal greetings; but Richard managed, by touching the toe of his daughter's slipper under the table, to communicate to her the fact that his heart was in the right place, notwithstanding appearances to the contrary. Mrs Delavel poured out Sue's coffee, but otherwise took no sort of notice of her; and Sue did not speak to her mother – a circumstance which pained the poor girl very much afterwards whenever she remembered it.

It was a perfectly silent meal. The master of the house propped his newspaper against the slop-basin and absorbed himself in matters outside the domestic circle as far as possible; and immediately after breakfast he made haste off to business, without a word to anybody. Sue and her mother were left alone, and the silence continued. They usually spent the morning in the breakfast-room, which was a cheerful apartment, having a substantial table near the window, which commanded a lovely open prospect of the bay. It is not, we may observe in passing, the easiness of chairs and sofas that makes the comfort of a room; or not that only. It is the convenience and sufficiency of its table space. Because the modern drawing-room is so ill-furnished in this respect, however charming in all others, its occupants can rarely make life interesting and active therein; a table large enough to spread one's elbows on in the neighbourhood of the hearth, or in the light of a big window, according to the season of the year, would just make all the difference. It was because of that table in the Delavel breakfast-room that Sue and her mother lingered there of a morning, for they had choice of several sitting-rooms beside. Here they scattered their needlework, their books and newspapers, their drawing or writing materials, with a sense of ample accommodation that was restful and satifying to mind as well as body, and which they did not seem to be able to find in the same degree elsewhere.

On this particular morning Sue would have been very glad to exchange her favourite corner in the angle of that pleasant window for any other in the house where she could have been alone, but she would not leave the room without permission, and was too proud to ask for it. She sat down with her hands before her, and a meek air of waiting for orders. Mrs Delavel also sat down and glanced over the newspaper while the breakfast things were being removed. As the tray was going out she spoke for the first time. 'Tell the cook to come to me.'

It was her custom to visit the cook in her own quarters every morning at this hour; today the cook was summoned to the breakfast-room for consultation and instructions. This, of course, was in order that Sue should not be left unguarded. The interview was a long one, and the girl turned to the table, on which stood her work-basket, and began to sew by way of relieving the irksomeness of her position. As she sewed she listened and longed for the sound of the door bell and the announcement of Lord Boyton's arrival. Never – up to yesterday – had she dreamed of the possiblity of welcoming him as she was ready to do now.

And he came early, as if he knew how badly she wanted him. He came at the very nick of time, just as the cook was retiring to her kitchen, with the bill of fare for dinner in her hand. He entered with a beaming face, wearing his flannels and canvas shoes, and Mrs Delavel smiled and was gracious to him, according to established habit. Sue sprang to her feet and threw down her work, and held out her hand with unprecedented cordiality; she felt almost ready to kiss him for so opportunely coming to her relief.

'I'm afraid I'm rather early,' said he; 'but I thought it would be better to have our game before it got too hot, don't you know.'

'Oh, much better,' said Sue. 'We'll go now. I'll just get my hat' – She broke off and looked at her mother, with a quick change in her face. 'Mother, may I be allowed to go upstairs to fetch my hat?' she asked stiffly.

Mrs Delavel's answer was to touch the button of the bell, and to order the maid who thereupon appeared to tell Hannah she was wanted. Hannah came, looking very surly, and her mistress said to her, in her calm tones, 'Hannah, Miss Sue wants to get her hat. Will you go with her, if you please?'

The girl left the room with flaming cheeks and swelling breast, leaving Lord Boyton to stare after her with his mouth open. Half-way up the stairs she turned to her sour-faced nurse, and said in a deep, thrilling voice, 'Hannah, I feel as if I could *choke* you.'

'I dare say you do,' responded Hannah, taking no offence. 'And I don't wonder at it. If she's going to do this before folks, I'll have no more of it. I'll get the master to interfere. There's reason in all things.'

And then she flung her arms round the old woman's neck and kissed her. 'Never mind, Hannah, I'm happy,' she cried, with a little sound in her throat, half laugh and half sob. 'I'm happy, in spite of her!' Which was perhaps the hardest thing she ever said of her mother in her life.

'What makes you happy?' inquired Hannah.

'I'll tell you all about it some time,' said Sue.

She ran downstairs with her hat on and her racket in her hand, watched by Hannah from the corridor above; and she believed she was going to enjoy a little liberty in the companionship of her confidential friend. She had her letter that he was to post in her pocket; she had her head full of information that she meant to pour into his sympathetic ears as soon as they reached the tennis-ground. Mrs Delavel hated to be out of doors in the heat, unless in pursuance of her social avocations; she was never on the tennis-ground to admire and applaud the splendid battles that went on there almost daily between her husband and daughter in the cool weather; she had never yet thought it necessary to chaperone the latter person when Lord Boyton enticed her thither for a game. With him, at any rate, if with no one else, Sue expected to be considered safe.

But she was disappointed. On reaching the lower hall she found her friend awaiting her with a disconcerted expression on his face, and beside him her mother in her garden hat, neckerchief, and gloves. Not a word was said. The two young people exchanged a blank look, and then, with all the spring gone out of them, trailed out of the cool vestibule into the burning sunshine, Lord Boyton walking beside his hostess, and holding a white umbrella over her, Sue bringing up the rear, and slashing the heads off the flowers with the edge of her racket as she passed.

The tennis-court, cut out of the sandstone cliff, surrounded with high trellises to keep the balls from bounding into the sea, lay half-way down the garden. It was a tennis-court of the most luxurious pattern, perfect to play on and pretty to look at, with its trellis screen covered with flowering creepers, and its charming arbour in the corner, and its comfortable seats all round; but neither Lord Boyton nor Sue found any pleasure in it on this occasion. Mrs Delavel sat under her umbrella, on a level with the net, and watched them so closely that they could not exchange a word in private, nor was there any opportunity for passing the letter from one pocket to the other. Under these circumstances Sue wielded her racket with an off-hand recklessness, and Lord Boyton swung his to and fro with a languid carelessness that betokened an utter want of interest in the game on either side; and after half-an-hour of disgraceful play they tacitly agreed to make a failure of it.

'Lord, how hot it is!' exclaimed the young nobleman, who got hot very easily. 'Too hot for tennis. We'll have to wait till we get to New Zealand, eh?' Then after a short silence, he continued, 'Look here, Miss Sue, let me take you out on the water – that's the only cool place. Let's get the boat out, and have a quiet row down the harbour, eh? Mrs Delavel, you don't like the water, I know, but you can sit on the terrace and watch us, and you'll see what good care I'll take of her. We won't go out of your sight, and when you wave your handkerchief we'll turn back. Eh? You can trust her to *my* care, I know.'

'Certainly I can,' said Mrs Delavel sweetly. 'But who told you I did not like the water? I like it very much, and if you feel inclined for a row I will go with you with pleasure. I couldn't let you take my daughter alone, of course – not because I could not trust you with her, but because it would not be proper.'

This was not at all what Lord Boyton wanted. However, he could not gracefully go back on his proposal; and Sue, who saw herself doomed to strict captivity, thought it would at least be more tolerable on the water than in the house, and was anxious to keep her friend beside her as long as possible. So they repaired to the boathouse, and the girl, with her quick, strong hands, got the boat ready while the young man made a show of doing it.

'We'll bring it round to the steps for you, mother,' she said; for it was as unseemly for Mrs Delavel to get into the boat in the boathouse as to get into her carriage in the stableyard.

But this little dodge failed, of course. 'Thank you,' she replied coolly; 'I prefer to get in here.' And she stepped in as she spoke, assisted by Lord Boyton, and sat down in the stern, fairly in the middle of the curved seat.

'I think I shall have to sit there, mother, to steer,' said Sue politely.

'I think,' replied Mrs Delavel icily, 'that I am as competent to steer as you are.'

'Oh, certainly,' rejoined her daughter. 'Only you are not used to it, and I thought perhaps you wouldn't care for the trouble.'

Mrs Delavel calmly drew the ropes round her waist, without deigning further remark. Lord Boyton took the oars, and Sue sat down on one side, with nothing to do but to watch their performances.

They had not gone far before the expert young boatwoman perceived that helm and oars were in the hands of arrant bunglers. Mrs Delavel had never steered a boat before, in spite of having lived by the sea all her life, and, like others in the same position, imagined that no practice was necessary – that anybody could do such a simple thing as that. She gently tugged at one rope, then at the other, with the result that the boat turned exactly towards the point to be avoided instead of from it; and she did so with an unruffled air of dignified ease, as of one who knew her business perfectly. Once, when they were in imminent danger of colliding with a ferry-boat, Sue instinctively made a snatch at the rope, and was rewarded with a rebuff that determined her to interfere no more, but to let them muddle on as they liked. And presently Mrs Delavel, aware of her inefficiency, though scorning to own to it, gave up pulling one way or the other, and contented herself with holding the rudder level with the keel, and leaving the whole responsibility of guidance to Lord Boyton.

The performances of that young man were little better than her own. He had always been too fat and lazy for this kind of exercise, and his style was the style of the conceited amateur anxious to show off before ladies. He spread his legs and arms, and splashed and tugged, and panted, jerking the boat from side to side, and generally making a most ungraceful exhibition of himself, while fondly imagining that he was doing splendidly. As Sue watched him, too kindly disposed towards him to hurt his feelings by criticism, she could not help comparing this mode of progression with the flying sweep of the boat through the water yesterday, and picturing the man who sent it along so quietly and so powerfully with his clean-cutting, regular, almost silent strokes. What a ludicrous contrast to that noble and capable person was this self-sufficient little podgy lord, whom the world of great folks flattered and coddled, but who was such a duffer and ignoramus after all?

She was thinking this when she suddenly became aware of their too close proximity to a mail steamer which she had been watching for some time. The little boat was taking a course of its own towards Bradley's Head; the big ship was coming up at right angles to it on the way to its berth at Circular Quay; and while Sue's attention was wandering for a moment to thoughts of her lover, Lord Boyton was contemplating the feat which was to make that day memorable in the annals of Sydney Harbour. At first he thought he would; then he thought he wouldn't; then again he thought he would – just to show the ladies how clever he was. He who hesitates is lost, and if he had not hesitated he might have done it easily; but because he hesitated he was just half a minute and a dozen yards or so short of the time and space that was necessary to enable him to cross the bows of the Orient liner in safety.

Sue awoke to a perception of the catastrophe too late to prevent it. 'Look out!' she cried sharply. 'Look out! Oh – you *idiot*!'

Further expostulation was rendered impossible by the sudden pouring of salt water down her throat.

CHAPTER XXXVIII

●

The Broken Bonds

Richard was sitting in his office, talking to Noel Rutledge. 'What I want you to do now,' he said, 'is to come into this business; to have duties and a salary at once, a partnership by-and-by, and my place when I am gone. You need not protest and make objections – you're under no obligations to me; I'm thinking of her interests, not yours. I have no son, moreover. I'd like to make a son of her husband, if I could – for I suppose you'll be her husband some day, though it will be a long day yet, by all appearances. . . .'

And just at this point a clerk knocked hastily and loudly at the door, and at the same moment opened it to usher in the bearer of ill news.

'Please, sir, your boat has been run down in the harbour, with Mrs Delavel in it, and the young lady, and a gentleman who was rowing them. He got foul of the mail steamer – the Orient boat that's just come in. And they're all on board her now – she stopped to pick them up – and they're trying to bring Miss Delavel round. The other two are all right, but she's not sensible yet. They think the ship struck her, for she didn't rise, and they were some time before they could find her. They're just hauling the steamer up to her berth. Will you come at once, please, sir? The captain sent me to tell you.'

Ricahrd, who had sprung to his feet, stood fiercely staring during this breathless recital; then he snatched up his hat and ran down to the quay like a man pursued by a pack of wolves. Noel Rutledge ran beside him. The people in the street ran after them, calling to each other to ask what was the matter, but the two men did not exchange a word. The father dumbly ground his teeth; the lover prayed involuntary, inarticulate prayers. It was a dreadful moment for them both.

The ship, when they reached her, was still in process of being hauled in to her place. There was a river of water between the black wall of her side and the coping of the wharf too wide to bridged by any gangway at present; but the crowds of people on her decks were within speaking distance of the crowds on the shore. Richard hailed the captain on the bridge.

'How is she?' he shouted, in a hoarse, thick voice, that made all the bystanders turn to look at him.

'Your daughter is all right,' was the answer from some one on the deck below.

The father's breast heaved with a bursting sigh of relief; his hard eyes softened and filled. He turned to his companion with a little laugh. 'Why do they make fools of us like this?' he cried in an unsteady voice. 'You see it's all right.'

'God be thanked!' ejaculated Noel fervently. And then Richard remembered that his wife was in the accident too.'And Mrs Delavel?' he called questioningly.

There was a moment's pause, and then the captain called back, 'Wait a moment, Mr Delavel. We'll have the gangway out directly, and you can come aboard and hear all about it.'

The crowd on the wharf whispered together, and cast looks at the tall grey man which were by no means congratulatory, but he did not heed them. His precious Sue – the only one who had been in any real danger, as he was told – had 'come round', and he had no further anxiety.

The captain received him on deck with a grave face. 'Well, Mr Delavel, this is a sad business,' said he, as he shook hands. 'But I can honestly tell you it wasn't our fault.'

'Oh, I know that,' replied Richard; 'I know whose fault it was. I'd like to wring his neck, the damned young fool.'

'Well, he *is* a fool,' said the captain; 'I never saw a bigger one, that I know of. He tried to cross our bows when we were already right on to him – when a child must have seen it was impossible. However, you can let him alone. He's properly punished for his stupidity. He's crying downstairs like a baby – you never saw such a pitiable object.'

'Well, there's no great harm done, fortunately. It's a lucky thing there were no sharks around. My girl is all right?'

'Oh yes; she came up like a cork. She's a plucky young lady that; it would take a good deal to drown her, I fancy.'

'And she wasn't stunned? She didn't get a blow?'

'No; nothing but a ducking, which she didn't seem to mind a bit.'

'Where is she?' Richard looked eagerly around, and was vaguely surprised at the expression of the scores of faces watching him, and at the fact that passengers were not scampering off the ship in their usual hurry.

'The ladies have just taken her down to put dry clothes on her,' said the captain. 'I insisted on her getting dry. We had a deal of trouble to persuade her; she wanted to wait to see you first; but she'd been dripping on the deck for the best part of an hour, and I didn't see that it would do anybody any good for her to get an illness. So I told the doctor to make her go down.'

'I should think so. Why did he allow her to wait so long? Though I should have thought her own sense— By the way, where is Mrs Delavel?' He asked this question in an abrupt, sharp tone, that betokened a dawning sense of the situation. All at once he understood that something serious had happened, and that he had not heard the story correctly. 'The messenger told me my wife was in the boat, but that she and Lord Boyton were safe – that only my daughter was insensible when she was taken from the water.'

'He made a mistake. It was your wife – not your daughter – who was insensible. In fact, Mr Delavel, I've got very bad news for you. I was in hopes somebody had told you, but I see you don't know it.' He stood with his back to the door of his own cabin, holding the handle in one hand while with the other he waved all spectators to a distance; and, looking at him, Richard knew what he was going to say. 'We must have struck her when we struck the boat – she's got a wound on the side of her head; she did not come up like the others – and there was a little difficulty in finding her. The short and long of it is, Mr Delavel – well, you understand, don't you? We tried for over half-an-hour to restore her, though the doctor said the moment she was brought up that it was no good. He thinks she was killed by the blow before she went into the water at all.'

Richard felt stunned, and looked so; and the captain broke off suddenly, with the idea of summoning the doctor or the brandy bottle. But after a brief silence, during which a hundred pairs of pitiful eyes were fixed on him, the stricken man pulled himself together, and hid away his emotions from the public gaze. He took a step or two towards the closed door, and said quietly, 'Is she in there?'

'Yes, she is in here. But – but. . . .'

At a sign from the other the captain desisted from remonstrance, turned and opened the door, followed his visitor into the cabin, and then stood aside and blew his nose for three minutes without stopping.

He thought of his own wife, with whom he spent a blissful honeymoon twice a year, and of whom he dreamt a lover's dreams at such times as duty gave him sufficient sleep for the purpose, and imagined himself in the position of this other husband, widowed in a moment – so cruelly, so unnecessarily. It seemed to him too terrible for words. He was obliged to blow his nose a good while before he could face his crew and passengers becomingly.

Richard walked into the little room, where he had often smoked his pipe with the skipper and talked of ships and cargoes. He had always seen it so smart and trim, in its handsome simplicity of arrangement, with all its polished drawers and cupboards; but now its ship-shape neatness was gone, and she who in life had been the spirit of order had brought the disorder into it. She lay on a sofa beside the littered table, her body in its wet garments, wrapped in a blanket, her head loosely bandaged in blood-streaked linen, her hair lank and dripping, lying in masses over the sodden pillow, the salt water trickling from the loose ends still. Her glazed eyes and her drawn blue lips were partly open – there had been no time to think of appearances – to soften the hideous change in the face that had been so fair but an hour ago. Nothing was left of the beauty of the living woman, and the beauty of death, that is so much talked of, but so seldom seen outside the poetic imagination, had not replaced it yet.

Her husband looked at her shudderingly, and hid his face, and grieved for her with his whole heart. He only thought of what he had lost, not at all of what he had gained. Memory brought him the picture of her as he saw her that day, so long ago, when she was nearly drowned at Dunstanborough, and he carried her ashore in his arms – the pretty gentle girl who had clung to him and depended on him, whose innocent life had been his to guard and cherish; and it was terrible to him to think that he had not known her danger now and been at hand to save her from it. Her beauty and sweetness and the comfort she had been to him were new discoveries at this moment; all the bitterness and emptiness and loneliness that she had made him suffer were forgotten. All her faults were blotted out. And he had sinned against her so much and so long, and he could make no atonement for it now, nor ask for her forgiveness.

Sue came in a few minutes later, and drew him away from that dreadful sofa, and made him sit on another one, and lay his head on her young breast. And when the captain went out to leave them together, and she began to speak of what had happened, her first words were those which we so rarely utter until it is too late – 'Oh, poor mother! If only I had not vexed her.'

Poor mother! Poor wife! Poor thing! All Sydney spoke of Mrs Delavel that day in those pitiful terms. But she was not poor. She had had her good things in this world, and she had passed through the great trial with hardly a pang. Oh no, she was not – she never had been – poor. They are poor who, like Don Quixote, hunger for better bread than is made of wheat; who cherish an impossible ideal of life – think from time to time they have reached it – taste the divine bliss of fulfilment for a moment, and fall back, cheated, to an ever-deepening consciousness of starvation and failure. She had known no honest want; her narrow nature had had a full measure of satisfaction – had, indeed, received more than it had asked for, more than it could understand or value. She had been rich and fortunate, as things go in this world, and not poor. Yet the hearts of her child and husband, and of all her friends and acquaintances, bled with pity for her fate, and, in the case of the two former, not with pity only, but with passionate unreasonable remorse.

CHAPTER XXXIX

•

Nature Unadorned

On the evening of the funeral Mrs Blundell came to talk to Sue about Lord Boyton, who was on the verge of delirium tremens with grief: and the girl put on her hat and went to Mrs Blundell's house to administer what comfort she could to that poor young man.

'I won't be long, dear,' she whispered to her father, who was standing at the library window, gazing blankly out. The drawing-room where she had received her visitor was lighted up, but this room was in semi-darkness; he had been alone there since he returned from burying his wife, and no one had liked to disturb him. 'I would not leave you for anything else. But I can't bear to think of that poor boy!'

'Nor can I,' replied Richard grimly. 'But go, my dear, go; I am glad for you to have something to do – some one to be with. I don't feel as if I could talk even to you tonight, Sukey. I'm best alone, old girl. I thought – I thought I'd go out to the camp presently, if you don't mind. The house feels so close. I should sleep, perhaps, at the camp. You wouldn't think it unkind of me, would you?'

She told him she wouldn't think it unkind of him, though it hurt her a little that he should want to get rid of her in these first hours of their common desolation. Then he took her in his arms and kissed her solemnly – a kiss that stilled the momentary pain – and she went off with Mrs Blundell, and saw him no more till breakfast time.

As soon as she was gone he left the house and descended the garden to the boatshed, got out a small outrigger – rather a dangerous craft for night use in those shark-haunted waters – and put off for his lair in Middle Harbour. It was warm and still, but the freshness of the sea was in the air; and it was delicious to him after the muffled chambers of death and mourning, the atmosphere of inquests and funerals that he had left behind. The mists of twilight were clearing off, and the dark outlines of the shore growing sharp on the delicate sky, where the thinnest thread of a new moon was palely shining. He pushed his peaked cap to the back of his head, and lifted his face, and opened his heart to the influences of the sweet free night. This was what he wanted – to be alone with nature, whose genuine child he was – alone with that mystery of comfort to which we give the name of God.

As he skimmed along in his arrowy little boat, leaving wharves and houses behind him and drawing nearer and nearer to the illimitable sea, there dawned on him a sense of new beginnings that he had not allowed himself to recognise till now. In this great space of lonely night, face to face with his natural self, he dared to feel that he could go to the camp now without any fear of consequences. He was conscious of his liberty, though his thoughts were shapeless, and his whole mind set to the gravest key – conscious that his life was given back into his own hands, and that he was a young man to all intents and purposes still.

The camp was wrapped in the shadow of the hills; only the lantern at the top of the flagstaff, replacing the flag which had hung at half-mast all day, marked its site amongst the trees. Without a glance at the glow-worm light, Richard guided his course across the waters of the cove straight to the invisible landing-stage. This was his real home, and he could have found his way to it in the blackest night. As he drew alongside he saw a movement among the bushes. 'That you, Bo'sun?' he called, in a low voice.

'Ay, ay, sir,' the old man answered, and hurried to take the boat and fasten it.

'I'm going to sleep here tonight, Bo'sun, but I don't want anything. You can turn in when you like.'

'All's ready for you, sir. I expected you'd be coming tonight. Is – beg pardon, sir – is the young lady bearing up pretty well?'

'Yes, thank you. She always bears up.'

The old fellow was full of sympathy that he did not know how to express in an acceptable manner. 'They let that young gentleman off too light, sir,' was the way he put it. 'They ought to have tried him for what he done.'

'Oh, he's punished enough. Don't talk of it, my man. I've come here to be quiet for a little while.'

'All right, sir.'

The Bo'sun said no more, but went to light the lamp in the tent and to get something in the way of supper ready – food and drink being the natural assuagement of grief which he felt it incumbent on him to offer, whether it were accepted or not; and his master took a walk along the sands for an hour or two to be out of his way.

Pacing up and down that narrow strip of solitary beach, with the boom of the Pacific billows in his ears and the free sky over his head – lying afterwards in his little bed within the open tent door, not sleeping for a moment, but keenly awake and alive in every nerve – Richard Delavel did what he had come there on purpose to do. He looked around upon his life, took his bearings frankly, and set the course for the rest of that journey which had hitherto given him so little choice of road.

A few nights later, at Darling Point, the housekeeper got up from her bed, slipped on a skirt and shawl, and descended the stairs to the library, where lights were still burning, though the clocks had just struck three. She did not knock at the door, strange to say, though she knew her master was within; she opened it with an air of authority and boldly confronted him.

'Mr Delavel,' she said, in the tone of a mother remonstrating with a wayward child, 'why don't you go to bed? Sue is as restless as you are, listening for you to come upstairs. Though she won't say a word about it to me, I know the child is fretting dreadfully at the way you go on, and no wonder. You might think of her a little.'

As she spoke, Richard, who was pacing one long strip of carpet to and fro, turned and paused in front of her, and she looked at him curiously. 'Poor man,' Mrs Blundell was saying to the crowd of eager gossips that thronged her drawing-room for authentic information; 'poor man, he doesn't seem as if he could bear the house now that she is gone. The servants say he walks about all night instead of going to bed, like a person out of his mind. And I don't wonder at it. A more perfect wife never breathed, and he was simply devoted to her. She had not a wish that he did not gratify.' Which statement from the mouth of the deceased lady's dearest friend was generally accepted and endorsed. Because, being rich and highly placed, the husband was naturally credited with the solid virtues of respectability, in despite of his intellectual oddities. A black sheep was not recognised in one who had done so well in the world, whose establishment was so handsomely appointed, whose birth was so noble, whose chosen partner had been such an extremely distinguished person. But a black sheep he was all the same, as old Hannah could have testified – only Hannah was such a miracle of discretion and conscientiousness that it was of no use to ask her questions. As in the case of the woolly quadruped, the unconventional colour was engrained in his constitution. He did not make himself black out of *malice prepense*; he was born so; he could not help it. No broken man was he as he faced his old servant, who had been his friend almost since he was a boy. There was a virile vigour in his tall frame, a fiery spirit shining in his deep-set eyes, such as few young men could boast of. He was all awake to his finger tips, with quick blood running in his veins, though it was past three o'clock in the morning, and he had not had a proper night's rest for a week.

'Why don't I go to bed?' he said, repeating her words. 'Because bed won't hold me, Hannah. I want a strait-jacket to keep me down.'

'I think you do want one indeed, sir,' she returned, setting down her candle and proceeding to shut the windows, which were open to moths and mosquitos as well as to the sweet night air blowing up from the sea.

'I must go, Hannah – I must go,' he went on, taking a restless turn round the room. 'I have been hesitating about the day on account of Sue, but I was just making up my mind when you came in. I must go at once – I can't stand it any longer. I don't know where she is. I can't be certain whether she's alive or dead, even. I *must* go and find her.'

'Not yet, sir, surely,' said Hannah, 'when that poor dear is hardly cold in her grave. Why, the whole place would cry shame on you.'

'And do you suppose I care a brass farthing about that?'

'Well, perhaps you don't. But you'd care about breaking your daughter's heart, at any rate.'

'Yes – if that were in question. But it isn't.'

'You don't know. She's thought a deal about her mother since she lost her – more than any one'd think for.'

'I understand that, Hannah. I know what she feels, and I will not shock her if I can help it. The worst thing will be leaving her – and leave her I must. I can't ask her to go with me this time.'

'No, I should think not! And it's to be hoped she won't guess what you've gone for. It would shock her so as she would never get over it. And,' continued Hannah, looking into her master's glowing eyes, 'if Miss Constance is the woman I used to take her for, she'd be just as shocked – and more.'

'No, Hannah, no. She'll be above all that. It would never occur to her to be shocked. She knows better – all these years have taught her better than to be so trivial. Do you know how old she is, Hannah? She is forty-four. Think of it – forty-four! And she was only a girl like Sue when – when – oh, it seems like yesterday! I can see her now, stooping over me, with the tears in those beautiful eyes, when I was too ill to speak and answer her. I can hear the very tones of her voice – that sweet voice that was so full of truth. She used to know my thoughts before I spoke them, and feel everything that I felt as if we had one heart and mind between us. And now – now! We have lost all the best of life, and have only a fag end left. Good God! how have I borne it? And you ask me to *wait*!'

'Don't say "lost", Mr Delavel,' said the old woman solemnly. 'Life has not been lost to them that's done their duty. And your duty you've done, though you do talk so wild.'

'I made a contract, Hannah, and I fulfilled it – yes, I can say that. To the best of my power I fulfilled it. But now I am free – now I may think of having a little happiness for myself – at last, at last, before I die. I'm nearly fifty, Hannah; I can't afford to waste the little time that's left.'

'There's better things than being happy in this world,' said Hannah.

'Is there? I don't think so.'

'There's a world to come, where, if we do what's right, all we suffer here will be made up to us,' she added, 'if you'll only believe it, my dear.'

'But I don't believe it, Hannah. I can't believe it. And if I did it wouldn't make a bit difference. Who cares about another world? Nobody wants it in place of this one, however much he may pretend – because it is the custom to pretend. I don't, anyhow – I don't. I'd give all my chances of happiness in another world to be young again in this – to be able to set the clock back for about eight-and-twenty years. To live over again, and to have *her* to live with me, would be heaven enough for me.'

'Oh, for pity's sake, don't talk like that,' Hannah sternly remonstrated. 'It's tempting God to send a judgment on you.'

'Tempting God!' he repeated, in the same tone of reckless passion. 'If there is a God – of the kind you are thinking of – you may depend on it He knows more about it than you do, and sees the whole matter in quite a different light. He wouldn't require me to pretend to Him that I am sorry that poor soul is dead, when the sense that I am free is turning my brain with joy. He wouldn't wish me to leave *her* to pine on now, after all the trouble and solitude of these twenty-five years – just because it would look like a disrespect to one who can know nothing of it, who cannot be hurt by it, to do otherwise – just because it would offend the senseless prejudices of shallow people to whom it can be of no possible concern.'

'Well, I can't talk to you,' said Hannah, whose old voice began to shake. 'You don't seem like yourself – I don't know you as you are now.'

'Because I *am* myself – my real self; that's why. I have been wearing a disguise so long that you don't know me without it.'

'I wish you had worn it for ever, sir, before you'd shown yourself so hard and heartless.'

'Hard and heartless? Did you say heartless, Hannah? My good woman, if I were heartless I should be sleeping in my bed at this moment, a dull and solemn mourner of the most correct pattern.'

'To be glad that she is dead, dear soul, that never did you any harm,' cried Hannah, with deep indignation. 'Well, husbands are queer things, as I've known to my own cost. But I never thought to hear *you* say such a thing as that.'

'I say it because I feel it,' he replied. 'I am aware that it is in very bad taste, but that doesn't make it the less true. Do you suppose people are never glad when their relatives die? They are, very often – they can't help it – only they pretend they are not, because it seems so shocking. I don't pretend – at least, I need not pretend to you. The fault is not always – not all – on the side of the survivors, Hannah. I don't think I am any worse than those who pretend a grief that they don't feel. I was never unkind to her – never in my life, that I can remember. I did not kill her – I would have kept her alive as long as I possibly could. I think – I hope – that if I could have saved her by the sacrifice of my own life, I should have done it without a single moment's hesitation.'

'I am sure you would,' said Hannah.

'But,' he continued with that unwonted fire blazing in his eyes, 'since dead she is, I *am* glad – I am, I am! I am glad as a man who has been kept in prison is glad to be let out. It is not my fault – I would be sorry if I could. Some day, Hannah – some day, when we have been dust for a few hundred years – perhaps for a few score only – people will wake up to see how stupid it is to drive a man to be glad when his wife is dead. They are finding out so many things – they will find out that too in time.'

Hannah took up her candle quietly, as if accepting the situation. 'What do you think of doing, sir?' she asked, in the formal tone of one awaiting orders.

'I think of going on Saturday,' he replied promptly. 'That is, I mean to go on Saturday without fail, if I am alive and able. I shall tell Sue that I am going on a journey – she need not know the particulars, and you will take care of her till I return. You and she can manage everything. I – we – shall not come home much before the end of the year, I suppose, out of respect for the feelings of the moral public – or the feelings of the child, rather. When I find Constance I shall marry her then and there, but I shall not tell anybody – not even you, and I shall keep her somewhere where there will be nobody to gossip about us until a sufficient interval has expired.'

'You are making very sure,' said Hannah. 'How do you know you'll find her?'

'I'll find her, if she's above ground,' he replied.

'She's probably married, with a dozen children round her.'

'No. She is free, as I am.'

'How do you know?'

'Never mind how. I do know it.'

'You won't find her at forty-four like what she was when she was twenty. She'll be old and changed – grown plain, perhaps.'

'She'll never be plain to me. And she may be as old as Methuselah, toothless and tottering on a pair of crutches – I don't care. She'll always be my own Constance Bethune while there's a bit of her left.'

'May be years have changed her in other ways besides looks. She mayn't care for you now; there's been time enough for her to grow out of it, and that's what most folks would do.'

'May be the sun won't rise tomorrow, Hannah; we can't tell – we can only hope it will. I shall go to bed without any doubts, for my part.'

'It's today – not tomorrow; the sun will be up in a couple of hours. Are you going to walk about here till the servants come downstairs and find you?'

'No; I'll go now. I'd have gone long ago if you hadn't kept me talking.'

CHAPTER XL

———•———

His Misfortune, Not His Fault

Sue came to breakfast looking as if she, too, had slept little, though the temperature of Sydney at this season of the year could account for faded cheeks and languid limbs to anybody's satisfaction. She wore a white gown of thinnest lawn, with a few black bows about it. Her father was attired in white also, with a black necktie loosely knotted over his shirt front. The barbarities of crape and woollen stuffs, with the thermometer registering ninety in the shade, were not for these free-born creatures, who paid no heed to custom unless they saw good reason for it.

The breakfast-room was deeply shaded with drawn blinds; the snowy table, with its bright equipment, glimmered indistinctly in the dusk. Father and daughter kissed each other in silence and sat down to their meal side by side, the girl in the mistress's place behind the silver kettle, the man on her right hand; and it was some minutes before they could see each other clearly. It was not, however, necessary that they should see each other in order to be made aware of the variations in their respective minds and moods. If they had both been blind they would still have understood each other better than other people could understand them. For nearly all the week Sue had felt in her heart what her father was thinking of, and this morning when he spoke his thought for the first time she was not at all taken by surprise.

'Sukey,' he said suddenly, as with a great effort, 'I am going away from you for a little while.'

The colour rushed into her face, and a trembling seized her. Though she had known it was coming, it was as bad to bear as if she had not known. The sense of shame and disappointment in him that had first visited her on the Observatory Hill made the blood tingle in her veins, for she knew very well what he wanted to go away for. The outrage upon conventional decency was nothing to her; the outrage upon the austere susceptibilities of youth and virgin womanhood was great and sore. 'To America?' she inquired, in a low, cold, husky voice.

'No; to London.'

'When?'

'On Saturday – by the P and O.' Neither spoke for a full minute, and then he continued, 'Do you think you will much mind being left, you and Hannah? I shall give you full command, full liberty in every-thing, my dear – trusting only to your honour to carry out certain wishes that I'll tell you about presently. You are not afraid of so much responsibility, are you?'

'There is no question of my feeling in the matter,' she answered, in a voice that suggested her mother's. 'I am your daughter; it is my business to submit to whatever you choose to put upon me.'

'I am putting nothing upon you, Sue. I am hurting nobody. I have to go away. It is a greater wrench than you think to leave you, but I *must*. I can't help it. And you would not like to go with me.' After a pause he added wistfully, 'Would you?'

'Father, you would not ask me,' she replied with proud severity.

'No – no.' He saw that she understood. He read her mind like an open book. 'But I want you to be as happy as possible while I am away. Will you tell me what arrangements you would like best? Will you go to New Zealand with Hannah for the summer, to begin with?'

'Oh,' she cried with a shudder, 'don't talk about New Zealand now!'

'To Tasmania, then? You ought to have a change of some sort.'

'What does it matter where I am? My health is perfect – I don't want change. I am as well here as anywhere else, if – if this must be.' She dashed away a passionate tear, and straightened herself. 'You ask me what arrangements I would like best,' she continued, with a touch of defiance. 'Let me marry Mr Rutledge before you go, and then you can wash your hands of me altogether.'

'I have not the slightest intention of washing my hands of you for a long time to come. And I don't intend you to marry Mr Rutledge till you know a great deal more of him, and of life generally, than you do now.'

'I am of age, father.'

'I know it, my dear. That makes no difference.'

He got up from the table, with a grave and patient air that rebuked her rebellious spirit, justly rebellious as it was; she remained sitting and silent, and allowed him to have a long conversation with Hannah in the hall, and then to take his hat and leave the house, without exchanging another word or look with him.

When he had gone she dashed up to her room, flung herself on her bed, and abandoned herself to a perfect hurricane of grief. Hannah heard her sobs, and knew what they meant, and when the old woman went in to scold and sympathise she took quite a different tone in reference to the cause of trouble from that which she had used to her master a few hours ago. Now she defended him with an outspoken vigour that would have astonished him considerably had he heard her. And for the purposes of his justification she entered upon that history of the past which had been such a well-kept secret.

'If you'd known all that I know,' she said, with evident pride in her superior position, 'you'd not have been so hard on him, you'd not be so took aback as you are, my dear.' And then, as he violence of Sue's opposition to her reasonable remonstrances abated, she began the story. And the girl could not help listening to it.

'It was all done, past being undone, before you were born. It was a pity, God knows, but I won't have him blamed for it. I saw it all from first to last, and if it was my dying breath I'd say he didn't do wrong, nor she either. I used to live close by her when she was a girl; and when he was only a boy, though a married man – which we didn't know then, and nobody would have thought it to look at him – he was in her mother's house ill. He had inflammation of the lungs, and we never thought he'd get over it. Mrs Bethune was so crippled she couldn't stir about, and they had only one young servant; Miss Constance did nearly everything for him, and what wasn't fit for her to do I did. My good-for-nothing husband had gone off and left me, and I was waiting for him to come back – more fool me! – and I had plenty of time on my hands; I used to sit up o' nights to let her rest, and I'd keep dropping in all day to see if I could help her. No mother ever slaved for a sick child more than she did for him. "He *shan't* die", she said to me, and she shut her teeth just same as I've seen him do many a time; "I won't let him die", says she. And she'd kneel by his bedside and give him drops of brandy and water on a feather for hours without stopping, when the poor boy was lying like a log with his eyes gone back into his head, and even the doctor said it was no use.'

'Anybody would have done it,' said Sue.

'But anybody *didn't*,' replied Hannah, with a slight tightening of the lips; 'and that's where the mischief was. Not a word would I say against that dear creature that's gone, Lord knows, but all the same she left him to shift for himself when 'twas her place to have been at his side and helped him. How she and him came together in the first instance – well, they were boy and girl, I suppose, with nobody to advise them. It was before he'd fairly grown up to know things for himself, and certainly she couldn't have cared much for him' —

'*Don't!*' groaned Sue; 'I can't bear to think of it. You're as bad as he is, Hannah – you think *nothing* is sacred.'

'My dear, justice is justice. It's for his sake I speak so plain. She stayed at home to keep herself comfortable, and let him struggle as he might, and let strangers do for him what she should have done. That's where it was. And that's why things went wrong. He wanted her to come with him, and she wouldn't come; and when he fell sick she should have been there to nurse him, and she wasn't. And so others had to do it, and others got the reward. 'Twas only natural. He was not like most men – he was always grateful and thankful; and he was a born good husband – about the only one I ever came across. He'd have poured himself out at her feet; he'd have paid her a thousand times over. But she gave him away to Miss Constance, as one may say, and it was natural he should love the person he owed his life to; he'd have done it if she'd been an ordinary woman, instead of as sweet a young creature as ever a young man set eyes on. From the moment he got his senses back he was so that his heart's blood wasn't good enough for her. I remember, when he began to look about him, how he'd watch the door when she was out of the room, and how his poor hollow eyes would light up as soon as she came in again – and no wonder! She had a face that the very larrikins in the street would turn to stare at. And she kind o' took to him from the first, just as he did to her. She'd stand over him when he was asleep, and look at him with such a look. Ah, poor young things! The Almighty didn't make either of 'em like common people.'

Sue wept silently, and the old woman babbled on.

'They didn't know what they were doing till it was done. I remember when he first began to feel that he ought to tell her his secret; he got restless and sleepless, and was all thrown back, and we couldn't think why when he was getting on so well. Indeed, I don't know when she first knew it; it was a long time, because I suppose he felt that telling her would be like giving *her* a hint, which she was the last person in the world to want, dear soul, so proud and good as she was. He tried to hold himself back from loving her, instead – to pretend he only felt brotherly affection for her; and that, of course only made bad worse. Then poor young Bethune died, and the old lady seemed to lean on him; and then he got a situation, and it seemed natural that he should go on lodging where he had already made his home – it gave him opportunities to pay back some of the kindnesses they had shown him. And so – and so – well, it had to be, I suppose.'

Still Sue said nothing, and the conversation flowed on.

'It was I who helped her to get away in her uncle's ship without him knowing it. Ay, my poor girl, how she cried that night when we were packing her things. He was at his own little house that he had just taken – the house you were born in, my dear – a bit of a place with four rooms and a lean-to kitchen. "Mrs Brett", says she – I can see her now, with the tears running down her sweet face – "Mrs Brett, if I go away he will settle down, but if I stay where he can find me he will have no chance. He'll never do wrong", says she, "if I don't tempt him, and if there was no other way of preventing that I'd drown myself in the harbour this very night", says she. Oh, she took things hard, just as he did; there was no shilly-shally about her. And so she went away like a thief in the night, and when he came to look for her and found her gone he was like a man possessed. He was like a devil. It was the only time I was ever really afraid of him. And what a lie I told him to please her, that was the soul of truth. He asked me if I knew anything about her going, and I said no. I said no, and I stuck to it; but I knew all about it, and I went to live with him as his servant because she begged and prayed me to do what I could for him – to look after him and help him, and be all the comfort to him I could. And all the years I've been with him I've known what's been in his heart. I've never said a word to him – or hardly ever – nor he to me; he has never let on to anybody; your poor mother never guessed – she wasn't one of the noticing sort, the precious dear, which was lucky for her; and he was always careful over her not to let her feel anything wanting; but he couldn't hide the truth from *me*. I could see that he never got over thinking of Miss Bethune. And I shouldn't wonder if she never got over the loss of him either. There never were two people who were so much to each other as they were – they'd have died and welcome to do each other the least little bit of good. And yet I dare say,' concluded the shrewd old woman, shaking herself out of her sentimental mood, 'I dare say, if it had been so that they could have kept together, they'd have cared no more about each other than folks usually do.'

CHAPTER XLI

●

The New Departure

Meanwhile Richard repaired to Pitt Street, summoned Noel Rutledge, now an officer of the establishment, to his private room, and for the third time made the announcement that he was going away. The news was no surprise to the young man; he thought it natural that the bereaved little family should desire to detach themselves from the sad associations of their home, and also to get out of the summer heat, which was what everybody did who could afford to do it. But when he heard that one of the pair was to go and the other to be left behind, and what an extent of time and distance might separate them, he could scarcely believe his ears.

'Don't stare at me like that, man,' said Richard irritably. 'I am quite in my right senses, I assure you.'

'I beg your pardon,' said Noel. 'I can't help being surprised. At such a time – and never having been parted from her. . . .'

'I dare say she will explain it to you if you ask her,' the other interrupted. 'But please don't ask me – take it for granted that I have good reasons for what I do.'

'I shouldn't dream of asking you, or her either.'

'Well, sit down,' said Richard with sudden gentleness, laying his hand on the shoulder of his friend. 'Sit down and let me tell you how you can help me while I am away.'

'Only tell me what I can do,' responded Noel, 'and I'll do it, whatever it may be.'

So they sat down and talked things over.

'I am obliged to leave my daughter behind,' Mr Delavel said, 'because I am going upon business that she is best out of. She would hate a lady chaperon, so I'm not going to inflict one on her; my old housekeeper will be an excellent duenna, and Sue can be trusted with her liberty, though her poor mother didn't think so. I shall instruct them to write to me by every mail, as I shall write to them, and if time is of importance they must telegraph. While in any immediate difficulty, that they find more than they can manage by themselves, they may apply to you, Rutledge. And when I say that, you will understand what enormous confidence I place in you – in your honour as a man, in your discretion and judgment, in the sincerity of your regard for Sue's best welfare.'

'I am more proud and touched than I can say,' replied Rutledge earnestly. 'But don't you think, Mr Delavel, considering all things – considering that you are going so far, and are likely to be absent a long time – considering Sue's youth, and the accidents and discomforts that may befall lone women who have no man to fall back on. . . .'

'The gardener will sleep in the house,' interrupted Richard. 'He has been with us fifteen years, and is the most faithful servant in the world, with pluck enough for an army – if it's burglars you are thinking of.'

'Burglars – and other things; female gossips, for instance. Don't you think, Delavel, there's a better way of settling things – a way that would leave you with an easier mind about her?'

'No,' said Richard quietly; 'I confess I don't see any better way.'

'If – if' – Mr Rutledge blushed and hesitated – 'if you had not consented to our engagement I wouldn't have dared to make the suggestion. But you have accepted me as your son-in-law. In principle it is the same thing whether we are engaged or married.'

'My good fellow, it isn't at all the same thing,' was Richard's prompt reply. He leaned forward with his arms on the table, and looked with stern gravity at his companion.

'I knew,' he continued, 'that that bright idea would occur to you, and I've no doubt Sue would approve of it if you submitted it to her; but I want you to give me your word of honour that you will let the marriage alone till I come back again – no matter what she says or does – no matter how expedient it may appear to you. I'll tell you what it is, my boy – I have such a horror and dread of making things irrevocable, until every possible test has been stood, that I'd rather – I'd rather *anything* should happen to her than she should do it, even though I honestly believe that you are the right man. I'll take every possible precaution against harm touching her while she's alone, but if burglars and scandal-mongers do their worst, it will still be better for her than that she should run the risks of a hasty marriage. I know what I am talking about, Rutledge; it's not for the sake of thwarting you. I'll put no hindrance in the way of your seeing all you can of her. You won't go to the house, of course, because we must consider *les convenances* to a certain extent – unless, as I said, there should be some urgent and unforeseen necessity for it – but Hannah will let you meet sometimes, and you can write every day if you want to. You can take a look at the place before you turn in of a night, and if she puts a lamp in the window to show you all's well it might ease your mind, and there's no harm done. In all this I trust you to take care of her – not to let her get gossiped about – not to make too free yourself, nor to let her be reckless. It is a great charge, Rutledge, a delicate and difficult one, and I leave you unfettered – it shows what I think of you. Only in this one thing I want a solemn promise from you – that you will not marry her till I come back; unless, of course, I die abroad and am not able to come back.'

It was not without a struggle that Rutledge consented to bind himself, but he gave the required promise subject to certain contingencies that were never likely to arise. He took over his trust with a due sense of its sacred and serious character and an intelligent recognition of all that it involved, insomuch that Richard, when he went home to his lunch, felt that he had safeguarded his daughter as far as human means could do it. Another man would have told him that he had ingeniously contrived to expose her to the only danger that was worth taking into account.

There were but two days in which to make all preparations for his journey. On Thursday morning he announced his intended departure; on Saturday morning he left Sydney by sea. He went by sea because it was his habit to travel that way, and for business reasons; also because up to the last moment he expected his daughter to go as far as Melbourne with him.

All those two days Hannah bustled about, packing his clothes, taking his orders, making elaborate arrangements for the new domestic administration. But Sue did nothing to help her father – she could not. The testimony that her old nurse had advanced in condonation of his offences had its effect in reconciling her to them later on, but at this time she only thought of it as an aggravation of the insult to her mother's memory – the mother to whom all had bowed in life, but whom no one considered now that she was dead and no longer able to resent insults for herself. Annie's child had the natural instincts of a child; moreover, she had the natural feelings of a pure young girl, not yet acquainted with the more tragic joys and woes of human life. That her father should go away some day in search of 'that woman' – for thus did Sue now designate her once admired friend – she had prepared herself to expect; but that he should bury the companion of so many years as if she were no more to him than a dog, and rush off immediately, with such undisguised exultation in his freedom, to the arms of another, no matter whom, was a thing gross and low to the delicate-minded, inexperienced creature – a degradation of the idol whom it was so necessary to her to respect. 'He thinks nothing of either mother or me, or of what is right, or of what is becoming – of nothing but the gratification of his own selfish desires – just like any common man.' That was how she viewed it. And so, instead of giving him help and sympathy, she left him to his confederate, Hannah, and spent her time alone in bitter meditation, or in wandering miserably about the house, collecting her mother's little personal belongings, the photographs of her that were scattered about, all the sacred relics of her late presence and sovereignty, and carrying them to her own room, which she made a sort of shrine for their safe keeping from the dishonour to which they were subjected elsewhere.

Saturday morning and the time for parting came before she had fully realised what was happening. She did not offer to accompany her father to Melbourne; she did not even offer to go down to the ship to see him off. She shrank from showing herself in public, and from doing anything to countenance his proceedings. When his cab came to the gate, and Hannah called her to say goodbye to him, she went downstairs with a tight feeling in her throat and her heart ready to burst with grief, but still passionately resentful – unable to forgive him even at this melting moment. She walked into the library where he awaited her, and instead of rushing into his arms, came to a standstill just within the door and stood there like a statue.

'Well, my dear, I'm off,' he said. 'As you didn't seem to want to hear anything about it, I've given full directions to Hannah. Sukey – Sukey, old girl – do you feel as if you could give me a kiss before I go?'

She still stood by the door without moving, except to put her handkerchief to her eyes and heave a strangled sob. She really didn't feel as if she could kiss him under the circumstances, even though he was going away. After waiting some minutes, he gave a quick, short sigh, opened his watch and shut it with a loud snap.

'Have you anything to say to me?' he inquired, in a still gentle but quite changed voice. 'Do you want to ask me anything, Sue? The ship sails in half-an-hour.'

Then she put down her handkerchief and looked at him with wet, indignant eyes. 'What am I to say to people when they inquire for you?' she burst out. 'Am I to tell them you have gone away to be married again?'

He did not answer at once, but stood looking at her. She felt the pettiness of her speech the moment she had uttered it, and dropped her eyes to the floor, blushing furiously. 'You may tell them that if you like,' he said quietly; 'it won't hurt me. I no more care what you say to people, or what people say to you – as far as I myself am concerned – than if I were living in another planet.'

Then she sobbed aloud, and somehow found herself in his arms. But she only stood and wept while he embraced and kissed her; she did not return his caresses.

'Old girl, I am sorry for you – I feel for you from my very soul,' he murmured, as he held her to him, 'but I know it is hopeless to try to make you understand that – or, indeed, anything. You are too young. You will know more some day. Don't cry, my darling. Kiss me, Sukey.'

But still she did not kiss him. She allowed him to lift her chin and press his lips again and again to her mouth, her brow, her cheek, her silky hair, yielding passively, but making no response. And suddenly she found herself alone, lying on the library sofa with her face buried in the cushions; she heard the sound of the cab wheels die away in the distance; her opportunity was gone.

And then she realised what had happened – realised it to the full – as we generally do when it is too late. She ran upstairs like a wild creature, and stood for an hour on the topmost balcony of the house, indifferent to the luncheon gong and Hannah's threats of sunstroke, and watched the departure of the mail steamer in a condition of speechless despair. It was a beautiful sight to see the manoeuvring of the ship as she came out into the fairway and rounded to her course, a beautiful picture, set in that exquisite framework of wooded shore and sapphire sky and sea; but it wrought upon the poor girl to such an extent that she could hardly forbear to shriek aloud. The relentless monster calmly bearing off her father before her eyes – her father, from whom she had never parted before, and had now parted in coldness – the sight drove her to desperation.

And he was quite as miserable as she was. 'Shall I let the ship go?'

he asked himself, as he was rattled through the streets. 'Shall I take the train next week instead, on the chance of her relenting? Why – why – *why* must we always be torn two ways like this?' But by the time he reached the wharf and the ship he had made up his mind again that he must go, and that he would make no change in his manner of going.

It was a beautiful night at sea, and he walked the deck in the moonlight when common passengers had to lie abed. His dissatisfaction and restlessness would not let him sleep. He could not plan his plans and dream his dreams for thinking of his 'old girl' and her solitary wretchedness. 'But she'll come,' he said to himself confidently; 'she'll never let me go away like this. I shall see her on Tuesday morning at the latest.'

He arrived in Melbourne on Monday, drove at once to the office of his firm, and plunged into business with an ardour that astonished his subordinates, who said they never saw a man bear his grief so gallantly. He succeeded in adjusting all his more important affairs by eleven o'clock on Tuesday, and then, claiming an hour of privacy in which to write letters, sat with his watch open on the table before him and listened for his daughter's step.

At exactly twenty-five minutes after eleven he heard her voice in the outer office, asking if he was in his room; and a moment later she flung herself unreservedly into his arms, and cried, 'O father! father!' in a tone that assured him of forgiveness for all his sins.

'What, Sukey – what, have you come to see me off after all?' he exclaimed, with a shake in his voice and a moisture in his eyes. 'Ah, Hannah, you're looking after her – that's right. Just take her to Menzies' and order a good lunch – I'll join you there in ten minutes. And look here, if you haven't got enough clothes and things for a week or two, go and buy some more. You shall go as far as Adelaide with me, Sukey.'

And so she did. She went on to Adelaide with him, transhipping into an in-coming mail-boat at that port; and after two days of quiet walks and talks on deck – talks like the old talks that were the habit of her life – she parted from him in a spirit as tender and loving as heart of father could desire. It was weak of her, perhaps, but it made her feel happy afterwards – and him too.

CHAPTER XLII

●

'We'

It was in August of the next year that Richard Delavel returned to his house, having accomplished the purpose for which he left it. He would have made a further concession to popular prejudice had not Sue written in May to ask him when he was coming back. She had never been directly told that he had married Mrs Ellicott, nor even that he had found her; but she readily divined the circumstance from the tone of his letters and the fact that for several weeks together they were dated from the same place – Mustapha Supérieur, on the flowery heights above the Bay of Algiers.

'It has been like paradise,' he wrote to his daughter in April. 'It has been the divinest spring-time. Oh, such evenings, Sukey! – when the last flush of the sun is gone from the Djurdjura ranges, and the twilight comes, and the moon shines through the vine trellises; and such dawns as you never saw when we come round to the sun again – I watched the light grow in the sky behind those cloudy peaks this morning until the dazzle blinded me, and I thought of you, old girl, and wished you were here to see it with me. But I know how it would have been – you would have looked at the mountains and the sea, and the white houses shining, and you would have said a Sydney harbour sunrise was just as good, if not a great deal better. Well, perhaps. At any rate, the days that follow would be preferable now. It is getting too hot for the invalids here. A hammock in the garden, or a long chair on the terrace of an evening – that's all. No more clambering up and down the walled lanes at all hours of the afternoon; and as for that blazing staircase of a town, that was so delightful to rummage in when the weather was fit for it – of course that's out of the question. I must look for a cool place in Switzerland – the Alps will be beautiful before the tourists come – but I shall find nothing like the air of the camp, Sukey, the delicious air that will blow off the sea for the next few months. I shall pine for the camp as the summer comes on.'

Sue knew very well for whom the heat was dreaded, for whom the long chair was placed on the terrace and the hammock under the trees – not for his own robust and hardy frame; and his allusion to the camp was perfectly understood. If he pined for the camp, she pined for the day that would restore him to his place, having by this time tolerably accustomed herself to the new condition of things. She wanted him back, at any price, as soon as she saw a chance of getting him. So she wrote, as a postscript to her last May letter, 'When are you coming home?'

He replied by telegram, 'Immediately,' though he had not intended to return for months. He understood her question to mean that she wanted him, that she accepted the stepmother, and that she cared for Mrs Grundy no more than he did. 'We return immediately,' he wired on the day of receiving her letter; and he named day and route. And the news, which presently leaked out and flooded the place, causing pain and grief to all proper people, brought joy unspeakable to the heart of the one person to whom, if to anybody, it should have been unwelcome.

That evening, when it was quite dark, she put on a fur cloak and stole down the terraced garden to the sea wall at the bottom, and leaned upon the low stone balustrade like Juliet upon her balcony. In two minutes a little boat came stealing alongside and made fast to one of the short pillars; and Romeo stood up, planted a foot on the basement wall, and leaped over to his lady's side.

Let not the discreet reader suppose that this was a constant, or even a frequent occurrence; it only happened just once in a way, under the compulsion of a mutual longing for close quarters that was more than poor human nature could resist. Noel Rutledge, who lived at the camp when he was at home, had early established a habit of rowing or sailing up to Darling Point, 'bescreen'd in night', to have a look at the house that sheltered his beloved, to satisfy himself that all was quiet and safe; and, thinking it might give her a sense of security, had informed her of what he did, and suggested that she should make some signal if it should happen at any time that she needed his help. And the way she acted upon this advice was not to set a lamp in a window, but to descend the bosky garden and lean upon the white bulwark that divided her from him – the mask of night upon her face, certainly, so that a casual observer could not tell her from the kitchen maid, but her dim shape unmistakable to the eyes of love. The first time she did this he rowed up to the wall and inquired, 'What is it, dear?' in accents of alarm. She said, 'Oh, nothing; I only wanted to know if you were there.' And it was seldom that she had any better excuse for calling him. When the moon was bright he would draw near, but not too near, and whisper across the water, 'All right?' And she would whisper back, 'Yes.' And perhaps she would remark that it was warm, or cold, or that she and Hannah were going somewhere tomorrow; and he would warn her not to catch a chill being out so late; and they would exchange a soft good night, and he would slowly draw away, and the mystic night would swallow him. But when there was no moon he dared to run his little boat up to the wall, and if he found her there – feeling her presence rather than seeing it – he would steady himself with a hand on one of the pillars of the balustrade, and have several minutes' conversation with her. From that he went the length of tying up his little craft, so that he could stand upright and kiss his sweetheart over the top of the wall as she leaned down to him; and that naturally led to his getting over the obstruction – on a night when it chanced to be pitch dark and stormy, and the wind was blowing her hair into his face, and she clung to him and told him she could not bear to think of him out on the black harbour waters alone in his cockleshell of a boat in such wild weather. There was no question of unlocking the gate at the landing steps; he was over the wall in the twinkling of an eye, and the welcome he got on the other side was such that he was constrained to repeat the exploit on a subsequent occasion, conscientious scruples notwithstanding. He was but a man, and 'the woman tempted him.' By this time Sue had got far past the A B C of her experience in love; she was learning with a thoroughness that left nothing to be desired.

On this particular evening, after receiving her father's telegram, she had an excellent excuse for inviting her lover into the garden, and invited him accordingly. 'Come over for a moment,' she said, as he tied his boat to the balustrade; 'I have something very important to tell you.'

So he leaped over, as a matter of course. It was quite dark on the little strip of lawn, and the flowery banks overhanging it enclosed them in the solitude of a desert island. They were as invisible and inaudible from the lamp-spangled water as from the star-strewn sky. Therefore they put the important something aside for a few minutes.

When by-and-by they sank upon the bench on which Sue and her father used to sit in earlier days, she communicated her piece of news.

'And he says "we", Noel; "we return immediately". I have been studying his letters closely for weeks to find that little word, and he has been so careful not to use it. As if I didn't know that it was "we" as well as he did! It has been "we" from the day he went to Algiers, when he did not write for a fortnight, and then sent me a note about as long as an invitation to dinner.'

'And you were so jealous – poor little girl!'

'I am jealous now,' said Sue. 'It never goes out of my head that he is mine no longer. And he used to be all mine. I was everything in the world to him.'

'Well, I am all yours instead, and you are everything in the world to me – and always will be.'

'Oh, I wonder shall I? This sort of thing shakes one's confidence in the fairest prospect.'

'Then we won't look forward – we'll be content with the present. Sue, when he comes back and finds how matters are between us, he will be satisfied that I am the right man, and he will let me have you.'

'Oh yes; he'll let you have me fast enough when he comes back. I should think you need not have much fear of that. *She* will be all in all, and I shall be *de trop* and a nuisance to both of them. He'll be thankful to any one who'll take me off his hands and out of his way.'

'I thought so,' said Noel. 'You have *not* got over it.'

'But I have, quite – quite; it's only just now and then, when I think of it, that I feel a lingering nastiness for a moment. Only for a moment, really. My poor old daddy – that I should grudge him his bit of happiness! It's a happiness that he hasn't been within miles of before, all the years he's lived. He would never grudge me *mine*, bless him!'

'You are two such intensely human creatures you can't help yourselves,' said Noel, smiling. 'If he hadn't his own consolation, he would find it hard to look on at yours and be shut out – I believe he will find it hard as it is. That day when he met us in the north-west passage – do you remember? – for the first moment he could not bear it. But, oh dear me, in this world, where we have such a short life and such a lot of trouble in it, if only there were more of us with such generosity and fellowfeelingness!'

'*He* is generous,' said Sue, colouring; 'but I am just a mean, selfish, jealous wretch. However, I'm not going to be nasty now – oh, I will *not* be nasty any more. I have had a struggle to submit to it, but I have got over that – yes, I really *have* got over it this time. I am so glad he is coming home – I am glad to have him happy. It is his right. Noel' – with solemn emphasis – 'I am convinced that the marriage system is altogether a mistake – an anachronism – a clumsy contrivance for keeping society together that we ought to have improved upon long ago.'

'I have been expecting to hear you say that,' he returned, with a quiet laugh. 'I have such work to bring you up to the reasonable point, and I no sooner get you there than you at once rush off away from me, ever so much farther than I can follow you.'

'But don't you think so, Noel?'

'No, I don't.'

'Oh, I am sure you do. Look at my poor mother, thrown away upon a man who could never find any comfort in her, though he tried his best. To another husband – say a good, quiet-minded clergyman, or an English squire of the old school – what a treasure she would have been! What a happy life she would have had! And look at my father, pining like that for all those years, everything spoiled and wasted. And all because of a little error of judgment when they were boy and girl, before they were old enough to know what was good for them. Oh, I have been thinking about it seriously, and I am sure it is all wrong – I don't care what you say.'

She was in the full swing of a new idea, a new revolt, and scorned the cold suggestions of his more settled mind; but this attitude, to which he was well accustomed, never prevented him from putting his gentle check upon her intellectual imprudences – a check to which she yielded more or less, in spite of feminine protests.

'It will be all wrong when the time comes for it to be all wrong,' he said; 'but so far it has been as right as possible – in my humble opinion.' And when she flew out at him for his disloyalty to the doctrine of universal liberty, which was his professed religion, he only patted her on the shoulder and said that people generally got their liberty as they got fit to use it. 'You are not historical, you headlong reformers, and you always want to destroy the old house before the new one is built – to break down the carved work thereof with axes and hammers instead of taking it to pieces gently, so as to have all of it that is good and beautiful to use over again,' he proceeded, at such times as she would allow him to speak.

'You are such a compromiser,' she complained, 'and you never used to compromise. I hate you to be so cautious – just like common people.'

'Oh, it isn't caution. I am quite ready to take my part in the bustle of preparation when the time for changes comes.'

'And hasn't it come? Or, if it hasn't, can't we make it come?' She rapidly adduced the unanswerable stock arguments in support of the right of men and women to that freedom in the management of their conjugal affairs which they claimed and received in matters of so much less importance – showing that she really had an intelligent grasp of the subject; and she asked him how he had the face to tell her that a system which denied this right and ignored all the laws of nature and of common justice was a good system, and suitable to such an enlightened age as they were supposed to live in?

She was for ever flaring up in this way at something wrong in the established order – and he loved her for it; but she could never make him indignant and impatient as she was. It was not in his sober nature. And now he respectfully but firmly refused to admit that marriage – marriage as it stood – was not a good thing.

'It is a form of slavery,' said Sue. 'And slavery never was a good thing yet that I know of.'

'Oh, yes. In your light, superficial way you can only think of it as a horror to shudder at – a thing altogether abominable – that's of course; but, like our marriage system, it was an enormously good thing, quite the best thing possible, before the time came when in the natural course it had to make way for a still better. What an advance in civilisation to save one's captured enemy and make him useful, instead of battering his brains out with a spiked club! And feudalism, too, that you rant and rave against – what a noble institution was that as compared with the systems it superseded! What an enlightened sense of duty and order it showed, as against that of the slave days! It was entirely the right thing in the right place – only its place was *then* and not now. And so with the Church, that I am sorry to say, my dear, you sometimes scoff and sneer at – which is all the same as sneering at one's mother when she has grown old and past work. The Church, as we know it, has had its day – its grand and splendid day, which will be done justice to by-and-by when this struggle is past – much ampler justice than we do it now. We are outgrowing the Church, in which our social arrangements are more or less included, as we have outgrown slavery and feudalism, and' – suddenly he paused, and the ring of spiritual passion that Sue loved to hear came into his voice at last – 'and we are awaiting the next development. Not *ready* for it, Sue, but waiting – growing – preparing for it – clearing the ground a little just about our feet. What will the next thing be, I wonder? Oh, how much I should like to know!'

'And *don't* you know? Can't you see at all?' she questioned wistfully.

'Can't I see?' he echoed, with a little laugh. 'My dear, only think of the time things take! Why, *The* Reformation, which was a trifle to this, was a matter of some 300 years a-doing.'

'*Everything* seems to have time with us,' she mournfully rejoined. 'All these tremendous things go on to completion, and we are hustled away before we have hardly made a beginning.'

'We may go on too,' said Noel. 'We can't tell.'

'Ah, *we* – not you and I, Noel!' And she put her arm round him.

'We must not think of it,' he murmured, clasping her to his breast. 'It unnerves us.'

They were always dropping out of their lovers' talk into sudden solemnities of this sort.

CHAPTER XLIII

●

The Goal

Romeo wrenched himself from the enchanted garden and dropped over the wall into his boat, kissed his lady's stooping face and outstretched hands, and drew away into the darkness with lightly-dipping oars that made no splash in the still water. As he rowed down the harbour to his quiet home a smile played upon his face, and peace and contentment filled his heart. Never at any time had he been a discontented or restless man; in all his battles and perturbations he had seen his way and maintained a steadfast soul; not fighting with necessity, like Richard and Sue, whom he resembled in so many things. He was tougher and steadier, less exigent and self-conscious than they were; there was no 'wild drop' in the wholesome current of his blood to make living the tragical matter that it was to them. But still he had found life difficult. Now the easy time had come, the happy time for which he had paid in advance, the holiday that was the due reward of the patient labours of his youth. His worldly affairs were improving daily. All things being equal, press work was more congenial to him than his new profession, but having adopted the latter for sufficient reasons, he had cheerfully adjusted himself to its requirements, and never thought of hankering after anything else. So, with his calm but effective energies concentrated upon his proper business, he naturally succeeded in it, to his own satisfaction and that of the office generally. And he had cleared his character wonderfully by becoming incorporated with the great 'concern' in Pitt Street, and the affianced husband of Miss Delavel – if he had cared about that. A great many people were ready to recognise him in the street and to let bygones be bygones now. Mentally and spiritually he was tranquil and cheerful. He had passed through the torturing transition time between the first doubt and the last conclusion, and, recognising that the Power which created him had made him responsible for himself, rested in the quiet determination to be worthy of his manhood as far as in him lay – to do his little part well, to whatever mysterious unseen end. There were things that 'unnerved' him, but these he would not think of. It was the part of a man to accept the fate he could not alter with dignity and fortitude, with courage and cheerfulness; and it was also his part to make the best of what he had and not throw away the possible in futile reachings after the impossible. A good many of us understand this quite well, but very few of us can act up to it, chiefly because our physical brains and stomachs are not in the requisite state of health. Richard could not do it, with his thin-skinned susceptibilities, nor Sue, with the hereditary passion in her blood; but nature had given Noel Rutledge the temper of the philosopher, who is born and not made. He took things as they came, and did not quarrel with destiny, which seemed to him a feeble sort of thing to do. In Richard's place he would never have pined for an impossible woman for twenty-five years, 'spoiling and wasting' everything, as Sue rightly described it; to his mind a man had no business to let himself spoil, whatever happened; and his secret judgment upon the late proceedings of his friend was more nearly that of the commonplace world than his ladylove supposed. In which the reader will perceive that he lacked some fine qualities if he was over-rich in others, which is the way of things in this world. But he was happy in his limitations as well as in his large-eyed wisdom; they were so many protections to his spiritual tranquillity and his peace of mind.

He rowed down the harbour in a windy darkness that suggested a dirty night at sea, and smiled as he thought of the fireside rest that would soon take the place of such lonely journeyings. The girl whom he loved – but whom, if he could not have had her, he would have managed to do without – was every day more dear and charming to him, with her beautiful crude generosities and enthusiasms, her unsophisticated human nature, that held such a splendid store of material to make life out of; and his habitual patience had been tried by the conditions of present intercourse as nothing had ever tried it before. Now his probation was nearly at an end, and the prospect before him held all that man could wish for.

The Bo'sun's lantern stood on the landing plank to light him home. It was never hoisted on the flagstaff now at night, nor did the bit of bunting flutter there by day; the old man hauled down the flag when the vessel that carried his master passed out through the Heads, rolled it up, and stowed it away in his sea chest. 'When they signal the ship that brings him back,' he said to Noel, whom he saw looking at the bare pole, 'then I'll run it up again.' And Noel said 'All right,' for he thought it a very proper notion.

The Bo'sun made a further distinction between his master and his master's *locum tenens* by leaving the latter to tie up his own boat, and in a general way Noel was not waited upon with enthusiasm, though his simple wants were attended to. Had this come to Sue's knowledge she would have swooped down upon her humble admirer and given him as sound a rating as he had received from any skipper of his acquaintance, but of course she knew nothing about it, and Noel cared nothing. His nightly presence at the camp was an unaccustomed check upon his servant's liberty and propensities which he did not expect to be welcomed, and he was satisfied with the usual reward of virtue for having much improved the Bo'sun's health by keeping him from the rum bottle.

This young man did not use the camp to mope and dream in, except as he dreamed in his healthy sleep. He did not pace the lonely shore of a night, struggling with the problems of life and human action. No sooner did he set foot on land than he called for his supper, which, being brought to him, he devoured with an appetite that any growing schoolboy might had envied. Then he lit his pipe and took the last new book from his pocket, and enjoyed his hour of intellectual exercise just as much as if there had been no exciting interview in the garden at Darling Point – the memory of which, however, glowed all through him with the effect of wine. By-and-by he found himself beginning to doze, and then he jumped from his chair and undressed and put himself to bed; and from the moment he laid his head on the pillow until the sun was up next morning he slept that sleep which comes neither to the just nor to the unjust unless their nerves and digestions are in perfect order. There was a howling gale outside the heads, and the breakers crashed against the rocks like cannons firing. The blustering wind shook the canvas of his tent, and even ruffled the bedclothes about his face, and a fine salt spray, blown straight from the ocean over the racing ripples of the Sound, bedewed his placid forehead and his ruddy beard until they shone wet in the gleam of the South Head light when it travelled directly over them. But none of these things disturbed his rest. His comfortable, soft snore was audible through the night, quiet and even as a ticking clock.

A happy man, indeed!

Sue did not rest so well as this. She had to wake at intervals to listen to the storm, and the sound filled her imagination with a vision of staggering ships that she could not choose but dwell on. She even rose from her bed and went out upon the balcony, with a fur cloak over her nightgown, to realise the blackness of darkness beyond the lamplit harbour, and the velocity of the gale that lonely mariners had to cope with. Ships naturally represented to her one of the most important interests in life, and the abstract sea had a solemn fascination that drew her as with a spell of enchantment. In wild moods like this it roused an inarticulate passion in her young soul— that intensity of exalted feeling which we describe as inspiration when we speak of some of its results. Wagner's Ride of the Walkyries would fitly express the whirl of formless emotions that strove in her heaving breast as she stood out for a moment in the night and the storm, with the wind shrieking past her at the rate of eighty miles an hour. The vital current in body and soul was fresh and strong, the forces of womanhood in their full power, and the richness of her experience at this moment of life present to her quick consciousness, and realised as we seldom realise good things until we have to part from them.

She strained her eyes to pierce the darkness in the direction of the camp; she could have seen nothing of it in the broadest day, but she thought she knew the exact spot of blackness which indicated its site; and she pictured her lover awake as she was to the voices of the night which put into such eloquent music the feelings and fancies of her heart. How should he sleep out there, at the very gateway of the sea, with wind and waves both thundering in his ears, and his heart surcharged with happiness until its fulness was a positive ache? She thought of him watching as she was, uplifted in soul, withdrawn from vulgar earth: and she longed to be with him that they might share the solemn hour together. She leaned over the railing of the balcony with an impulse to reach towards him. 'Ah, my dear,' she called aloud in her impassioned young voice to that vision of him that she imagined, 'my spirit is with you, though my body is here. And in a little while we shall keep these sacred vigils together.'

But when that time came, she found, not only that he could sleep and snore in the sanctuaries of life, but that she could too. And if she was happy in her maiden ideal to the contrary, she was happier in the possession of a nature which enabled her to adjust herself to the inevitable real without loss of any quality of character that was worth keeping.

And the father, of whom she thought so much tonight, when not absorbed in contemplation of an approaching honeymoon at the camp – how was it with him?

He had found his mate. He had reached his goal. The hunger of his craving nature, 'all the longings of his body and soul,' were assuaged at last. But love like his, which had been a tragedy from the beginning, was bound to be a tragedy to the end. It was what it was because he had suffered for it so heavily; the measure of his satisfaction was in proportion to the time he had waited for it. It was in the nature of things that a bliss so exceptional should come too late, or, if not quite too late, late enough to make a tantalising agony of its brief possession.

Of course Mrs Ellicott had not gone to winter in Algeria merely for pleasure and to kill time. A woman imbued with so deep a sense of the responsibility of life, and so much in need of active occupation to defend her higher from her lower self, had other haunts and pursuits, and it was in these others that her lover had sought her in the first instance. But when he heard of her at last, he heard that she had been long ill – ever since she had left Australia – and that the doctors had sent her to a warm climate in a last effort to save her life. Thither went Richard after her, on the wings of love and terror, and when he found her – she was asleep, and woke up to see him kneeling at her bedside – she was considered to be actually dying. He was able to justify the haste in which he had rushed to seek her, straight from poor Annie's new-made grave, by his conviction that had he waited a week longer he would have had his pilgrimage in vain. It was his coming in the nick of time, he believed, that saved that precious life.

'You used to say when I was ill, "He shan't die – I won't let him die"; and you kept me alive by sheer strength of love and will – kept me that I might see this day. O Constance! you must live for me! I can't lose you now – I can't – I *won't*. It would be too awful a thing to happen even in this cruel world.' Thus he wrestled with death for possession of his beloved, as Hercules for the body of Alcestis in Leighton's picture; and though the doctors pronounced her shattered with rheumatic fever, and with a failing heart that could never recover itself, the fact was that Mrs Ellicott began to rally from the moment that her old lover appeared upon the scene. It was a more serious and obscure disease than any the doctors knew of that had been sapping her vital powers, and for this he brought the remedy.

The first thing he did, while she was still hovering between life and death, was to make her his legal wife by the simplest and briefest process, in order to clothe himself with authority that nobody should be able to dispute or share. Then he took her into his own hands, and never left her again for an hour night or day. Money he poured out like water of course. The best physicians in the world were called to her bedside, and all the sick-room luxuries that science had thought of; and when she was able to be moved from a not very spacious lodging he selected the best house he could find, asked to see its tenant, and offered that gentleman terms to go out of it which even a British nobleman, taking bad times into consideration, could not bring himself to refuse. Thither she was tenderly carried, further up the heights than she had yet been, where she had terraced gardens and fountain courts and Mediterranean views that were a dream of beauty; and there the honeymoon was spent, and the bridegroom said it was 'like Paradise'.

Like Paradise! when one was too weak to walk without assistance, and the other grey-haired, haggard, strained with a constant fear that his treasure would slip through his fingers before he had fully grasped it. Little like Paradise would those young folks at Sydney have thought it! In his Arab villa at El-Biar, and in his present home in Switzerland, Richard in all his raptures had never tasted rest. While Noel slumbered at the camp like a new-born infant, and Sue watched the storm with a sense that she herself was safe from all perils and dangers whatsoever, the man who had 'gone through the whole campaign' was finding no peace in victory – so far. The stress of fierce and overwhelming anxiety, the agonising force of his wild man's passion, the terrible consciousness of the many years gone and the few years left – a mingling of bliss and anguish that words cannot describe – fevered his brain and consumed his strength; and he found the satisfaction of his heart's desire quite as hard to bear as its long frustration.

Yet, doubtless, the finest flavour of life – call it happiness or not – was his.

CHAPTER XLIV

•

The Prodigal's Return

'Well, since it is to be, we may as well make the best of it,' said
Hannah to Sue, when the contents of the telegram were disclosed.
This pretended resignation did not disguise the real cheerfulness with
which the old woman looked forward to the installation of the new
missus – a complacency that, in a confidential housekeeper who had
virtually controlled the establishment, spoke volumes in the lady's
praise. Almost from the first – from the night of her interview with
her master, when duty and decorum required her to oppose it –
Hannah had accepted the inevitable with more than a good grace; but
she had endeavoured to dissemble the fact, because to expose it would
have been to hurt Sue's feelings deeply. Now the girl's relief and
satisfaction at the prospect of getting her father back so soon, and the
extravagantly generous frame of mind, that was a reaction from the
grudging one she had cherished until she was ashamed of it, disposed
her to be cheerful also and to fall in with Hannah's most hospitable
designs.

'I'm sure your father'd wish us to have the place nice for her to
come to,' said Hannah tentatively. 'And he'll grudge no money we
like to spend in doing things up for her.'

'Certainly we'll have the place nice,' said Sue. 'There is only one
condition I must make, Hannah – that it is not my mother's room we
do up for her.'

'Of course not. Who'd think of such a thing? She must have the
big room over the drawing-room. The blue room next it will make a
beautiful dressing-room if we get a door knocked through in the
recess where the washstand is. Come upstairs and look. If we're going
to do things properly, it's as well not to lose time in setting about it.'

'You seem to have thought it all out already,' said Sue, with a returning pang of jealousy.

'Oh, well, there's been nothing to do but think,' replied Hannah; 'and of course I knew she'd be coming some time.'

On the morning following the receipt of the telegram and her interview with her lover – a delicious morning, with a bright rough sea and only a breezy reminiscence of the gale – Sue cast herself into the business of preparation for the prodigal's return with her customary whole-heartedness.

'We'll have in the bricklayers to make the doorway into the blue room at once,' she said to her factotum, bustling round as if they had two days instead of two months before them. 'I don't know whether father would approve of our knocking the house about under ordinary circumstances, but he'll forgive anything that's done for *her*. And then we'll have the painters, Hannah, and they shall paint the walls of her room in beautiful colours – or we'll hang them with Morris chintz, or leather paper, or some art stuff; and we'll take out the old furniture and put new in. She shall have the easiest sofa at the window and the softest armchair by the fire, and Eastern carpets – the best that money can buy – and pictures; and a great big writing-table full of drawers, and a Japanese screen all over gold embroidery – the prettiest things that money can buy, Hannah. We'll go and hunt for them while the bricklayers and painters are at work.'

'She won't care for grandeur,' remarked Hannah, who had an intimate acquaintance with the new mistress's tastes.

'I dare say not. But my father will want her to have the best of everything, and I wish to please him.'

'Well, my dear, you'll please him more than you've any idea of if you only do the half of what you talk about.'

Sue was not a person to do things by halves. Having determined to treat the interloper handsomely, she gave effect to her intentions in the noblest manner. When the travellers arrived at Auckland – having come via America, Honolulu, and New Zealand to avoid the Red Sea heat and for other reasons of their own – and her father wrote to request that the large-spare room might be got ready for Mrs Delavel, and the things out of his dressing-room put into the adjoining chamber; when he further ventured to hope that Sue would give her stepmother a kind welcome for his sake, and because she was rather delicate, and would be tired after her travels, the young housekeeper was able to smile serenely at his unnecessary anxiety.

'They will be here in four days,' she said to Hannah, 'and they will see that we didn't wait to be told what we ought to do.'

On the day the ship was expected she went boldly to the office in Pitt Street and asked to see Mr Rutledge, feeling practically liberated from the restraints to which her orphaned condition had subjected her. 'Oh, isn't it nice?' she exclaimed, as she sank into a chair in her father's room. 'Noel, dear, don't scold me for coming; everybody knows the reason, and it is so lovely to be free! Hannah and I have shaken each other off – she hasn't a thought to give me now, and I feel it such a relief to be rid of her, the dear old thing! I should like to walk about the streets with you, Noel, all day, till the ship comes in.'

'I'll walk about the streets with you, if you like, with the greatest pleasure,' he answered, closing the door for a minute that he might kiss her blooming face, which was evidently impatient to be kissed. 'But. . . .'

'No buts, Noel. Come along. Let us enjoy the novel sensation of lawful companionship in the most public places we can find. I have the carriage in town, ready to be called the moment we know the ship is coming. And it may be here any minute. Let us go out and wait for it – and talk.'

They went out accordingly and roamed the streets, for Noel considered that his first business was to attend to her, in the absence of Hannah – and they had a delightful day. Wandering to and fro, on the look-out for the steamer's signal, whilst seeking lunch and tea and pleasant places to sit down in occasionally, they had long hours on their hands, which would have wearied anybody but themselves. They felt no fatigue, however; their legs ached, but they did not know it. Between the little bursts of vague impatience, when they looked at their watches and wondered how much longer 'she' would be, they absorbed themselves in conversation about matters that thrust all lesser matters out of mind.

'Now, Sue,' said Noel, as twilight gathered and the street lamps began to shine, 'I should have got the message at the office as soon as anybody, and there would have been plenty of time for me to send to Darling Point and get you and the carriage before the steamer was hauled in.' The steamer had entered the Heads when he spoke, and they were standing on the wharf in a crowd of people. Hannah had been apprised of the travellers' approach, and the Darling Point carriage, full of down cushions and possum rugs, was waiting close by. Nothing would induce Sue to sit in it, of course.

'I hate a carriage,' she declared, 'and I love to be hustled in a crowd – with you. I like the contact of my fellow-creatures, Noel – I like the streets, and the common people – to be in the thick of it like this. It feels as if we were really out in the world together, you and I. Oh, how horrid it would be to be married to a rich man, and be condemned for life to sit perched up over people's heads, out of everything that is genuine and interesting! But I was never meant to marry a rich man.'

'Clearly not,' said Noel, pressing the arm that clung to his tightly to his side. 'Still, even a poor man doesn't like to see his wife's toes trodden on by hob-nailed boots, and tobacco smoke puffed into her face. Come the other side of me, dear.'

'Oh, you must get rid of those prejudices,' she retorted, while allowing herself to be gently pushed to windward of a democratic pipe. 'A woman is a man's equal, and able to meet what comes just as well as he does. The day is past when she needs to be taken care of by her husband or anybody.'

'No, it isn't. Not a bit of it.'

'Oh yes, Noel. Now don't be an antiquated Philistine if you can help it. You know as well as I do. . . .'

'Here she comes,' he interrupted softly; and nipped in the bud an eloquent exposition of Miss Delavel's latest 'views'.

The steamer came along through the fast gathering darkness like a pillar of fire, ringed round and round with electric lights; and for half-an-hour Sue watched it in silence with a quickly beating heart, thinking only of the meeting so close at hand. It was the very ship that had taken poor Mrs Ellicott away not so very long ago, when it seemed so certain that they would never see her again. Sue remembered the miserable day, and gave credit to the pair who, for the sake of doing right and to protect each other, made their sacrifice so much heavier than it need have been. The memory disposed her to be very sympathetic now, though she was her mother's daughter. As the great vessel was slowly warped up to its place, towering high over the heads of the crowd on shore, she looked up and saw her father leaning on the rail of the upper deck, and a slender fur-clad figure at his side. The clear radiance in which they stood fell upon the girl's face, and they recognised each other, and each waved an impressive hand.

'Oh, my darling! my darling!' she murmured in an impassioned exultant whisper, trembling from head to foot.

'Were you addressing me?' inquired Noel calmly.

'*You*? no, indeed! Oh! to think of having him back again – my own dear.' Her voice shook, and her bright uplifted eyes shone with sudden tears.

'He isn't your own,' said Noel, 'now.'

'What do I care? Let him be anybody's, so long as I have a bit of him. Come – come; they are putting out the gangways. Never mind the crushing. I'm too substantial to be crushed.'

Her lover steadied her with his calm demeanour, so that she recovered her self-possession by the time she gained the deck. There her father met her, eager and excited too, though holding himself in check; he had his wife sheltered in a corner, and was evidently waiting to see how she would be received. Taking in the two figures at a glance, the girl held out both hands to her stepmother, drew her into her arms, and kissed her with ungrudging heartiness, first on one pale cheek and then on the other. 'I am glad father has brought you home,' she said; and when he heard the words Richard said to himself that he would make up to Sukey for *that*. He was not kissed himself in the electric-lighted crowd, but he felt no loss on that account. 'Well, daddy!' was enough for him, and 'well, old girl!' was enough for her, in conjunction with a hand-clasp that nearly wrung their fingers out of joint.

'Bring her away to the carriage, father dear,' said the happy girl, who knew how generously she was behaving, and enjoyed her own generosity as much as anybody. 'Let's get her home out of the cold. Noel will look after the luggage for you.'

Noel was introduced to Mrs Delavel, and they all talked about the voyage and the late arrival of the ship for a few minutes; then the precious person was escorted down the gangway and through the seething crowd, half-a-dozen arms being thrust out to protect her, and was tenderly placed in the carriage and tucked up in fur rugs as if they were bedclothes and she was in bed. This being done, and Sue seated at her side, the two men disappeared for some minutes, and when they returned stood talking on the pavement for several minutes more. Taking advantage of the opportunity, the two women exchanged a confidential word.

'My dear,' said Mrs Delavel – the street lights illuminated her face, and it looked very thin and worn – 'I can't thank you for your welcome. It overpowers me.'

'You have nothing to thank me for,' returned Sue, colouring deeply. 'You have a right to be welcomed.'

'Oh no; one has no right to anything of that sort. And I – I have given you a great deal of pain, I know. I feel it acutely, though I may not seem to have felt it.'

'You could not help that.'

'No. I have not been able to help anything.'

'I am sure of it. He would not let you – he would sweep all before him. I don't blame you – oh no. You had to think of him first, as he thought of you first. You were very brave and good when you saw you *had* to be – once – before – you know when; but now, of course, there was nothing – only a prejudice that didn't matter, and my feelings. I *did* feel it.'

'It would be strange if you didn't, poor child.'

'But that is over now. I don't care so long as he is happy. He ought to have been happy as he was – all those many years with all he had – but if he *couldn't* be, why, I suppose he couldn't. He's happy now, at any rate.'

'You have put the crown on his happiness,' said Mrs Delavel gently. 'I was afraid you would not have felt able to welcome him – or, rather, to welcome me in this way, and that would have hurt him. But you are his child all over – high-minded and unselfish like him.'

'Oh,' said Sue honestly. 'I can't deny that I've had a hard fight not to be jealous and nasty. You see I used to be everything to him. *You* would feel it if you were in my place, wouldn't you?'

'I should, indeed.'

'And my mother,' whispered Sue; 'how can I forsake her, now that she has nobody. . . .'

'Hush, dear, hush – I know.' Constance put out her hand from under the fur wrap, and Sue seized it and held it. They could say no more, but they had come to a perfect reconciliation.

'Well, good night, old fellow – I'll see you in the morning,' cried Richard from the crowded pavement; and he jumped into the carriage and sat down in front of his wife and daughter. 'Home!' he shouted to the coachman, and he repeated the word lovingly under his breath. 'Home at last, Sukey! Old girl,' and he leaned forward on her knees, and took her disengaged hand and kneaded it between his strong palms, 'old girl, this is something like coming home'.

'You are welcome back, father,' she responded, quick tears rising at the sound of that thrill in his voice. 'You are dearly welcome – both of you,' she added, after a moment's pause.

CHAPTER XLV

●

'Evening Coloured With The Dying Sun'

As they drove through the lighted streets father and daughter chatted of those common everyday affairs that make such useful conversation in the tragic crises of life – little matters of domestic interest and current gossip that were of no sort of importance, except to give them the pleasure of hearing each other's voice again. Mrs Delavel sat in her corner and listened to them with enjoyment, but without breaking into the dialogue. Every now and then her husband leaned forward and touched her knee and asked her if she was tired, or if she felt rested, or if she was cold or warm, and if she liked the night air, or would prefer to have the carriage closed. He talked about all sorts of things, but his attention was occupied with her.

'What, isn't she well?' asked Sue at last, struck by this excessive solicitude.

'She says she's well,' he answered, 'but she isn't well enough to satisfy me.'

'You would never be satisfied,' Mrs Delavel interposed.

'Wouldn't I? Nothing keeps me from being satisfied now but the want of a touch of colour in your face and a shade more substance in you generally. With that, I should be the most perfectly satisfied creature that breathes the breath of life, either in this world or any other.'

'Oh, we'll soon get her all right,' said Sue cheerfully. 'She just wants rest.'

'You are going to rest now, Constance,' her husband said, smoothing the fur on her knee. 'That is to be the business of your life from this hour.'

'And we'll take her out on the water to get an appetite,' said the practical Sue. 'We'll give her a long day at the camp, father, and mutton chops for dinner. That will set her up. Do you know that old Bo'sun got drunk and burned down the big tent, father? He did; but Noel had it put up again, and I don't think the old fellow has ever been drunk since. It was such a shock to him.'

And here the carriage turned out of the noisy, bright shop streets into a dim an quiet one that soon became a silent road, bordered on either hand with gardens that did not hide all their beauty in the darkness – gardens over the shrubs and lawns of which the travellers looked out and looked down upon the bosom of the harbour waters faintly shining under the stars. Richard leaned over to his wife and said in a joyful whisper, 'You are nearly home now.'

The gates stood wide open to welcome them; so did the hall door; and the hall within was full of lights and of flowers in tubs and Oriental jars and bowls, looking like a Belgravian vestibule on the night of a great reception. And as the carriage dashed up old Hannah came out, in a new black silk dress and a new white cap, to receive her master and mistress.

'Well, Hannah, I've *got* her,' the former said simply, in a tone that conveyed a great deal to her ears.

'Is that you, Mrs Brett?' said the bride in her clear voice, which vibrated a little, as she descended into the old woman's outstretched arms. 'You have not quite forgotten me, I hope?'

'No, Miss Constance,' replied Hannah vigorously, 'that I haven't. You're not one of them that is easy forgotten.' And, a little to Sue's surprise, the two women – both dignified and undemonstrative, each in her way – fervently kissed each other. 'It's *you* that's been forgetting *me*,' continued Hannah reproachfully. 'Coming and living here for weeks and months, and never letting me know – *me*, that used to know everything. How *could* you?'

'I did not know you were here,' said Mrs Delavel earnestly. 'Nobody told me. I never imagined you were with him still.'

'I've never left him from that day to this,' said Hannah, in a proud tone of triumph.

'Come, let her in – let her in,' Richard broke in impatiently. 'She must not stand about in the cold, talking. You can talk presently. Come in, love – come in to your home and resting-place.' He put his arm round her and took her up the steps and into the hall. The other servants were gathered here, waiting to be introduced to their new mistress, and to one and all she extended her hand and spoke a word or two, while he held her by the elbow as if anxious to push her quickly through this business and on to her room, where she might rest. He greeted the old faces with a hurried, kindly, absent-minded nod. 'Mrs Delavel is tired,' he said to each in turn; 'she'll talk to you tomorrow. Come, Constance, don't stand about, dear; come upstairs and get your things off. I suppose you've got a good fire in her room, Hannah?'

'Father, don't insult us,' said Sue. 'We've got her everything she wants. Come up and see for yourself, if you have any doubts about it.'

Sue held out her hand to her stepmother and led her up the brilliantly-lighted stairs to the beautiful room upon which so much time and pains had been spent, and flung open the door proudly. It was a vision of comfort for a winter night and travel-tired eyes, if ever there was one; infinite thought and carefulness, a moderate amount of taste, and a great amount of money had achieved a success that left nothing to be desired. It is not everybody – it is not, in fact, one person in twenty – who can, or does, so arrange comfortable furniture as to get the comfort out of it. She had managed this, partly because she was free from the bondage of fashion, partly from that natural instinct of benevolent sympathy and hospitality which makes a hostess do things right without knowing it; which shows her how to group guests for her dinner parties, for instance – another apparently simple matter, in which nineteen women out of twenty fail. The bridal-chamber had an air of spacious luxury, combined with an air of homely cosiness that made it seem to breathe welcome from every article in it. There was a bright log fire on the hearth, and, beside the capacious soft armchair and within the gorgeous screen a little dainty tea-table, with the teapot standing ready and the kettle boiling. An inner bathroom resounded with the bubble of hot water, and the dressing-room opposite revealed its substantial masculine appointments through its open door. Wax candles shed a soft light on a toilet-table fit for a queen or a prima donna of the stage; flowers stood there, single blooms and buds mixed with delicate ferns, the choicest of the choice. Daintiness of every description met the suffused dark eyes of the bride and the bright keen glance of the bridegroom as they crossed the threshold together.

'*There!*' said Sue. And she waved her hand around.

The subsequent five minutes crowned her with the full reward of her labours. Her father pretended to ask her how she dared to trans-form the house in that fashion when his back was turned, but ended by catching her to his breast and hugging her vehemently; and his wife wandered round the room to inspect and admire her pretty things, with a smiling appreciation that left nothing to be desired, but with a secret pang at her heart as she thought how precarious was her tenure of this paradise of love.

She was placed in the soft armchair, and tenderly divested of her bonnet and wraps.

'There's one thing I haven't got for you,' said Sue, 'and that's a maid. I didn't know whether you'd bring one with you.'

'She doesn't want a maid,' said Richard promptly. 'I am her maid.' And he knelt down on the Persian hearthrug and began to unbutton his wife's boots. It was an occupation that Sue did not like to see her father engaged in, and she attempted to take it from him; but he put her aside. 'I always do it for her,' he said simply. 'I do everything for her.' And he drew off the boots as a doctor would draw bandages from a wounded limb, and gently chafed the slender, black-stockinged feet, first one and then the other, between his palms.

It was too pathetic for ridicule. When her wraps were off and she sat in the broad light of fire and lamps and candles, it was clear that Constance had changed a good deal since Sue had seen her last. She was pale and thin then, but she was paler and thinner now. Her always refined face was refined beyond the requirements of beauty; the delicate nose had become more transparent, the large eyes larger and more lustrous and pensive; the tell-tale line of jaw and throat, which marks the passage of a woman's years when nothing else will do it, was sharper. She had aged more than she should have done in so short an interval. And when Sue noted this, and then saw with what passionate solicitude her father looked at the fading creature on whose frail life he had staked his all, the last remnant of 'nastiness' vanished from her heart. She forgot even to feel embarrassed or *de trop*. She slipped away as soon as she had made the tea – her father stood over her while she did it, to see that she did it right – and he seemed not to notice her departure. He sat on the arm of his wife's chair and held the saucer while she sipped from the cup, and between her sips drew her head to his side, on which she leaned with an air of great weariness and ineffable repose. But though the girl felt more 'out of it' than she had expected to feel, which was saying much, she no longer felt aggrieved. If it was a small thing to them whether she went or stayed, there were now aspects of the situation that made it a small thing to herself also.

On her way to her room she met Hannah marching along the corridor to offer her services to the new mistress, and she warned the old woman not to expect to be let in.

'I shall be let in,' replied Hannah, in a tone of pride. 'Many's the time I've helped to dress her when she was a girl. She'd rather have me to wait on her than anybody.'

'No, Hannah, she'd rather have her husband, and he won't let anybody else touch her. It's my belief he sews her tuckers in.'

Hannah took this for spite, and marched on to her goal. However, she was kindly thanked through the closed door by her master, and told that she might come back in half-an-hour, when Mrs Delavel was dressed. Sue intercepted her nurse's retreat in order to say, 'I told you so,' and then hurried over her own toilet that she might be in the drawing-room when that half-hour was up.

She was standing there, in front of a roaring fire, surveying the festive garnishings around her, when her father came in alone and shut the door behind him. Oh, rapturous moment! She was in his arms, crushing his shirt front and the flowers on her breast, kissing him with all the passion of her heart, sobbing with the inexpressible ecstasy of having him all to herself, if only for a few minutes, again. And his caresses were as warm and eager as her own. He called her his dear old girl, his good old Sukey; he asked her how she had got on without him; he talked about Noel Rutledge; he was the same unequalled father that he used to be in the days when his daughter was to all intents and purposes his whole family.

And then, presently, she noticed that he became inattentive and fidgety. His eyes were fixed on the door; his ears were strained to catch the rustle of a dress on the stairs.

'Sukey,' he said, 'if you see me behaving like a fool, don't mind, old girl. I can't help it. When she's out of my sight I always have a sort of feeling that I may never see her again. It's force of habit, I suppose. I think I'll just go up and fetch her.'

But at that moment they heard the sound of voices in the hall. Hannah threw open the drawing-room door, and Mrs Delavel entered. She wore a trailing tea-gown, soft in colour and texture, falling from her throat in long folds – a graceful dress that gave full effect to her natural dignity of carriage and to the lines of a figure that had once been perfect. Her face had a tinge of clear colour from her warm bath, and the excitement of dressing, and coming forth to take her place as the mistress of the house. Her eyes were bright with repressed emotion, and she carried her noble head with an air that betokened a temporary victory over her fatigues. She was a beautiful woman still, even though she was forty-four.

In her character of hostess Sue stepped forward into the room, took her stepmother's hand, and led her up to the fireside. The husband stood on the hearthrug watching them, gloating on the slender figure, beside which the girl looked like a stalwart dairy-maid in her exuberance of youth and health. As she approached him he held out his arms.

'Well, how do you feel?' he inquired eagerly. 'Not too tired, after all this? I think you ought to stay on the sofa and have your dinner brought to you – eh?'

She laughed and said no; then reflecting a moment, said yes – she would. For she knew it would please Hannah to wait on her, and please Sue to have a *tête-à-tête* meal with her father.

The decision made Richard anxious. 'I'm afraid you *are* very tired,' he said. 'I ought to have made you go straight to bed. However, you must go directly after dinner.'

'I will,' said Constance. 'In the meantime, I am as well as I am happy, if you will only believe it.' It was an assertion that he required of her a hundred times a day, and she would have given it if she had been dying.

Dinner was announced, and she was tucked up on the sofa, a table was swept bare of its flowers and ornaments and wheeled up to her side, and Hannah was summoned. Father and daughter went to the dining-room hand in hand, and sat down by themselves at the gorgeous dinner-table. There was, of course, a dinner of an elaborate and choice description for this festive day, but Richard glanced over the menu merely to select such delicacies as were suitable for his invalid wife, and showed no manner of interest in it on his own account. He ate little, but talked much, sending the servants from the room when their attendance was not actually necessary, and all his talk was on one subject.

'You think her looking ill, don't you, Sukey? You see a great change in her – I saw you did when we were upstairs. But that's because she's had a bad illness and hasn't quite recovered yet. She gets better every day – she will soon be all right if she's taken care of. What wine is that? The black seal, out of the corner bin? Sure? You got it out yourself? All right, she can have that. Do you remember that day when we saw her off to America, Sukey? Oh, my God, it makes me shudder now when I think of that day! Well, she was broken-hearted – like me – only she was not so strong as I was; and when she got to 'Frisco she was laid up with a fever – my darling!' He made a little quick moan under his breath. 'She had rheumatic fever – but it doesn't matter what they called it, it was just that she couldn't keep up the effort of living any longer. And it left her heart weak, it left her shattered. When I found her she was dying as fast as she could – she was gone so far that I wonder I ever brought her back. But I think she's all right now – oh, I'm sure she is all right now. I wish her children had lived. I can make up for everything else, but I can't make up for them; and yet I know I should have been jealous of them – I couldn't have borne to have them in the way. *You*' – he looked at her wistfully – 'you'll help me to keep her from missing them too much, Sukey?'

'I'll do all I can, father,' she gently answered.

'My dear old girl! And she thinks a lot of you, Sukey – I know you can be no end of comfort to her in all sorts of ways. After all, a woman wants another woman; a man can't be everything.'

'I think you are pretty well everything,' said Sue.

'Well, yes; I'm quite sure a man was never *more* to a woman than I am to her, and I doubt if there's another living who's as much.'

'And you, father, dear?' inquired Sue. 'You are as happy as you imagined you would be?'

'*Happy*!' He drew a long breath and was silent for a few seconds, as if words failed him. 'I daren't say how happy I am, Sukey – I'm afraid of tempting Fate – and if I could you wouldn't understand what I meant by it.'

'You always say I can't understand, as if I didn't know what love was!'

'You are too young to know that sort – things have gone too well with you. What's that line of Browning's? – " 'Twas not the morn blush widening into day" – that's your case – "but evening coloured with the dying sun, while darkness is quick hastening". The morning glow is all fresh and new – it has to warm the earth, to dry the dews of night, to quicken dormant forces that wake up slowly; but the evening glow has in it all the fire, the growth, the fruition of the day. One must have gone through it all – one has to have suffered and wanted, and taken one's full experience of life – one has to be growing old and getting towards the end of things' – He paused, for a fresh

course was being served, and gave his attention to preparing a plate
of tit-bits for his wife.

All through dinner he was jumping up at intervals to see that she
had what she liked and an appetite to eat it; and, as she did not wish
for sweets, he would not look at them, while the dessert was spread
in vain. As soon as coffee was brought – which he dissuaded her from
taking, lest it should keep her from sleep – he told her she must go
to bed, and as he gave her his hand to lift her from the sofa, he
studied her all over with a searching gaze, which told plainly how
insecure he felt in the happiness he had boasted of.

'*What* can I do to make you look a little stronger?' he cried; and
there was an indescribable yearning tenderness in his voice, and in
the eyes that gazed into hers, and in the hands that he passed over
her hollow shoulders. 'What can I give you to fatten you, Constance?'

'What can you give me to make me young again?' she answered,
gently mocking him. 'No, Dick' – shaking her head – 'my complaint
is past cure. I am an old woman, dear – that's what ails me – only
you will perversely shut your eyes to it.'

He wrapped her in his arms with a sudden, savage energy, held
her head hard down on his breast, and laid his cheek upon it, with a
low long deep groan that shook the heart of his daughter when she
heard it. In that irrepressible cry all the solemn strength of his passion
and suffering was expressed – the anguish of frustration that love had
been to him from the beginning, and seemed likely to be to the end.

CHAPTER XLVI

'Like A Basking Hound'

Like Balzac, Richard Delavel had had no flowering spring-time in his life, no warm and fruitful summer, but entered upon an autumn which seemed to promise compensation for all his past privations. It was the most perfect happiness, on both sides, his and his wife's – when it was apparent that she still continued to improve in health – that mortal creatures can attain to, so long as they were together and able to forget their ever-haunting fear and dread of losing it. When they were obliged to separate for a few minutes or hours, the restless anxiety with which they awaited each other's reappearance, and the celerity with which they despatched whatever business had called them apart, was a source of amusement to the young spectator – that is to say, it amused her then; it does not amuse her now. She had the inclination of a young person to look upon them as old people who made them-selves slightly ridiculous by forgetting that they were old – keeping up fashions that were inappropriate to their time of life; but she has come to understand it better now, as one grows, by experience in such things, to understand a fine picture that was once nothing but paint and canvas.

When they were together their content was absolute; and they were together at all times when they were not driven by the direst necessity to separate. If he went to the office, which he did very irregularly in these days, either she went too, or he was back at Darling Point before there had been time to miss him. In the middle of the morning he would break in upon his family, just as they had settled to their *tête-à-tête* with books or work-baskets, and look round the room with an eagerness that suggested a fear lest Sue might have murdered her stepmother and buried her body during his absence. His evident relief when he saw her peacefully sitting in her soft chair, enjoying a woman's gossip with her young companion, exposed him to many gibes from the latter person, who, however, could never make him feel ashamed of himself. He would give them a bright-eyed greeting and sit down between them, and fan his heated face with a newspaper, and say he really must superannuate himself, because he had become useless as a man of business. He would make the poorest excuses. 'I could think of nothing but you two sitting here. . . .'

'You one, you mean,' Sue would interpose.

'And really it isn't necessary for me to slave at the office now that I've got Rutledge to represent me. Sukey, my dear, your young man works in a manner that would surprise you. He has evidently found his vocation in ships.'

Sue would say she was glad to hear it. And then he would get a book and read to them till lunch time.

On one of these occasions – it was hot weather, and they were spread on long chairs in the hall, which, being open to the roof, was the coolest place – he happened to see Sydney Dobell's poems lying about. He read 'Home, wounded,' and asked Sue whether she remembered reading it to him at the camp 'in the dark ages' long ago.

My soul lies out like a basking hound.

When he came to that line he shut the book, and laid his head back, and closed his eyes. 'I know what that feels like now,' he said.

No longer did he shut himself into his library when he was at home, and keep his man's interests to himself. Not a letter did he receive or write without showing it to his wife; whatever business he had on hand, great or small, he told her all about it. They were companions in everything – the truest mates that ever had, as he said, one heart and mind between them. Intellectually they were equals; spiritually they were sympathetic in every respect; in person, in temper, in all that made them the exceptional people that they were, the one seemed the natural and necessary complement of the other. The way her father sat in his armchair, when he could see her in the armchair opposite, was something quite new in Sue's experience of him. He basked in peace. Peace, indeed, was no word for it. His very soul was satisfied. All his old restlessness was 'laid' like the devils of Scripture that Hannah had been wont to liken it to, and at the same time all the dulness that had so often oppressed his heart and brain was gone. Once again he read philosophy and science aloud in the evenings, but the air that took his fine voice now was electric with intelligent sympathies. How they understood each other! – 'to the finest fibre of their being', as Jane Eyre says. At certain passages that struck him he would look up, and she would be certain to look up at the same moment – certain to have been struck, too, and by the same thought as he. And then when they talked – and such brilliant talk it was – the manner in which they evolved each other's ideas, and shaped them to beauty and meaning, was an education to Sue. She had never known what her father had in him before.

But sometimes she felt her position of mere onlooker at all this love and happiness to be intolerable, and sometimes – for she had plenty of human nature in her – she said so. One day she broke down and wept, and told her father she couldn't bear it any longer, and if he would not let her marry and go and live at the camp with Noel (a subject that he obstinately refused to listen to for several months) she would have to run away and do it without his permission. The Darling Point house was no sort of a home for her, she said, however perfect it might be for other people.

Richard was dreadfully shocked and remorseful. 'Old girl, I can't tell you how hard I try to help it,' he said, 'but I can't – I can't!'

'Father, dear, I don't want you to help it,' she replied, remorseful in her turn. 'Do you think I would want you to help it? *Am* I that sort of person? But – but, oh! do let me be married, and feel that I have somebody of my own!'

It was five months after his return, and he began to feel that he had held out long enough. It happened to be about the right time of year for the P and O voyage to Europe, and part of his plan was to despatch his daughter thither for her wedding journey. She was full of schemes for a working life; she wanted no bridal tour, she said, and her heart was set on living at the camp, where she and her husband would be unmolested by the idle world of fashion, which would surround and absorb them if they established themselves in a brick house. She detested that world; she didn't intend to have anything to do with it. It had scorned and persecuted the best man that ever lived when he was most in need of kindness, and she would not allow him to be patronised by it now that his circumstances had changed. If he showed an inclination to allow it himself – and sometimes he did – she flew at him with a red-hot indignation that was fine to see. As for money, she would not have it, simply. 'Father, if you weigh us down with a big income at the first set-off you will *cripple* us,' she said, with a tragic earnestness that neither of the men dared to laugh at.

'Don't you think Noel might manage to bear the weight of responsibility represented by a couple of thousand or so?' Richard asked her gravely.

'No, father, a couple of thousand is far too much.' She reminded him of that great maxim of human conduct which Constance had long ago impressed upon her mind, and which she and Noel intended to follow in the subsequent ordering of their lives – 'Take all, but pay'; and pointed out that it would be no kindness to load them with debt, which was what the giving them a fortune would amount to.

'You'll have to have it some day, Sukey.'

'I don't see why, father.'

'Oh, yes. I am not going to upset my affairs and give myself a lot of trouble just to make things easy for you.'

'Well, if you leave your money to me, I shall make ducks and drakes of it. I just warn you beforehand.'

'All right. I'm sure I don't care if Noel doesn't.'

The suggestion of a carriage – to which for years she had been as much accustomed as to a bonnet – was enough to put her into a fever of revolt. Rich or poor, nothing, she passionately declared, should ever induce her to have a carriage of her own. Industrial and economic points of view were humbly put before her, but she would not glance at them for a moment. She was strong enough to walk and ride in the 'bus, like other people; a carriage, in that case, was merely a piece of vulgar luxury and ostentation, and as such was indefensible. 'No, it is *not* affectation,' she pleaded, fancying that the sympathies of her male auditors did not run to the required length. 'It is not mere red-republicanism; it's just that I want to pay for all I have, and that is a thing I could not possibly pay for.'

'If you could take out some of the poor folks in your carriage – invalids, crippled children, old ladies who were too infirm to walk – girls who thought riding in a carriage the height of earthly bliss – you wouldn't mind having one then?' said Constance, smiling.

'That would make a difference,' replied Sue. 'That *would* be paying for it. But I should have to find those people first. And even then,' she added, after a pause, 'I shouldn't like to patronise them; and they wouldn't, if they were worth anything, like to be under such an obligation to me – except the children, of course.'

'The children are the first consideration,' said Mrs Delavel. And

Richard looked at his daughter to warn her not to talk of children before the childless mother.

So what Sue wanted was to marry the man of her heart and live at the camp with him, far from the madding crowd of carriage people; there to fashion a system of life that should satisfy her conscience and her peculiar tastes. But when all had been said for and against this scheme Richard coolly closed the discussion by informing her that he wanted the camp for his own purposes. She immediately proposed to found another, but the proposal was set aside in favour of his own plan for the completion of her education by foreign travel before she settled down. About this he had made up his mind, and no arguments were allowed to unmake it.

He had never returned to his native place to show his family how prosperous he had become – had never taken his daughter out of sight of the Southern Cross. His native place had lost its attraction for him when his mother died, and while his father lived and the edict of banishment was not formally revoked, he had maintained an unshaken determination not to set foot on British soil. Keppel, his favourite brother, had committed suicide; Katherine, his favourite sister, had married his enemy, Delavel-Pole; Roger, when he came to his kingdom, took over the paternal animosity or indifference to the black sheep as a part of his inheritance – or so Richard concluded from the fact that his elder brother made no sign of remembering his existence. And these things, and his own ever-growing sense of alienation from the traditions of his aristocratic race, took from him, as the years went by, all interest in his home and all desire to revisit it. A Delavel who had married a girl of the people and taken to trade, who had identified himself with a locality that was infinitely more unfashionable than Clapham or Camden Town, was not expected to turn up again, he used to say; and, for himself, he honestly declared that a return to the solemn state and rigid conservatism of the ancestral house would bore him more hideously than words could express. But he wanted Sue to see the world; moreover, he wanted her to see Dunstanborough – a desire that poor Annie in her lifetime had steadily discouraged, while constantly whetting her daughter's curiosity with the most gorgeous descriptions of the magnificence of the family seat. So when, after Sue's outburst of tears and pathetic appeal for some-body of her own, the marriage was decided upon, the grand tour, which in these days is only limited by the boundaries of our planet, was put into the programme as a preliminary to the self-denying, world-serving life that the young folks had set before them.

'Go and see everything first,' said Richard. 'You'll never have such a chance again as you've got now. Go while you're young and learn what the world is made of – it will make all the difference in your social efficiency by-and-by. Take her round, Noel, and show her what's doing, and don't think of money or office work or anything for a year at least – only of making the old girl happy and giving her things to think about. Sukey, you know I don't say it because I want to get rid of you.'

'Oh yes, father; if you'd wanted to get rid of me you'd have done it before now. And if you think it right for us to go and give ourselves up to pure idleness and pleasure for all that time, why, I suppose we must do it.'

'It won't be idleness,' he rejoined promptly. 'It will be the most profitable of all employment – for the present.'

In the early part of February the wedding took place. It was a simple wedding, and a private one, because our bride and bridegroom, holding advanced opinions, considered the public function a coarse and barbarous business, that should be out of date with delicate-minded people, educated to appreciate the sacredness of the occasion. They simply went out for a walk single and came back married; and, having had lunch at Darling Point, got out the boat, rowed themselves down to the camp, and there lived for a fortnight like Adam and Eve in Paradise, without even the Bo'sun to spy upon them. Noel made the fires, and Sue cooked the chops, and they rambled and boated and read choice books and reclined on the sand to watch the ships go by, and were supremely happy.

They returned to Darling Point for another fortnight, and then they started off on the grand tour. And the splendid raw material in Mrs Rutledge's mind underwent a useful process of manufacture during the subsequent two years.

CHAPTER XLVII

———•———

Two Years Afterwards

Two years afterwards Mr and Mrs Rutledge returned to Australia –
the latter greatly matured by her experiences, as we have said – and
found the elder members of the family still in the same world together,
and still cherishing a hope that they would be allowed to remain there
for a considerable time to come.

The travellers came overland all the way from Adelaide, in order,
since they were coming home, to get home as quickly as possible.
Whether that journey was a bad thing for Sue, whose health at this
juncture was such as to require more care than usual, was a question
much debated in Hannah's sitting-room next day; but at the time she
felt it no more than she was accustomed to feel such things, which
was not at all, provided she had a bed of some sort for the night hours.
The racket of express trains, which when long continued reduces an
ordinary woman to the condition of an old rag, found no weak place
in her admirable constitution – an inheritance to be put to the credit
of the ill-starred marriage of which she was the result, the blending
of the fiery, nervous, finely-cultivated Delavel strain with that of the
tough and solid yeoman race representing her maternal ancestry. She
slept in her tight berth, shaken by the jar of revolving wheels, as she
had slept in several gales of wind at sea, like an insensate infant,
waking each morning with nerves and digestion undisturbed.

Her father was at the station to meet her on the hot morning of
her arrival, as glad to get her back now as she had been to get him
back two years and a half before. In defiance of etiquette, she stepped
out of the train straight into his arms, and kissed him on the platform
before all who cared to remark upon her behaviour. Noel was in
danger of being overlooked, in spite of his great stature and noticeable
handsomeness, but his time came in a few minutes, and he used the

interval to collect his baggage, which the others had no thought for. The dressing-bags and odds and ends were tossed in the carriage, and they were soon bowling through the poor streets, which by some law, municipal or divine, environ all important railway stations, towards the statelier city and the lovely shores of Darling Point.

'I need not ask how Constance is,' said Sue, looking at her father's keen-featured face, which was full of life and brightness. 'You wouldn't leave her like this if she wasn't all right – at least, you wouldn't have done it two years ago.'

'I wouldn't do it now,' said Richard, with a quick smile. 'But she's pretty well – as well as she ever is, I think. You can't expect a disembodied spirit to grow fat. She made me come, and wanted to come herself, but of course I wouldn't hear of it in weather like this. She has to keep very quiet in summer time.'

'I wonder you haven't taken her out of Sydney before now.'

'This year,' said Richard, 'she wished to stay at home. She thinks, and so do I, that heat affects her less than travelling. Do what you will, you must get shaken up more or less, and that seems to try her heart, which is the weak place, you know. Remember that when you meet her, and don't be boisterous, old girl. She's all right while she's quiet. I make her lie on the sofa – I've invented a new sofa for her – when it's hot, and I row her down to the camp when it's cool, or I take her for a drive. Do you notice that we've got another carriage, Sukey? Indiarubber tires, you see; they don't jar her so much. And it's hung in a new way.'

'Well, I am glad she is all right,' said Sue. 'Since that's the case, I don't mind saying that I never thought, when you brought her home that night, she was going to live and keep well all this time.'

'All this time!' he repeated. 'Sukey, the time has flown like the wind – it has been *no* time – it has simply *raced* away. It seems but a month ago since you and Noel left.'

'Evidently you haven't missed us,' she said, laughing. 'You didn't find time hang heavy on your hands for want of *me*.'

'Have you found time hang heavy?'

'Often and often. There are moments when I would have given my ears for the square of magic carpet, to be transported home again for a little while.'

'Leaving Noel?'

'If necessary. He is just as dear as dear can be' – throwing a bright glance at her husband, who sat before her — 'but he couldn't keep me from wanting you.'

'You've never had to feel the want of him yet,' said Richard. 'However, I'm not prepared to say that I haven't had a hankering for you now and again, old girl. Habit is strong, and we'd got so thoroughly used to one another somehow. I'm glad Noel doesn't mind bringing you home for a bit. We needn't hurry about looking for a house, Noel; it's too hot for that work. It will be time enough when winter comes, won't it?'

Noel looked with a little anxiety at his wife, and declared himself quite ready to postpone everything for the sake of giving her immediate rest and quiet; and furthermore intimated that all domestic arrangements were absolutely under her control.

'Well done!' cried Richard, with a heartiness that would have set at rest any doubts as to the security of her hold upon his affections, had she entertained doubts, which she didn't for a moment. 'Then we four won't part again, Sukey. If you must have a house of your own presently, we'll buy out the people next door.'

'We should have to part if Dunstanborough came to you,' said Sue gravely. 'I suppose you understand, father, what the death of Uncle Roger's poor boy means for you?'

'It means nothing, Sukey. Roger's life is as good as mine, and if not, it's all the same. Dunstanborough may come to me, but I shall never go to it.'

'Why not, father? There's a dreadful whisper going about that Uncle Roger's illness is cancer.'

'God forbid! I don't believe it.'

'If it should be so — if you *should* inherit while you are still comparatively young and strong — there is such a lot that you might do to improve the place and reform abuses!' (By this time Sue had strong views on the land question, which she burned to put into practice.) 'It would be such a chance for helping things on — it would be such a position of power and influence — as surely no man qualified as you are ever had before! You would go into Parliament — you would fight with the leaders, the pioneers — you would set such an example as no country gentleman ever set before, with all your money to back you. It is the poor people who have hitherto preached the rights of humanity, and because they are poor their motives are discredited; all of them put together have not the moral weight — the power to affect public opinion and fashion and custom — that one rich man would have, doing what you could do, if you were Mr Delavel of Dunstanborough, which, I can see, is like being a king in a small way. Poor Uncle Roger has done nothing for anybody but himself – *none* of them do – and it's enough to make one's heart bleed to see the things that go on. I must tell you all about it by-and-by. But *you* – well, you wouldn't have to complain that you were unable to pay back to the world the value of what the world gave you, if it gave you such an opportunity as that.'

He smiled at her unabated enthusiasm, and shook his head. 'I shall never take it, Sukey.'

'Why not, father?'

'Because, my dear, Constance could not stand the climate.'

That settled it, of course. She had nothing more to say. The idea which crossed her mind so often – that, Constance being possibly laid in an untimely grave, he could remain 'comparatively young and strong' to pursue the business of life without her – never by any chance crossed his.

The carriage turned out of the hot streets into the familiar, shady road to which the mansions of the wealthy and exclusive presented their front gates, and in a few minutes Sue was welcomed by her stepmother on the doorstep of her home. Constance was looking, she thought, a little more shadowy than when she saw her last; but her complexion was beautiful in its transparent purity and softness, her eyes bright, her whole face suffused with inward happiness. She wore a loose gown of thin white silk, tied at the waist with a silk girdle, and a little fine lace about her throat. She was forty-six, but her last years had not aged her; they had made her look young. This so struck Sue that she remarked on it at once, and sent her father who had been waiting for the verdict in a nervous agony of apprehension, into raptures of delight. Mrs Delavel made her own anxious inspection of her step-daughter, and was also reassured. Tanned with sea-wind and sun, flushed with heat and excitement, dirty, sticky, tousled, with her girlish trimness all gone for the present, it was still evident to the most casual observer that the state of Sue's general health left nothing to be desired. It was quite evident to Hannah when she came into the hall to greet her nursling, but Hannah would on no account acknowledge it. She was filled with indignation at the iniquity of husbands who could allow their wives to be knocked about in ships and trains at a time when nature plainly ordered them to stay quietly at home.

'You ought to have come either a good deal sooner or a good deal later,' she muttered with a severe face, 'and you would have done if there'd been a woman to manage things.'

'She is her own manager,' said Noel, who overheard the remark. 'She insists on doing what she likes, Hannah.'

'Don't tell me,' retorted the old woman, who had never considered him good enough for her child. 'It's a husband's place to prevent his wife from doing what she likes.'

At which there was a little merry laughter, and Noel bade Sue remark that Hannah was on his side, and that her words were the words of wisdom.

'And now, my darling, come to your room and get undressed and cooled and rested,' said Mrs Delavel, taking her step-daughter by the hand, with a motherly tenderness that poor Annie would have been unable to feel or show. 'You must get a little comfortable before you can eat anything to enjoy it.'

'You ought not to go upstairs, Constance,' Richard hastily interposed.

'Just this once, Dick,' she answered. 'I will go slowly.'

'Then let me help you,' he rejoined. And he almost carried her to the first landing, with an arm round her waist, leading Sue with his other hand.

'How does she get to her room usually?' the latter inquired. 'A lift?'

'I don't live upstairs now,' Mrs Delavel explained. 'He thought stairs were not good for me, so he had a new bedroom and dressing-rooms built below. O Sue! he does spoil me in such a preposterous manner!'

'Well,' said Sue gently, 'it pleases him, and it is evidently good for you.'

She found herself installed in that very chamber over the drawing-room which she had herself prepared for Constance on her home-coming as a bride, and the other rooms on the same floor, all beautifully furnished – in simpler but finer taste than she had displayed when the matter was in her hands, and with equal comfort – were placed at her disposal.

'You will have your independent home presently,' said Constance, 'but in the meantime – and indeed always, where-ever you may be – you and Noel must feel this your home too. Here is your sitting-room, dear – your bedroom that used to be – and there is a den for your husband, and a room for your maid, if you care to have one –

and a nursery. I have made your mother's room a nursery for her grand-children, darling – you don't mind that? It seemed a good use to put it to, and it is so large and airy. Hannah took care of everything that came out of it. But don't trouble to look round now. You must undress and have a bath, and rest.'

'Constance,' said Sue, with a little moisture in her bright eyes, 'father strictly enjoined me not to be boisterous and hug you, because he said you couldn't stand it, and you don't look as if you could; but will you please understand that I would crush you to a jelly if I dared.'

In the afternoon the two women, stretched on two couches in Mrs Delavel's room downstairs, had that woman's talk for which they longed, while the men chatted over their pipes in the smoking-room.

'Now, I want to know,' said Sue, 'what you meant by that private postscript, in which you begged me to come home as soon as I could. What did you want me to come home for? It always seemed to me that, however valuable my company, my room was just a little more so, if anything.'

'I was not so well as usual,' said Constance, 'and I was afraid of something happening to me – and your father with nobody to fall back upon. Indeed, I have been in a fidget all the time, more or less. Imagine what it would have been if I had died suddenly, and you on the other side of the world – only servants with him!'

'We won't imagine anything so dreadful,' Sue replied. 'If I had known you were feeling like that, I would have come home long ago. But you are not *really* nervous about yourself, are you? It's only father's fuss?'

'It is always a nervous thing to have a heart like mine,' said Mrs Delavel. 'It may, and I trust will, hold out as long as I want it; but on the other hand it may, the doctors say, stop suddenly at any time. And the dread of leaving him alone – without you – has been a perfect torment to me. At last I felt I must try to hasten you back. I did not know when I wrote that you were not quite in a condition to be hurried – and you *have* hurried. I hope it hasn't hurt you. The voyage would be beneficial, as you are such a good sailor, but you should not have taken those two immense railway journeys, with only the one day in Melbourne between them. Hannah is quite right about that.'

'I'm none the worse. Nothing hurts me. I only wish I could give you some of my strength. But tell me, Constance, honestly, you don't – putting your heart aside, and hearts don't seem to matter much, as long as you're careful – feel as if things were going wrong with you, do you? Oh, you really *mustn't*, you know. Father could not stand it.'

'I don't know,' replied Constance. 'I frightened myself while you were away, but now you are back I am at ease.' She rose from her sofa with a happy, girlish air. 'I feel today as if I had taken a fresh lease of life, now that that weight is off me. I dare say I shall be a tough old woman yet. And here is Hannah with the tea. Call the gentlemen, Hannah; they will like to come and have some with us.'

CHAPTER XLVIII

'While Darkness Is Quick Hastening'

It was a happy little family that sat down to dinner that night. Sue was rested and refreshed, and her stepmother, who had an unsuspected fund of brightness and humour at the back of her seriousness, in a mood of positive gaiety, which was all that was needed to inspire their male companions with the spirit appropriate to such an occasion. How often the younger members of the party recalled the pleasant scene; the pretty festive table – the graceful woman who presided over it, looking as they had hardly ever seen her look before, with such a shining exhilaration in her soft, dark eyes – the keen-faced host, still in the strength and beauty of his manhood, to whom she seemed to have given the elixir of life. They were all young together in that delightful hour, taking no thought for the morrow, and not seeing the shadow under which they laughed and joked.

Sue and her father were the chief contributors to the conversation, which never flagged for a moment. They were too full of news and too eager to impart and receive it to think of their digestions. She had to tell him about Dunstanborough, the reality of which had so far transcended her colonial ideas of such a place; to describe its present aspect, and what was changed and what was unchanged. Though he had thought little about it for so many years, he was keenly affected by the associations her eager tale revived, and his interest in it was wonderfully enhanced by the fact that Constance had seen his home (having made a pious pilgrimage thither in the year that Sue was born), and had as correct a memory of its features and surroundings as he had. She had thoroughly explored the green woods and quaint gardens, as a casual tourist graciously permitted to 'do' the show-place of the county, and been conducted over the stately, ancient rooms by that same dear, fat old housekeeper who had nursed him as a baby and sent him hampers of cakes and pastry when he was a boy at school; therefore she was in a position to sympathise with his disgust at the news that most of those old rooms had been modernised beyond recognition, and that the moat which had girdled the grey walls for centuries had been drained and filled and converted into gravel paths and flower beds.

'But I think that was a very wise thing of Roger to do,' she said. 'My instincts as a nurse prevent me from seeing any beauty in stagnant water under your bedroom windows, however beautiful it may look in the eyes of the thoughtless.'

'It was fed from springs, Constance.'

'It had scum and duckweed on the top of it, Dick, and it was certainly dangerous to health, my dear. Roger was quite right to do away with it.'

'Father would have done away with it himself,' said Sue, 'before letting you sleep under the ancestral roof, if the place had been his. And yet,' she added, 'poor Uncle Roger, with all his sanitary precautions, has not been able to keep sickness away. That poor boy! Just turning seventeen, father – just finishing at Eton; and he was so like the old photograph of you at that age. We saw them all at church when we first went to Dunstanborough, the time when we just poked about by ourselves, and nobody knew us. Such a handsome family they were, in their huge chancel pew, raised a foot or two above the common people, so that everybody could see them.'

'You couldn't see us in my day,' said Richard. 'We had blue curtains all round us.'

'Oh, there's nothing of that sort now. Open benches, with carved ends -- everything modern and orthodox. The only difference in the squire's pew is its shape and size, and its carpet and cushions. And there was Uncle Roger, stout and proud looking, with his nose in the air – he was not ill then; and his magnificent wife and his three beautiful daughters, and that dear boy who died only a few weeks after. I did nothing but stare at them all church time. It was Christmas Day, and the church was decorated – you never saw such decorations! They said the ladies at the Hall and a lot of people staying there did them. And Mr Delavel-Pole walked up the aisle in a cope and things, all the colours of the rainbow, with a boy carrying a cross four feet high before him.'

'The same old Max!' ejaculated Richard. 'And what does he look like, Sukey? Have years softened his asperities at all? Is he rotund and sleek and double-chinned? He ought to be.'

'No, he has a severe, ascetic look. He is spare and bony and hatchet-faced. A very unsympathetic sort of man, apparently. And he gave us a nasty, hard, dogmatical sermon, all about the authority of the Church – nothing but the Church, the Church, from beginning to end, till one got sick of the very word – not a bit of human feeling in it, not a thought that was of any use to anybody.'

'Dear old boy! I know his style. And to think of Kitty, who used to be such a merry little soul, taking up with the likes of him! It must have been that she never saw anybody else. How does she seem to have stood it, Sukey? Is *she* spare and bony too?'

'Aunt Katherine,' replied Sue, 'is rosy and plump, and has every appearance of enjoying life. Report credits her with having the upper hand of Mr Delavel-Pole, and she is certainly a powerful person in the parish. You should have seen the sharp watch she kept on the Sunday-school children; they shook in their shoes under that eagle eye of hers, poor mites!'

'Ugh! He's spoilt her. And what about Barbara? If any one had told me one of my sisters was to marry that hypocritical prig, I should have been sure it was Barbara. She seemed cut out to be the ogress of a Sunday-school. And she's an old maid, after all, poor old girl!'

'Yes, and a very sour old maid too, poor thing. The gossip of the village has it that she loved Mr Delavel-Pole, and was broken-hearted when he married her sister, and would never look at another man.'

'Good Lord!'

'Certain it is that she and Aunt Katherine are not on speaking terms. If they meet on the road they cut each other dead. I was very friendly with Aunt Katherine when we went to visit them last year, after Uncle Roger found us out. She used to want me to tell her about Australia, and took a lot of interest in things; but Aunt Barbara would never have anything to say to me. She regularly turned up her nose at me, as if I'd been a black gin or a convict. Aunt Barbara,' said Sue judicially, 'seems to me to be a Delavel all over.'

'She always was,' said Richard, 'true blue to the backbone. It would be just like her to turn up her nose at you. I wish she'd married her precious Max – they'd have been a pair. And little Kitty might have had a chance. However, I'm glad Kitty has the upper hand of him. She had a spirit of her own, I remember, and wouldn't allow herself to be sat upon. Well,' – after a pause and with a twinkle in his eye –

'and how's your other Aunt, Aunt Rhoda? Rhody they used to call her in the old days. I hope she's well and thriving. I hope you went to see her when you were paying family visits, eh? She was a sensitive person, was Rhody – very apt to feel hurt if she was neglected by her relations.'

Sue's face grew crimson, and after a moment's hesitation she broke into an embarrassed laugh. Her father had left her to find out for herself how the case stood with respect to her maternal antecedents, and the discovery had been a considerable shock to her. She had a vivid recollection of the Morrison family as they appeared in their pew in the nave of Dunstanborough Church on that Christmas Day of which she had been speaking – Aunt Rhoda coarse and red faced, a mountain of flesh, with coarse-looking girls and boys beside her, the girls wearing fly-away hats turned up at the side, and silver lockets and chains round their necks; and Uncle John grey and bent-backed, dull-eyed and stolid, physically and intellectually on a level with his own farm labourers – and of her feelings when she realised the discrepancy between the facts as she saw them and the fiction that poor Annie had imposed upon her. She also thought of that visit to the farm which she dutifully paid – how her aunt had commenced the interview with cake and wine, and honeyed words and obsequious-ness – had then proceeded to wound the filial susceptibilities of her niece by professing Christian forgiveness towards one whose pride, that would not allow her to acknowledge her own flesh and blood, had been brought low, even to the dust; and ended by unpacking the whole store of bitter grudges that the dead woman had provoked and spreading them before the indignant eyes of her living representative. It was a grotesque and painful memory.

'Never mind,' said Richard, with mischievous enjoyment of her confusion; 'you shall tell me all about her by-and-by. There's a tale to be unfolded, I can clearly perceive. Eh, Noel?'

'We got on with the uncle better than with the aunt,' said Mr Rutledge, with becoming gravity. 'We made a point of seeing Mr John Morrison a second time.'

'You did, did you? And you told him all he would naturally want to know?'

'Everything.'

'That's right. That's what I wished. And' – gravely – 'you think he was satisfied, Noel?'

'Yes. But he's a crabbed old stick. Times are hard for farmers nowadays, and I think his struggle to make ends meet has soured him.'

'I expect it's Rhody has soured him. But to do her justice, she was a capital business woman. I thought she'd have managed somehow to put money into her husband's purse.'

Then the talk fell upon the hopeless state of the agricultural interest, and how the Dunstanborough property, with its mortgages and dower charges, would have been bankrupt over and over again had it not been for the new watering-place; and Sue rushed into the burning land question with her characteristic ardour, and then into a moralising account of her uncle's splendid establishment, and the impressions she received from her sojourn therein. Her description of the rigid state and ceremony to which she and her husband were subjected, and how like fishes out of water they felt, was very graphic and amusing; and the picture she drew of Uncle Roger in his pride and power and his human helplessness – the Lord of Dunstanborough, who had all the good things of life apparently, but could not save his only son from the common destroyer nor himself from the clutch of malignant disease – was a pathetic one that drove the smiles from all their faces for a minute or two.

It was Lord Boyton who introduced the Australian Delavels, in her person, to the chief of the family – poor Lord Boyton, who had flown home a broken-hearted little man after manslaughtering Richard's wife, and had not been heard of since. He was sent for to Dunstanborough in the autumn following the death of the heir, when the head of the house was mournfully considering how to open communication with the next in succession – sent for to report what he knew of that now important person; and it oddly happened that he ran across the Rutledges the day after leaving Roger's house, where he had been giving a glowing description of the charms of Richard's daughter.

The unexpected meeting was a great joy to himself, apart from the family amenities to which it gave rise. When his old friend met him with such cordiality and kindness – when he found that she was married to the man of her choice – when he heard, moreover, that her father had married also – his load of self-reproach was wonderfully lightened. And as for Sue and Noel, the fortnight they had spent with him in his Irish castle was one of the pleasantest episodes in the history of their travels. She had to tell her father all about it, and make him take the enhanced interest in Lord Boyton that she now felt.

'He hasn't 20,000 a year, father, nor a quarter of 20,000, nor anything like it,' she said enthusiastically.

'My dear, I never for a moment supposed he had,' said Richard.

'And he has married a girl as poor as himself, and not an heiress, who would have helped him out of debt and difficulties,' she continued, in a glowing tone of eulogy. 'I always did say there was a lot of good in the dear little fellow, and there he proved it beyond a doubt.'

'Perhaps the heiresses wouldn't have him.'

'Nonsense. Of course they would. You don't know the social value of a title at home, evidently.'

'No doubt the present lady had the title in view. She can hardly have taken him on his own merits. A nasty little drunken beast. . . .'

'Father, he is nothing of the kind. He is struggling to cure himself of his bad habits for her sake, and that alone is proof that they love each other. She is a dear, bright, sweet-tempered creature, who must have had lovers by the score – isn't she, Noel? – and she chose him and he chose her; and it's just delightful to see how happy they are in their dilapidated old castle, with their crowd of slipshod servants. He really doesn't know which way to turn for money to live on. I was *so* pleased!'

It was a summer night, and there was a full moon, and everybody who knows Sydney harbour knows how it looks under those circumstances. Our four friends, on rising simultaneously from the dinner-table, stepped out of the open windows to gaze upon the enchanting scene, and to breathe the salt air blowing freshly from the sea. They did not go down the stairs and winding pathways, because Constance was not allowed to climb, but gathered on the upper terrace, and from that altitude, as from a watch-tower, looked through a frame of rustling foliage upon the lovely distance of shimmering water and shadowy shore.

'Oh,' cried Sue, with tears in her eyes, 'there is no place like home, and no home like this home!' She was leaning on her husband's arm, but her father stood on the other side of her, and she laid her cheek on his coat sleeve in the old caressing fashion. 'I certainly am the happiest person on the face of the earth tonight,' she declared, with the emphasis of strong emotion – 'the *very* happiest, without exception.'

'Oh, I think you must make one exception,' said Noel, laughing.

'Two – three,' said Constance.

'Absit omen!' cried Richard, putting up his hand. 'Don't talk so loud, lest that old hag with the shears should hear you.'

CHAPTER XLIX

●

The Wages Of Love

Before they separated, Sue asked her father a laughing question. 'And what have *you* been doing all the time? I have been giving you a full account of our adventures, but you have told us nothing.'

'There is nothing to tell,' he answered. They were dawdling in the hall, lighting their bedroom candles; as the yellow flame rayed upward over his face she noticed that he was a little greyer, but otherwise as alert and bright and handsome as ever. 'Constance and I have been standing stock still, simply.'

'Haven't you done anything?'

'Not a mortal thing. We didn't want to.'

'Fancy two people doing nothing for two whole years!' exclaimed Constance who was drooping on his arm, looking rather white and weary, though smiling still. 'O Dick! its dreadful! We ought to be ashamed of ourselves.'

'It seems to me,' said Sue, 'that though we've talked so much about paying back, we've done nothing but run into debt the whole time. There is not one of us that has earned his salt, so far. Noel dear, now that we are home again, we must bestir ourselves, and set these idle people an example.'

'She has done her work,' said Richard, covering with his own his wife's beautiful hand, which looked very white and slender on his coat sleeve. 'I'd like to have as good a record to show. And she shall do no more. She wants to rest now, and she has honestly earned her rest.'

'But you haven't.'

'Perhaps not. But I am going to take it, because if I don't rest she won't. I can't be bothered with your schemes, Sukey. You must work them by yourself.'

'But I haven't the money for my schemes. You have. All that money lies on my mind, father – when you think what it might do!'

'Take it, then, and do what you like with it.'

'Oh no; it is yours, and the responsibility is yours. . . .'

'Well, go to bed, old girl – go and talk about it to Noel. Here's Constance looking as white as a ghost – she's had a heavy day of it, and she must go and settle to sleep as quickly as possible. Good night, child, good night. It's good to have you back again. But you mustn't be too severe on us poor old folks, who have never had a real holiday till now.'

When her father had kissed her, with all the old lover-like warmth, Constance followed with a maternal embrace that was not less cordially responded to. 'You see how it is,' said the elder woman. 'You will have to pay back for him as well as for yourself. Remember it when the time comes and the money and everything is yours – that he left liabilities behind him; and be his steward and deputy, and discharge them in his name.'

She said it lightly, with a smile; but her step-daughter understood that she meant it very seriously, and answered her with another close and silent kiss. Then they said good night all round, and separated. Sue climbed the stairs with a lagging step, hanging to her husband's arm, and Constance was conducted to her spacious ground-floor chamber by her inseparable companion, who was still the only maid she had or wanted.

As for poor Annie – if we look facts plainly in the face, a proceeding quite contrary to civilised custom – the place that had known her literally knew her no more. Her twenty-five years of domestic sovereignty simply went for nothing. What else could be expected in the case of a husband who had regarded himself as her captured bond-slave from the first, and in the case of a child who had taken the part of that conventionally unfaithful spouse against her? In her lifetime she had had but the letter of their allegiance, and not the living spirit; and now that she had been a few years dead, though they kindly and tenderly remembered her from time to time, they did not mourn for her any more. This to the general reader will prove, not that Annie was in fault, but that she had a bad husband and a bad child; and indeed no excuse is offered for them, except that they are here set down as they really were, and not as they appeared or as they ought to have been – which is a cruel process to which we are never subjected in the world of real life, and which therefore does them a certain injustice. In the world of real life a legal mother who conforms to rule is never allowed to be judged on her intrinsic merits, never required to reap what she has sown, like the poor folks who are not hedged with the divinity of a like status. She is to be revered by her intelligent grown up family, whether she be hard or tender, selfish or unselfish, noble or ignoble; and if they don't revere her they are never to own it, even to themselves. This is all right, of course – everybody feels it so – but at the same time it is not quite sincere or natural; and Sue, like her father, was terribly prone to lean to nature rather than to the supreme authority which regulates our affairs. Faith was once defined by a Hindu Christian convert to his missionary teacher as 'believing what you know to be untrue'; and the people who can perform that feat can, no doubt, love those whom they know they cannot love; but our two poor friends were morally too simple and clumsy to do either. And it is still a question whether, in the general process of examination and judgment to which all our institutions are being brought, the conventional mother may not have to justify her claim to filial duty and honour which she has done little or nothing to deserve.

At any rate, the melancholy fact remains that Sue did not miss her mother very much, and had no sense at all of wanting her.

She went to bed feeling as happy as she had recklessly described herself when her father warned her that she was tempting fate, but she was much more fatigued than she supposed or allowed, and inclined to be wakeful and restless. Her bedroom arrangements, devised by the thoughtful stepmother, were such as to make sleep easy even on a Sydney midsummer night. Four brass poles, fastened to the floor, held a gauzy canopy about twelve feet square over her head, and from the light rods connecting them hung the airiest film of mosquito curtain, enclosing her as in a large transparent tent. Within this she reposed in spacious comfort, with that room to breathe which she always needed for body and soul alike, and without the windows stood wide open to the night breeze. She could see the moonlight on the water as she lay, without lifting her head from the pillow – she could feel the wandering airs that came up from the sea – through the light veil that protected her from the tormentors. After the cramped quarters she had occupied in ships and trains, the space and softness and delicate purity all about her were delicious. She talked to her husband for a long time, in spite of his gentle remonstrances, until the sound of his breathing indicated that he could no

longer take part in conversation. Then she looked at the harbour
lights, watched the revolutions of the South Head beacon, thought
about her schemes, little and big (how she and Noel could begin to
pay back for 'value received' during the last two years, where she
should look for a monthly nurse, and so on), and instead of growing
drowsy as the night wore on became more acutely wide awake and
active minded every moment. Her admirable nervous system was a
little strained by the excitements of the day, following upon a long
railway journey.

Towards three o'clock in the morning, when feeling the first symptoms of approaching slumber, she was startled by the sound of a
banging door downstairs, a hurry of feet, a bell ringing loudly, and
her father's voice calling to somebody in a voice that made her heart
stand still. She knew in a moment what that wild shout meant, ringing
through the silent house in the dead of night; only one cause could
account for it. Springing to a sitting posture, she shook her husband
violently, and, as the cry was rapidly repeated, he too heard it, and
came to full consciousness of its meaning with a bound.

'Run, Noel, run! Constance is ill, and father is calling us,' she cried.
And she got out of bed and groped tremblingly for the candle.

He promptly put her back again, and implored her, if she loved
him, to stay there – not to come downstairs unless he sent for her.
Then he snatched at his dressing-gown and ran, as she bade him,
closing her chamber door behind him. He was almost overpoweringly
tempted to turn the key, but did not, knowing the uselessness of brute
force to prevent her from injuring herself if persuasion would not do
it. He could excuse Richard for not thinking of his daughter when he
made that terrifying noise, but it was natural that his own first anxiety
should be on her account, lest the rude shock should upset her.

Of course Sue found it impossible to obey him. When she was left
alone she lit the candle at the little table that stood within the gauze
tent, and put on her slippers and dressing-gown, her heart thumping,
her hands shaking, her ears strained to catch every sound dowstairs.
The whole house seemed alive in half a minute. The servants were
calling to one another and running hither and thither; the front door
banged, and the front gate; all the signs of a dreadful catastrophe
were audible. She felt it would be maddening to remain alone and
idle when she might be of more use than anybody, and that at any
rate she must learn the worst. So she blew out the candle, lifted the

tent curtain, and by the light of the moon made her way downstairs, where gas was flaring in all directions.

The door of her stepmother's room was open, and all the windows thrown up. At the farther end, in the recess of a large window that overlooked the bay, was a little group of four people – her father, Noel, Hannah, and poor Constance, who was fighting, through the last hard two minutes of her life, trying to breathe, while something clutched at her breast and strangled her. She was sitting in a large armchair, just as she had been lifted from her bed, gasping for air, but otherwise making no sound, while her husband held her up in his arms and howled – no other word could describe the noise he made – howled like a wild beast tortured, not loudly, but with a concentrated force of savage anguish that was indescribably dreadful. He was trying to get her to drink some brandy – a supply of which he always kept in a cupboard near her bed – while Noel held the glass, and Hannah wildly flourished a bottle of smelling salts; all their efforts being obviously futile. The poor woman was past help; she could neither speak nor swallow. She looked up at her husband with a pathetic helplessness and consciousness of their mutual agony; and he clasped her and cried over her with that terribly howling cry, as if he and not she were in the throes of a cruel death. It was a scene that haunted Sue for many a long day, like a frightful nightmare.

But it was only for a minute. As she ran through the long room towards them, Noel and Hannah calling to her to go back, she saw the end of the struggle. Constance lifted her arms to her faithful mate – a sudden, desperate sort of gesture – and he caught her up bodily, carried her a step or two, rocking her as he went, as one sees a mother rock a child in a paroxysm of pain, and then laid her on a sofa – that sofa which he had had made on purpose for her, to be better than all other sofas – where she had lain in the afternoon, and prophesied that she was going to be a tough old woman after all. As he laid her down she gently sank out of his arms, sank back upon the pillows, limp and still; her delicate head rolled a little to one side, and there rested as if she slept; her pretty hands fell open, palm uppermost. They smoothed her white gown over her placid form, and Richard, looking at her, ceased to howl, for he saw that she had ceased to suffer.

It was not yet daylight when the doctors, who had come too late, were shown out of the house. Mr Delavel spoke to them quietly and rationally, and thanked them for the useless efforts they had made to reverse the decree of fate; then he desired the servants to return to bed, kissed his daughter, and went back to his dead companion, locking the door behind him.

'Now, come upstairs,' said Noel to his wife, wearily. 'We can do no more for him.'

'And don't come down again,' added Hannah, 'for it'll do you harm, and do him no good. As for comforting him, you'd comfort him as much as that fly buzzing round that candle. He'll stay there with her to the last minute, and he won't want anybody else. It's my belief he won't let us lay a finger on her now she's dead any more than he would when she was living. Ah, dear me, it was only yesterday that I wanted to brush her hair, and he wouldn't let me. He said he liked to brush it for her himself. Well, I don't know what he'll do, I'm sure.'

'It will kill him,' said Sue.

CHAPTER L

●

The Wild Beast's Lair

Sue lay on a sofa in her own chamber, shattered out of all self-control by the shock she had gone through, and it became clearly apparent to her husband as he looked at her that the tragedy of the day was not yet over.

'Look here,' he said, holding her hands, and gazing at her with an appeal in his eyes that no words could express, 'this is the greatest call on your courage that you have ever had, or probably ever will have. If things go well with you now there will be consolation for all of us – the only possible consolation for him – not to speak of me. I can't help you, my dearest, but you can help us – him and me, and yourself too – beyond all measure if you can brace yourself up to be calm and steady till the crisis is past. You were never like common women, Sue, to give way when others depended on you. And you will not let your safety be threatened by dangers that you can keep off by being brave and resolute – will you?'

At once she sat up and rallied whatever heroic spirit she had in her, controlling the sobs that had been shaking her frame. She promised him she would try not to give way, and bade him have no anxiety on her account. Then she whispered to him that she was afraid she was not well, and would like to speak to Hannah.

Hannah, being summoned, was constrained to recognise the fact that troubles seldom come singly in this world. She discovered, not at all to her surprise, that Sue was kept from going to her father by something more than an anxious husband's wish; that out of the great deep which had just absorbed one precious life, another might come to the mourning household before the day was over; and the knowledge roused her in a wonderful way. No bereavement, however terrible and overwhelming, can dull that strongest woman-instinct, that mother nature, that deep sex sympathy to which the girl's circumstances appealed; and in a moment Hannah had dashed away her tears and concentrated all her solicitude upon the heroine of the great experience that was so near at hand. The grief-muddled brain cleared as by magic; the trembling fingers became quick and capable; all that could be done to meet the sudden emergency she thought of, and did without fuss or delay – producing from various mysterious sources the necessaries for the occasion, which could not be disinterred in time from the European luggage. When the official person who had been summoned, and of whom she was bitterly jealous, arrived to take command, there was nothing for her to do but to look round and signify her august approval, and then retire for lunch and gossip to the servants' hall.

Noel came upstairs towards noon, and found the two old women making a slight commotion, and Sue in the thick of her struggle to be courageous and calm.

'Don't mind me,' she said with a wan smile, when she beheld his anxious face. 'Tell me how *he* is.'

'Well,' said Noel, when after much questioning an answer was got out of him, 'he has great pluck. He's very quiet – quite himself, and talking rationally1 He is concerned about you. He will be coming to see you presently. But not, I think, until *she* is gone.'

'When will that be?'

'Tomorrow evening. I wanted to attend to all that for him, but he won't let me. He'd rather do it himself. He said I was not to leave you. And he wants us to keep Hannah – he says she would be comfort to you just now; but I think we'll send Hannah downstairs. It's not right that he should be without somebody he can speak to.'

'Oh yes, we'll send Hannah down at once.'

She rose to call Hannah, who had left them *tête–à–tête*, when he checked her, and drew a letter from his pocket. 'Here, he sent you this,' said he.

'What, a letter! He was able to write me a letter!' She took it with trembling hands, as if afraid of it, and tore it open. Yes, it was in his own bold handwriting, and just like the letters she had had from him before.

Dear Sukey, Don't grieve about what has happened. She's out of pain – it only lasted two or three minutes – and I was never more thankful in my life than when I saw the end of it. Noel tells me you are not well today, and he thinks more troubles are at hand. Keep up your heart, old girl, and don't fret about me. I've been expecting this any time for three years past, and was quite prepared for it. Don't let it upset you, my old girl. If anything can comfort me it will be to hear you are all right.

Sue laid it down with a moan. 'That is just a sham,' she said; 'a pretence, to try and impose on me. As if he could impose on me, knowing all I know! He has done it to ease my mind – to help me through. Oh, my poor, poor old daddy!' She broke into wild sobs, that went perilously near to being shrieks, for about a minute, and then resolutely calmed herself and smiled in Spartan fashion at her distressed husband. 'However, if he can be as brave as that for my sake, it's the least I can do to be brave too,' said she. 'Don't you worry yourself about me, Noel dear; I shall be as right as possible.'

And so she was. For a long afternoon she bore her sorrows and sufferings without complaint, drawing more comfort from her own heroic mood even than she gave to those about her. To have something to do was the first need of body and soul under the circumstances, and she could not complain that her task was a light or unimportant one. Until the shades of evening fell she upheld herself for the sake of upholding the men she loved; and then nature forced her to rest, and forced her also to feel conscious of a simmering happiness in the depths of her heart, under all the weight of black disaster that overshadowed her.

As the dinner table was being laid – that function which seems so much more important than life or death – Noel, with a full heart, crept stealthily downstairs; and Richard came out of the room where his dead wife was lying to receive the information that Sue had a daughter, and that mother and child were 'doing well'. He was quite composed and quiet, but his son-in-law did not dare to look at him.

'Give her my love,' he said. 'It's better for her not to see me now, but tell her I'll come soon. Tell her not to worry about me. And take care of her, Noel – take care of her while you can.'

'No fear of my not doing that,' said Mr Rutledge.

And then Richard congratulated him personally, asked a question or two about the child, said good night and locked himself up again.

To be brave under the circumstances of that tragical day was not Sue's hardest task, though it seemed so. The day that followed, when she lay still in her bed, with the sweetest baby that ever was seen cuddled up to her breast, was an infinitely greater trial to her. It was the day of the funeral, and it was sultry and stormy, with tempests of rain driving upon the windows; and to have to lie in her utter power-lessness and think of what her father was undergoing made conscious-ness a torture that pain and effort would have relieved. She was kept in ignorance of the funeral arrangements, but, though she was sure he would evade the ghastly customs of his kind as far as the law would allow him, she knew there were cruel necessities that he would have to bend to – necessities that he had calmly accepted in the case of poor Annie, to whom established customs only were appropriate, but which would seem to him to put a sort of public indignity upon the sacred person of her successor, the beloved woman on whom the wind of the vulgar world had hardly been allowed to blow. He could not carry her in his arms to the boat and row her down to the camp by the light of the summer moon, and dig her grave in the sea-shore scrub, and lay her where no one should know of her resting-place but himself; he would have to see that precious body treated like common bodies, and to expose his anguish to the gaze of the streets. And the day was wild and wet; at the hour when she would be taken from him the rain would be driving into his stern, set face; and when he came back to his empty rooms at night – oh, what a vision of desolation and loneliness rose in his daughter's mind as the night drew on! And she could not be there to remind him, with her arms enfolding his down-beaten head, that he had still one little shred of something left, poor and trifling as it might be.

The next and few following days were still worse to bear. She was all the time watching and listening for her father to come to her, and he did not come, and no one could or would give her any clear account of him. The nurse and Hannah and Noel himself all answered her appeals for truthful information in that palpably insincere, would-be soothing manner which is so maddening to helpless invalids; and then it was dragged out of Hannah that her master had gone to the camp immediately after the funeral, and had not been heard of since.

'Why couldn't you have told me so at once?' moaned Sue, who had a touch of fever as the result of their well-meant tactics. 'Of course I knew he would go to the camp. It is the natural place for him to go to.'

But she was disappointed that he had gone without seeing her first, and she soon began to worry herself as to what he was doing there. She begged Noel to go and see, and several times he implored her to excuse him on the ground that he could not bear to intrude on the suffering man who had gone away from them all to be alone with his grief; but at last he yielded to her importunities, and one morning set forth in Richard's outrigger to Middle Harbour.

He was gone all day, and when he came home at night he was very reticent and grave. After questioning him till she nearly lost her temper, Sue got out of him by degrees that her father was not very well. 'It's just a bad cold,' said Noel, with that affectation of ease and cheerfulness which he supposed to be good for the nerves that it set quivering with irritation. 'He must have got a chill at the funeral – he was wetted to the skin as he stood by her grave; and of course he hasn't been taking care of himself, and it has settled on him.'

'A chill!' echoed Sue. 'Yes, I should think so! It's a chill in his soul – in all the currents of his life – that he'll never shake off in this world.'

'And I thought it would be better for him not to be alone any longer, being so seedy,' Noel continued, 'so I've sent Hannah down to look after him.'

'You've sent Hannah down! To the camp? Oh, he'll never bear to have her there, Noel, even though she is Hannah. A woman servant at the camp? What a preposterous notion!'

'Well, of course he can send her back if he likes.'

'And so he will fast enough.' She was silent for a little, and then a vague suspicion of the truth came into her mind, and she looked at her husband earnestly. 'Noel, you don't mean that you have sent down Hannah because he is too ill to come back to the house?'

'Oh no,' he replied carelessly, and thereby perpetrated the first downright lie of his life. He hoped it was not a lie, but said to himself that if it was he couldn't help it. 'He prefers to stop at the camp now.'

'Ah,' said Sue, only half-satisfied, 'the camp is to him what his lair is to a wild beast; he always goes there when he is hurt. But I'm sure he'd rather be at home at Darling Point than at the camp with servants waiting on him.'

The days passed, and Hannah did not return, and Noel was absent from morning till night. He said he had to attend to business – another lie, in intention if not in fact, committed for the sake of the sick wife who was not thought to be yet in a condition to bear the truth. But presently his business kept him out at night too, and then she divined the sort of business it was – that it had no connection with Pitt Street. The truth was 'broken' to her at last, as, in spite of all drawbacks, her naturally fine health came rapidly back to her, and she learned that her father had not lost his cold; that it was rather worse – indeed, much worse; that doctors had visited him at the camp, where several servants were now installed in addition to Hannah; that, in short his condition was considered critical, though of course there was always hope while there was life.

Then Sue took matters into her own hands, and defied husband and nurse to prevent her. She put on a hat and cloak, wrapped her fortnight-old baby in a shawl, and bade Noel straightway get out the boat and take them with all speed to Middle Harbour. The nurse mutinied, and would have resigned her office on the spot, or been discharged for impertinence, had not Noel interceded and propitiated her; he made no protest on his own account, but only set himself to minimise the risks of the expedition as far as human means could do it.

In the strange way that things happen in this world a messenger arrived with a telegram a few minutes before they set off; and when the telegram, addressed to Richard Delavel, Esq., was opened by his son-in-law, who had authority to conduct his business correspondence, it was found to be dated from London, and to be a communication from the legal advisers of the great Delavel house. The message ran thus: 'Roger Delavel dead. Return immediately.'

CHAPTER LI

•

The Bo'sun Hauls Down The Lantern

The heat of the day was over, the hard glare mellowed to that lovely peach-pink mist, that impalpable veil of evening colour, which neither pen nor paint-brush can describe – sunset-tinted exhalations of the city and the sea – through which the harbour shores loomed faintly like a land of dreams. The air was still, but sensibly freshening from the south; the bay was smooth and shining as a sheet of glass, just delicately breathed on by the twilight haze; everything was hushed and tranquil, like Wordsworth's sonnet – quiet as a nun, yet with suggestions of eternal motion in the background, where the great Pacific billows rose and fell. On how many summer nights like this had Sue and her father stolen away from the dinner table to cool and rest themselves on the water after a hot day; paddling as far as the camp, perhaps, and sitting there for a while to smoke and meditate, to talk over *Mill on Liberty* or *John Morley on Compromise*, returning by the light of stars or moon to fall into inevitable disgrace for being out so late. Memories of those happy hours crowded upon her as she watched her husband getting out the boat – *their* boat – she standing idly by with her baby in her arms. Husband and baby, that so soon push father and mother from their place, had not dethroned the beloved one, of whom she was less flesh of his flesh than spirit of his spirit, and they could not console her at this moment, when she realised that boat and camp would soon be his and hers no more.

She took her accustomed seat and the familiar tiller ropes, the stout nurse and the child on one side of her being balanced with sundry bags and bundles on the other; and Noel, in white flannels, well open at the throat, pushed off from the landing steps, planted his feet firmly, and bent himself to the task of getting over the distance between house and camp in as short a time as an Oxford-trained oarsman could do it. The clean sweep and dip of the blades, the speed and power of his noiseless stroke, were beautiful to see, and even in her sorrowful preoccupation Sue could not help being proud of a husband who could row so well; it was too dusk to see the straining of his unpractised muscles and the beads of perspiration that trickled down his face.

Fast as he rowed, it was almost dark when they swept into the little cove, where the white tents sheltered under the hill. Though the curve of the beach was defined by the tiny thread of surf sent across the Sound from the ocean breakers, and the open water still reflected the fading sky, the wooded heights and the bosky shore were all one velvety blue shadow, in which nothing was distinguishable but the Bo'sun's lantern on the top of the flagstaff, except when the beam from the lighthouse, like a policeman's bull'seye, was turned upon that quarter for a second or two. They almost touched the jetty behind the bushes before they saw the two figures standing there – the poor old sailor, who was the unconsidered scullery-maid of the camp, evidently stupid with rum or grief or want of sleep, waiting to take the boat; and Hannah, pushing before him, craning over the water to see who was coming.

'That you, Miss Sue?' she called, as the dip of the oars ceased and the boat drew near. And on Sue answering that it was she, Hannah uttered an ejaculation of thankfulness in a tragic tone that was anything but reassuring.

The nurse, disappointed of her coadjutor's support, here firmly intimated that Mrs Rutledge would not have come if she had been able to prevent it, and disclaimed all responsibility for the consequences of such an imprudent step; but nobody heeded her or the dictates of prudence – except Noel, who hurried her away to show her her quarters, and what she could do for the comfort of her special charges during the night. They carried off the bags and bundles, and Sue lingered a moment with the baby, to speak with Hannah alone behind the hedge. She upbraided the old woman for not summoning her before. 'I *could* have come, Hannah, long ago,' she cried; 'and he *must* have wanted me!'

'No, my dear, no,' said Hannah. 'Everything has been done for him that mortal creatures could do, and all his anxiety has been to keep you from knowing. But now – well, it's no use hiding it from you, for you'll see it for yourself – now it's nearly over, and 'twould be too cruel to keep you from him.'

When she heard that, Sue broke into wild words of rebellion and despair. She *could* not part from him – she could not bear it! *Why* should he die, who was so strong and healthy, when other people got over it?

Hannah said it was God's will, in a solemn, reproving voice; then she took the question from a much lower standpoint. 'He's dying because *she's* dead – because he can't live without her. If she'd been here to nurse him, like she was when he had the same complaint before, no doubt he'd have got over it. But now there's no chance for him – I felt from the first there was no chance. Oh, dear me, I wish he'd never set eyes on her, that I do! It's pitiful to see him die so lonely, with no hope, human or divine to cheer him – no comfort, except that she's gone first, and is spared the pain of seeing him suffer. He thinks of nothing but her, and he ought to be thinking of other things. He bears it all quietly enough, because he's a man, and he'd be ashamed to rave and cry, but he isn't resigned a bit – he isn't in any state to die, my dear, and that's a fact.'

'My darling,' murmured Sue passionately. 'Not fit to die, when he's lived as he has lived! He never made pretences in his life – he's not likely to begin to make them in his last hours.'

'I don't want him to pretend, Heaven knows, but I want to see him thinking about his Maker that he's going to meet, and not casting himself away for a poor, sinful, earthly creature like himself. But there, it's no use – nothing will turn him. Seems as if things had gone crooked from the beginning, and were never going to be straightened up, not even on his deathbed. He's dying like a heathen, and not like a Christian man – and I can't bear to see it.'

'What are names?' protested Sue. 'There are good heathen and bad Christians – good men and bad men. He is a good *man* – that's enough for me. If he's a bad man' – with wild incoherence of speech, though with perfect clearness of thought – 'he's better than any of the good ones that I have ever known.'

Hannah passed over the protest, which did not seem to her to touch the point. A death-bed, in her view, as in that of many worthy people, was like examinations at the end of the school term; on its report depended whether the candidate for immortal honours 'passed', or whether all his preparation was to go for nothing. To be a black sheep in life was one thing; to fly in the face of sacred use and etiquette in the hour of death was quite another. It was the difference between a boy playing pranks in the school-yard and turning somersaults in class under the eye of the head-master.

'There's Mr Pilkington has been here again and again, and as long as he'd breath to speak, your father refused to let him come near him. "Keep that snivelling idiot away from me", he said – and those were his very words; "Keep that snivelling idiot away from me; I've enough to bear without that." '

'So he has, indeed,' said Sue, 'and I won't have Mr Pilkington worrying him. What does he know of the needs and trials of a man like my father? Why, my baby might as well set up to teach him!'

'Give it to me,' said Hannah, putting out her arms. 'The precious lamb, it's a sad start in life she's having. And go in and see him, my dear, and try if you can't make him think of the things a man in his position ought to think of. You could always do more with him than anybody – except *her*. Do, while he's got sense and reason left, get him to understand that there's a God above who has sent him these afflictions to bring him to Himself, and a world to come where it'll all be made up for if he'll only repent and believe.'

'O Hannah!' cried Sue, 'I'm afraid *you* have been worrying him!'

'I wish I could have worried him,' Hannah replied. 'But it was just speaking to the empty air; he never so much as heard me.' And, weeping in the shelter of the darkness tears that in her hard old eyes were much more impressive than ordinary tears, she took the baby from the mother, and carried it to one of the small tents, whence its little voice, piping shrilly through the airy silence, was heard at intervals all night.

Sue gave it up without another word, and entered the camp by a different path. What a changed camp it was from the dear place she had always known! – the neat footways and flower-beds that had been the Bo'sun's pride, all crowded with strange litter, lights and figures flitting about, the whole place humming with subdued life. And, oh, what a changed face on the pillow of the bed in the big tent, from the keen-eyed, wide awake, spirit-lighted face that had been used to lie there in unmolested solitude in the bygone summer nights!

The worst of his sufferings were over, though he was still in a dull agony of semi-suffocation, too weak to cough air into his choked-up chest, and rapidly nearing the stage of insensibility which would practically be the extinction of life. His hands were already cold, there was a film over his bright eyes and a dragging rattle in his throat; his breathing was terrible. Sue felt for one wild moment not only that the sight of him in this extremity was more than reason could bear, but that to live through future years with the memory of it would be utterly unendurable. She flung herself down at his bedside, spread her arms over him, and uttered the only word that could express her love and grief – 'Father! father! father!'

It woke him up in a way that astonished the doctors, who had not expected to hear him talk again.

'What, Sukey, my old girl. . . .' He had no voice left, and could only articulate a syllable at a time, but she understood him. She made a sign to his attendants, obedient to a sign from him, to withdraw from the bed and leave them together. And then they passed through an experience the nature of which was known only to themselves, and is not to be described in these pages.

By-and-by, when they had accustomed themselves a little to the tragedy of the situation, Sue did make a poor attempt to carry out Hannah's injunctions. 'Can't you see any glimpse – any hope at all – of anything to come after, father?'

'No, Sukey,' he said; 'I can't.'

'No one can tell, father! It is all so much beyond us! You remember Arnold's paper in the *Fortnightly*? You *may* find her again, after all.'

'Ah,' he responded, in a groaning whisper, 'if I could – if I could! But I don't want an angel or a spirit – I want *her*. And she's gone, Sukey – and I'm going – and it's all over. And ' – looking at her with a look that broke her heart – *'we've only had three years out of fifty!'*

This, it became apparent, was the one thought absorbing him – that life was over for him and her, and that they had only had three years out of fifty. It did indeed strike even his daughter, so like himself as he had made her, that it was dreadful to be overwhelmed in such an hour with an aspect and result of life that was comparatively so ignoble. To have the faculty to discern the proportions of things, to stand as he stood now with the Infinite around him, and to concern himself only with this local detail – it showed how, in the moral as in the physical world, thwarted nature was but another name for disease. The cruelty of the fate that had tantalised him was too fresh to be forgiven; it shadowed his spirit and intellect as the oncoming night obliterated the fair features of shore and sea.

'I haven't been what I ought to have been,' he admitted – his nearest approach to thinking of 'things a man in his position ought to think of' – and he struggled desperately to make his old 'girl' understand him, dragging out his toneless syllables, bit by bit, with an effort that he could not have made for anybody but her. 'I haven't done what I ought to have done with the opportunities I've had. I should have paid back more. I know she felt that – I felt her feeling it. But I was crippled for want of her, Sukey – crippled, crippled – that was the reason. And when I got her at last, to lose her in three years – only three years out of fifty!'

He fell into a stupor of exhaustion after his long speech, and the doctors came forward to attend to him. Sue passionately appealed to them to make another effort to save his life, for she said he talked so sensibly, he was so perfectly aware of what he was saying, that she could not think he was so far gone as they supposed. It was only the accumulations in his chest that he could not cough up which were choking him; couldn't they perform tracheotomy or something, to give him room to breathe – to give him one more chance?

Of course they said they couldn't, and stated reasons why they couldn't, but it was impossible for her all at once to relinquish the thread of hope she had despairingly clutched at. 'Father,' she cried, in the sweet wild voice that stirred him to consciousness as long as anything could stir him, 'listen – I want to tell you something. Uncle Roger is dead, fater – the telegram came today – and now Dunstanborough is yours. Won't you, oh *won't* you try to live – you have got strength yet, and if you make a struggle for it, if you make an effort to cough and rouse yourself, you may yet pull through – and we will go home, my darling, to your own old home, and do all that splendid work that is waiting for us. Do you understand? You could pay back all then – it's what *she* would beg and pray for, father, if she were here.'

He was drifting farther and farther away from the sound of her voice, but was arrested for a moment by this potent pronoun. 'She couldn't stand the climate,' he whispered huskily. And then a gleam of intelligence, touched with the spectre of a smile, came into his suffering face, and he said – 'Max will have it; Max stands next.'

'And would you let *him* take Dunstanborough, and keep everything back? It will be worse than Uncle Roger – it will be like the dark ages again. . . . o father! father!' She laid her head on the bed and sobbed. It was no use. He did not care for Dunstanborough; he did not care to live; he did not hear what she was saying; the deep waters that had engulfed him were closing over his head. It is seldom that last words are so *à propos* to the occasion as novels and death-bed gossip imply, and these happened to be the last that poor Richard Delavel had the power to utter – 'Max stands next'. Perhaps he gave a kind thought to his old enemy in this supreme and final moment of conscious existence, but it is more than likely that he didn't.

His eyes, that had dreamily followed the movements of his daughter, slowly settled to a blank fixedness as her image faded from them; his breathing grew slower and slower. Lying just within the tent door, to get all the freshness of the air from the sea, he was bathed every minute in the radiance of the electric beam; it quenched the lamplight as it passed, and revealed the subtle changes in the dying face with the distinctness of day. Noel Rutledge watched for a while while, and then lifted his wife from her knees and bore her out of the tent and through the garden to the beach, where he sat down under the bushes and folded her in his arms. There was no moon, but the night was beautiful. The little waves rippled at their feet; the great breakers filled the air with the sound of a distant organ. The spacious silence was unspeakable.

'Oh, *what* does it all mean?' wailed Sue, in an anguish of bewilderment, overwhelmed by the terrible mysteries with which she was confronted. Her husband had no answer for that question. They could only cling to one another as they had never clung before.

The hours of the night passed, and at three o'clock in the morning they heard the flapping of ropes over their heads and the tinkle of the tin lantern against the flagstaff. The little yellow smudge that had been enough to show them the path between beach and tent was effaced, and when the lighthouse turned its ray upon the ships at sea the camp was lost in darkness.

'What are you doing, Bo'sun?' said Noel, rising to his feet. 'It isn't sunrise yet.'

'Sunrise or sunset,' the old man answered solemnly, 'it's not wanted there any more.' And, when he had hauled down the lantern, he hauled down the running rope, leaving the pole bare.

They left him fumbling, and returned to the tent. Looking down on the bed as the electric beam passed over it, they saw that Richard Delavel had ceased to suffer. The life that had so ill-satisfied him was at an end.